# BETWEEN WORLDS

book two in the Heaven's Scent series

## TANIA COOPER & RICKY COOPER

Other books co-written by these authors:

Heaven's Scent
Love, Life and Naughty Bits


Books written by Tania Cooper:

Too Broken to Love
Too Easy to Love
Happy Little Horrors anthology
Cold – coming in 2016


Books written by Ricky Cooper:

Designated Infected
Designated Quarantined
Alienated anthology

# DEDICATION

To anyone who ever dreamed and
was brave enough to scratch, claw, and
fight to make it come true.
We believe in you.

The boast of heraldry, the pomp of pow'r
and all that beauty, all that wealth e'er gave
awaits alike th'inevitable hour
the paths of glory lead but to the grave

*"Elegy written in a country church yard"*

# 1

## Straying the Path

## ALBION

***How could she?!*** **How could she turn her back on all we were,** all I had given; not only to her, but to us? All I had lain bare to ensure we two survived against all that had been set in our path. Sacrificing my own kin to see her safe, carving a path into Heaven itself to see her free from the lingering spectre of death and yet, there she is, bedecked in satin and lace, walking into the embrace of another.

I fall into their gripping hands, talons digging into my flesh, my blood dripping to the ground beneath my torn and tattered knees. I feel them, bone shards sinking deep into my arms, tips scrapping bone as I am hauled upright.

I no longer care what they do to me, all I was, all I am is tied to the love I hold for her, the love for my Angel; and now, well, now all I am is this empty shell held between two gaolers.

I feel fingers curl into my hair dragging my head upwards. Lucifer's grinning face hanging inches from my own, a diamond edged glint in his eyes that at any other time would have made my blood run cold, but now, all it promises is the tactile distraction of my internal pain and torture. I find my mind wandering, pondering the limits of my endurance, of what my soul can withstand, then everything washes through me once more. The loss, the sheer overwhelming destruction of my entire world; even now as I am held here, pinioned like a butterfly on a pin between these two mountains of blood thirsty muscle, I find crimson tears creeping free, searing my eyes and scalding my flesh as they carve paths through my skin.

'Bring him; we're far from done with this slab of flesh, and what I see before me now, well, it will certainly be a thing of raw and unbridled malice.'

Lucifer leans in, his breath hot on my skin, the stink of Hell's pure essence leaching from his pores, coating my throat and tongue in a stain so rich I fight for every whisper of breath.

'You will be vengeance made flesh, and by the time we are done with you Weisser, you will sing to the glory of my name.'

He lets my head drop, my chin slapping against my chest as the last dregs of my resilience leaves me. I let my eyes slip closed wanting nothing more than to feel the blessed release of darkness and death, and yet, I see her.

I see the soft curve of her breasts, the supple flow of her body over mine. I see her face, the shimmering violet of her eyes, and the glossed rose tint of her lips as she whispers those words I had so longed to hear from her. How many times has she uttered them to me only for them to end in a lie? Skin peels from my feet as I am dragged back down the hill side, the sting of raw flesh on stone raising naught more than a bristling of a tear before thankfully I am sent tumbling into the waiting arms of oblivion.

'It's at points like these Albion that I certainly do so adore the resilience of youth. You see, there's little in these worlds that's ever escaped my sight. Not your dalliance with that piece of Angelic fluff.'

He steps past me, away from my sight, his heavy trembling aura curling around me as I feel my body tighten, my soul already yielding to his teasing, flowing like putty in his hands. I know I should resist, I should fight to remain the man that she fell in love with, that she called her own, the man that owned her mind, body, heart and soul. But, after what I witnessed, after all that was shown me, why should I? She didn't wait for me. Without her, what else is there for me to fight for?

'Not the way my younger brother Gabriel, fathers winged messenger and fluttering mouth piece, fawns over her; nor the way Michael and his *'flaming sword'* spies treachery at every turn. It's of little surprise that he came to me to wrest her from your talons Albion, goodness knows the spoilt brat had little stomach for doing it himself.'

His fingers run through my hair dragging my head backwards, his eyes boring into my own, his lips curl, glowing teeth glittering as I watch the skin around his eyes char and blacken. The bones of my neck crackle and grind as he drags my head ever further backwards. His skin sloughs away, the meat suit peeling like blistered paint. What lies beneath chills me, a deep rippling malice that seeps through his fingers and into my soul.

Never before have I born witness to something so malevolent, something so purely Evil, that it has made me want to vanish from this world and into another, just so I can be sure my soul is not completely tainted by its presence.

Yet here I am, my body lank, my soul all but dead as I stare into the eyes of my maker and all that they offer, and, I go willingly. I trip from this precipice and plunge head long into the void that spans before me. No more will I be this shattered form; no more will I be the man betrayed by the Angel he loves; no more will I be the Demon that fell for his enemy.

'Now Albion, we shall truly see what cloth the vaunted son of a Hell Knight is cut from.'

✦ ✦ ✦

The door crashes closed, darkness enveloping me like the maw of a cat closing around a mouse. Nothing stirs, not me, not the gutter dwellers that curl through the open sewer that spans the width of the room, not even the air itself dares to breathe.

I sit and wait, nothing more, nothing less. As the darkness takes hold, the whispering begins to seep in, softly at first, almost like the lingering kiss of a summer's breeze. It wafts through me, caressing my sweat licked skin as it slowly takes hold. I feel it, creeping, burrowing, gnawing away at all that made me the man she fell for.

I push myself into a corner, chains rattling, skin scraping as I curl my beaten and shattered body onto the handful of straw that is supposed to pass for a bed and yet still they whisper. I shudder, cold fingers of teasing malevolence slither through my mind, shattering dreams and cursing nightmares, all the while my old self, my righteous self, the man who loved, is slowly ground away and what's left in its wake. I cannot bring myself to name it.

✦ ✦ ✦

The whispering, all there is, is the whispering. I cannot remember a time where there was silence. Even when I close my eyes and try in vain to slip from the waking world, off into one that is free from the howling of these children around me, the whispering is there.

I cast my eyes around me, their giggling voices dance from corner to corner, shrouded by the blackness that soaks these walls. I drag my talons from where they lie trapped beneath my meat suit. The feeling of them slicing through my own flesh makes me want to vomit, bile rising through my gullet searing my tongue like acid. I raise my hands, the collar around my neck biting deep into my flesh as I drag one chipped and yellowed claw down the stone that surrounds me. The shallow rent joining the four before it while I slowly slump to the floor, the whispering and giggling closing in.

I draw her memory tight to me as their laughter closes in. I feel their breath hot and wet against my neck, the click of their nails on the cold wet stone, the silk slithering of their tongues against my ear as their whispering begins once more.

The pain that fills me makes me wail in agony, my heart heaving in my chest as they claw at my mind, the soft chattering of glee filled children echoing around my cell. Time drops to a crawl as I feel my skin part, claws raking over muscle and sinew, each tick of a talon, each pluck of a finger reverberating through me. I whim-per and beg and still they come, plucking fingers and whispering voices.

✦ ✦ ✦

The door swings open, dead light bleeding through the dark as a shadowed and shrouded figure, its shape all too familiar and yet all too foreign, hauls me to my feet, my body limp, lifeless in their grasp as I stumble along beside them. The mark in my chest aches, its edges burning with a septic bite as I smell the sweet scent of gangrene taking hold.

I am cast to the floor, my body thumping dead to the reed strewn stone. Feet shuffle past my eyes as fingers curl through the chains around my wrists and heave, my body, sliding over the dried and desiccated reeds to the splintered oak table in the centre of this blood smeared room. The heady scent of copper and offal fills my nostrils as the ring of iron on iron teases my ears.

With a whimpering plea I am hauled from the floor, the rattle of chains through pulleys bouncing off the walls as my arms are dragged over my head. Hooks bite into my hips as I feel the tug and tear of their tarnished tips, my skin popping open as I am pulled backwards onto the oak slab.

The words resounding in my head like a choir of the dead. *Glory be his name, glory to the name of Lucifer.* I feel it run from my soul, a torrent of heat and hatred, drowning me, consuming me. Glory is to his name. But even now as I lie there, my eyes trembling behind my lids I see a flash of gold, a glittering of violet, but can I find its source? No, try as I might to trace its origin within the vaults of my mind, all I find is the whispering, the choir of the dead.

*Glory be his name. Glory to the name of Lucifer.*

'So Albion, are you ready to submit once more, to pledge yourself to my service and become the tip of the spear once again?'

I smell spice in the air, the soft perfumed scent of birch and apple blossom as they crackle in the hearth behind the shadowed figure before me. I feel the soft clasp of supple fingers, shiver with the brush of feathers over my skin, the world around me dropping out of focus as violet eyes and pursed rose tinted lips fill my vision, the warmth of breath over my neck and cheek making my skin tingle with want and need and all the while, the scent of apple blossom and birch.

I taste her name on my tongue, I hear the laughter, feel it wash like water over my mind, but still that whispering remains. Burrowing, burning deeper into me, searching, clawing, tearing the tattered shreds of my will asunder as his question once more unfurls in front of my eyes.

His eyes dart away from me for the smallest of moments, drawing my own with them, my heart tumbles in my chest as I watch the shadow behind him dance over the roughhewn stone. Rippled wings and willowed form flowing behind me, I watch the shadows fingers trace along my shoulders. Can it be, can it be her; can she be here, shut away from the light, twisted to his bidding; tormented by her betrayal of me to the point of falling into the waiting arms of the Fallen Angel that holds dominion over this twisted den of lies and deceit?

Her name boils through me, coursing through the torn and butchered remains of my mind like water, washing aside everything in a bid to claim what was rightfully hers.

I feel the name trip from my lips, little more than a harsh croak falls from my cracked and parched throat. I strain at my bonds watching the shadowed figure before me sigh and set the cup and saucer down, arms ensnare my shoulders as a cooing, sickly sweet voice shivers through my ear and down to my core. The impudent film soaking everything in its putrescent slime as the words rail against all that is fighting in vain to break free from the gaol of my own existence.

'Ari ... Arianwen ... *Arianwen!*'

I scream the name, her name, the name of the Angel who owns me, me the man, not the chastised and bound Demon that sits between these two shadows of former souls. Ebony hair tumbles past my eyes, strands catching in the blistered and scabbed flesh around the edges of the Sigel carved into my chest.

I snap my head backwards, skull meeting flesh and bone as I hear the crumbling crackle of cartilage fighting to fill my ears as my echoing voice rolls around the room.

A sharp snap draws my eyes as I watch the room turn over itself, fists and feet filling my vision while I continue to scream her name. Even as darkness filters through my eyes, her name is all that finds it way free.

*'Arianwen!'*

Her name echoes through my mind, through my soul, the itching tickle in my skull screaming in agony as I let her name sear my lips and continue to scream. My nails tear from my toes; burning ash searing my bloodied flesh as I thrash against my gaolers grips. All the while I continue, continue to let her name burst forth from me, continue to call for the one who completes my soul and heals the bleeding wounds that carve paths through the tattered remnants of my spirit.

And yet, I suddenly cease, my heart freezing, settling like the ice of a harpies kiss when my eyes alight on the figure before me. Blazing violet eyes and hair as golden as the brightest of dawns greets my gaze. Lilith smirks, the vile twist of her lips making my soul tremble with hate and sadness. How can she possibly have taken the form that sits before me? A form that is second only to the owner of the name that is still echoing through the halls around us both.

'Albion, my dear, sweet, Albion. Oh how you have fallen from grace, tumbling like a sparrow cast from its nest.'

Her fingers trace my chin as she crouches before me, the sneer still etched on her face as I sink to my knees, all strength and will leaving me.

'Why all the fuss, all this horrid noise, why scream for a simpering, mewling piece of heathen cunt, when you can have me?'

She traces her fingers down my scarred stomach, her nails tracking the groves carved in my flesh as she slips her hands past the ragged waist of what is left of trousers. Her cold, dead grip ensnaring my limp length as she squeezes, coaxing my soul dead flesh to life.

I feel the heat of her breath on my ear as she snakes her tongue over me.

'I know you Albion; I know the depths of your depraved fantasies. How does it feel to have me in this form, the svelte, luscious, curvaceous form of your lover, how does it feel my little half breed?'

She squeezes me tight, her nails sinking into the soft skin of my sack as her palm slips along my thickening flesh. I do not want this, this vile harpy clothed in the skin of the woman who owns my heart and soul. Even as she stirs the lust of my loins, I feel bile and disgust rising through me. I cannot abide this, the feel of her hands around me makes my soul want to scream in anger as her hand closes and slowly draws along my shaft. The vicious glint in her eyes say it all as she drags her nails across my skin, her palm smoothing the slick exuberance of my responsive length. Cold courses through me, waves of boiling revulsion at every squeeze, every pinch of her nails, even as I feel my limit begin to rise and my sack shrink tight.

My teeth sink in my lip as I bury my grunts of release deep in my throat. The self-loathing and hatred that sears through me is overwhelming as I spill my seed into her sliding palm. She smiles as my liquid warmth spills over her. I feel her let my jerking member go as she cups her hand catching as much of my unwanted release as she can, before, with malicious care, she slips her hand from within my tattered trousers.

A sultry hum leaves her as she stares at the pearlescent fluid sliding over her hand.

'Such volume from my lustful Demon. Is this what you have to offer me in the future my handsome slayer?'

She brings my flowing seed up to her smirking mouth as I watch, my stomach turning in upon itself as her flicking, snake like tongue slithers past those rose tinted bringers of lust lapping up the fruit of my loins, my pearl milk trickling over her lips. My gorge rises searing the back of my tongue, the hollow chuckle that ghosts from her throat skewering my heart as she swallows the pearl essence of my loins.

'The taint of treachery and defilement is a very acquired taste, but one ...'

She skates her hands down her body as she sighs.

'That I could very much get used to, especially when this form is so … energetic. No wonder your feathered whore took your mind and lust.

Her finger tips trace my jaw once more before, viciously and without warning she claws her hand and rips her nails through my cheek, the edge of her smallest digit scrapping my skin, my lid snapping closed as blood spatters against my eye.

I grunt in pain as she grins, her fingers dripping with my blood and skin, claws sinking into my shoulders gouging bone as I am hauled to my feet, nothing left within me can find the will to offer resistance, seeing her draped in my Angels form could mean one thing and one thing only, death found her before I ever could.

'Was there any need to ruin his face like that Lilith?'

A shadow draped form steps from a corner, my mind whirling as I am dragged away from them all, words fading as I strain to hear all that is being said.

'There was no need for it, but there was certainly a lot of enjoyment to it.'

'And taking her form, taking Arianwen's form, well, even I find that a bit … much. After all, I am rather adept at taking on the skins of others, it is, after all what I was born into.'

'It still seems, brother, that Albion doesn't see his little shape shifter friend for what he really is does he?'

'No Lilith, he doesn't, and for now, I'd like to keep it that way, at least until I'm deep enough in his confidences and mind to get what I need.'

# 2

## A Little Death

## ARIANWEN

**Dark fear tries to weave itself around my senses, but I will not** allow *it*. I will not allow its vicious claws anywhere near mine and Albion's unborn child. I will straighten my spine, I will mask my features, I will calm my entire being, I will not let them see the secret I hold within. Nobody will ever harm the miracle my love and I have created.

A fierce protective sense strengthens me like an armour of lead wrapping itself around all of my body's responses, shielding it from the hateful glare of the towering leader in front of me. I take a slow deep breath and let it out with my first step towards the door Michael is holding open for me.

I remove my eyes from his and focus on the wooden carved foyer before me as I step towards the doors that will remove me from the hate that is seeping from his every pore. Just as my steps place me under it, he grabs my arm in a vicious vice like hold, his nails driving the lace that covers the flesh on my upper arm into my skin, as he draws me closer to his large form.

'If you think for one second that the urge to hang your traitorous arse has gone from me, you are sadly mistaken you whore. The only reason you live is because my brother cannot see past his blinding obsession for you, and to eliminate you would cause more problems than it would solve. I need him to focus on the issues at large within our world, so maybe, after he has finally had you in his bed, his mind might actually return.'

Michael twists his grip, making me wince in pain as I try desperately not to utter a sound as he leans closer to me.

'So you will do everything he demands of you, from now until well after you are wed? How hard can that be considering you have already spread your legs for that Demonic scum? Surely it will be much easier to spread them for one of your own sweet Angelic kin?

'But make no mistake. The day will come when you'll pay for your sins Arianwen. Until then, know that I'll be watching your every move. If I catch you returning to the enemy … I'll kill you on sight!'

As the last savage word drips from his harsh lips, he pushes me through the doorway. I stumble and take a few steps to right my footing as I look up, thankful that the ancient carved doors that lead to the main chapel are still closed. The two attendants holding the curved metal handles raise their eyebrows in concern at my entrance as one begins to take a step to help me. I place my hand up to stop him and plaster a fake smile on my face and whisper that I am a little nervous, which gains me two understanding smiles. I take a step towards the large entryway, waiting for the heavy wood to heave open and guide me towards what feels like a little death of my true self.

My invisible armour begins to slip as the magnitude of Michael's words starts to seep into my aura. I know I have to go through with this, to not only ensure the safety of my family, but also the safety of the cherished gift I am cradling within. But, with Michael's ever watchful eyes upon me, how will I ever get a chance to seek out Albion and grace him with our joyful news? Joyful yes … but also very dangerous. The danger Albion and I will face is nothing compared to what our child may have to endure. If either side were to find out that a child will be born and possibly possess the power we create when we are together, then their safety will never be guaranteed in either of our worlds.

The sound of a heavy weight dragging along stone has my mind snapping back to the now, and the gazes of my entire kin suddenly lies heavy upon my shoulders. I am stunned frozen for a moment, all eyes trained on my form before the fluttering in my stomach reminds me of what is at stake if I do not go through with what is expected of me. If I do not take a step in the right direction, I could lose everything that I have or ever will hold dear to my heart.

I brace myself as I step off the stone of the foyer's floor and onto the sleek shiny wood at the beginning of the chapel's isle. There are crowds of people standing in between the old curved pews offering me sweet smiles as the choir sings soft slow hymns in the background, but I barely notice any of it. My vision is slightly blurred by the blinding light that is streaming through the old stained glass windows that adorn the entire pointed roof, and I can hardly hear the musical notes that are filling this grand chapel as the sound of my heart beating erratically is booming in my ears.

Each step I take feels like lead has filled my shoes as I look straight ahead and see Gabriel and my family waiting for me at the end of this long isle. I try as hard as I can to conceal my senses feeling my control slipping the nearer I get to the end. A sweat starts to break out over my brow as my hands begin to shake. My heart feels as if it is trying to jump out of my chest as my breathing begins to hasten. The dread of what I have to do is saturating my aura and starting to blacken my soul.

I have to control myself better, I have to conceal the fear that Michael's words have instilled in me. I cannot show any weakness in front of my entire kin, especially the leader that is smiling at me as I am only mere feet away from him. My throat is dry making it difficult to swallow as I try and use every trick I have been gifted with to conceal what my body is currently experiencing. But it betrays me. I feel as if I have no control over myself as Gabriel reaches for me, silently asking for my hand to be placed in his and as our hands make contact. My stomach turns violently and sends a burning heat up through my chest and into my head. The world begins to tilt sideways before I hear Gabriel shout my name and everything goes black.

✦ ✦ ✦

I can vaguely hear my name being spoken as I feel myself being jostled in somebody's arms before I am being slowly laid down onto a soft surface. A hand is gently pushing hair away from my face as I hear muted voices surrounding me. My eyes feel too heavy to open as I try and remember where it is that I am.

'She was still too unwell for such a large amount of pressure to be placed upon her. She should have had more time to rest,' I hear my father's concerned voice say.

'I'm sorry I rushed this Elek. I would never have pushed the ceremony forward if I knew Arianwen wasn't well enough to attend. The last thing I want is for her to become more ill.'

I hear Gabriel respond, his voice very close to my head, just as I feel a wet cloth placed upon my forehead. This snaps me out of my daze and has my eyes flying open to see the very concerned stares of my family and Gabriel, who is gently holding the damp cloth to my heated head. I blink rapidly as my mind races to control my reactions to everybody's stares. I know they cannot see it, but I feel open and raw, as if they can all instantly see the secret I so desperately need to conceal. Before I can think of a response or a way to move away from their watchful glances, Michael steps forward from behind me and leans in to speak to Gabriel quietly, but makes it obvious to me that he means for me to hear his words.

'Why don't you take her back to your private chambers to rest in quiet away from these crowds, and I'll go and inform the gathering that the ceremony will resume tomorrow.'

My stomach starts to turn again as I force myself to sit up. There is no way I am going to Gabriel's private chambers on my own or with anyone else for that matter. I deliberately stare at Michael as I speak up.

'I'll be fine I promise. I just still feel a little unwell from the past few days, but if I could just have a glass of water and a few quite moments with my family, I'm sure I'll be able to walk back out there to finish the ceremony.'

Michael glares daggers at me as my mother steps forward making Gabriel take a step back as she places her hand on my cheek.

'Are you sure Arianwen? You look a little pale. Today is only a presentation ceremony, so I'm sure it can be arranged for a time when you're feeling yourself again. I think it may be better that we take you home now before you fall further ill.'

Her worried eyes make me wish I could tell her what I am really feeling. That I am so very happy with the little miracle that is growing inside of me, but I hold real fear for the safety of its father because I can only now faintly feel him within my heart and soul. That I am terrified with the knowledge I will one day have to leave her and the rest of my family to protect the grandchild she may never get to meet. That I feel as if I do leave, it may leave her, my father and my two young sisters in grave danger. That I feel as if the weight of two immortal worlds lies upon my small shoulders and if I make one wrong move it will mean destruction for all who live in these realms.

But instead, I draw strength from the tiny being I hold within, who has turned my worlds upside down and inside out and find the strength to erect the mask I must wear to conceal the truth. I take the glass of water from the out stretched hands of my youngest sister and take a few small sips as I choose my next words carefully.

'Mother I couldn't possibly disappoint all our kin who are excited to attend such a rare ceremony. I just need to drink some more water and take a few deep breaths, and I'll be able to continue. I'm feeling much better already.'

I smile brightly at her and everyone else in the room as I take a few more sips of water. Out of the corner of my eye I see an attend-ant walk up to Gabriel to address him.

'Arianwen is the third and final young lady, so the rest of the ceremony shouldn't take much longer if you'd like to continue sir.'

It looks as if he may say no, and I really need this presentation ceremony to be over with as soon as possible, so I swing my legs off the soft couch to the ground and stand up as confidently as I can, trying to show I am more than capable of continuing.

'I'm fine to continue and don't want to keep our kin waiting any longer,' I say as I draw forth an overtly sweet smile.

'Then let's continue shall we?'

Michael proclaims a little too brightly as he starts ushering everyone out of the door. Mother grabs my hand and gives it a little squeeze, guiding me out of the room as we follow everyone out into the grand chapel where all of the babbling voices instantly turn silent.

I plaster a small smile on my face as I again take my place at the front of the aisle, standing closer than I would like to Gabriel. He stretches his hand out, expecting me to place mine in his, but as I do my hidden miracle turns again. I now know that it is Gabriel's presence that is upsetting my child's aura. Can they sense the darkness that lies beneath his exterior? Or does it know that this male holding my hand is not their father? Whatever the reason for such a reaction I must do my best to conceal what my body is going through.

Instead of listening to the ancient words the master of ceremonies is reciting, I am saying a silent mantra to my miracle within, *'Please stay calm, I will keep you safe. Please stay calm, help me to conceal'*. I repeat it over and over again, and my fluttering little one seems to understand. I must have zoned completely out because before I know it Gabriel is squeezing my hand slightly for my attention. When I look into his eyes I see nothing but concern which confuses me for a moment, before I realise one of the attendants is standing directly in front of me with an opened book I am expected to read from.

I pull myself together with a small smile as I begin to repeat words that will never hold meaning for me. I will never truly pledge myself to be in the running for Gabriel's hand in marriage, and I pray to my God that he understands what my intentions are and helps to guide me to my intended fate in life. This is not where I am meant to be, it is simply a means to an end, a small part in the greater plan of my life.

Did God know this is where I would be standing today? Did he know what condition I would be in when I took my place here? Is it more than fate that is guiding these recent events in my life? All of this unknown would be warring me down if I did not understand the importance of staying strong for the miracle Albion and I have created.

Albion.

It should be his hand grasping mine. It should be his distinct scent washing over my being. It should be his heat I feel beside my body. It should be his aura our child is sensing. Instead, I stand here, before all of my kin, before all of our leaders, before my dearest family members and pledge I am happy to be considered a candidate for marriage to one of our greatest living legends. An Angel that has for centuries helped protect everything we believe in, everything we fight for. Yet I feel pain at my deceiving thoughts, at the truth I hold within. I am standing here to not only protect my family from a threat I am not even certain would harm them, but to also ensure the safety of my unborn child.

But, I know any safety would only be a perception, not a guarantee. What I am taking part in today is buying me time, not freedom. It will give me the much needed time to carefully consider my next move, my most important move, which is to reach Albion without being seen so I can finally grace him with our exciting news. Yes, the danger is too great to bask in this excitement, but it is still a miracle that we will both embrace and cherish until our last breaths.

I am now ushered to stand side by side with the two other contenders to Gabriel's hand in marriage. They are both such sweet young ladies I have had the pleasure of knowing their entire existence. They are both very quiet and shy, yet have the grace and poise to become a bride of a leader. Their work amongst our community has not gone unnoticed, nor has the fact that they both eagerly want to become his wife. Honestly, compared to these two innocent sweet girls, I do not see how I would be seen as a perfect fit to stand beside our leader in the union of marriage. The biggest reason being my calling as a Reclaimer. Not only is it seen as not very ladylike in the traditional sense, the danger it brings is not something that is welcomed for the other half of such an important partnership. Which is why I suspect I have not been chosen as a pretty statue to stand quietly at Gabriel's side, but rather to be used for the gifts I possess in my calling.

My ability to go where the rest of our kin cannot tread, may one day be used for a reason that is anything but good. Now that I have seen first hand the connections that Michael has with the Devil himself, I am more certain that Gabriel's blatantly obvious desire for me is to serve his dark intentions more than to have a pretty young thing beside him who can provide him with pretty heirs to his leadership. Can these brothers with dark ties truly be trusted to make a decision that is for the best of our world?

I am snapped out of my wayward thoughts by the clapping of our kin surrounding us. We are now, one by one, required to walk up to Gabriel and bow down on both knees, while he dips one hand into an urn of our holy water, raises it over our head, and lets the pure water of God drip over us, as a sign of his commitment to be wise in choosing the most suitable bride to help lead our kinsman by his side. A very old and outdated ceremony in my thoughts, but seen as a must in others eyes.

When it is my turn to reach him, he offers a warm smile before I bow my head and gracefully fall to my knees. And as I feel the first drop hit the golden strands of my hair I hear him whisper softly so only I can hear, 'I hope you are well soon my dearest Arianwen.'

I cannot help but internally shiver at what I hear as false sweetness in his voice, but myself and my hidden secret both conceal our reactions in the face of all these eyes trained on us. With my best composure intact, I rise slowly, nod my head as expected and turn to stand with the other two presented girls. The master of ceremonies concludes this presentation ceremony and wishes us well. We all return to where our individual families are waiting and begin to move slowly out of the chapel behind all of our fellow kin.

As we make our way through the beautiful gardens of Eden, I feel a tinge of pain at my deception in front of this world's fellow men and women, who I all hold dear to my heart. I have been grateful for eternity to be a part of this amazing world, and I have been honoured to serve our great Lord. But, I feel my life has taken an unexpected turn for a reason. Like no matter how hard I would have tried to fight it, the same result would have happened eventually anyway. Despite the danger I am in, and the danger that will continue to surround myself, Albion and our child, this all seems to be a part of a master plan.

Once we arrive home everyone begins to fuss over me. My sisters are excited I was the centre of so much attention and despite there being three girls presented today, everyone could see that Gabriel only had eyes for me. Then my parents are checking I am okay and telling me I still look slightly pale, and I should rest for the remainder of the day. I nod and smile, unable to push the words out past the lump in my throat. Who would ever want to harm my beautiful family? The only reason would be me, because of my recent actions and the pain I feel in my heart at that thought, just about has me falling to my knees.

'Arianwen, you look ill child. Let's get you to bed and we can all talk about our excitement at dinnertime.' Suddenly I am feeling as weak as I look, my strength slowly fading. With concerned looks upon their faces both my parents help me into bed, my mother pulling my blanket up and fluffing my pillow, as my father wanders out and comes back with a glass of water and a muffin. I am glad when they both retreat quickly and leave me to this much needed quiet.

'How can I do this? How can I do this without the man I love by my side?' I say to myself as today's proceedings start to weigh heavily on my shoulders. Great love is never an easy path, but will we ever have a chance to enjoy this love that has truly captured us both? Maybe someday, but the sad thought is that it may never be amongst my immortal world that I cherish so dearly. The thought of leaving my home and the people I love is just about my final undoing.

Just as I feel the first touch of moisture gather in my eyes, I hear soft voices making their way towards my room. My mother opens my door slightly and smiles when she sees that I am still awake. 'You have a visitor Arianwen.' She steps aside to reveal Gabriel standing politely beside her. I am stunned into silence for a moment before I realise they are both waiting for my response. I sit up straighter and nod slightly, as it would be highly suspicious if I was to refuse his visit, and take a deep breath, willing the threatening tears to subside, as Gabriel turns to face my mother and thanks her for allowing him to check on me.

He moves confidently towards my bed and nods at the edge as

if asking may he sit as my mother closes the door. I nod again, not trusting my voice as he sits down gently beside me and looks at me with what can only be described as affection and concern. Gabriel seems to be just as good an actor as his brother Michael. The man that sits here with me now seems so far detached from the man, who not so long ago, confessed to watching me bathe in our sacred lake, the same man who has smirked at my discomfort at being alone in his presence without a chaperone. A man who now feels too comfortable in paying me visits in my personal haven.

'Arianwen, how are you feeling now that you are able to rest? I was so worried by your fainting spell and the loss of colour from your beautiful cheeks my sweet Angel,' he coos as he leans in and runs a finger down one side of my face. I cover my true reaction with a shy smile as I break his stare and focus my eyes on my hands gathered together in my lap. 'I agree that it may be wise to rest for a while. It's been a long day,' I add, hoping he will get the hint that I would really like him to leave.

He continues to run his finger over my cheek, until he brings it under my chin, forcing it up so I have to look into his eyes. 'I regret letting Michael talk me into moving today's ceremony forward. I should've been more aware of the toll it may have taken on you since you've not been awake long since your ordeal with the dark ones. I promise to put your needs first from now on. A man should always put the wellbeing of his woman first, and I promise that's how it will be.'

My shock at his words must register plain and clear on my face.

'Arianwen, surely you must know by now that the other two young ladies presented to me today were only there as a formality? How can you not know you are the only woman I see, the only woman I need, the only woman I want. If I had my way, I would abolish such ancient formalities such as today's ceremony and shout it from the roof tops that you are the woman I have chosen as the other half of my leadership. The other half of the man that I will become.'

I am stunned at his words, but surprise myself with the controlled composure I present in front of him. I will not let him or his words rattle me. The words that have spilled from his mouth hold no meaning to me. I know, it is all an act. The words, his body language, is all a lie, and I will not fall for any of it.

'Thank you for your concern. I'm sure a little more rest will see me back to my normal duties soon.' His frown surprises me and so does his next words. 'Please do not push yourself too soon Arianwen. I want you well and happy, not exhausted and drained. I don't want to experience you fainting in my arms again. In my arms ... yes, but not unconscious. It's a feeling I don't think my heart could take again.'

I do not know how to respond, his words seem so genuine, but I know they are not. My silence and distraction gives him the opportunity to move in closer. By the time I realise his face is right in front of mine, it is too late to move away without raising suspicion. I am frozen as panic saturates my aura. I know he is about to kiss me, and I feel trapped in this moment, a moment that may shatter my false composure.

I must not flinch, I must not flinch. I repeat this mantra as I brace myself for Gabriel's intimate touch. His lips are so close to mine that I can feel the heat of his flesh, his scent seeps through my pores and his stare is intense. He reaches up and runs two fingers across my jaw as he leans in and softly kisses my cheek, pulling back slightly to see my reaction before leaning in again and this time placing his lips on the corner of mine.

Outside I do not react, and I am proud of myself and my little hidden miracle for knowing how important this moment is to not show our true response. But inside ... inside I feel as though my heart is slowly shattering, piece by piece, falling to a dark and bottomless pit as a kiss by another man feels like an unthinkable betrayal to the man I love.

Gabriel once again looks straight into my eyes gaging my reaction to such intimacy. A small, almost shy smile graces his lips as he leans in again. But, this time he connects with all of my lips and with more pressure. I control my breathing, almost stilling it for fear of gasping in disgust. This man, a man who is supposed to be one of our greatest leaders alongside his brother, is very attractive on the outside, his features would be called alluring to most females of our kin, and his personality can be quite charming to most I suspect, but I know better. I have felt his darkness, I have seen it up close when he has cornered me alone, and now I believe not one, but two brothers may have some sort of alliance with the Devil himself.

His smile broadens when he pulls back again. 'Arianwen … thank you for not pulling away from me. You have no idea how much that means to me.' Unable to form a word past the vile that has risen in my throat, I offer a small smile and lower my eyes to try and break his stare, but this only encourages him. I feel his hand move slowly across my jaw, his fingers gliding into the hair at the back of my neck, his grip firm yet still gentle. He lifts his other hand under my chin, raising my face to once again stare into his intrusive eyes.

I freeze my reactions, not giving into to the bitter resentment that rises inside me, but his reactions are all loud and clear. His pupils have darkened slightly, colour has risen in his cheeks and his breathing has fastened. My brain is in overdrive, thinking of a safe way to pull away from this situation, but I need to keep him happy, I need to not raise awareness to my true feelings, I need to keep this man on my side in order to eventually slip under his and his brother's radar. But, how far am I willing to go?

When he presses his lips to mine this time, there is more force behind them, more eagerness, and I start to shake at the thoughts of how far he will want to take this. I pray, I pray to whoever can hear me to save me from this situation, to save me from the feelings of guilt that are washing over my aura. There is a slight tap on my bedroom door, breaking the spell that Gabriel was under. He pulls back and straightens up just as my mother opens the door.

'I was just wondering if either of you would like a tea?' I deliberately stifle a yawn with my hand when Gabriel turns my way. He smiles at me sweetly then turns back to my mother. 'I think Arianwen needs some sleep, so I will decline the offer.' He raises and turns towards me, leaning down to place a chaste kiss on my head.

'Rest my sweet Angel. I will check on you tomorrow.

Goodnight.' He bows his head towards my mother before leaving the room and home. I do not have the focus or strength after what just happened to talk to my mother so I shuffle down to lie on my pillow and pull my blanket up tight around my chin and close my eyes. My mother whispers goodnight as she quietly closes the door, and the moment I hear the handle click the tears begin.

My heart is shattering under the enormous pain that is shooting through my entire being. I need my love so desperately in this moment. I know I need to be strong for the life that is snuggled so preciously inside my womb, but I can no longer hold it together. I miss him, I need him and his scent is getting weaker and weaker, and it has me beyond panicked. He needs me too, I know he does, but I have no way of reaching him. How long will I have to wait, wait until I can safely slip away from my world? The not knowing is what hurts the most.

I am struggling to catch my breath as my tears flood my pillow, tears that are more human than Angelic, tears that have never been a part of my world until my heart and soul found its missing piece. Until I fell in love ... with a Demon.

# 3

## Resurgence

## ALBION

four weeks later

***Glory be his name.*** Those words resound in my head, a mantra I carry with me always. *Glory be his name, the one who gives. Glory be his name, the one who takes, and glory be his name, the one who never forsakes. Glory to the name of Lucifer.*

I dive from the edge of the building, my body rolling as I land amidst my prey; their startled fear laced screams make my grin deepen as I draw my blade, her exultant wail making my body shiver as I turn, slashing, hacking at the soft flesh around me, the warm patter of blood on my skin making my body clench as I relish in the abundant slaughter.

I grab one Reclaimer by her smooth throat, lifting her from the floor as I line the tip of my weapon with the shallow dip of her navel and slowly press forwards. She thrashes and kicks as my blade sinks through her, blood oozing around the invading steel, as I watch with widening eyes, sinking into her soft pliant warmth.

I chuckle deep within my throat as her eyes begin to dim, her mouth gaping like a drowning fish. The soft pat of those paling slips of flesh her final eulogy as I slowly twist my blade, blood sliding over my fingers as I push it deeper.

The hilt tears at her skin as she shudders, a wet gargle rising up from this skewered Angel as blood runs free of her lips, the glittering blue wash spilling down her pert breasts, soaking the thin cotton dress that clings to her form as she begins to crumble to nothing.

I lift my hand, staring at the warm glow of the pile of ethereal dust that was once my prey. The spiced wind cuts through her disintegrating form dashing her across the compass like so much like discarded trash.

My tongue dances across my fingers, tasting death and frailty on them as I swallow the glittering syrup of my latest kill. Memories twist through me, images of a life now lost to everything. I smile, the look of utter incomprehension and fear making me swell against the laces of my codpiece only to all at once shatter as a set of blinding violet eyes fill my mind.

Moans of ecstasy making me sink to the floor, my mind screaming, agony lancing through my skull as I once more feel the tickling claws of my mentor sink into my very soul. Why does this vixen tempt me so, who could hold such a power over me? My blade tumbles to the ground, its wolfen core screaming as I sink my talons into my skin tearing at my scalp until blood runs free, the copper scent of my own life mingling with the all encompassing aroma of Angel dust and fear, as pain scours all from my mind.

My knees shake and quiver as I force myself to my feet, my heart hammering in my chest scraping my weapon from where it lies screaming in the blood soaked dirt. I can barely stand as I move my steps uneven and ragged. What was that, those images, who was that? I cannot fathom the answer, though one thing I do know, one thing I am utterly and unequivocally sure of, whomever it was, whatever it was, was no Demon.

My blade screams in the back of my skull, its need still not sated, the ever present cry for death and blood soaking my mind like a tide of ice. I turn, my sight shifting, the world bathed in a myriad of colours as I watch the glittering trails of the dead and repentant. The turn of wings draws my attention, the heavy thunk of armoured feet hitting cobbled dirt filling the air behind me, tightening my grip on the hilt of my blade.

The stench that fills my nostrils is all I need, to know who it is that dogs my shadow. Rotten meat and boiled blood, it is not a scent one can easily forget.

'You're doing well for a new convert Albion, how does it feel to be fully realised in the eyes of our King?'

I turn, his form a billowing curtain of black and red, the pulsing wall of malice and decay that flows from him is stifling. I feel it, like a band of iron around my chest, the sheer wanton, hedonistic need to feed and consume. How can one body hold such contempt for life? Something stirs within me, a bubbling seed of doubt at the kinship I share with this Demon before me. I know that I hold within myself the same malevolent power. I have shown as much with the heathen whores I sent to the ether only moments before and yet, as I stand here staring at the shifting shadow of energy and anger, I cannot help but feel this seed take root. Am I truly this Evil, am I truly as malevolent as they all think I am?

I cast my eyes down to the blade in my hand, her wailing cry still for now as she hums in sync with the weapon on the hip of the Demon addressing me.

'Thank you brother, it's most gratifying to finally be able to see myself for what I am. I was lost for a long time, my eyes clouded to my own potential, but thanks to our Kings guidance, I can finally come to understand all that I am.'

The words ring hollow in my ears, even as I know they hold shreds of truth. I know none of it really comes from the truth of what and who I am. I am the son of a Demon Knight, not some bootstrap pauper dragged up from the pits for the sake of breeding a killer. Blood of millennials flows through my veins, I carry in my very footsteps the lineage of a genealogy that stretches back to the creation of Eden.

So why do I find it fitting so ill? Why can I not accept the role before me, the path of a Hunter and Killer? Why am I so damned torn as to my true vocation and purpose? My blade hums in my hand sensing my trepidation as my kinsman's hand flexes edging towards his own weapon. I know I had best say something more before something goes awry, and yet, as I feel my lips curl, I relish the thought of sinking my blade into his chest and hearing the caw of my weapon as she rejoices in her meal.

I shake the thought away, my hand finding the sheath on my hip as I push my wings free.

'Brother I must bid you farewell for now, meet me in the Undercroft tonight, we can continue our discussion then, I have a patrol to finish.'

Before he can reply I am in the air, my wings pushing me aloft. The soft kiss of heat makes me shiver as a thermal catches the thin skin that sheaths the fragile bones of my Demonic heritage. I close my eyes, letting my body flow on the winds twisting, curling, and tumbling through eddy and stream as I rise as high as I dare. Ice begins to crackle in my hair as the bitter chill of the skies cold kiss washes over me. I pull my wings in sending my body plummeting towards the floor, the dusted ochre of my home, giving way to the florid green canopy of the forests that surround Eden. I feel my chest heave at the sight of those gates. Why am I so drawn to them? Pain lances through my skull, my wings flaring as my feet skim over the dusted lip of the fall, my body contorting, curling as I land with a bone rattling thunk.

I stifle a cry of anguish as I feel my shoulder shatter at the impact. What damned affliction has taken hold of me? My fingers tear at my scalp as I writhe, violet eyes, rose tinted lips, a crystal laced laugh, all of it sending shards of blood rending agony through my mind.

My voice finds freedom as I roll to my knees, my forehead smashing into the floor as tears stain my cheeks.

'Who are you? Why do you haunt me so?'

I crawl, my fingers, raw and soaked in my own blood draw me to the edge. I need to be free of this place, to find solace and quiet if but for a moment. With little care for myself, I pitch head first from the plateau my wings snapping open as the only place I have to call my own draws near.

'Albion, brother, come with me. You need to silence the voices, and there is only one place that can do it. Come brother.'

'Alp, what … what are you doing here … how did you?'

My world folds to black as I feel Alp haul me to my feet.

✦✦✦

Silence. Silence is all consuming as the door slides shut behind me. Nothing can find me here, nothing except for the emptiness of my own mind. I know this place, I know its meaning and yet, I do not recall a time I have ever set foot in it. I trace my fingers over the dust choked animal pelt on the bed, its plush stuffed mattress moulding around my hand as the mingled scent of my own skin dances with another. It flirts with something softer, almost feminine, a whispering fragrance that stirs a feeling in me so strong that for a moment, one fleeting second I can see its owner.

Their willowy form soft and nubile, dancing against the soft glow of the torches around me, gossamer silk and cotton sheathing her delicate form as she steps towards me. I draw my eyes up her lustful silhouette hoping to gain a hint of recognition, but as I find my gaze alighting on her face, there is nothing, a craven hole of dark and emptiness greets my eyes, even as I watch the tender hand rise to my jaw and her form dissolve into smoke, the sight of her face eludes me. I cast my hand through this spectral taunt, anger breeding hatred as I turn from the taunting wraith of a long deceased memory.

I take a step, my knees buckling, my body a dead weight as I plummet to the floor. White, incandescent agony wracking my entire form, sealing me in a cocoon of pain. The eyes, those eyes, her eyes, the iridescent orbs filling my mind, turning me inside out as I clutch at the sides of my head.

My voice echoes through the cavern as I scream, my throat burning with the force of my pleading exultation.

'Who are you?'

My words ring through my ears as exhaustion claims me, my eyes fading as I crumble to the floor. I can still hear my words, but now, even as I feel the warmth of this place close around me, I am all too tired to care and tumble headlong into the waiting arms of my own exhaustion and the violet eyed temptress that waits in the dark.

I wake, my body sheathed in sweat, my scars singing with heat as I feel their claws in my mind, the kneading call of my keeper. I feel the searing choke of hunger in my chest as I heave, my stomach full of naught, but bile and acid. My head swims as I try to rise, the call of my master pulling me as the scent of my own burning flesh fills me.

My feet draw me towards my dresser, and the bowl of water atop it, the iced water making me flinch as I break the seal, the crackle of frozen water shattering the silence around me.

I feel it, cold against my face and neck. The hiss of my scars sending up twisting coils of steam as the frigid water traces through the runes and patterns carved into my flesh. I stare at the human meat coating my body, its pink skin glistening with sweat already as the heat of my masters call begins to rise. I know if I ignore it for much longer this form will immolate, the swine flesh burning to cinders around me.

I close my eyes for a moment as I once more soak my skin in the crystal waters before me and there they are; the eyes, those iridescent violet eyes. So foreign and haunting, yet comforting and familiar in a single glance, how, where, who, all are questions I cannot venture to answer. Even in the echoes of my mind, all that grows is madness and silence. Like lines in the sand my mind wanders, searching for an answer that is gone before it is found. A voice breaks the silence around me, my eyes snapping open as I turn to face its owner.

'Infuriating isn't it Albion, the unattainable memory dancing like leaves in the wind. Tell me brother, do they perchance look like this?'

I watch the face shift, eyes twisting from the dancing green that were once an iridescent violet. They take me in, surging through me in a single glance, as if within them is held the key to resurrecting the sun that once illuminated my mind. A land, where now, naught but darkness and fear hold sway. I screw my eyes tight as I begin to whimper, my knees buckling under me as the figure begins to speak.

'Don't fight it brother, don't fight it, let it take you, carry you. Forget all that you were, become all that you should be, forget it all, don't fight it.'

'I ... I ... I can't, I need to know, I need to know!'

I clutch at the sides of my head willing myself to remember, wanting to remember now more than ever whom these haunting orbs belong to, but it is for naught, for as much as I try I cannot find the owner of my suns resurrection.

'No you don't brother, forget it all, let it slip away, just let it slip away.'

Black takes me once more, my head sinking against the stone floor below as I feel hands clutch at my skin, the shadowed figure twisting, dancing back to its true form as I find an ice laced comfort take hold.

'Alp?'

'I'm here brother, I'm here. Come on, let's head home.'

With the eyes still haunting my every glance, Alp helps me as I drag my armour back over me, the leather and mail sitting heavy on my shoulders, pulling it tight and making my way towards the door.

✦ ✦ ✦

Smoke ensnares me, the guttural caw of my kin clamouring for supremacy against the driving beat of the music that pummels my senses. The rippling rhythm pours over me as the salt tang of sweat and lust soaks my tongue. I shiver as my loin's burn and pulse races.

'Albion, brother, join me.'

'Not tonight Alp, my mind can't take much more.'

'Ah, be a man, here, drink.'

I take the Bruvou from Alp's outstretched hand, his face a mask of twisting emotion as he smiles. My brow furrows, a slim line of alarm filters through me as I sip softly at the drink in my hand.

'Ah look everyone the great and vaunted Albion Weisser is too sensitive to drink like a man.'

'Fuck you Alp.'

I tip the stone carved mug to my lips, pouring the sickly thick liquid down my throat. A strong scent catches at my senses, familiar yet foreign. I know it from somewhere, and yet I cannot fathom where.

My mind swirls, the drink in my stomach boiling like the waters of the river Styx. I let the cup slip from my grasp shattering like glass on steel on the floor as I begin to stumble. I turn my eyes to Alp's, his smirk making fear grip my core as I watch his eyes dancing for the briefest of moments. The shimmering green swirling into an iridescent violet and back again. I push myself away, my arm rising in a futile gesture as the press of flesh, grasping hands, and the sickly sweet scent of another's breath on my lips and cheek drags me into the fold.

I duck my head surging through the crush, head spinning, those violet orbs soaking me, drenching my body in a nerve shredding deluge that has me quaking like a toddler lost in the rain. I finally reach the door to my cell and send it slamming shut behind me as I blessedly find solace in silence.

✦ ✦ ✦

*I am running, my feet scouring the floor as I feel my lungs burn. Nothing can shake the feeling of my being watched even as I twist and turn through the alleys and pathways of the world that surrounds me.*

*I feel the earth shake, ground buckling, my pathway falling away at my heels as I struggle to keep from descending head first into darkness. I cast my gaze about me, the violet eyed wraith greeting my every glance. Iridescent orbs wreathed in black, face lost beneath the darkness. Beckoning hands and soft sensual moans, the shade calls to me, even now as I am running, running for my very life, they call, faceless violet eyes that, all at once seem so familiar and yet oh so strange.*

*I stagger stone crumbling as I drag myself upright, scurrying on my hands and feet like a chimp. My heart hammers in my chest as I hear the soft air filled gasps of the shadow behind me.*

*'What do you want from me? Who are you?'*

*Hands ensnare my throat, lifting me from my feet as I fall into the black; tumbling, twisting, gossamer robes curling around me as the shadow swallows me whole.*

My shoulders kiss the ground, chilled stone shocking me from my sweat soaked sleep. I lie gasping, my chest heaving as I feel tears sting my eyes. Who is this faceless maiden that so haunts my dreams and stalks my days?

I crush the balls of my hands into my eyes, even now as I lie panting amidst the sweat drenched sheets of my bed, the cold stone biting my flesh. One thought rises through my mind, its solitary presence echoing in the blank cavern that has opened up within me.

Who is she, who is this faceless Demonette that plagues my mind?

I roll onto my knees and rise, legs shaking, struggling to lift my weight as I stagger to the small bathroom in my cell. Reaching out I turn the tap listening to the piping echo and clank in the walls around me. Ice laced water crashes down over my fear and sleep heated skin, frigid balls of cold rolling down my back as I lean against the wall.

Her face pierces my mind as I grind my forehead into the roughhewn stone; blood seeping from my brow, mingling with the water at my feet as it drips from my chin and snakes down the wall. I cannot shake the gaze from my mind, the iridescent eyes that gaze out at my soul from within a pitiless void of black; the sheer bewitching stare bores through my heart, lancing me to the core with a single glance.

Yet even as I feel my own blood mingle with the frigid waters that pound down around me, something unerringly familiar strokes at my memory. I know those eyes, two piercing orbs that hold so much comfort and fear within them, but like mist through grass I cannot catch hold of just what so stirs my mind.

I curl my fingers into my palms as I beat at the wall, all my will soaking away as I crumble to my knees. Skin striking stone as I drag flesh from bone, the pain washing my mind clear as the eyes of my unknown temptress slowly fade from my mind's eye. I stare at the shredded flesh that hangs like burnt silk from the walls of my shower; the edges curling, whispering with smoke and sulphur as it begins to turn to ash as water hisses against my raw flesh. My red hued skin makes my stomach clench as I feel another form whisper from within, the pale skin and sapphire blue eyes that stare back at me as I turn to the mirror behind me. Anger and anguish flow within them as I turn my head, the foreigner before me matching my movements. I reach up, my talons clawing at my cheek as I watch the pale gauntlet coated fingers touch the face within the glass.

I know that face, I have worn it, I still wear it, and yet, as I look into the eyes that hide within the sheet of silvered glass, I know it is not mine. It is a shadow of something I used to be and whatever I was, it is not what I am now. I feel my stomach lurch bile searing my throat as I vomit into the sink in front of me, viscous ooze and steaming acid burning my tongue spattering across the travertine sink below me.

Taps twist in my grip as I watch the water flow, washing away the deluge of my confusion. Crystal clear liquid fills my palms as I lift them and send it splashing over my face. I cuff away the dangling strings of saliva and mucus before once more letting my gaze rise to the mirror. I grunt in relief as I find naught, but my own face staring back at me, my sulphurous eyes glowing with anger and confusion as I twist the taps closed.

The stench of alcohol and sweat fills my senses as I push my cell door aside, the mind bending heights that tumble away before me make my head spin as I step towards the stairs. Piles of groaning gasping flesh fill my path as I reach the base of the stair case, skin glistens and bodies writhe as I watch one supine form arch as she pushes down upon the slathering Demon beneath her.

The sounds of skin striking stone draws my attention as I watch Alp drag himself free of one glutinous mass. His grinning face meets my eyes as he stands as naked as the day he was cast from his mother's loins.

'Albion, where were you? The Harpies and Sirens were in particularly amorous forms last night.'

I turn my gaze away as he stretches, his length slapping against his thigh.

'Brother as much as I enjoy our morning conversations, I do prefer them when you're dressed. I've no more desire to see your third eye than I'm sure you do mine.'

Alps eyebrow rises as he smirks, his body shifting; flesh and skin moving with fluidity as he morphs into a woman. Skating his hands down the curves of his own, now feminine body, Alp grins.

'Does this form please you more Albion?'

He lifts his hands to his chest teasing and twisting the cherry flushed nipples that adorn the pendulous breasts filling his hands. I shake my head, a mirth filled smirk playing across my lips as I turn away from him, my shifter friend.

'The only person "that" is pleasing is you Alp. Now, if you're done playing with yourself go get dressed, we've a patrol to make.'

✦ ✦ ✦

Heat soaks me, my padded, chainmail lined leather armour clinging to my body, swelling and tugging with every movement I make. My feet slip through dust and sand as I make my way along the cliff edge. The echoing call of crashing waves draws my gaze for a moment, my mind folding as I watch the echoing blue fall again and again, against the crimson cliffs below.

'The tides pulling heavier, something is looming on the horizon.'

Alp's nodding form teases my peripheral vision as he moves to a crouch beside me. The smell of the ocean swirls through me as I pluck a handful of soil from beside my foot, pebbles and crimson dirt clinging to my palm as I let it slowly slip from my closed fist. Wind catches the dust sending it dancing through the air, swirling and twisting as it is buffeted by the turbulent spray as it rises from the water soaked cliffs.

A heavy pulsing rolls along my spine, my hackles rising as my hand slips to my holstered pistol. Alp nods. I watch his skin suit take hold, his eyes turning to me as I grimace, my red sun burnished flesh rippling as the sallow pink flesh of the pigs encases me. I stare at my fingers as my talons sink beneath the veneer of humanity. Rising to my feet, I roll my shoulders breathing in deeply. Salt stings my tongue and throat as I lift my weapon free and turn away from the cliff edge.

'It would seem Alp, that the heathens are moving sooner than we estimated.'

The pulsing begins to grow, sending a blistering heat through me. Alp shivers as he glances at me, a nervous tick pinching at his eye, the guttering shadows of Gabriel's minions floating across the amber orb that hangs high above us both. My scalp itches as I watch one of them pause, the beat of their wings thrumming in my ears as they hang in the air, silhouetted against the horizon.

'Their movement and concealment isn't what I thought it would be Albion. This one certainly doesn't know how to maintain a modicum of stealth, and given their proximity to our territory, one would think that would be their priority.'

I watch the figure, their shape all too familiar. The sheer arrogance that oozes from them drowns everything as my eyes draw them into focus, the rippling haze of iridescent heat that shimmers at the hovering Angels hip, makes my heart seize. There is only one Angel in all of Heaven and Hell that carries a weapon with such an over bearing aura.

'Michael.'

The name slips from my lips like oil over water, my very soul burns with anger at the name and yet, deep within my core I know it is pulling from something far more ingrained. A burning hatred so raw and pure that nothing in this existence would ever come close to measuring the equal of it, in this life time or any other, fills my senses.

'The Arch?'

Alp turns to stare at me, his gaze wide with fear as I spy him from the corner of my eye. I nod slowly as Michael's lips lift in a sneer of self assured pride, pride that flirts with the edges of vanity, a vanity so self indulgent that it shines like a nova. With a heavy beat of feathered wings he turns, the snide, malice filled smirk burned into my vision as I watch the heathen peacock disappear into the haze of the new day. I glance to my left, Alp's hands reflexively twitching around the hilt of blade, the soft growl of my own echoing my friend's nervousness. I lift my hand free from my caster, the heavy leather holster grinding against my thigh. My fingers stroke the hilt of my blade, its cooing sending a soft, warm shiver through my mind.

I motion catching Alp's attention, his gaze following mine as his eyes land on what holds my ire. The thoughts of Michael and his flaming phallus washed clean as we follow the litany of Sleepers that are crawling their way through the rocks and dust below us. I nod towards the right of the traverse, Alp slipping into the shadows, his body twisting as he shrinks and moves ever deeper into the darkness.

I cannot help but feel a smirk twitch my lips even as my heart begins to sink, pain lancing through me as those eyes, those faceless violet eyes fill my mind. My teeth sink into my lip as I fight the urge to scream, my gorget pressing tight to throat as I lift the bavier into place, the thick chainmail lined leather sitting snug over the lower half of my face.

A soft whisper flirts with my ears, my name drifting from the lips of the wind as I frantically cast my gaze in all directions, the soft intonation dragging at my mind. I know the voice, I know those eyes and yet, nothing in the world can pull it from the cavernous vault that has so swallowed all that ever filled my mind. Names, faces, places, people; all of it, everything, is just gone. Not even the faces of my own parents remain, just the turgid shapes and shadows of a world I know I should belong to, but can never find a way back into.

I turn my mind outwards, the Sleepers slowly inching towards Alp, his slim frame wedged into the gap between two orbs of granite, rifle sling wrapped around his arm as he takes aim at the feathered scum below us. Yet, try as I might to block out the shadows of everything that came before, everything that haunts me, I still see them dancing through the ravine below.

I watch them, the Sleepers, their black leather clad bodies shifting, all but dancing, through cleft and crevice as they make their advance. I watch one, their hooded form twisting against stone and dirt as they inch their way into Alp's sights. Their head swivels, eyes locking to mine. Those violet eyes, that face a blank slate of bottomless black, body sheathed in darkness and deception, try as I do to find its name, I cannot. I cannot dredge from my mind the name that I need, the name that paints itself across my heart and soul, the name that is forever etched into my bones. I know, once uttered I will be forever free of this torment, but, a part of me. Something dark and twisted does not want that freedom, and I am not sure I truly deserve it either, no matter how much this faceless spectre tries to wrest it from me.

The snapping whine of a long caster being fired yanks me from my reverie with a heavy crash. I leap forwards, my blade sliding free as my feet find purchase on the body of one Sleeper, its chest collapsing under my weight as I send them tumbling into the dirt in a gasping mass of blood and flesh. The howl of my blade stings my mind as I feel the handle warm in my grip, the stench of blood filling my nostrils as the rhythmic crack of Alp's long caster sends another winged heathen into the eternal sleep.

# 4

## Fading

## ARIANWEN

**I move through the motions. Day … after day … after day. My** movements almost robotic, my responses practiced. Everyone around me seems to believe I am happy. Happy with all the attention I am receiving from Gabriel, happy with all the compliments from my kin on what a wonderful wife I will be if I am chosen. Happy with the joy I see on my parents and sisters faces at the prospect of me standing beside one of our most admired leaders for eternity.

Eternity.

Never is there a word with such infinite finality, and yet, my current situation is anything but final. It is just a façade to hide behind, just a temporary fix to a problem so grand I feel it may swallow me up, never to be seen again. Maybe that would be easier? But no, I will not let my thoughts trail down such a dark path. I have a tiny little life depending on me, and I am the only parent it has at the moment.

Albion's scent has been fading more with each day. It has been almost five weeks since I last saw him, almost five weeks since I was last held tightly in his arms, almost five weeks since I last felt my heart truly beat a steady rhythm. I am fearful for his safety, for his soul. Who knows what kind of treatment he has had to endure since Michael and Lucifer torn us apart. A painful shutter racks my body as my soul whimpers in pain.

I have yet to find a safe moment to try and make contact with the man who holds my heart in his hand. I have been watched very carefully by Michael and Gabriel. I have not been allowed to attend a calling alone. If it is not Gabriel accompanying me, it is one of his generals, and all of my callings have been on the outer edges of the village, which is strange, but I like to think that it is because someone higher is watching out for me, keeping me from Lucifer's attention. But, this extra surveillance has also drawn the attention of my entire kin upon me. I am stopped on a daily basis by well wishes and interested people who only now want to know every little thing about me. What food I like or my favourite flower, all mundane things. If only they knew what was lurking beneath my surface.

I feel as if I have not had a moment's peace to myself in so long. The only little bit of quiet I receive is when I go to see the Bookkeeper with the excuse of collecting stories to read to the young ones, something I have been doing on a daily basis. It is the only time I am not followed or carefully watched. Even Claire the Bookkeeper seems to sense I desperately need this time alone. If only they all knew what I was really doing in the basement of books.

I research, gathering every piece of information I can find on the last and only child born of an Angel and a Demon. Some are truths, some are myths, but I soak up every word I can find. I need to be prepared for anything that may come our way. I also research other immortal worlds in case the worst comes to pass. I do not want the unknown to take us by surprise. I just wish I could share all of this information with Albion.

I have been strong during the daylight hours, keeping busy, masking my true feelings in front of everyone. But when night falls, so do I. The minute I retreat to my personal bedroom, the instant the door slips shut and I hear that familiar sound of the handle clicking into place, my internal struggles start to flow over, and my scattered emotions end up all over the floor before I even have a chance to lay my head on my pillow. I try to hold it back for the sake of my little hidden secret, but I just cannot. I use up all the strength I have throughout the day. When I smell the familiar scent of apple blossom, or see a bright red or blue flower in the same tones as the crystals in my cloak, or every time I hear a calling and step foot onto the forgotten forest floor, I use all my strength to mask my pain in those moments. Those once joyous memories now tainted by the night I was ripped away from the man I love, from the Demon that owns my heart, from the father of my unborn child.

At night is when I let it all go.

I know it is not good for the child, but my body takes over, and I have no control over falling apart under the dark night stare. I look after myself. I rest when I need to, and I eat constantly for the sake of my little miracle, but by the end of the daylight, I feel so weak. I do not know how much longer I can do this alone before my health and the health of my unborn child is affected.

Maybe today is the day to end all my worries. The leaders and their council, including all Generals, will be attending a meeting. This will be the first time they have all been busy at once. This may be the only chance I get to sneak into the forgotten forest without being followed.

I put on my sandals and grab my cloak and lay it over one arm. I use that arm to cover my stomach. I am still not showing to the outside world, but just in case, I do not want to take a chance. I walk slowly through Eden, wondering through the flower lined paths, smiling and saying hello to those I pass, looking as if I do not have a care in the world, even though underneath the surface I am starting to panic slightly the closer I reach the edge of my world.

Thank the Heaven's my senses have become heightened more with each passing week of my pregnancy. I was always in tune to everything around me, but it seems now that I can consciously think of one person and instantly sense their aura and know the exact location they are currently at, so before I cross the border of my home and under the larger than life stone protectors of our world, I stop and concentrate on first Michael's and then Gabriel's aura, making sure that neither have left the great hall. From what I can gather, the meeting is still in place and every important member of our leadership is in attendance.

I reach the ancient Dragon Gatekeepers and take a moment before I take a step over the border. The last time I passed these borders, I was unconscious and being dragged with a bag over my head. The memory of the moments just before that will haunt me for eternity and beyond. The deep seated fear I felt when my eyes alighted upon Michael, standing beside the Devil himself, is a feeling I never want to relive again. The deception that soaked through my aura, knowing that one of my own kin was consorting with the enemy, was devastating.

I take a deep cleansing breath, calming myself as much as I can, ready to set all of my senses on high alert and send a silent prayer to the Heavens above for my safe return. Even though my first step onto the leaf covered floor of the forest is without a sound to the surrounding world, it sounds like a howling tornado inside my head. My heart is beating so fast it is sending my blood through my form at twice the normal speed, as I scent Albion stronger than I have in weeks. Baby can sense it too, if the two kicks it just delivered to my stomach is anything to go by.

I move with extreme care, using my abilities to sense all movement within this dreary haven between worlds. The usual forest critters are scurrying about, and I can sense two fellow Reclaimers entering the village of the condemned, but so far no Hunters, no imminent danger is lurking. I move deeper into the forest, still staying a distance from the village, until I find a small clearing that is well hidden. And then I wait. I wait and hope, praying that my love can sense me here, and we will finally be reunited after all these weeks.

As I wait, I imagine his eyes as they bore into me for the first time after our long absence, the fire in his pupils as they glisten with need, the slight rise of one side of his lips that turns me inside out, the lowering of his shoulders as he sighs in relief at finally having me within reach, his hands bawling into fists and slowly releasing as he tries to gain control of the love and lust that roars through his body, his feet walking slowly towards me ready to claim what is his. And when he finally lays those plump red lips upon mine ... all my worries will wash away in our sea of ecstasy, never to return ... for at least this small moment in time.

Seconds feel like minutes, minutes feel like hours, hours feel like days as I wait for any sign of my love's awareness of me here. Panic threatens to rise within my aura as the day passes by without Albion seeking me out, here, desperately needing him, desperately wanting him to feel me, to come to me, to see me, to see the small signs of our child growing within my body yet ... nothing.

I still scent his presence deep within the confines of Hells walls, and I am at a loss as to how to send a silent message for him to come to me. He has always known I have entered the forest within my first step and meet me almost with my second, but now ... I stand here alone after hours of waiting, knowing the longer I stay here, the more danger I risk to not only myself, but our baby hidden within, yet, I cannot leave. After waiting all these weeks to finally seek him out, I am unable to physically walk away without being encased in his arms.

I close my eyes and send everything I have to him, my thoughts, my scent, my aura, everything I have to try and draw him from whatever prison he is encased in, desperately pleading silently for fate to please bring us together again, to please let us be one in our time of need, but I receive nothing, but deafening silence. And pain.

Pain threads its way from my head, down my spine and all the way to my toes as I pace back and forth and begin to lose all the strength I have been holding onto these past weeks, knowing that I will have to return to my own world soon before my long absence becomes too noticeable. But, how can I possibly return to all of that with no hope to hold onto? I need Albion to tell me that all will be okay, that we will find a way to be together, that our child will be safe always, that we never have to part again.

I fall to my knees as a million years of tears start to flow down my face with the grief of having to walk away, not knowing when I can return, not knowing if he is all right and not knowing how to reach my love without walking directly into Hell itself. As great as my love for Albion is, I have the responsibility of a little life growing within my womb I have to protect above and beyond everything else. Where once I would have stormed through the village and found a way to sneak behind Hells gates, I now have to return to the safety of my own world and think of another way to reach my heart, my soul, my Demon.

As I take a deep cleansing breath and rise to my feet, preparing myself to leave my hope on the dead and dry forest floor, my senses become aware of an all consuming force, a force that awakens every cell within my body and has my heart beating hard against my ribs as I raise my eyes quickly to look into the other half of my soul. But alarm floods my aura instantly. Albion stands on the other side of the clearing, but the man before me, is not the same man I was torn from weeks ago. Something is different, something is very wrong, his distant stare breaking my heart as I try to quickly come to terms with what is in front of me.

He is still divine in every way, his large form seeming to have grown in our absence, his hair longer hanging down one side of his solid jaw, his lips still as red and plump as I remember them, his shoulders broad with strength, his hands still gloriously large hanging by his sides, his muscles still rippled under his tight leather clothing. But ... his eyes are not the eyes of the man I fell so deeply in love with.

They are slightly lazed over, but that does not dull the menacing stare he is giving me that is full of confusion but also of hate. The eyes I am staring deeply into do not belong to my Albion. Fear starts to wind itself like poison ivy through my veins as I notice that his breath is coming hard and fast as if he is having trouble controlling his temper.

Without meaning to, I take a step back out of protection for our unborn child before I stop myself and stand firmly in place. Regardless of what the Devil's magic has done to the other half of me, I will not leave him in this state. But, not knowing what has happened to him or the spell he seems to be under, I need to proceed with caution.

'Albion,' I say softly, hoping that his name from my lips will bring his focus back to me, back from wherever his mind is trapped, but instead of recognition filling his eyes, he flinches back a little and frowns deeper. 'You need to leave,' he says in a tone I have never heard from his mouth before. It is deep and it is threatening, it makes shivers crawl all over my skin, but I will not back away.

'Albion, it's me, Arianwen.'

I plead, but there is no recognition in his eyes, just fuming anger that is barely contained. 'You need to leave,' he repeats louder this time, but I will not flinch, I will not leave, I will get through to him. He is mine, and I will not give up on him.

'I'll not leave you here like this. You're just lost. Search deep within, and you'll find me, I promise. I'm a part of you and you are a part of me; our souls are one, this is just the Devil's games at play, and I'll not let him win, you'll not let him win Albion. Fight harder!'

I plead with as much passion as I can as he still stands there like a statue, a very fierce angry statue. I watch as he swallows hard and then takes a deep breath before releasing the words that will shatter me to pieces.

'You need to leave before I'm forced to kill you!'

His roaring words echo around the quiet of the forgotten forest as my heart breaks and falls to the pits of despair, as I witness the man I love barely able to hold on to the control he is gripping so fiercely. I cannot leave him. But ... for the safety of our hidden miracle, I take a step back ... and then another ... and then another as tears silently fall down my pale cheeks, my eyes refusing to leave his, his lost and confused and angry eyes; eyes that once looked upon me as if I was as precious as the air that he breathes.

Just as I am about to step out of his stare, I see his frown deepen in thought, before he is no longer in my sight. I still continue to take slow steps backwards, unable to think straight, unable to comprehend what just happened, unable to physically let go of my love, my life, my all, who stood before me as a stranger. A stranger so clearly under the control of Lucifer's mind games, games I will not let him win. If Albion is unable to fight, I *will*.

I will find a way to free my love.

As I turn around to concentrate on taking careful steps, baby takes that moment to lash out with five consecutive little kicks, sharper than ever before as a tidal wave a nausea takes my breath away and has me stumbling to my knees, retching all over the forest floor. I have a feeling that baby is just as devastated at what just happened as I am. As much as I know I need to fight, fight for us all, the grief that washes through my aura is overwhelming.

With silent tears still raining from my eyes, I rise to my feet and carefully make my way back to the safety of my world. I need to think. I need to come up with a new plan. I need to find a way to beat the Devil at his own games. But, right now I need to rid myself of the grief of not seeing the Albion who loves me, the Albion who would do anything for me, the Albion who would love the child I hold within.

I blindly make my way over the border between worlds, not hearing the sympathetic whimpers of the stone Dragons, then through the garden of my world and into the comfort of my own home. It is late and my family are all home, busying themselves in the kitchen when I come stumbling in, forgetting to wipe the tear stains from my face. All eyes are upon me, and the room falls silent at what I can only imagine is utter devastation poured across my face.

'Arianwen, what's happened?'

My mother says in panic as she reaches out for me, holding onto my shoulders as she takes a closer look at my face. Think quickly, I say to myself before I cause them all more worry. 'I think I've been overdoing it lately, I feel so exhausted and weak. I think I may need to reduce all the extra duties I've been taking on lately.'

This lie flows easily off my tongue because it is mostly truth. To keep myself from the grief of missing Albion, I have thrown myself into anything and everything that involves our world. This has also had the advantage of keeping Michael and Gabriel from watching me too closely, allowing me time each day to slip away from all my extra duties to head to the Bookkeepers cottage for research.

But, in amongst it all I have made sure to look after myself and ensure I am eating all the essential things baby needs. But, I must admit, I am exhausted for many reasons. It feels like the weight of the worlds may never leave my shoulders. My mother frowns at me, looking very carefully into my eyes making me think she sees too much. *Oh no.* What if she can tell I am with a child? A mother's intuition is a powerful force, something I have recently started to learn. Before I start to panic, mother starts to move me towards my bedroom.

'No wonder you're exhausted, you've taken on way too much lately my daughter. You're already a favourite to win Gabriel's heart, so if all this extra work you've been doing these past few weeks is an attempt to prove you are worthy, then stop. Your kin already knows what a wonderful person you are and that you'd make a wonderful wife to our leader, so you've nothing to prove. Please slow down before you make yourself sick. Go rest on your bed for a while, and I'll bring your dinner in when it's ready.'

She kisses my head lightly, pushing me slowly towards my bedroom door, before letting go and returning to the rest of the family in our kitchen. I want to let grief have its way, but I know that it is not good for baby. I am a little frightened of what the stress has already done to our precious child, but under the circumstances, I feel I am doing the best I can.

I close my eyes with the intent of resting just as my mother commanded, but as soon as I do, all I see are visions of Albion. His lost glassy gaze, his tense hardened pose, his angry stare and the harsh tone of his words. A sob escapes my mouth before I can stop it with my hand flying up to clamp over my lips, not wanting to let another one pass.

I have to control this. I must not let it boil over. I think of baby. I think of its strength in being conceived against all odds and what it has had to endure in its small time of existing. I have not been able to flourish and rejoice in my pregnancy like most new mothers. My emotions have been sorrow, pain and fear, not exactly the best building blocks to the start of a little life. I have to strive to give it the best possible start in life despite what is surrounding me.

I take a deep breath and gain control of my emotions, vowing from this moment to enjoy what I do have within reach. My barely visible baby bump, my hands resting under the slight swell of my stomach as I stare at it lovingly, a wonderful supporting family who will always love and care for me unconditionally, a beautiful home filled with the most glorious peaceful garden ever to exist, and a community of caring faithful kin whose purpose it is to make people's lives better on a daily basis. I am a very lucky girl to be a part of this world.

I wish I could find a way to stay here for eternity, with Albion and our child. Surely God can sense the Good in him? Surely he would understand our child was made out of pure love? Surely he would not support Michael banishing us from this world because of a love we had no control over? We are good people and have done nothing to deliberately hurt anyone. But a Demon is a Demon, so maybe he would never be able to look past that.

The unknown is what is making my heart ache and my soul scream. I have to make sure I am prepared for any outcome that may come our way and do what I can to protect the ones I love. And just pray, pray that none of them are hurt along the way.

# 5

## Violet Calling

### ALBION

**Dust drifts, hanging in curtains across the slaughter that lies** before me. I listen. The thick crush of feet through wet dirt makes me turn. Alp's blurred form moves towards me as I turn to face him, my gore streaked armour hanging from me like wet linen as I breathe deeply, my lungs stinging.

'They certainly put up a valiant effort. It didn't help, but it was valiant none the less.'

Alp's words make me nod as I pull my bavier down past my chin, the stagnant blood tinged air stains my mouth. Dust clings to my teeth as I drag sweat laden phlegm and grit from my throat. I glance at my companion, his stance easy and face set in a satisfied grin as he moves from my side strolling amongst the twisted corpses of our enemies. Their slowly dissolving forms glowing like the moon as he kneels, lifting one from the floor by her hair, the back of her head naught, but a gaping hole.

My mind burns as I watch the head turn towards me, the features slack and lifeless as I watch the skin begin to slough free, an ebony black void left in its place, as a soft silken voice rolls free from below the violet eyes that now hold sway over mine.

'Albion, I need you Albion, I need you. Come find me Albion. I need your warmth my sweet Demon, come find me, the darkness Albion, free me from the darkness.'

A hand clasps my shoulder, my blade rising sharply as I react on sheer instinct, my mind shredded by the overwhelming emotional torture of what lies before me. A guttural howl echoes in my ears, but all I can see, all that registers on any level of cognitive thought is that voice and the violet eyes that spear my soul.

I cast my gaze about me as spectres rise from the fog of dust and grit, faceless shadows of a svelte and tender figure, all of them glowing with an incandescent light as orbs of violet pin me in place. I scurry back, my body colliding with the ravine wall as my blade slips from my grip lodged in whatever had so grasped me moments before.

'Who are you, what do you want from me? Leave me be spectre, I can't free you from what I can't find.'

The shivering vaporous forms of black close in around me, hands clutching, grasping, curling into my armour as they try to tear it from my frozen body. I cannot tear myself from their grip; my entire being is pinned to the earth beneath me. I try to scream, to beg for clemency from the shadows that are drowning me in their depthless black, but nothing, not a whisper of sound will rise. I feel my lungs burn as they pour down upon me, the words pouring from them, the begging, pleading lament filling my ears as I slowly begin to fade, the edges of my vision dancing with light.

I feel a hand across my face, my bavier long gone, torn from me in the frenzied clutching of the shadows that had been dancing over my prostrate form. My face burns with the impact as I hear it ring across the cavern's walls.

'Albion, snap out of it!'

The voice is all too familiar, the panicked tone that fills it though is not. I turn my gaze towards the sound, slim features, fear and pain pinched eyes locking with my own. Alp's arm quivers as it grabs my shoulder, the wince all too clear to me even in my current state. I tear my eyes from his, casting them around me, searching for a sign of the wraiths that had so lain siege to me moments before.

'Where, where are they?'

Confusion dances in his gaze, sheer puzzlement vying with a

wary apprehension of me. I lift my hand to his arm, Alp twisting away from me as I move. A soft wetness fills my palm as I make momentary contact, the sodden bandage that covers his arm drawing my eye as he speaks.

'Brother, we're the only ones here. There's nothing else aside from dust and empty armour.'

I open my mouth to speak, but, I cannot form the words. What had I just witnessed? Was it some malediction of my own making or a twisted incantation cast upon me at the moment of death by one of the malodorous Sleepers? I still see them when I let my eyes slip closed and yet, by Alp's accounting, there was nothing here to begin with. But, if there had been nothing here, then how could it have felt so real? How could the pressure upon my form have kept me stuck to the floor like a moth on a pin?

No, I know they were real. I felt them as sure as I can feel the beating of my own heart. But, what of Alp's own accounting, could he be lying? I pinch the bridge of my nose as I lean forwards, the passage of my own thoughts making my brain boil inside my skull.

Even if there was nothing here, it still leaves me with one truth. The shades I had seen were very much a reality and those eyes, those damnable eyes even now in my waking hours, can find me no matter how much I try to hide from them; and if they can find me here, then what sanctity do I have, for even my own mind is not safe from my faceless torturer.

✦✦✦

We sit the cool air around us both, pale and calm. The sodden bandages on Alp's arm doing little to assuage my guilt at harming a man who is my brother in all, but blood. I turn away slightly as I lift my drink to my lips, the ice cold water rolling through me, sealing my stomach in a swathe of vacuous ice.

I hear words, I hear a voice, I know its Alp's but, it ceases to register. The prattling of my brother fades into a warped twisting vortex of noise and pain, as the eyes once more swim to the forefront of my mind.

'Albion, come find me Albion, I need you to find me.'

The voice echoes around me as I rise to my feet, my mind snared drawing me towards the door. Hands grasp at me trying to halt my flow, but the pull, the voice, my need to finally reconcile all, is drawing me onwards washing aside all in its path. I cannot deny it, I cannot avoid it, it will not let go. Those eyes, that voice, I need to know what they mean, from what or where they come. They are so familiar yet, nothing I can do can pry from my memory their origin or even the face to which the violet orbs belong, and still they call, one unending all consuming call.

The heat of the day strikes me like a hammer sapping the air from my lungs as I feel my heart race, the call resounding in my head rising to a scream as I turn my body moving of its own volition as I begin to run. Buildings zip past me, the sallow hairless apes cowering as I cast them aside, my need to find the source of my torture filling every fibre of my being.

The echoing call burning my mind, the soft musical voice pouring from deep within my soul, begging me to find it, begging me to bring it home.

My heart beat quickens as the fall opens out before me, the sheer drop sending a rippling ball of trepidation and excitement in equal measure. Without a dip in my stride, I cast myself forwards, arms open wide as I fall into the waiting arms of the wind, my armour rippling around me.

Trees flash and branches snap as I tumble through the canopy, my body rolling across bough and limb as I move like water over stone. The calling, my calling screaming in my skull, dulling every-thing around me, even as I feel one supple pine limb lash across my neck, the welt rising like a boiling red serpent. I come to a stop with a bone rattling thump, needles and dead wood bursting around me as I hit the floor.

Drewen and insect alike begin to whimper and flee, the sentient spires of lumber twisting away from me, vainly trying to flee my path as they strain against the world beneath their roots. The woods fall silent as I slowly rise to my feet. I hate this place, but I know it is where I need to be, my sirens call growing by the second.

I move my body numb to everything except that call. My feet

guide me as I blindly follow, my eyes shifting the forest before me dancing with energy, pushing aside branch and bush and then as if a veil is lifted, I see them. My heart leaps, finally finding the source of what has plagued my very soul. I take a tentative step forwards as the eyes meet my own and yet as they do, despite my jubilation, I feel anger pour through me, taking in who my minds torturer truly is.

*An Angel.* Anger sours my throat; a heathen, a feathered harlot of the spoilt titan that calls himself the one true creator. My blade snarls, my spine tingling as I feel my palm itch for the caress of my blades handle, but despite the screaming of my lineage and the swirling cauldron of hatred that has so been ingrained in me, I find myself speaking. Telling her to leave, telling her to flee my presence and yet, even as I do, I feel a sorrow so clean and pure that crimson tears begin to threaten to make themselves known.

She protests, railing against all I am saying, calling me by my given name, pleading for me to fight, against what I do not know, but still she pleads.

I stand there, my words coating the air around us both as she finally begins to retreat from me, my mind screaming at me to follow, but all I can do is watch, the sadness within me mounting as she finally disappears from view. My mind is a twisted mess; a seething cauldron of snakes in tar has replaced every semblance of logical thought. My violet eyed temptress, the one who has dogged my very soul is an Angel, an Angel, the very beings I have pledged my life and soul to send to the eternal sleep, and even now, is walking away from me back into the sheltered dominion she calls home.

I sought this heathen out in the vain hope of finding solace and peace for my tortured memory and yet, I found what? Absolution? Explanation? No. I found nothing but more confusion and questions so twisted that I would never find their ends if I was given eternity.

I sink to the floor, my body rooted to the spot. I am a Demon, a Hunter, a winged embodiment of malevolence and hatred and yet, as I watch the leaves twist at her departure, the wall of greenery having long ago swallowed her whole, I find myself questioning whether or not that is what I truly am. I have never up until now lain eyes on that violet eyed woman, that, I thought was true. But, if I have never once seen her until now, then, how can she haunt my dreams and mind? And her name, the one she had so earnestly pleaded for me to know, Arianwen, even now as I play it through my head, I know I should know it. I know I should now feel this confusion melt from me as memories I desperately want to remember flood through, but, I cannot; there is nothing there, nothing but darkness in a mind filled with silent confusion.

✦ ✦ ✦

Anger burns in my heart, searing me shut to everything that seeks to wrest emotion from my charred and twisted soul. My blade coos as it feels my ire begin to run, tracing paths of luminescent rage through my blood. I rise to my feet, wiping blood from my eyes and turn, my wings shearing through my meat suit, the pain a soothing balm quirking my lips as I relish in the delicious sensation of feeling my flesh part.

My eyes shift as I take flight, leaving the quivering woods to its fear and inadequacy, rising above the forest and the fall. My clothes ripple as I follow the currents, dancing through stream and eddy, searching for some source of entertainment.

My fangs slip free as I grin, my gaze alighting on a nubile young Reclaimer; the winsome little strip of flesh flitting from shadow to shadow as she moves towards whatever soul is calling to her. The stupid little strumpet has not even noticed my presence. I follow her path as she dances into a doorway, her light shining like a beacon in a storm. I sigh inwardly as I fold my wings back and tumble from the sky like a stone. Dust and debris rises, my body shrouded, my silhouette casting a shadow across the floor and wall as she spins. Her eyes give me pause, the summers that pass in them are all too few as I watch them brim with fear. She stumbles back as I take a slow measured step towards her, my blade slipping into my hand.

'Your name?'

My voice roars in the silence even though I am barely above a whisper. She stares at me, her body shaking as she scrambles into a corner, a small dagger appearing in her hand, the stump of a blade is barely bigger that a paring knife; the diminutive little tool of a kitchen maid as she peels a potato, and yet, this cowering strip of fear soaked fluff is holding it before her like the sword of Damocles.

I bat her hand aside, sending the strip of poorly edged steel skittering away as she whimpers, eyes glistening with unshed fear.

'Your name.'

I am all but nose to nose with this child as I lift my weapon setting the point against her chest, its cold countenance in line with her pounding heart. I feel it rise and fall with the heaving of her chest as she begins to hyperventilate, her face, flushed with the terror of what is to come, and I cannot help but feel amusement.

'One last time, your name; tell me your name before I run you through and send you to the eternal sleep.'

She stutters, her name tripping from her lips in a tangled mess.

'Arianell ... it's Arianell.'

I pause, the name striking a chord deep within me. I pull my blade away slowly, a small speck of red blemishing her dusted skin. I move away from her as I turn slipping my blade into its sheath ignoring its hungered and indignant screams.

'Go. Go now before I change my mind.'

I listen to her scramble to her feet, her rapid departure echoing as I hear a whimpering thank you flirt with my ears as the beat of her wings fills the air. Arianell, her name so strikingly similar to the name of my torturer, Arianwen; the violet eyed woman who haunts my nightmares. Even now, as I seek to fulfil my lineage, she is there in the facets of my mind, controlling, contorting all I do into some tainted mirror image of itself. I am a Demon and yet, with this Angel at the edges of my mind I find myself doubting all I am, all I was raised to be, all I know I should be. But with this Angel, this *Arianwen*, I feel my doubt rising. Am I truly the murderer I have been led to believe I am?

I step out into the ridged furnace of purgatory, heat haze rolling from the roofs around me in waves. The shimmering, boiling air falling away, like water over glass as it coalesces into glistening pools between the buildings.

I walk in a seemingly directionless daze, my feet carrying me onwards without preamble or purpose as I move through lane and thoroughfare, the destitute and dead souls that inhabit these wall less prisons scurrying from pillar to post as I pass, furtively glancing in my direction, eyes wary, darting from me to their supposed salvation.

'Vermin.'

My muttered curse making one of the hairless scum whimper as it fades into the darkness of an open doorway. My feet carry me upwards, away from the noise, away from the putrid swine stench of the foetid pit that surrounds my homelands. I feel the heat break, chilled winds pushing aside the layers of sweat, bathing my skin in a soothing blanket of ice.

I watch the world below me, my path slowly ascending the rock and dust strewn mountain side that rings my homeland. The pit, the gaping maw that leads into Lucifer's kingdom sits shimmering and sulphurous, its charred edges, blistered like the dead core of a rotting tooth. How can this Angel claim to know me, a Demon born of Hell and malice, my father, a Knight of the pit, second only to the King of Hell? I am everything that she should despise and yet, she stood there, pain clean in her eyes as she stared at me; no not pain, it was something else, something deeper. A look I have only ever seen once before, a look so pure and open that it can come from only one place. No, it couldn't be. She is an Angel, a being of light and a minion of the heretic creator.

How could an Angel claim to love me, love a Demon, the absurdity is laughable and yet, that is the only thing that I saw in her eyes, love, for me. Who is she? She calls herself Arianwen, but, before today I have never laid eyes upon her. Pain lances through my skull as I collapse to my knees, images flaring like stars behind my eyes, sinking my fingers into my scalp, screaming, feeling my brain boil in my skull.

Glimmers of memories, images, sounds, it all flows through me, a flood of noise and confusion that tears my mind to shreds. I sink to the floor, my body curling into the foetal position as I claw at my scalp. My fingers bloody and tattered, I can make no more sense of what I am seeing than I could stop the sun from rising.

Flashes of skin; of those violet eyes, her eyes; gasping moans, whispers of my name on her lips, soft near tender declarations of love and devotion. All of it, pours forth as I slowly begin to regain my sanity, my mind sifting it all, pushing myself to my knees, my hands lifting my head from the dirt as I gasp for breath.

This is not some hexing or bewitchment, nothing in any tomb or text could make something that vivid or vexing. No, this is real, her devotion, her pain, is real. It is not some malediction of fate or design; this was ripped from me, from us both. Twisted and scoured from my mind by a hand I once sought to serve, that sought to feed a lie, but one I know now should have been bitten. No Angel would ever love a Demon out of spite, and no Demon would ever love an Angel out of fear.

What I saw in her eyes was real and what she saw in mine, what I made her see, was a lie cast through me by the one person I thought I could truly trust, but then, he was cast from Heaven, and they say that the greatest trick the Devil ever made was making man believe he was not real. So if he can fool the creations of a God into thinking that, scouring the memory of an Angels love from my mind would have been akin to closing a door.

I carry on upwards, the memories squirming, churning in my mind. Nothing complete, nothing more coherent than the charred and tarnished remnants of a burnt photograph. Faces dancing past my mind's eye in flashes, voices echoing in my ears, gasping moans of ecstatic pleasure teasing my flesh as I push higher into the cold and snow capped mountains around me, searching for that point, searching for that one place I know I can be free of everything.

The plateau spreads before me, piercing the clouds, jutting proudly from the face of this millennia old mountain. I move, buffeted and freezing, winds biting through my clothing as if it were paper. I glance over the edge, the dizzying heights doing nothing more than making my stomach tighten. The thrill of the fall beckoning me, calling to me. Many a young person, Demon and Angel alike has ventured here whether it was at the challenge of kin or the lust fed dare of some tart, they all bar none cast themselves from the edge and into the frozen waters below. I hunker down, the winds passing over me as I feel my wings itch, moving like worms in dirt as I fight to keep them contained, the lake partially frozen over now, of that I am certain.

Only a fool would leap from here, a fool or someone looking to meet their end. I smirk. I know I am neither, but, no one has ever accused me of having the sense not to do it. My feet carry me away from the edge, my heart hammering in my chest as I turn and sprint towards the waiting arms of the open air. Leaping out, I cast my arms wide embracing the moment, before I turn and plummet head first towards the ice layered lake below me.

Water bursts around me as the ice shatters, cold searing my lungs and skin, my mind washed clean by the bitter shock. I close my eyes as I breach the surface, water glittering as I gasp, breathing in the frigid air. I bob for a moment like a cork in a bowl, my mind empty, silent for the first time in what feels like a millennium, nothing but silence greets me and as I lay back, shattered ice and chilled water entombing me. I relish in it. Ice begins to form over my arms and legs, its chill seeping into my bones scouring me clean and yet, there she remains; the Angel of my nightmares, Arianwen, my violet eyed torturer. How can one woman hold such sway over a man such as me? I am a Demon. I should be as callous and uncaring of her as I would a dead rat and yet, here I lie, in a lake of shattered ice and frigid water unable to scrub clean the sight of her from my mind.

The vision of her face, the moment she saw me in that clearing sears my brain, the pain, the hurt, the sheer lack of understanding as to who and what I am, has become more than I can truly bare. My breathing slows as I begin to sink into my own mind, images slowly becoming clearer, words, and places, scents, and sounds, all swimming into focus one by one as I lie in the ice bound waters.

One thing overall seeps through my mind, one irrevocable point; she ... this Angel ... my torturer, was in some semblance of reality, mine. My heart seizes in my chest as the weight of all that I once had crashes down upon me. My mind turning in upon itself as I begin to question my very sanity; how could these memories be mine, how could she have been mine? Yet, these memories are no seed of a malicious hand, they are no subversive fabrication, they are real and yet, I still cannot bring myself to admit that they truly are mine, even with the self revelation that all I think I know comes from the machinations of a vain and vicious King.

I lie in my ice encrusted coffin for what feels like eternity, unwilling to move from the silent dance of my mind, even as the call of my King sears the scar on my chest. The scent of my burning flesh rising as I feel the water around me begin to warm from the heat that boils from the glowing rune hacked into my skin. I pry and twist my form, the crystal white layer shattering as I push myself upwards and quickly move towards the shore.

✦ ✦ ✦

'You took your time Weisser. It's not something that I expect from my personal Hunter.'

I kneel as he speaks, the movement involuntary, ingrained in me from the moment I took this path, although, it is not something that I relish in doing. Something inside me screams in anger and disgust every time I find myself prostrating before this fallen Angel.

'I beg forgiveness sire, I was involuntarily detained during your summoning. But I'm here now. What is it that my King requests of me?'

Lucifer smiles, his ivory teeth glowing with the ethereal light of his former kin. I watch with a bubbling trepidation as he moves away, his hand beckoning me to follow as he moves towards his personal balcony. I step to his side, my pace rapid as I stumble slightly before catching myself and settling in at his right hand.

'Albion, many things can transpire in a person's life, they can be cast from their home as I was, they can be subjugated and down trodden as the people of the village are by us, and my former kin or like you, they can be pushed to a point so far beyond their limits both mentally and physically that they ...'

He stops and looks at me, a glimmer in his eyes that I have never once seen before makes me pause. I flinch involuntarily as he sets his hand on my shoulder and smiles. Not maliciously or one pasted in place to hide his real meaning, just smiles almost fatherly in its appearance.

A soft chuckle leaves him as he watches my sudden reaction. I watch him turn away from the window, my feet rooted to the spot as I stand unsure of myself in the light of such an unprecedented and unnerving turn of events.

'You're a powerful man Albion, one that could be and should be destined for greatness, and one that I'd hoped would come to be my protégé, alas that fell to the wayside due to a rather unfortunate turn of events. But, I have a soft fix in mind for that calamity.'

He picks up a small decanter and pours a measure of the softly bubbling liquid inside into two cut crystal tumblers in front of him.

'What would you say if I were to tell you that you've been chosen as a suitor for one of the daughters of Lilu, a man you should know as the father of your father's commander Gilgamesh.'

I stand stunned, the tumbler in Lucifer's hand unclaimed as he smirks ignoring the unintentional slight. My head swirls in a vortex of fear and panic as I cycle through the clutch of names that sit in the back of my mind, one appearing time and again.

'My Lord, I am fully aware of the honour this is, but I must know the name of my would be betrothed, before I can give my final answer.'

Lucifer slowly sets the tumbler aside, his eyes fogged and blank as his lips curl, a knot twisting in my gut as I can already sense the name that will be slowly worming across his lips in a moment, and as he begins to speak. I know my worst fears are realised as my fate is once and for all sealed to the hand that feeds my misery.

'Lilith.'

# Maybe Never

## ARIANWEN

*Her precious rosy cheeks are glowing in the sunlight, as her* adoring father holds her up high into the sun's rays filtering through the gardens tallest trees. Her eyes, so much like my own, wrinkle in joy at this new game. Her plump lips, a mirror image of her daddy's, curl up in a smile as he brings her back down to plant a kiss on her tiny forehead, her little hands taking this opportunity to reach out and snag a lock of his long dark hair without him realising, until he goes to rise her up again.

'Oww,' he grumbles as he brings her back down and tries in vein to pry his hair away from her tight little fists. 'Damn she has some strength in those tiny fingers,' he says more with pride than chastisement. 'Come on baby girl, let daddy go you cheeky one.' She ignores him of course, now too busy trying to pull his hair into her slobbering mouth much to his amusement. 'There are much yummier things to snack on than my hair pretty one. Is daddy's baby girl hungry? Then let's go sit with mummy shall we?'

Albion brings our infant daughter over to me where I am sitting in the shade at the base of a tall oak tree, resting my back against its solid trunk. As soon as she can smell her mummy she starts to fuss in her daddy's arms, desperate to reach her source of food. Our baby girl seems to always be hungry. As Albion swaps our fussing child to his other arm, getting ready to hand her over to me to nurse, I *unstrap one tie of my white dress and let it fall, exposing my very full and now slightly moist breast. I take her from his arms and settle her in her favourite position as she latches on a now dripping nipple. She sighs heavily as she finds the sucking rhythm she wants.*

*Looking down at our precious miracle, I grin, not only at the happiness she has brought to our lives, but at the tilted lips I know her father will be wearing on his face when I lift my head. I raise my eyes and there it is. That dopey grin he gets on his chiselled handsome face every time I feed our child. It is a mixture of curiosity, joy and dare I say it ... heat. Yes, he finds it slightly arousing that my breasts can provide the single life force for our child's needs are also the same breasts that can keep him captivated for hours, especially now since they have more than doubled in size.*

*I elbow him softly to snap him out of his trance and much to my delight, he blushes at being caught thinking dirty thoughts about what our child is suckling at. I giggle, unable to stop myself which only makes him blush more. Who would have thought a Demon could blush and do it so beautifully?*

I sit up straight in bed, my heart pounding loudly in my ears, as I franticly search my surroundings for mine and Albion's child, to only cruelly realise it was just a taunting dream. Tears spring to my eyes as my hands cup my tiny baby belly, needing to feel our child is still within me, wanting to make sure our precious one is still safely tucked where it should be. The tears begin to fall and I let them. I need the release after witnessing the future I so desperately want, the future we all so desperately need.

Seeing the man I love yesterday stare at me as if I was a stranger, is tearing my soul *apart*. But, if I give into the grief that is threatening to strangle me, then the Devil has won ... and I will not let that happen. I will find a way to drag Albion from the spell he is so obviously under and bring him back to the light he deserves to bask in. Our child needs us both, and I will move Heaven and Hell to make sure that is what it gets. I may have woken up shattered, but I will start this day stronger. I will fight and I will win.

With fierce determination I get out of bed, dress for the day and grab an apple from our kitchen table as I make my way out the front door and head to the only place I will find the answers I need. I walk through the winding paths of Eden, smiling at my fellow kin as I continue to walk, moving with haste, my head down, not wanting to get stuck in conversation.

Just before the Bookkeepers cottage comes into view, I am stopped by a very large figure standing in the middle of the path. As I stumble to a stop, I look up to the wicked croaked grin of Michael.

'Well, well, well Arianwen. It seems that you have taken a keen interest in literacy of late. Do you feel our little ones education has been lacking? Or are you reading to broaden your mind? You would think such a clever Angel as yourself already knows everything she needs to know in this life, so what is it that you are seeking I wonder?'

My words are frozen in my throat as panic starts to set in. Surely the Bookkeeper has not told Michael or anyone else for that matter what I have been reading? She has left me alone each time I have come to read. Knowing I need to speak quickly or his suspicions will grow, I say the first thing that comes to mind.

'There would never be enough written information to fill one's mind. I love the written word and want to pass that passion onto the next generation of our kin. The little ones love it when I find a new piece of history they haven't heard before.'

I know he is not convinced by my slightly rushed words, but he does not say it. He just stares ... and stares, as if waiting for me to break first. But I will not. I will not show Michael the weakness he wants to see. He continues to stare and so do I. I will not back down and give in to his stand over tactics. And this makes him *furious*. His face starts to turn red, and I can see him clenching his fists so tight his knuckles are turning white as he quietly pants in anger.

After a few more minutes of silence, he releases a low growl and turns and stomps away from me. I release the large breath I did not even realise I was holding. As much as I am determined to stand up to Michael, I know his power and the power of his friendly enemies, so I will make it a point not to antagonise him in the future. I really do not need to be a target to him any more than I already am. I continue the few steps towards the Bookkeepers cottage, and when I reach it I am greeted with a kind smile from Claire, with the door open waiting for me.

'I knew you were coming and I have some tea ready. Will you have a cup before you head down to the library?' I am surprised she wants to have tea due to the fact that the last few weeks I have just been coming in, smiling with a quick hello as I walked past and straight to the winding staircase that would take me down to the library where I would hide for hours.

Not wanting to be rude to such a lovely lady, I nod politely and step inside her quaint cottage. We each settle at her small table in front of her window as she begins to pour the tea. Her eyes have questions so I sit quietly waiting for her to speak first.

'Are you okay Arianwen? You have been looking slightly pale of late. Are you unwell?' *Damn.* She is one of our cleverest kin. I know I may not be able to talk my way around the truth, but for the sake of my child's safety I have to.

'I'm fine Claire, just a bit exhausted. I think I've been over doing it a bit lately, so I'll cut back on some of my duties.'

I smile sweetly at her, but her wise eyes tell me she knows there is more to it than just exhaustion. 'Are you in trouble dear? If you are, I may be able to help. I'm here for you if you need me.' Her kind and caring words bring tears to the back of my eyes, so I look down and take a sip of my tea, silently composing myself before I answer her questions.

I know she is a loyal kin, but if I told her my troubles, would she be loyal to me or our leaders? If it came down to it, I think she would have to be loyal to the ones who rule our world, not some girl who fell in love with the enemy of our kin. I have no one to safely turn to and for now I do not have the support of the man I love. I swallow the emotion that is threatening to spill over before I answer her. 'I'm fine, there is no trouble here. I just need to slow down a bit.' I smile as sweetly as I can as I look into her wise eyes.

I place my tea cup down and mumble a thank you as I head to the stairs, ready to find the answers I need to fix my complicated life. As I descend the spiral stairs leading to the library, I think back to my lost kin, Anatiamoros and wonder if I could have shared my secret with him. What would he have said? Would he have been able to help me out of this dangerous situation my heart has placed me in? His wisdom is something I am missing in my life on a daily basis. Why did fate have to take him away? Why is fate so cruel as to cross mine and Albion's paths, gift us with love and a child then tear us apart? Why?

These questions well up through the emotions I am struggling to contain, so as I take my last step off the staircase. I vow to push them aside and concentrate on what I do know. That I am going to fight hard to find an answer to all my woes.

I feel like I have read thousands of books by the time I look to the roof, giving my neck a much needed stretch as I hear the door at the top of the stairs open and then slowly close again. I quickly and quietly close some of the books I have opened in front of me about the one and only documented case of a Demon and Angel creating a child, not wanting to raise suspicion as to what it is that I am seeking and hold my breath, hoping it is only Claire who is descending the stairs. When I feel her aura, I let my breath out and pretend to read one of the books I have collected to read to the little ones tomorrow.

'You have been down here so long I thought you may be hungry so I brought you some of my strawberry savarin,' she states happily as she places a small plate with a slice of the cake on it beside me as the smell of warm strawberries floats around the room. I smile and say a quiet thank you, then take a small bite as I continue to pretend to read. She wanders down past a few book cases, seeming to search for something herself, claiming, "here it is", before walking back towards me. I pretend to be engrossed in my reading as she places the book down beside me, before walking back to the stairs and making her way back up to her cottage.

The minute my eyes reach the title of the book she placed, they start to water as I struggle to breathe past the lump that has formed in my throat.

*The Angelic baby.*

I slap my hand over my mouth to stop the sob that is threatening to leap out as the tears start to crawl down my cheeks. I feel a mixture of relief and fear. Relief that someone knows, but fear for what that means. I know Claire has the kindest heart, but she is also very loyal, as all my kin are. A knot forms in my stomach at the unknown.

I close all of the books I was researching, still unclear on what my destiny may hold, and place them back on the shelves, cradling just a few to read to the little ones later today, as I nervously make my way back up the stairs for the inevitable fate of having to look the Bookkeeper in the eye now that she knows.

With every step I take up the winding staircase, my imagination gets wilder. Has she told someone already? Will Michael and his guards be waiting for me outside her cottage? Will I be taken into custody for questioning? Will I be banished from my world? My head is spinning by the time I take the last step up to open the door.

I instantly feel that it is only Claire within her cottage and relief floods my system so fast I feel slightly faint as I take a few steps into her cottage. I look up and my eyes stare directly into Claire's, and it is clear by her frown that she can sense my apprehension. She offers me a beautiful smile as she slowly takes a few steps to stand in front of me, reaching down, taking my hands in hers.

'Congratulations Arianwen. Maybe it was a surprise to you, or maybe not under the best of circumstances, but whatever the reason, whatever the situation, you have been granted the gift of a child by God and the happiness that comes with that will eventually outweigh all of your woes, I promise. And remember ... I'm here for you, you will always be safe under my roof.'

She embraces me in a gentle hug, and I cannot help but squeeze her back tightly, desperately wanting to convey to her the impact that her words have had on me, unable to force my words out past the lump in my throat. I hold onto her for what feels like forever, willing my tears to stay at bay, knowing if I let them out with the emotions that are welling up inside, I would fall to the ground.

I eventually start to let go and take a step back, composing myself the best I can as I offer her a bright smile before turning and heading towards the door, needing some fresh air to ease back these raging emotions. I turn and open the door, relishing in the bright sunshine that warms my body as Claire comes up behind me, placing a soft hand on my shoulder. 'It'll all work out for the best my dear. Enjoy, be happy and look forward to meeting your little gift one day.' I smile but move quickly, determined not to fall into a blubbering mess by her words.

I take deep breaths, walking through this beautiful piece of Heaven, thankful that I am a part of this world. My kin live a simple life, not needing the complicated material things of earth's current times. To them, we would seem to be living in the dark ages, much like their medieval world of old.

We are hard workers, devoted to our kin and our families; wanting nothing more than a peaceful life, with our duty to deliver peace and protection to all of mankind. I relish being able to fulfil my role and then as a Reclaimer, to help those human souls who wrongly find themselves at the foot of the Devil, reach their creator and find the eternal peace that they deserve. We Angelic beings are blessed to serve the Lord of all.

Just as I feel the peace of this world start to calm me, it begins to be rattled by the hushed voices I hear coming towards me. It is Michael and Gabriel, and they are approaching me fast. At this moment, there is no other path to take, and I do not have the time to turn around without being seen, so I quickly duck behind the large trunk of a tree and hope that they pass quickly.

'The force may have been dimmed of late but it is still there, lying just under the surface, maybe waiting for us to let our guard down. I will not let that happen. We have to remain on high alert until its source is discovered.' Michael's voice is low, but no less menacing as I hear him and Gabriel come to a stop.

'There has been no sign of this mysterious entity for weeks, brother, and we have had every available soldier out looking, for what, we still don't know, but we are losing kin for no solid reason. Being on constant watch for something we know nothing about is just making everyone nervous. I think we need to relax a little.' Gabriel tries to reason with his brother. I do not need to hear any of this, but have no way of escaping this situation without being detected, and I do not need to be questioned by both brothers.

'I have my suspicions as to what the source may be, I just need more time to confirm it.'

'Patience then brother, I'm sure all will be revealed soon. Until then we continue with our patrols and sending out spies into the forest. We will not let our guard down.'

When Michael said he has his suspicions, my scalp prickled. He knows I was sleeping with the enemy, but has never mentioned our connection to the force that rocked all of the worlds, but it would not take much for him to put two and two together.

I know they have not sensed me yet, and I feel overwhelming relief when they begin to move on towards the great hall. I let out the breath I was holding onto tightly, and when they are out of sight I move back onto the path and make my way quickly home, knowing the danger that looms over me is anything but gone.

Lost in my own thoughts just before my home comes into sight, I feel a sense of danger begin to crawl over my skin as I realise exactly what the cause of it is. He steps out from behind a small house and stands there, in the middle of the path, looming over me with a vicious grin on his face.

'Did you really think I didn't know that you were eves dropping on the conversation I was having with my brother? You seriously underestimate my intelligence Arianwen, but I'm quite aware of yours, and I'm waiting for you to prove my suspicions right. So save me the time and tell me exactly how you and your Demon lover created such a disturbing force that you have all of the immortal worlds scrambling around like frantic rats, all trying to find a way to save their own hides.'

He steps closer with each word until we are standing nose to nose, but I will not back down and give him the satisfaction of making me wilt beneath his harsh tone. I know I need to be careful, but I do not want to give him any more fuel to use against me.

'I've told you before, I haven't seen anything that has caused such a powerful shift in our worlds, nor am I or Albion, responsible for such a thing.' His face turns red at my denial, and he seems to grow larger with anger, but I stand my ground until he reaches out and grabs a handful of my hair before I have a chance to escape his impending grasp. He yanks harshly causing me to yelp in pain as he then brings his head down hard upon my own. I briefly see stars before I ready myself for another possible blow. But, he just brings my face up to his again before continuing with his tirade.

'I am no fool, so stop treating me as if I am. Tell me the truth Arianwen, and it may spare your families lives. Because you see, your alliance with the enemy not only affects our worlds, but also the people in it. Do you want to be the cause of your kin's death or the death of one of your ... sisters shall we say? Hmmm. Think about it Arianwen, do you want their blood on your hands for eternity?'

I know what he is trying to do, and internally it is working. His words are twisting my heart as I would want nothing more than to see all of our kin and my family safe. But, the force that mine and Albion's love caused, would never be a source of Evil. I feel deep within my soul that one day our love will be called upon for Good and not Evil. So I will mask the pain his words have caused and draw on my little one's strength to stand strong in the face of such malice.

'We didn't create such power or a force of any kind. We were just star struck lovers, nothing more, nothing less. You, yourself worked with the Devil to separate us, so maybe you should ask his opinion on what this mysterious force could be.' I regret those last words as soon as they leave my mouth, knowing that they are just poking an angry bear. I brace myself for what I know is coming. With him still holding my hair in one hand, he sends the other across my cheek, the force echoing through my skull, making my vision blur as he then pushes me face down into the soil at my feet, before crouching over my head, whispering in my ear.

'How dare you use such an accusing tone with me! You have no idea what it takes to keep our world safe. You are smart enough to know that one needs to keep their friends close but their enemies closer, so from time to time, if it benefits me and our world, I will call upon an old foe for a favour just to keep the status quo in our court. And what do you think it would do to our world and the people who live in it, if they were to discover that one of their most beloved kin has been cavorting with the enemy? My brother's infatuation with you is the only reason you are alive, because Reclaimers die out in the forgotten forest all the time, so it would have been an easy lie to tell our kin that you simply died doing your duty. But believe me, the day you are no longer needed, will be the day I make you pay for your sins. It'll come one day Arianwen, when you least expect it.'

With that, he pushes my face into the dirt, then rises and stomps back down the path and I stay still. Am I shocked about the way one of my leaders has treated me? No. I have always felt the anger surrounding Michael, but I am a little surprised he used his force across my cheek, such a hard injury to explain to others. But I will raise, I will brush myself off and I will remain strong, because without strength, I would just shrivel up and cave into his threats and that, I will not do.

# 7

## Life Over Death

## ALBION

**I stagger away from Lucifer's chambers, the vision of his all** knowing and all too self satisfied smirk burned into my mind. My head swirls with a vortex of hatred, revulsion and confusion. Lilith that heathen witch. How can he expect me to pledge my eternal life to that embodiment of malice and hate? I stumble, my knees buckling as I feel my heart and stomach seize as one. Acid bile sears the roof of my mouth as I heave, my body rebelling with a ferocity only surpassed by the hatred I hold for that carrion whore.

My feet carry me forwards, the ground slopping away from the burning pit of hate and anguish that is my Kings chambers. The pulsing rhythm of the Undercroft shivers through the soles of my feet. The doors fall away from me as another of my drunken and amorous kin staggers through, the grin on her face all too plain as she looks me up and down, the lust in her eyes as blatant as her state of dress. She smirks as she watches my eyes travel over her sweat glistened skin, the pursed nakedness of her form calling in even the most stalwart of gaze.

'See anything you like *Master Hunter?* I see something I like, and I like it a lot.'

She cups her left breast as she moves towards me, her fingers teasing her nipple as she grinds against my side. I turn away, my hand cupping her face as I push, sending the sodden harlot sprawling as she screams in a drunken half cackle.

'Only time I would lay with a drunken lump of carrion hole such as you, is when no better option remains for the continuation of our people. Until then, remove your naked drunk visage from my sight.'

I feel her eyes on me as I move into the croft, the thick miasma of sweat and alcohol coating my throat and tongue in a paste so vile that I doubt anything will ever scrub the taint free. The auras mingle, blending into one oppressive tumult of uplifting energy, energy that burns through my veins, igniting my nerves in a blazing wall of blinding white. The thudding base line rolls through everything, my chest vibrating as I try to breathe through the wall of sound assailing my senses.

I move through the crowd, assaulted by grasping arms and gyrating hips. I feel searching fingers trace across my loins, cupping and squeezing. A firm hand makes me stop, searching fingers sinking into the leather seat of my trousers. I turn, my head a mess of conflicting thoughts and emotions playing through me as I come face to face with the miscreant cupping my buttock.

The glittering taint of insanity drips from her eyes, the cruelty that stains her smirking lips makes my blood burn as she steps closer to me, her hand finding its way to my wrist. The sway of her hips and tilt of her head scream death and seduction, all of it oozing from the succubus that stands before me, the embodiment of lust and perversion that stands gazing at me through violet eyes.

'Albion, I have to say, you're looking decidedly delicious today.'

She holds my gaze as I pull away from her lingering grip. My throat constricting as I feel her grip tighten, her jaw clenching as she struggles to contain her true nature.

'You're not leaving me are you Albion? You only just got here.'

I set my hand atop hers, my talon sinking into the skin between her thumb and index finger. I watch with a tinge of amusement as her eyes water with suppressed pain as she fights not to cry out.

'I am afraid, Lilith, that much to my *dismay* I have to go. I'm on patrol before dawn and need my rest.'

I feel her hand loosen around my wrist as I sink my talon deeper into her flesh. I drag her hand from me as she whimpers, my grip grinding her bones against each other as I watch her legs quake. She drags her hand away from me, her bilious green blood staining my talon as I watch it drip from her hand, spattering the floor beneath us both with an acidic hiss. She glares at me, her eyes narrowing to reptilian slits before she scurries off, disappearing into the rippling wall of gyrating flesh.

I trudge through the rapidly thinning crowd, bodies moving from my path as I push my aura outwards, the Revellers sensing more than seeing my presence, their bodies quailing despite their overt inebriation.

My cell door crashes closed behind me, the din of my kin's revelry fading to naught but a murmur as I sink bone tired and weary onto the bed in the corner. I fall backwards, my head scraping the coarsely chiselled stonework and even now as I lay here, I am too tired to care. Too tired to even attempt the simplest of tasks, like shucking my boots from my feet as I sink deep in a fitful sleep.

The world around me fades, sinking to black as my eyes slip closed. The dull thrum of the music below fading to nothing as I sink deeper into my dreams.

✦✦✦

*Leaves tickle my skin, my clothing hanging loose as I rest in the warming rays of the dappled sun. My eyes snap open as something tugs at the bindings of my trousers. I lean heavily against the tree trunk behind me, the violet eyed Angel that straddles my hips leans in, soft lips brushing over mine as she nips me, drawing my lip between hers.*

*The soft pull of her teeth on my skin makes me rise, my length pushing against her fingers as she pulls my bindings apart. I lift my hips as my hands rise ghosting along her sides, a soft whimpering giggle rising from her as she squirms under my fingers. I pull her close as I ensnare her in my arms, my tongue finding hers.*

*Her hand drifts along my length, fingers curling around me as she coaxes me beyond hardness, the pressure of my throbbing length bordering on painful as she drags the sodden lace of her panties aside and slowly guides me home.*

*Her heat folds around me, the smooth silk of her core drinking me in as she sinks lower and lower on to my pulsing length. I thrust sharply watching her mouth open in a near silent moan as she grinds down onto me, our breathing rises locked in pure synchronicity as we both sink into each other.*

*Whispered words, too soft for me to hear, mingle with the moans of ecstasy floating around me as our pace begins to rise, the feel of skin on mine, the heat from her soft and supple form soaking me as I feel my limit near. I pull my lips from hers as she leans against me, groaning moans bathing my skin as I lean in, my lips skating over her neck as I nip at her skin.*

*The point of eclipse is nearing for us both as she sinks her teeth into my neck, her core gripping me tight as she draws me to her, her whimpering scream echoing free as she begins to tremble around me. I bite hard on my lip to keep from screaming as I feel my levies break, my seed spilling free in one exultant torrent as she milks it from my soul.*

*I am gasping, groaning, heat rolling through me, searing me to the core as I feel myself shrink, slipping free of the lust soaked woman astride me, yet, as suddenly as it all started she is gone, and I am once more alone in the woods. Silence envelopes me, my skin chilled and damp to the touch, the warmth and ecstasy of mere moments ago, gone, replaced by a depthless longing and loneliness.*

*I stare at the ground around me, footsteps leading away from me, the light scent of vanilla and jasmine flirting with my senses as I rise. My feet lead me, dragging me through twisting pathways, glades and rivers, hills and trails, all leading me to one inescapable destination.*

*A soft giggle draws my attention, a soft smile vanishing behind leaf soaked branches as I turn towards the tinkling laughter.*

*'Wait, stop!'*

*The musical laugh echoes over me as I push through the branches.*

*'Come and find me Albion, come and find me my love.'*

*I tear through the woods, her laughter guiding me, flashes of white, the soft caress of her perfume, drifting feathers drawing me deeper as I scramble upwards. I breach the top as woodland gives way to grass coated fields.*

*The ground rises sharply carrying me away from the forests and my lingering dalliance. I turn my gaze upwards as I pause, her silhouetted form standing arms out, calling to me as she turns away, her voice carried to me by the perfume scented breeze. I breathe in deeply as the words curl around me, beckoning me, teasing me, drawing me onwards as my feet dig in and I rise, my legs driving me up the hillside.*

*'Come find me Albion, please, come find me.'*

*I crest the hill, the satin swathed form of my Angel below me, framed by the glowing golden light of the noon day sun. She turns once more, violet eyes meeting mine. Even from here, my breath is stolen, her beauty flawing me in a glance as I watch her lips turn, pursing lightly as she sends a soft kiss to me before moving ever further from my grasp.*

*'Wait, Arianwen!'*

*She pauses, her name echoing across the valley that is rising around us both. I sprint forwards, my legs turning the ground beneath me to dust as I race to her side. I reach forth, my hands begging for her touch as I come within a hair's breadth of the woman who so owns my mind.*

*I feel her, the soft satin of her hair plays across my fingertips as she turns, her eyes brimming with tears. Her lips tremble as she looks at me, a single tear rolling across her alabaster skin before, with the whisper utterance of my name she is gone, and I am left stumbling and alone.*

*'Come find me. Albion, please, find me.'*

*I turn, frantic, my mind racing as I cast my eyes about me for any sign of her, of my Angel.*

*'Arianwen!'*

*My throat burns as I scream, her name echoing around me. A guttural cackle draws my eye, the sultry form of another standing atop the rise, satin blonde hair billows in the wind as she curls a finger.*

*'Come Albion, you know you want this.'*

*I move, my weapon finding its way into my hand as the figure turns and vanishes over the horizon.*

*'You know you want to see this!'*

*The words echo around me as I stalk onwards, anger burning within me, the fear and loneliness long gone. I know my Angel is out here somewhere. I crest the hill my eyes falling upon the crystal roofed chapel below, and there, bathed in white satin stands my Angel, curled within the grip of another. I sink to my knees, hands closing around me, irons closing around my throat and wrists as tears begin to flow.*

*'She was mine.'*

*Dry dead hair falls around my shoulder as I feel the heat of another's breath on my cheek, the vile scent of death closing my throat in an instant.*

*'And now, you Albion, are mine.'*

My throat is raw, my sheets soaked with sweat. I shift to the edge of my bed as I drag my armour from my slick skin. Was that real? Was all I saw the truth, or ... was it all some twisted machination of my King and his trained succubus? I drag my hand across my head, the stunted ridges of my horns catching my fingers, the sensation making me flinch as I play through the slowly fading dream. Arianwen, my violet eyed torturer, were we really all my dreams have made us out to be? If we were, then, why cannot I recall it all? Why does so much of it feel like a washed out chalk etching scoured from the pavement by spring's rains? But, if it was not the truth, then why, when I recall all that has just played through my mind do I feel such pain? Why does my heart know what my mind does not? Nothing I know makes sense to me anymore. How can it when even my own memories are not telling me the truth.

But, one thing I do know, Lilith, the vile whore of my fallen King, she is something that has no place in those memories, and if she is there, then I know my mind has been re-sewn, the only question that evades me that has any true pertinence as of now is … why, why was the owner of my heart scoured so violently from my own mind?

# 8

## Dear Strength

## ARIANWEN

**I take a moment before I open my eyes, to take a few much** needed deep breaths as I let the serenity of my surroundings soak through my aura, revitalising it after weeks of utter exhaustion and worry. I need this moment, but more importantly, baby needs it. My poor little one has had to start its early stages of life amongst a storm of extreme emotions and situations and yet, I feel at times, it is stronger than I. How can that be? How can such a tiny little life force give me the strength to see through each day? To say I feel blessed to have created such a little being is an understatement.

My hands cup the tiny bulge under my nightdress, as I take in all the comforting, familiar smells of my personal haven. The old wood smell of the carved bedhead my pillows rest upon wash over me as childhood memories flood my mind; I see the day my father brought my new bed inside this room for the first time. My two sisters and I used to share a room with three single beds tightly crammed in and though it was often fun to share the silly times we would have when settling down for the night, I felt so very grown up when I was not only presented with my own room, but a full sized bed to fill it. That freshly carved wood smell is still present today.

The softness of the warm and heavy quilt that is covering my body, hand sewn by my mother, always felt like a soft armour, protecting me from what was inside my sometimes night scares, always ready to fight away not only the cold of winters, but anything else that dared to seek me out in the dark. But, it is the scent of the meals that have soaked the walls of our family home that bring me the fondest memories, that and the laughter that often went along with a kitchen full of girls.

But, it is that memory that has tears springing to my eyes. My child, whether a boy or girl, may not get to share in such wonderful family moments. My parents would adore a grandchild to spoil silly, and my sisters would be just giddy over having such a beautiful gift as part of our family, and even though there may be a slim slither of hope I may be able to remain with my family, I do not hold such hope for the man I love, the man I worship, the one who has such a firm grip on my heart that has been having trouble beating without him by my side. To have him as part of this world seems almost an impossibility.

But, that will not stop me fighting for him. Fighting for him to come back to me, to be a part of me, to be a part of our child's life. If it comes down to choosing my world or Albion ... I will choose him.

I open my eyes and take a look around my bedroom and let myself enjoy the fond memories of it for just a minute more, before I sit up and swing my legs out from under the covers and place my feet on the old stone floor. I want my love, I want Albion, and I have an idea on how to bring him back to me, an idea on how to break the Devil's spell he seems to be captured in. I only hope that I am not too late.

I dress quickly and begin to search for the items I need. I want anything that may jog his memory, anything that may grab at his heart or soul, anything that will help him to find the path back to me. I grab a small bag and place apples in from the bowl on our kitchen table; I know it is a smell he associates with me. I then head back into my bedroom and kneel in front of my bed to reach for the box I have hidden under there. It has the dress that I just could not throw away, that Albion ripped when he first made me his, which still slightly smells of the both of us. In the same box is a collection of the red and blue crystals that he used to leave for me to find in my childhood. All of these things mean a lot to me, and I know are saturated with my aura. I just hope these small tokens of our memories are enough to break through Lucifer's magic.

With trepidation starting to crawl over my skin, I make my way out of my home, the place I feel safest at, and head to the world beyond my own in hopes of finally being able to hold the man I cherish once again.

It is quite early, so the streets of my home are peacefully quiet as I make my way to the edge of our world. When I reach the Gatekeepers, the giant Dragon statues whimper with the need to speak, so I stop to listen to what are always words of wisdom from their ancient lives.

'Proce'd with care child, f'r darkness wants thy gift. Thy ordinary is changing, be prepar'd f'r what it may endue with it. The Lord hath design'd thy fate, follow thy instincts, they will lead thou to thy true path.'

I frown at them, knowing what I heard, but struggling to fully comprehend the meaning of those words. Could it be true? Could my secret beliefs be right? That God somehow had a hand in Albion and I meeting? Does that mean he also meant for this life growing inside of me to have been created by an Angel and a Demon?

I start to tremble slightly, and my legs become weak as I slowly sink to the earth beneath me, needing a few moments to comprehend the reality that has just been put before me. We were meant to be. Our love was meant to be. All of it, being drawn to each other's aura since childhood, Albion always watching over me from the shadows and not knowing why, myself, always feeling as if a piece of me was missing somehow, finding each other and feeling whole for the first time in our existence.

But why were we torn apart? Why did Michael and Lucifer join forces to keep us apart? Why would God allow that if we were meant to come together as one? *I do not understand. I do not understand any of it.* Why the pain, the heartache, the stress and worry if in the end we are meant to be? It is all too much. My brain feels as if it is going to short circuit if I try and decipher the meaning of all that has happened since I first meet Albion.

I knew something greater was at work behind our coming together, but to think it was God who made that happen ... is hard to believe in. I want answers, I need answers and I need them now. With Albion's life on the line, and the life on my child to be in danger, I need to know everything to ensure all of our safety.

'Tell me, tell me why God designed for my path to cross a Demon and then for our hearts to be entwined? Why was a child, a miracle allowed to happen between what has always been arch enemies? Then why were we torn apart? Why?'

They are both silent for a moment before the other one speaks.

'Tis not f'r us to reveal thy path, the journey thou wilt take can only be yours to discov'r. Tis purpose to all of the creator's plans and yours is yet to be reveal'd.'

*No.* I need more than that. I need a reason why, I need a reason as to where this will all lead. I need to protect my loved ones the best I can and that is not with uncertainty.

'Please, I beg you. If you know anything that will aid me in protecting the ones I love then you must tell me.'

They remain silent, just like their stone features. For a moment I think they will not respond at all, so I resign myself to not having the answers I need and rise to my feet preparing to continue with my plan. Just as I take a step over the border and into the land of the forgotten, they start to growl, making me turn their way once more.

'Listen to thy heart child. It'll always send thou in the right direction.'

Then that is what I will do. I will follow my heart to the man who owns it. I will follow my heart along the safest path to ensure danger will not harm our child, and I will follow my heart to the fate that has so seemingly been laid out before me.

I turn and take the familiar steps upon the forest floor, the crunching of the leaves beneath my feet but a whisper, as I wind between broken trunks and thistle bushes, heading towards the clearing I last saw Albion in. My mind still warring with the Dragon's words and the meaning behind them, leaving confusion and an endless line of unanswered questions. But, I must try and push them out of my mind. I need my whole concentration and abilities to be focused, so I can use all of my energy to silently call for Albion.

I reach the clearing and my heart plummets as once again, he is not here. I know it may take time for him to make his way to me and I am prepared to wait forever if I have to, because after what I just heard, more than ever, I need to break the spell he is under. We have a greater purpose that we have to stand together for, but more importantly right now, we need a chance to rejoice, together; rejoice in the fact that we will be parents, and that is a joy I have not been able to fully feel without him.

The same scene plays out again. I wait ... and I wait. Minutes feeling like hours have passed by, emotions warring to break free as I struggle to gain control of all the swirling confusion, anger and heartbreak that is threatening to suffocate me. Baby starts to turn, and I know that is a sign to calm myself as it is affecting my little secret bundle which has had so much to contend with in such a short amount of time.

'It's okay my beautiful one, daddy will return to us soon I promise and everything will work out for the best. He's going to love you so deeply little one. We'll be together as a family soon.' My eyes start to water at the thought of us finally being able to live as a family. Yes, it may be a distant hope, but I will do all I can to make that happen.

I jump as I suddenly realise that Albion's scent is flooding my senses, drowning me in its strength and power and he is indeed making his way to me. Excitement and fear war around my head as I stare into the forest, waiting for the man I love to appear, yet nervous at what version of that may well appear before me today.

Then I see him, the love I feel surges through my body making my heartbeat erratic. He stares at me differently this time, frowning as if something about me is familiar. I need to remind him now, in case he loses whatever memory he has tugging at his being.

'Albion, it's me, Arianwen. Please try and remember us. We're in love. We're going to make a life together work. That's what we were planning before we were torn apart. Do you remember? Try hard my love, try hard. Do you remember your hidden home, in the cave? You took me there, we were together there, on the white fur that adorned your bed. It was our safe place. Please remember my love. I need you Albion.'

He whispers my name, but as I take a step forward, he takes one back, still frowning, emotions swirling in his eyes. I know he senses something, I can see it, I can feel it in his aura, but something else has a much stronger hold over him, something dark, created by the Devil. I have to fight harder. I have to win him back.

I step forward again, slowly and this time he just stands there, unsure of what to do. I bend down slowly to the basket I left at my feet and take out all of its contents and lay them down. He takes a deep breath in, his shoulders raising high, and I know he smells the apples and the scent of us on the torn dress. His eyes move over the items and land solidly on the blue and red crystals as his frown intensifies.

'Do you remember any of these? You always watched over me near the apple trees. This dress is from the first time our love joined together, do you remember that Albion? Do you remember making me yours? See these crystals, you left these for me to find all through my life. They mean so much to me and protect me wherever I go. Look deep Albion please. All of this is inside you, deep within your memories. Fight Albion, fight to break free of Lucifer's dark spell, please.'

With the mention of the Devil's name, his eyes snap up to look directly into mine. It seems as if he is angry, as if he believes I should not have said his name. I had him for but a few seconds but now he seems to be falling away again. I cannot let that happen. I *will not* let that happen.

'Albion, you need to remember, because not only do I need you, but so does our child!' His body jumps slightly, as those words hit him as hard as I needed them to. 'We created a child Albion, it's growing inside me. You and I created a miracle, a tiny little miracle that needs its daddy as badly as I do. Please my love, please come back to us. Find me Albion, find me, find us!' I am pleading with him, begging him to remember, but as my words sink in, I see a change in him, a dark, twisted change.

He stands taller, his face contorts in anger as he clenches his fists, making his veins strain against his knuckles. His frown is now an angry sneer as he takes two slow menacing steps towards me. I do not understand what has brought on this rage, but for the safety of our child, I step back. He growls deeply that has fearful bumps rising on my skin. He opens his mouth to speak, and I grip my heart with the venomous hatred that slips out.

'I remember. I remember you. You were walking down the aisle of a chapel towards one of my enemies, Gabriel. *You left me.* You ripped out my heart and married my *ENEMY*. Now you come and try to torture me with lies and flaunt the fact you are carrying a child that's not mine!' He continues to take steps while he is talking until we are stood toe to toe, his hatred so dark it is burning my aura, but it is his words that are causing the most damage.

'What did you say?' I whisper, still not believing what he is accusing me of, standing here in shock at what my ears are hearing. He remembers seeing me, but cannot remember the good times before that moment.

'I said, you are carrying my enemies spawn. I should kill you on the spot for creating another feathered heathen you sorcerous!' He screams those last words at me and at that moment ... something snaps. I slap him hard across the face. I slap a very large, very angry Demon across his face and I do not even care. The pain of his words is shooting through my every facet. The weeks and weeks of worry for this man, the concern about his condition and well being, the anxious wait to return to this wasteland to try and see him again, was for what? To be accused of throwing our love away to wed a man I *cannot* even stand to be near.

I do not stay to see his reaction. I turn and run. I run and run, not caring where I may end up. Heartbreak is blinding me to the rest of this world leaving me vulnerable and raw. I needed him, I needed his unrelenting strength, I needed his love, I needed his reassurance that yes, we can get through this, but now ... now what do I have?

Tears sting my eyes as I try and focus on where my legs are leading me. My hands instinctively holding my tiny belly as I run from the man who owned my heart, yet also shattered it to pieces within a few seconds. How did he even see that presentation ceremony? And if he could see it, and see me, why did not he come and try to see me, to take me away from all of that?

I do not understand how that could be his only memory of me. He thinks that I left him and ripped out his heart, but does not remember how lovingly I held onto his heart before we were torn apart. He looked confused by his own words, like somewhere in his memories I am there, and he remembers our love, but it does not make sense to him. Has the Devil destroyed his brain so badly that he will never remember the deep love and happiness we shared together? Oh Lord please no, I cannot lose him forever.

I blindly stumble over the border into my own world, not taking in the whimpering concerns of the Dragons, or the sobbing noise that is flowing from my body, as my brain is warring with too many things to be able to concentrate on one. All I know is that my strength is leaving me as my heart breaking encounter with Albion starts to take over my entire aura.

Baby is moving restlessly. I can feel its distress, but I am at a loss as to how to stop these turbulent emotions from overflowing. I take a few deep breaths, but it does not help in stilling my rapid heartbeat. I know I am about to fall apart so I do the only thing I can. I slowly unfurl my wings, letting each feather stretch out to its full length, then stretch up on my tippy toes and begin to rise in the air.

I need to get away, I need a place to quietly shatter, because no matter how many deep breaths I take, nothing is going to stop this devastating break down. The sun beating down on my skin, or the wind blowing through my hair does nothing to calm my being, as I struggle to stay in the air, not knowing where I am flying to, letting my instincts take me to a place I can be alone.

It is no surprise when I glance down and see the floating giant lily pads on the river beneath me. I try to land as gracefully as always, but my concentration has deserted me and I land with a heavy thump on the edge of a pad, and for the first time in my existence … I fall into the cold water. When I make it to the surface I am gasping for air, because in all my turmoil, I forgot to take a breath when I realised I was going into the water.

I grab the edge of a pad and slowly haul myself up and into the centre and just curl into a wet ball. Baby is moving franticly, and knowing that my less than gentle landing could have hurt my precious secret is the last straw that breaks me. I let out a howl of pain and anguish as the tears and emotions finally have their way and take control of my body.

'I'm sorry, I'm sorry, I'm sorry,' I repeat to my precious cargo as I struggle to take much needed air into my lungs. I try in vein to get my heartbeat to calm, but it is determined to leave my chest as it thumps erratically against my ribcage. The pain that is slicing through my aura is just about unbearable as I lie here, curled up, holding on tightly to my knees, trying to keep myself together enough to survive this devastating pain.

My mind does not know what emotion or feeling it should try and process first, there is just too much distress and conflict. The only thought that stands out is have I truly lost Albion? I howl in pain again as that thought starts to take hold and fester in my entire being. How can I possibly do any of this without him? What will happen to baby and if I have to reveal I am pregnant? What will my family think of me? Will it still put them in danger if it is just baby and I?

I know one thing for certain. Michael will in some way make me pay for my sins, even though I am with a child. If he has his way, I will be trialled for sleeping with the enemy and cast from my home, from my world and then how will I protect my child? A woman alone forced to find another immortal world to hide in. How will I protect baby? Despair starts to choke me as grief starts to wind its way around my soul.

Grief at possibly never being able to save Albion from Lucifer's dark magic, grief at the thought of leaving my home and not having my families support when my little miracle decides to enter this world, grief at not knowing if I will be able to provide and protect my child in a strange world. How can all of this be falling apart so fast if God had a hand in what started this all?

My life was peaceful and calm before I laid eyes on Albion, even with the danger of being a Reclaimer. I still loved the life I was living. My kin are gentle and kind people who live to help humans in need in some way or another. We may live in a beautiful garden created by God, and reap the rewards of the hard work we do, but we were still created to serve a single important task, and that was to guide the people of earth when they needed us to, be it in life or in death. Even though at times I felt a little different or as if something was missing in my life, it was still a happy life to live.

Now I have to think about baby and what will be the best for its safety and wellbeing. Should I leave soon, before my belly starts to show too much? Would it be safer than to let my family in on my secret and risk them also being made to pay for my crimes? I could risk asking for their help, but Michael could accuse them of collusion in treasonous action and that is a risk I cannot take. And if Gabriel wants to marry me solely based on the gifts I possess, what would happen when he and Michael figure out that my child's gifts could be much stronger, then what? Will my child be taken away from me when it is born? *No.* I would never in all of eternity risk that happening.

It seems I am only left with one choice ... to leave before anyone discovers my hidden miracle. I could ask the Bookkeeper for as much help as she can safely give, to prepare myself as much as I can before leaving for another world. Then I would have to carefully plan the right moment to leave so I have as much head start on Michael and his army as I possibly can get. Even then, there is no telling how far Michael will travel to get me back, especially if he finds out about baby.

I squeeze my eyes shut tightly, trying to ease the pain that is shooting through my head, but it does not stop the tears that are flooding down my face. Baby has had enough to contend with in its short existence without the stress of what is to come to keep it safe. Why would God allow all of this to happen? Surely, he didn't plan for Michael to make a deal with the Devil to tear Albion and I apart. I feel it in every part of my being that Albion was created out of Good and not Evil, so if I can feel it, surely God knows Albion was born into the wrong world. Was that why he allowed a child to be created between eternal enemies? Would he save my little family if he knew all that was going on?

God has greater responsibilities than to save an Angel who fell in love with a Demon I am sure, but I just cannot figure out the riddle that the Dragons told me. If Albion and I were destined to be together, destined to create a child, then why are we not in each other's arms right now? Oh Albion … how did the Devil take control of you so completely? And how can I possibly take your child away from you? If only you knew what was truly happening, I know you would fight with all that you have to save us.

The thought of leaving Albion behind has another wave of grief gripping my body so tightly I feel as though it could snap. I do not want the pain. I do not want to feel anymore. I wish I could go numb. Strength … where are you?

# 9

# In Memoriam

## ALBION

**My face burns, burns with anger, burns with pain. It burns** from the mark she left there, the guttering heat of a hand lain upon it in anger and anguish. My hand rises, tracing the path of flame that scours my skin. I know the words I spoke, the words she heard, came from me. Came from my mouth, pushed across my lips by my mind, but, they are not my own. The place they were drawn from was not of my own creation.

I move through the motions, tracking a path through the brush and flora, my feet carrying me as my mind sinks in upon itself. My anger burns as I think back upon the revelation that was heaped upon me only minutes ago.

A child, she is carrying a child. One she so eagerly claims is mine. I bitterly shake my head, how could it be, how could she be the bearer of my offspring, yet so willingly lay in the arms of another man and declare herself his wife? No that child is not mine, that whore is not mine. Yet, as I move through the edges of the forest, ghosts of memories fight for life, pushing at the envelope of my mind, pushing for recognition of a life my mind vehemently denies. But, if it is so false, if it is so filled with twisted images designed by another's hand, why do I feel so much pain? Pain at the way she looked at me, pain at the words that slipped from her with such surety and devotion, pain at the very idea of that child being mine. If all I know is false, then why, why does it pain me so?

I need to be free of this; free of it all, of the pain, the confusion, the utterly overwhelming and undeniable tumult of memories and ghosted falsity. But can I really erase it all? Can I truly wipe my mind clean of all that lead me to her? How can I destroy the last vestige of an event that has so changed my life and existence? I do not know the answer and it is one that I dearly need. I need to find my final choice, I need to find the point at which I can put an end to this all and finally make my mind my own, rather than leave it open to the vices of others and the playground of traitorous Angels.

✦ ✦ ✦

Water soaks me, the chill spray of the ocean battering my body as I slowly strip my armour free, the dock and beach behind me littered with the blood and sweat stained leather that has so long shrouded my skin. I can feel eyes upon me, watching, studying, wary and frightened, but too consumed by their curiosity to look away. Women gape at me, men glare, even as my weaponry hits the water stained wood beneath my feet. I ignore it all, let them stare.

Sheep, they are all sheep. Villagers wandering these black and soulless shores, searching for anything that they can use, the flotsam and jetsam collecting like the bones of leviathans on the shore line; all of them stand gawping, lost and cowed into obedience by mass manipulation as I toss my under armour aside and stand naked and open to the sun and surf. I need to lose myself, I need to find that quiet place only true isolation can bring. Dropping down onto the rusted dead sands I run, my feet digging into the coarse sodden grit. I feel it clinging to my every step as I draw ever closer to the water's edge. Without breaking my stride I dive head long into the crest of a rising wave. Cold drowns me, washing through everything as I fade into oblivion, my arms draw me deep as my lungs burn, pressure mounting, falling deeper and deeper into the bitter salt drenched waters around me.

Pressed against the farthest edges of my world, sharp grey cliffs rising like hate soaked walls from the crashing surf, I cannot fathom how anyone could find beauty in these poisoned swells of salt and decay. I can feel the harsh bite of the sulphurous taint that bleeds through everything, Hell's overflowing malice eating its way free of the very rocks it hides behind.

Light vanishes, swallowed by the depthless oceans that swirl around me. My lungs are screaming at me as I sink deeper into the black, my mind slowly fading to nothing as everything is washed clean. I stare about me, the sights of this silent world drawing me in as I reach out, my fingers brushing along the heavy hide of one of the ocean's greatest hunters. I watch as its finned tail pushes it silently through the water, the razor edged teeth shinning dully in the near non-existent light.

My vision dances with black as I near the edge of oblivion, my heart hammering in my chest as I begin to rise, forcing myself to the surface. I crash through the thin film of water, the sky opening out above me, the heat of the sun searing my skin as my sodden hair arcs backwards, water flying, glittering like diamonds in the sunlight.

I cast my eyes to the shore, the twisted paths and trails hacked free of the hills and cliffs drawing my eye as I see the very limits of the village and the pitiless grey and yellow smoke of my home staining the sky.

I float, bobbing like a cork in a fountain, my mind pulling me, drawing me onward to one irrevocable conclusion. I need to face my *Demons;* I need to rid myself of these memories once and for all, before they destroy me. I know that seeing her, seeing the Angel who was supposedly once mine will open doors I dearly need to stay closed, and yet, I know it is something that I must do, something that I need to do.

✦ ✦ ✦

I know where she will be, the Angel of my nightmares. She will be nestled safely in the arms of those coddling Dragons, away from the slings and arrows of the other world, my world, away from me.

I know where, in this walled and fenced cage, she will go. I know what she will do, what she will think. And yet despite what I know, I cannot draw on the memories of any of it.

The scent of apples hits me. I stand, trying in vain not to topple as my head spins, the scent and sensation of familiarity permeating everything. I reach forth, my fingers skating over the smooth skin of the green fruit as I grip and twist, the branch rustling as the apple breaks free.

I raise it, inhaling sharply before I sink my teeth into it, the sweet nectar rolling down my throat. How could I have forgotten this, how could this have been scoured from my mind? Images of my childhood flash through my mind, images of times I crept from that darkened hole in the ground, squirming through gaps and openings as I scurry through the village, before, with all the gall and care of an adolescent, I scramble down the cliff and to the overhanging branches of the tree to steal these very fruits.

I drop the half eaten apple to the blossom strewn floor and jump, my fingers curling over the branches as I haul myself upwards. I scramble like a lizard from branch to branch, my feet sure and planted, leaping outwards, my arms sailing before me as I grasp the fractured bark of another tree. Pieces peel away digging sharply into my stomach as I push up and onto the quivering limb.

I stalk forwards, the soft scent of water and lilies' reaching me as I breach the edges of Eden. The fluttering of cotton draws my attention, a hunched and fragile figure perched in the centre of the small lake, the lily pad beneath her shifting on the tide.

I watch her, her slim figure perched, on the living pad of pulsing plant life. How can she be the source of everything that has so plagued me, this slip of a woman? I let my body sag, the branch beneath me groaning softly as my weight settles in. I watch her shoulders rise and fall, the mumble of her sobs sending ripples through the water. The sheer cotton of her dress clings to her skin, her cream coloured flesh shining like star light through the soaked material.

The urge to hold her spears me, the chains around me, heart pulling, dragging me towards the drenched and broken woman that is mere feet from me. I feel myself moving, my legs pushing against leaf and branch as I slowly begin to rise when a pain lances through my very core, a sensation so deep and primal that I all but scream. My hands clutch at my chest as I watch hers fall to her stomach, my eyes widening as I feel the pain redouble, drowning everything in an effervescent light, and as suddenly as it appears it falls away, draining everything from me, all doubt, all pain, every shred of the man that had been so pasted over me falls away, and for the first time in what feels like an eternity I am, me.

I am Albion, son of Abara. Hunter and General of the Sixth Legion, and there, supine and haunted by fear and doubt sits the woman who owns my heart and soul. The woman I have fought Hell and Heaven for, the woman who taught a Demon how to love and now, is the woman who has given me the one gift only a woman can. A child. All she had told me, all that she so fervently proclaimed is true and that child, the one she now cradles within her, is ours, is mine. All the falsehoods fall away, and my real memories that were scrubbed from my mind, returns in all their glory.

Pain arcs through me, not at the doubt or fear of what is to come, or at the unbridled union of our souls that courses even now between us both, but at the knowledge that it was I, it was my words that have drawn such sorrow from the woman I love, the mother of my child. And what the Devil must have done to me, caused her pain when we both should have been rejoicing.

My child, even now I cannot help but smile. I, a Demon and Hunter, am to be a father, father to the child of an Angel and not Heaven nor will Hell shake me from it.

Not again.

# The Edge Of Never

## ARIANWEN

**I am falling ...**

Into oblivion, into a dark void in the centre of the universe where nothing makes sense and you cannot feel which way is up. Is that what it feels like to fall over the Edge of Never? The edge of our world, where only myths survive.

I have not thought about what is over that edge since I was told stories as a child, tales of histories long past, but most of the times, they were just scary bedtime stories passed amongst children. I remember many nights where my father would tell my sisters and I tales about what is over that edge and about the immortal people who sort that answer for themselves, never to return. As I got older and enjoyed researching our histories, I found out for myself that the Edge of Never is exactly that ... the edge of our world. Beyond it is just oblivion.

Trees and plants grow along the edge, the river that runs through Eden creates a waterfall as it makes its way over, water falling but never landing. It took until I was much older to even go close enough to the edge to have a look over, something most of our kin do as a curious child, but not something I felt compelled to rush. I remember the nerves as I took the steps closer and closer to the edge, anxious bumps rising over my skin as I crouched down and crawled the last few steps, finally hanging my head ever so slightly over the edge, to see what all the mystery was about.

First, all I could see was the mist from the falls, floating around the strong wind swirling in every direction. After a few minutes, I could see the shadow of the cliff face, its sombre gaze peering out from behind the mist. For but a short glimpse, it looked like the cliff face, with tree roots and vines jutting out everywhere, went on forever, before the clouds rolled by blocking my view. The scent of the wind howling past was fresh, filled with life, but was also mixed with something else, something ancient, something that screamed finality. It was hard to explain then and no easier now, but it smelt like you would expect the end of the world to smell. Just like that … the end.

End … such a final word. A word I never wanted to use in the same sentence as Albion and I, but that is exactly what this feels like, this pain, this ache, this … I curl up tighter as a new wave a grief hits me. I so desperately want to fight for him, fight for us, but how? I need to think of baby first, which is not what I have been doing lying here, curled up on my side, on a giant lily pad for what could have been hours, as I let the emotions take over my body and shatter my heart.

'I'm so sorry little one,' I stutter as I try and gain a steady breath. I need to let this go, all of this pain and think of baby and our future. I take a few more deep breaths and concentrate on my heart rate, willing it to slow, willing my soul to start putting itself back together again. But how do I move forward from here? I draw back the tears that threaten to fall again as I place a hand beside my body and start to lift my head. It spins slightly, so I close my eyes and let the peace of my world take over my senses.

I sit up on my knees, slowly taking deep breaths, trying to find myself, a self that will never be the same again after the love of a Demon captured my heart, a self that now has to find strength to move her child away from our world and any possible danger. I open my eyes and look up into the sun, taking its rays in as I fight to clear my head. I have to move on … even though … I feel like dying.

I place both my hands on my stomach, cupping my tiny bump, swearing with all that is within me to protect the most innocent of all the players in this chess game of my life, that I *will* protect it. Always ... forever.

I will fight, I will plan and I will win. I close my eyes and concentrate on the first thing I need to do. I have to see Claire, the Bookkeeper and test just how far she is willing go in helping me and baby. I will not knowingly put her in danger, but I am not naïve enough to believe I can do this without any help, so I will take any help she is willing to offer.

Then I have to start hiding supplies under my bed for my travels and for when baby arrives. Baby ... I will have to deliver baby on my own. I will not have the support of the man I love, I will not have my family nearby to offer advice or to pass down heirlooms to the newest generation. I will not have the safety of my world and my kin to cocoon us in. We will be on our own. If that is the only way to stay safe ... then so be it.

It may take time to organise all that I need, so I will have to make sure to continue my current routine as to not raise suspicion. I will still attend my callings, as well as helping the little ones to learn, and I will do as much as I can to help my kin in our daily duties. I need Gabriel and especially Michael to see no difference in my actions. I will carry on as normal.

But, how do I tell my family of my departure? If I was to tell them face to face, they would find a way to make me stay and that is a risk I cannot take. They may have confidence in our leaders accepting my condition, but I have seen their other sides, sides I am sure would not be so compassionate behind closed doors. Neither of our leaders would take too kindly to me carrying the child of a Demon.

How do I put it all into a letter, a letter saying goodbye and that I may never see them again? And how can I be sure of their safety once I leave? Will Michael accuse them of helping me to escape? He could easily come up with any story he likes as to why I had to leave our world. Could my family be held accountable for crimes I have never even committed? My family is wise, they will not allow themselves to become a target of Michael's rage. Their innocence and grief over losing me will shine through. The truth will win. I have to believe that.

My senses suddenly become very aware of a familiar being and just as my aura registers who it is … so does baby, giving its largest kick yet, as if it is desperate to get out and meet … its daddy. My head flies up, looking into the distant trees on the shoreline, desperately wanting to lay eyes on him, but also fearful as to what version of Albion they will see.

I see him, slowly moving out from behind the trees, walking to the water's edge, a look of utter shock on his face. I cannot tell what it means. As much as the love for this man is swirling around inside of me, I will not let his dark vibes anywhere near our child. As much as I am drawn to him, even now, when mine and baby's safety could be in danger, I do not trust the Devil's hold over him.

He still stares, mouth wide open, his eyes trained solely on my hands protectively holding onto baby, as I then witness this tall, strong, mountain of a man fall to his knees, clasping his hands over his heart as I sense all of the Evil hatred and anger that was suffocating his entire aura, disappear into dust, floating away with the wind, leaving behind the man that changed my world, the man I love, the man who currently looks absolutely devastated and overjoyed all at once.

As I witness his shocked eyes fill brimming with unshed tears, baby starts to move, tumbling around and around. I rub my stomach in slow circles, telling baby it is all right, that is your daddy, as I continue to stare at Albion, silently fearful that this could be a trap, the Devil playing us both, just to discover our little miracle.

He slowly raises his eyes to meet mine and I know, I know I am looking into the eyes of my love. Whatever dark magic was gripping his true self, has been broken, broken by the love of a father and child.

*'Arianwen … please forgive me.'*

He chokes on his words as his shocked stance now turns into true understanding of what has happened. 'No!' he whispers as he falls forward, one hand out stretched landing in the mud at the river's edge as his body seems to shudder in pain.

*'Please, please forgive me, please, please, please,'* is all that he can manage as his entire body faces the grief of our time apart, like

mine has had to endure all of these weeks we have been separated. I want to rush to him, I want to wrap my wings around him and cocoon him in my love, telling him it is okay, telling him we can move forward as long as we are together, but ... I cannot. Fear, fear for our child is holding me firmly in my place. This could all turn out to be the Devil's doing, or ... even Michael's.

My aura is torn in two. I have needed this man so desperately every moment we have been apart, yet, my maternal instincts to protect the child I am carrying is much stronger than I could ever have imagined, and it is those instincts that are keeping me in a cautious state of being.

'Arianwen, my love, I know I can never change what happened, I know that I'll never be able to repair the damage that was wrought by my hand, but, I need to know. I need to know, that you know it wasn't me, that those words were not my own. Nothing will ever erase from my mind the memory of how I betrayed you, betrayed our love, and betrayed our child. I just pray that somehow, some way, I can earn your love again. Please Arianwen, all I'm asking is for that one chance.'

He takes a deep breath and lets it out in a deep low growl. 'I love you. I know I have no right, after all that has befallen us; to ask for that love to be returned, but can you ... do you ever think you could love me again?'

His questions are tearing me apart. Tears flowing down my face at the pain in his voice and the breaking of his heart, as he believes I would stop loving him because of Lucifer's Evil curse. I want to tell him I love him, I want to shout it from a mountain top, but what is best for baby is keeping me in my place, frozen, unsure of how to move forward, how to trust the man pleading with me with desperate eyes.

'Arianwen, please my love, please come to me,' he asks in an almost whisper, with one tentative arm reached out for me, as if scared the answer may be no. But I still cannot move. Baby on the other hand, is trying to get to him on its own, desperate to be near to half of its creator. The fact that I know our child can feel its father, has me just about sobbing. But, the danger is still too great to cave to all of these emotions.

'I can't … I just can't Albion. What if all of this is a trap, what if the Devil is playing games just so we will expose our most precious gift? I won't take that risk.' He looks just about destroyed with my words, but after a few more seconds, understanding seems to dawn on him. He closes his eyes tightly while I hold my breath, waiting for a certainty I am not sure will come.

'He is gone Arianwen, my mind is my own. His hold over me is gone. Neither Lucifer nor my Hunter kin will ever lay a finger to you. We are too far within Eden's walls for them to find either us or our child. Arianwen, my love, trust your instincts, you know my words are true, that I'm speaking the truth. Please my little wing, tell me what I need to do to show you I'm me once more and it will be done.'

I calm the upheaval his sudden appearance has created so I can indeed scent if anyone is near. I close my eyes and can instantly sense that no one is close to us, no leaders that may stumble upon us; no Evil is lurking near the borders. The only beings near this lake are Albion, baby and I. But, it would not surprise me if Lucifer's powers could penetrate through to our world, especially with Michael as an ally.

'I'm finding it hard to trust my instincts at the moment. I'm not sure I can trust anything in these worlds again.' My honest words hurt my own heart. But Albion changes his stance. He rises slowly, standing tall as a determination takes over his beautiful rugged face.

'I trust your instincts and I trust you. I trust you to tell me the truth, the truth about what I saw from a cliff top overlooking a glass chapel. I gave you my trust, I gave you my heart, I know in my soul that couldn't have possibly been what it seemed. I know you, and I know you'd never willingly wed another man because, despite all the doubt, all the shrouded clouds and broken sunlight that shields your heart, I still feel the love you hold for me.

'Despite my failures, my failure to protect you, to protect our child; my failure to be the man you deserve, to fight through all that was cast upon me and see you for who you are, my love, my Queen, my soulmate, you still love me. I can feel it flowing through you Arianwen, it was that love and all it created that brought me back to you, now all I ask is that you now, trust me, even if it is only once more, trust me when I tell you *we* are safe and that I promise you, with everything I am and ever will be, I will *never* fail you again.'

I do trust him. I can feel the truth in his words and for him to still have so much faith in me, even when he witnessed me walking down an aisle in what so clearly looked like a wedding ceremony, while he was still himself, is just about the last straw my heart can take. I slowly stand up, pausing to give my legs a chance to regain their feeling after being curled up for so long. I then open my wings and take flight, hoping the freshness of the air will help wash away some of this emotional distress.

I land a few feet away from him, still unsure of how to approach him after all these weeks apart, but he is having none of that. He all but sprints the few steps that stand between us and before I can even prepare myself, he picks me up, crushing me to him in an embrace of love, lust, pain and heartbreak. I slowly wrap my arms around his neck which makes him squeeze me harder, trying to mould us into one. His mouth and nose buried in my hair as I hear him take a deep breath in, swallowing my scent all the way down to his soul, his fingers gripping my back tightly, scared I may slip away if he loosens his grip even slightly. His lips press hard against me, strong and sure as he begins to once again claim me as his.

Wetness fills my eyes and falls down my cheeks as I become overwhelmed with love and relief that I am, once again, in the arms of the man who owns me. My breathing is erratic as my heart works double time to keep up with the love that is flooding my soul. He then pulls back slightly, searching my eyes before his lips slam against my own. I can taste his pain, and it has me whimpering in sorrow as he tries to make up for the failure he believes he committed. This kiss is not hunger ... it is heartache, raw and weeping. We are barely breathing when he once again pulls back and looks into my eyes, into my soul.

'Is it real my love, is it real? What I can sense, is it ...real?'

The look on his face, the look of excitement and fear all rolled together as he holds his breath, awaiting my answer to whether I am with child or not, is the sweetest look that has ever adorned his handsome face.

'Yes my love, we created a child.'

His grunt at my answer is a painful one, pain at not being there for us from the start. He grips me tighter, before letting go and falling to his knees, his hands gripping my hips as he closes his eyes and leans in to lay his lips gently on my cotton covered stomach, the sight of him almost making my knees give way. His body starts to shake as he keeps his lips where they are, but winds his hands around my waist, holding gently as he breathes in his own child's aura.

'I'm sorry,' he whispers to our little miracle and it just about breaks my heart. He looks up to me with watery eyes. 'Arianwen, how can you ever forgive me for not being there for you both? How can I ever forgive myself?' He whispers the last few words as he once again buries his head in my stomach.

'You were not yourself Albion, you hold no blame in not being there for us.' He shakes his head slightly so I squeeze him harder. My emotions are playing havoc with my body as my head begins to feel light. I sway slightly and Albion's grip increases around me. 'Why are you so wet and cold? Surely that's not good for you or the … *baby*.' He whispers the word, letting it hang on his tongue as a sweet smile graces his lips.

'I'll be fine, I'll dry soon.' He frowns up at me and then slowly rises, staring into my eyes, both of us still not believing the other is in front of us. I almost lost him, I almost walked away from him. I close my eyes as the pain slices through me yet again, the truth that we nearly lost each other for what could have been forever, has me shaking.

'We need to talk my sweet Angel, but you're cold, I need to get you both home.' The words both and home has me sobbing and my legs giving way. *We almost lost him.* All my strength seems to have deserted me in this one single moment as I start to mumble hysterically. 'Oh Albion. I've missed you so terribly. I thought I'd lost you.' He places an arm quickly under my knees and lifts me, cradling me close to his chest as he begins to move.

'Shh my sweet Angel, shh. Let me get you home and warm,' he

whispers in my ear as I feel him moving quickly through the trees, heading towards the forgotten forest. 'I didn't marry Gabriel, I'd never had agreed to that I promise you Albion. It was only a presentation ceremony and the only reason I took part, was to buy us some time, to give me a chance to come up with a plan to find you again. Oh Albion … it's been awful.'

I cannot control the flood of emotions anymore. He continues to move with haste as I fall apart in his arms. The weeks of worry, worry about him, about baby's safety, about moving from my own world into the unknown, all comes crashing down upon me at this moment. His scent, once again, invades every cell in my body; his touch bringing with it more than just comfort, his entire aura, instinctively wraps itself around mine and babies. I can feel it, I can feel its Good and its strength and its love and its protection, claiming what is his. We are his and he is ours.

And I was about to walk away.

'*Albion,*' I sob into his chest, knowing that I had no other choice but to prepare to leave for baby's safety, but only now feeling the magnitude of that decision. Never feeling his soft caress on my face, never smelling his unique masculine scent mixed with the darkness of his world, never feeling his soft lips upon my head again like they are now. But, most upsetting is the fact that baby may have never had the chance to know what a great man his or her father is.

A man, not a Demon, as legend would have described him.

# 11

## Coming Home

### ALBION

**I listen to her breathing as she rests on the edge of our bed,** the settled silence of the cavern wrapping us in its all consuming blanket. It is not until you come home, come back to that point that you left so unwillingly, that you finally realise just how much of an aching hole it left inside of you. I watch her chest rise and fall as I pull the covers back, her legs moving slowly, her feet pushing them aside as I brush her dampened hair from out her eyes.

A soft blue lipped smile plays across her features as I tug gently at the sash at her waist, her body shaking as she stutters and gasps, the throes of the iced death playing through her.

'Darling, you have to get warm, please lift your arms.'

She grumbles and murmurs, but slowly raises them, her movements dulled by the frigid waters that had so entombed her.

I slip my fingers under the slim straps of her dress, sliding the cotton strings along her arms, the sluggish, sightless, sleep drenched movements of my Angel doing more to hinder than help as I finally manage to slip them free. The sight of her quivering lips makes my heart sink as I watch the panicked nightmares begin to creep in.

She squirms and shifts, her shivering doubling as the soaked dress begins to worm its way down her back. I lift her gently from the bed, her body curling in my grip as she soaks in the warmth of my skin. I hear her whimper in my grasp as water drips down her back, trailing across her backside as it dribbles from between my fingers.

'Fuck it. She can be mad when she wakes up.'

I set my Angel back on our bed, her dress bunched and twisted around her waist, her eyes crinkled and screwed shut as she fights against her bodies shaking. I drag my blade from its sheath, the muted growling doing nothing as I slip it carefully beneath the bunched lump of sodden cotton and yank. The razor honed edge of my blade shears through the soaked material. I watch it part, landing with a sodden splat on my Angel's frozen skin. Her face crinkles in disgust as the material sticks to her clammy and pale body. With care tempered by haste, I lift and quickly discard the soaked dress, the heavy thump of it lost in my need to see my Angel safe and warm. I quickly dispatch with her underwear, the same callous treatment meeting them as I snatch a towel of soft cotton from the floor and begin to carefully dry her off, before smothering her in the thick hide blankets that adorn our bed.

I turn, my heart hammering in my chest as I kneel before the fire place, my finger dancing along the logs as I watch smoke curl free. Flames flicker into life as the wood begins to burn, the thick scent of burning timber filling the cave as my eyes slip shut against the fierce, orange glow. I feel my skin begin to shrink before I stand and move back towards my still shivering woman, the soft chatter-ing of her teeth turning my stomach into a knotted mess.

I drag my armour from me, casting it aside as the trousers bunch around my feet, meeting much the same fate as Arianwen's dress as I send the mass of sweat stained leather skittering across the floor. She stirs as I slip the covers over us both, the heat from the hearth pouring across the room slowly, like treacle off a spoon, sapping the cold from the air in a steady irrevocable march. I know it will give her the heat she needs in time, but as my lips touch the edge of her shoulder, the iced pallor of her supple body tells me it be all too late in doing so.

I feel her twitch as I draw her to me, whimpering moans of fear trickling from her as I feel the cold of her skin seep into my bones. I shrink into myself as her backside meets my loins, I lift my leg setting it over hers, wrapping her completely in my embrace as I softly shush her back into the depths of sleep.

My eyes begin to droop, the heat of the room and the comfort of my woman being where she has always belonged, lulling me into a sense of deep security, my heart and mind finally in tune and at rest. The soft chattering of her teeth begins to slow as colour gently washes across her cheeks, the pale blue tinge of her lips giving way to the soft dusted rose pink that so soothes my heart.

I slip my arm lower, as Arianwen moves in my arms, my body shifting with her as she curls into me, her head resting in the crook of my shoulder, a winsome and contented smile playing across her features as I feel her lips on my skin. A soft, mumbled 'I love you' dances with my hearing. I set a soft kiss on her forehead as I smile, Ari's breathing slipping back into the steady drone of sleep.

Even as I lay here, content and happy for the first time since this ordeal began, I cannot reconcile the notion that I am to be a father, a father, me. A few months ago the notion would have made me howl with laughter, but now, as I lie here with my woman in my arms the proof is plain to see, a child, my child lies with us.

I trail my fingers across the top of her soft bump, energy coursing through my fingers as I feel our unborn babe move with them. I watch as her skin shifts; will it be a boy, or a girl, my mind races at the possibilities. Can I really say which I want more, know-ing life as I did, the death, the sadness, the rage, I have witnessed man and woman alike tear each other to shreds, neither weaker than the other, just … different.

'What would you want little one, which would you rather be?'

I feel them press against my searching fingers, Arianwen's skin bulging as if the waiting life within is reaching out, desperate for me to take hold of them. A sharp shock lances through my hand, images dancing through my mind as I watch my sleeping Angel's stomach dance with then life within.

'It was you, wasn't it little one? It was you that pulled your father back from the depths of madness.'

I shift, carefully moving as my woman sinks into the feather stuffed pillows behind me and sets my lips to the soft bump, the baby within pushing back against me as I feel the energy course through me. Tears prick my eyes, pulling away watching as the small bulge sinks back. I trace my fingers around the outline of one small bump and watch as it moves across her pale stomach as our child feels my fingers dance across their mother's skin.

'You truly are a wondrous blessing little one, so small and yet, strong beyond your understanding. You truly are one of the loves of my life, and I will do whatever I must to keep you and your mother safe. For you and your mother little one, I would burn the world.'

I press my lips to my loves stomach, my words little more than a whisper as I pull away.

'As long as there's air in my lungs and a beat to my heart, nothing will ever harm you, I promise.'

I settle back into the plush comfort of the bed beneath us, the heat from the fire sapping the final dregs of my resistance as my eyes start to slip closed. With a gentle coaxing shuffle I pull my Angel to me, a soft moan of contentment rising from the woman in my arms as she slips back into the spot she claimed long ago.

'Goodnight my love.'

I set a soft lasting kiss on the top of her head before finally letting sleep claim me.

✦ ✦ ✦

The metallic peal of metal on metal plays out around me, shimmering in my ears as the wind blasts across my bare torso. My hands ache from holding the sledge hammer for so long. My forearms are twitching, begging for me to stop but I cannot. I will not.

I send the pitted and dented face of the hammer down atop another rune carved post, the Demon steel sinking further into the stone with each blow. The hammer slips from my grip, landing with a clatter at my feet as I stoop and scoop the spool of iron cored chain from off the floor. The links sear my skin, the runes etched into them glowing a dull blue as I begin to thread it through the hoops that hang from the posts.

The sound of rippling canvas draws my attention, the slashed and weather eaten cot in the corner dragging my mind kicking and screaming back to the point where it all nearly ended. It was here, on this plateau where they found us, where Michael and his litany of spoilt pigeons corralled me and the mother of my child, stringing us up like marionettes for all to see. If I let my guard slip, I can still feel the ropes biting into my skin. I shut my eyes willing the feelings away as I reach the last post.

'Never again.'

I slip the last of the chain through the final post, the spike in my pocket shivering as it meets daylight. The chain sears my palm as I pass the spike through the final link, lining up the Demon steel spike with the sigil painted onto the plateaus wall, before I drive it home sealing the blood spell. The air thrums with heat and energy as the chain and posts begin to glow a blistered orange, before, with a crackle of energy that shimmered red, it fades, smoke whispering away on the wind.

The spell sinks through the stone, the entire plateau shivering as I finally let myself relax. The wind buffets me as I step past the barrier, my body tingling as the blood spell tastes my soul. I know it is boarding on paranoia and insanity, my mind teetering on a level so pale and vacuous that my logic has twisted beyond any semblance of normality. But, one thing stands clear and plain above everything in my life. My woman Arianwen, and the unborn babe she carries are all that is important. There is nothing but them, not my duty as a Hunter, not my Demon kin, not Alp or any of the other clamouring hoard that plague the Undercroft and my former home.

I will slaughter them all if it is what it takes to keep my woman and child safe. Then there is Michael, that sauntering Angel and his levy of mindless drones. None of them will ever tear us apart again. I let my eyes travel across the lands below, the twisting winds lifting clouds of dust high into the air casting dancing shadows across the rusted shacks and rotted canvas tents that make up the crumbling fringe of the village. I snort softly as I turn my back on the slowly burning horizon and the pathetic world it is slowly bringing to life. Village, that place hardly be-gets the word; it is a sprawling warren of mud huts, tin shacks, old falling down building and crumbling tents extend from the fall to the edges of the pit, from the foot of my mountain home to the very edges of the cliffs that fall into the whispering seas. No, a village is the last thing that place is.

My senses tingle as I step back past the barrier, my body turning, placing my back to the door and hidden stair way as familiarity and comfort washes over me, the scent of vanilla and lavender floating past me. I lean down, plucking the handle of the sledge hammer from the floor, my senses aflame as I turn the pitted and dented head to the sun watching the twisted reflection. She steps closer, her movements light, fluid, decked in a silence born of instinct and practice. If it was not for my heightened senses, the gift of my father's blood, then, I would not have even known she was there.

I feign ignorance, my eyes watching her as I pretend to examine the sledge hammer in my hands for a non existent chip, before with a clatter of wood and metal spiced with a joy filled squeal of surprise I spin, lifting my woman from the floor, her body light and supple as her legs snare my waist, her warmth settling just above my belt, pressing against the sweat blown skin of my stomach.

'My sweet, handsome Demon. I was worried when I awoke and you weren't beside me.'

Her lips snare me as I feel her tongue glide across my own, the soft caress of her flesh upon mine driving me to distraction. I feel her grind against me, the damp warmth of her core soaking through me, igniting my mind in a glowing stream of lust and desire. She bites at my lip as I carry her towards the staircase, an impish grin spreading across her face as I turn pressing her backside into the cold stone of the wall, surprise lighting her face as I stare deeply into the violet pools that hold my gaze.

'Honestly my love, with how you were last night I was expecting you to still be deep asleep, and my having returned long before you were even awake.'

She nips the end of my nose as she smiles, my lips finding hers, common sense searing through everything before I carry on down the path I so dearly want to.

'Arianwen, as much as I want you right now, I'm not walking

down a stone staircase with the mother of my child hanging from my hips, besides, it's precarious enough having you walk down them considering ...'

I let my hand rest on her stomach, the rhythmic beat of life rippling through my palm as she grins at me and places her lips at the corner of my mouth. She shifts her weight, her legs sliding along mine as her fingers track across my chest, her nails catching on the edges of my Hunters brand. I wince slightly as my teasing Angel leans in and plants a soft kiss on my chest, her lips slipping along my skin before I feel the heat of her breath on my nipple, her tongue snaking across it as she grazes me with her teeth, a sharp wince dancing through me as she giggles.

'My, my, my gorgeous Demon, that was one reaction I wasn't expecting. But, you're right, I know you're right. Still, a woman has needs Albion, even if she is carrying the child of a man she would die for.'

I stare at her for a moment before I move ahead of her down the stairs. Thoughts of her, our child, the world that was slowly rallying against us; all of it turning, tumbling through my mind, drowning me in a vortex of confusion and fear. Fear at hurting the woman I love, a fear that is has become all too real, fear at my inability to protect the ones I love, even from myself.

I love her, I love her above everything. But, is it enough, will it ever be enough to assuage the fear at what is to come, the guilt at what has gone and the unassailable self hatred of what I, in my twisted and confused state was all too willing to do?

The bed slowly dances into my eye line as the heat from the hearth pulses over me, my body running alive with a sheen of sweat almost instantly. I feel her, soft and pure, her arms encircling me, the soft caress of her hair on my back as she pulls me tight to her; the press of her stomach at my back making me smile as I feel her shift her body.

'Darling, go rest, I'll be but a moment.'

I twist in her grip, my arms finding her shoulders as I lean down. The caress of her lips makes my heart hammer in my chest as she moans softly into my mouth. I need to feel her, to taste her essence on my tongue. But, how can I when she is how she is, when she is carrying our child? What would even a careful dalliance do to the tender life she now holds within her? I pull away lightly urging my Angel towards the bed as I step over to the small basin beside the hearth.

'Are you really that nervous Albion? You won't break me.'

I chuckle slightly as I lean against the wall, Arianwen's words crawling through my mind as I feel my lust growl in response. Her eyes shimmer with desire as I turn to face her, my advance slow, my steps measured as I watch her devour me with her eyes. The glazed look of wanton, unrestrained sexual desire oozing from her as I reach for the laced thonging on my trousers; loop by loop, my fingers travel lower, my length straining at the ever widening gap as I watch her eyes drink me in. I push the coarse padded leather down my hips as I reach the foot of the bed, Arianwen's gaze never leaving me as my thickening length springs free, her eyes widening, lips curling into a sensual smirk of lust and need as I slowly coax my length to its fullest.

I grin slightly as I step free of my trousers and begin a slow crawl up the bed, Arianwen's legs parting as I trail my lips along her thighs, her scent filling me as I reach her haven, the soaked cotton of her panties bathing my lips and chin in her sweet nectar. My tongue snakes out, pushing the wet cotton between her flushed and pouting lips as I drag it up, over her bud. Her moans fill my mind as my senses flow free, drinking in her musk, the subtle aroma of my woman swirling around me as I tease her panties aside and set my tongue to her soft pink rose.

I feel her clench around my tongue, her fingers digging into my hair as I slip through her satin folds. Her breathing comes in short stuttered gasps as I delve deeper into her honey soaked silk. Her thighs close around me trapping my head to her sex, the smell of her driving me wild as I eagerly drink her in, my tongue dancing over every line and curve of her soft core. Her fingers rake my scalp as I suck at her tender pearl, my teeth biting down as I graze them over the shuddering bundle.

'Oh fuck!'

Arianwen's stuttered gasp fills my mind, and I cannot help but smile as I bite down harder on her pulsing bud; she grinds against me, my jaw aching as I feel her flood my mouth, my chin dripping as my scalp starts to burn, her nails tearing my skin as she begins to groan, soft whimpering moans punctuating every clutching twitch, every dig of her nails as she edges ever closer to a tumultuous peak. A spike of fear lances through me as Arianwen slips the precipice and falls head first into an arcing climax. Her thighs clamp down on my head pinning me against her as she floods my mouth, her cream pooling on my tongue as I eagerly swallow all that she offers.

I feel her fingers stroke through my hair, a soft contented moan rippling the air as her thighs release their hold on my head. I cannot keep the grin from my face, despite the worry that now courses through me. I rise, my mouth and chin lathered in my Angel's honey as I step back, her flushed face glowing as she stares at me with a lascivious smile. Beckoning me, she lifts one leg, the sheer cotton robe sliding along her thigh, revealing all to my gaze as she pulls the sash open.

Her eyes narrow slightly as she watches me hesitate as she pushes up on her elbows, her chest bobbing softly, her swollen and tender breasts drawing my eye as she stares at me.

'Albion what's wrong? You were all too eager a moment ago, very eager, but now ...'

She watches as I scratch at the back of my head, hesitating over what I can say.

'Now, you're standing there like a child afraid of their first swim.'

I cock my head to one side, casting a slightly hurt look towards the woman I love more than anything, before, finally giving voice to the worry that hides within me.

'Can we really do this? With what I am, what can happen ... in the heat of the moment ... can we really risk it for a moment of pleasure? I ... I don't want to hurt you, you or our child, and with all that has come and gone between us, I can't guarantee I won't. I know saying this now is a bit, well, beyond the pale considering what we just did, but I can't help the fear that I feel.'

Her smile is warm, filled with adoration and love as she pushes herself into a seated position, legs crossed as she cradles her small rounded stomach in her hands.

'We'll be fine my love, just ... not as vigorous as we were, show me how tender my Demon can be, show me the love I know is in you, the love that makes you hesitate for the sake of our child.'

# The Unknown

## ARIANWEN

**I shiver as his gentle touch raises bumps along my skin; his** fingers once again find their way across my stomach and gently spray out, softly holding our child hidden within. He is still holding back, even after my reassurances that it is perfectly safe to continue with our sexual exploits. It makes me love him even more.

His lips find my ear as his tongue darts out to taste my skin. The moan that escapes me echoes around the stone walls of our room, letting him know I want more, letting him know I could never get enough of him. This Demon knows my body better than I, and the path his mouth is taking is very familiar to him. His lips move over my shoulder and across my collarbone where he gives a little nip, before slowly heading to a place he knows will drive me crazy.

He sucks and nibbles his way down before finally reaching a very sensitive nipple. The first swipe of his tongue across the puckered bud has me screaming in ecstasy as he then sucks it entirely into his mouth. I can barely catch a breath as he continues to suck before letting it fall from his lips and uses his teeth to bite the end softly yet sharply, the effect flooding my centre as my bodies arousal slowly slides down my thighs. I feel his growl vibrate against my skin.

'Mmm, I do like the change in these. The extra swell is quite enticing my sweet Angel,' he says in a deep husky voice as he attempts to fit one entire breast in his delicious mouth. He nudges my chest harder until I am lying on my back, and he wastes no time in cupping the neglected breast. I moan long and loud as my body starts to climb again despite my exhaustion not long ago and the climax I have already reached within his arms.

He swaps his mouth to the other nipple, giving it the same attention with his rough tongue, bringing all of my nerve endings to life, building me up higher as he sends a hand slowly down my torso, once again stopping at my slight bulge, before continuing further down to the apex of my thighs, pushing a finger through my wet folds, arching my back, making my hips lift from the bed, forcing more pressure against my centre as I feel myself yet again, hanging on the edge of ecstasy.

He raises his head and reaches up to claim my lips, his tongue pushing through, dancing erotically with my own, claiming me as his. I am panting into his mouth when his torturous finger slips inside. He swallows my scream as my intimate muscles start to clamp down on his intrusion. He adds another which has me bucking up against his body. 'Please my love, be careful, I don't want you to hurt.'

I hear his words but cannot stop my reaction to the friction he is once again creating inside my heat. I missed this, I missed him. I feel frantic, so desperately needing to connect with him again on every level. Mind, body, heart and soul all need to feel him again. 'I need this Albion, I need you, all of you. Please, please my love.' He understands my desperation as he moves over and between my legs, his large knees spreading my thighs further apart, his fingers still enticing my wet centre, his lips rubbing slowly over mine.

He slips his fingers out, the feeling causing my muscles to pulse with loss. But then I feel his thick shaft press at my entrance, and I almost come undone. I whimper in need as he slowly pushes forward, only the tip of him entering before he pulls back slightly. I take what I need as I buck forward, my centre pulling him in and clamping tightly, never wanting to let go. He growls at my audacity, one large hand reaching down to push my hips back against the fur pelt on the bed.

'Easy Arianwen, we need to be careful.' I do not want careful, I want my rough and feisty Demon right at this moment. He eases in slowly, my head falls back as my mouth opens in a silent oh. His grip on my hips tighten, a warning not to push past his carefulness as he begins to move slowly out, then in just as slow. The feeling of his solid flesh dragging past my internal walls has me gasping, and I know I will not last much longer.

His pleasured grunt has my internal walls gripping his shaft harder, and when he goes to pull back again, I am lost, my climax ripping through my body fiercely despite our slow pace. He pushes back in through my tightness, and I clamp down harder as my body explodes, stars flying through my vision as I feel him also losing his control. He pulls out slightly then slams back in hard as he explodes with a roar, his seed flooding my centre as we both struggle for some much needed air.

'I'm sorry,' I hear his muffled voice as he buries his face in my neck. 'You have nothing to be sorry for my love,' I soothe him as my hands gently rub circles over his broad back, as we both come back down from our dance with ecstasy. He pulls out slowly, the combined lust of our lovemaking flows down my core and between my buttocks as I notice the frown that is masking his handsome face. I reach a hand up to attempt to rub it away. He moves to my side and gently rubs my stomach, feeling the movement of baby beneath his fingertips.

'See, I pushed too hard, baby is upset, I may have hurt it,' he mumbles fast, upset with himself. Will my poor Demon ever understand that I am not fragile? 'Baby is fine, it's completely normal for couples to continue to be intimate during pregnancy. Baby is probably just awake now. There's nothing to worry about.' I try to soothe him with words and my lips, slowly raining kisses all over his frown.

He continues to caress my stomach, a small grin appearing at the edges of his lips as baby seems to be following his gentle touch. I will never tire of his amazed look at what he had a hand in creating. It is truly a beautiful sight. But, that sight will change when I bring up the seriousness of our situation.

'We need to talk about our future my love.' His hand stills and his frowns returns, but he takes his time, thinking deeply before responding to my words we both know had to be said.

'I'll not let any harm come to our child or you Arianwen. I'll do everything in my power to keep you both safe. Our family will always be safe, as long as there is breath left in me and my heart still beats, I will keeps us three safe.'

'I wish I had your confidence and conviction my love, but I've seen both sides of Good and Evil, and I know that if they ever discovered our tiny secret, it would become a battle we would have to fight alone to keep our baby safe.'

'We will be long gone before they have a chance to discover us or our child. You're only truly showing when you are bare. You just need to ensure you wear your cloak everywhere for the next few days or maybe weeks before we're prepared enough to actually leave. We'll both go back to our lives and act as "normal" as we can until I find a safe time for us to leave. We'll find a place to live, me, you and our child. We will be a family my sweet Angel, I promise you that.'

'But where will that be? What world could be possibly safe enough if it is mostly unknown? I have researched Albion, I have read all the information available on the other immortal worlds, and there is just not enough to guarantee a safe existence. Except …' I cannot finish the sentence because that alternate world would come with much sacrifice and no guarantees we would be able to protect ourselves against its natural elements.

'Except where? Tell me my love, I may have heard the Old ones tell of it or be able to seek information from my own sources.'

I doubt his own kin would know as much about this place as mine, but I need to share with him my thoughts, because it could be the one place we could safely escape to … if I could just find out how an immortal can find a way into a mortal world.

'Earth.'

That one word has an immense effect on both of us. He does not have to say any words, I already know what he is thinking, because I have had every similar thought over the weeks we have been apart, and I have stolen every free minute I have had researching all possibilities from all worlds, including this unpredictable mortal one.

I know we would both be powerless there, we would have no guarantees of keeping any abilities we now have to protect ourselves and baby, we would be vulnerable to Earth's elements and its people, but, we would not have the threats of such powerful immortals breathing down our backs.

But, there is no known ways of an immortal travelling to that world. The only documented cases of immortals going to the mortal world is where they have permission from or been banished there, by the hands of God. And I highly doubt that if I requested a meeting with him that it would be granted, or if it was, I doubt he would be so understanding of me wanting to leave my world. And I'm still unsure of what hand he has had in all of my recent life events, so that meeting would be too unpredictable to even risk requesting.

'Arianwen, I may not be able to … well … protect my family there. No Demon that has ever been summoned to the human world has come back without some form of scar. The humans, the ones who call us to Earth, the Warlocks and Witches, they all found their names; if any human finds a Demon's name, they own us, the entire time we are bound to the mortal world, they own us. Baal, Arianwen, they found Baal's name, the only other person in all of Hell that was stronger than Baal, barring the first ones, was Lucifer; he became their plaything. How can we go to a world where people like that exist? The only members of my kind that have ever ventured there and returned unscathed, have been those who were sent unshackled, without a way to leave Earth, without a link to this one and even then; they were lucky to find a path home. Why do you think Gabriel, Michael and the other Arcs are the only Angels that have set foot in the human world on their own? No foot soldier, no one of a lesser station than them, be they Angel or Demon, would ever venture there without help.'

I understand his concerns all too well. 'I think the best thing for me to do is to continue to seek the help of the Bookkeeper. I could tell her that Earth may be a possibility and see if she can find more information before we make a decision.'

His frown increases and his grip on me tightens. His breathing starts to fasten which worries me at what he may be thinking.

'Arianwen ... if we were to go to the mortal world, we run the risk of becoming mortal. Which means ...'

A shudder takes over his entire body, and I can sense his aura darken. It is not a feeling I like at all.

'Which means, my love; it would mean ... I wouldn't have you for eternity.'

That thought makes my heart sink to the bottom of my stomach. I had realised that if Earth was to become a possibility, then there was also a possibility that we would all become mortals, but I did not comprehend the full meaning of that until now.

'If it's the only way to keep us together and to not lose you and baby, then I guess we would just make the most out of every day we have together.'

He grins, but it is tainted with sadness. I understand, I do not want to lose any time with the man I love, or the child we will have soon, but I also do not want to risk losing them if we were to stay here and battle for our safety. Any time we have together would be a blessing. He hugs me tighter, understanding washing over him as we both ponder our options.

'Let's just continue to collect everything we will need and be well prepared for when the time comes to leave, regardless of what new world we will end up calling home. As long as you and baby are in my arm's Arianwen, I will be a happy man.'

His words ring true in my heart. Any time together would be a blessing. 'Can you trust this Bookkeeper Arianwen?' His question does not surprise me. I had concerns when she first let me know she had discovered I was pregnant, and I am certain she knows who it is that I have created a child with.

'I had concerns my love, but she has told me I would always be safe under her roof, and I know her aura is true, so yes, I do trust her. But, I'll only keep the information I share with her to a minimum for not only ours, but her safety as well.'

He ponders my words for a few minutes, absent mindedly drawing circles around my quiet stomach, baby now settled and snug. 'I may have someone I can also trust in my world. He is of no Demon descent, but has been in the village for longer than I. He is quietly wise, knowing a lot about my world. I know there was a time that my father trusted him, so that says a lot to me.' My heart clenches at his mention of a parent. I know he has not had family in his life for a long time. For a normal Demon that would not mean a thing, but Albion has a different heart, his Good makes him feel more.

'Do you miss them, your parents?' He seems shocked at my question, but that look of surprise is soon replaced by the starting's of a grin.

'I do. I don't remember everything, there are some gaps I just can't bridge, memories I simply cannot grasp. I remember my mother's smile, it was like a new dawn each and every time, it was so bright, so pure and clean that she could only show it inside the walls of our dwelling. I can't remember a single time she ever smiled outside of my old home. I've memories of my father smiling down at my mother while he held her tightly in his arms, my favourite is of me peering round my bedroom's door and seeing them by the fire. It's the one time I clearly remember my father telling my mother that he loved her. I never did understand, as a child, why smiles were only allowed in our home, although now, it's all too apparent that maybe they were both different from all the other Demons I grew up amongst. When they were gone I found it hard to reconcile that fact, hard to believe that my parents were something different from all our other kin. I know my father came from a long line of Demon Knights, so how could he also have some Good inside him? Up until now, that fact had always lain beyond me.'

He pauses as the smile on his face grows, his hand finding mine. 'I remember my mother being more beautiful than anything I'd ever seen. There was no one in our world that could even be remotely compared to her. She stood out that's for sure. Maybe that's why my father was always so protective of her, I don't know. She was barely allowed to venture anywhere on her own. I remember us always being together. Now I know how strange that truly is. I'm thinking that maybe she wasn't always from our world. But why would an outsider choose to live a life in Hell?'

As soon as he finishes it dawns on me. Why would an outsider give up their life to spend it in Hell? There is only one reason.

'Love,' I whisper, his eyes widen with shock at my words as his hand tightens around mine.

Something stirs in my mind as I turn to face the man I love. Could Albion's mother have been a Fallen Angel? That would explain the Good within Albion's soul and heart, a trait he could have only inherited from his mother. Even if she did choose to live in the land of Evil, her genes would still be those of the light and would have passed down everything that was pure in her if she was to create a child with her Demon lover.

'Albion ...'

But before I can speak, he holds up a hand.

'I know Arianwen, I know what you're thinking. It does ... make sense. But you and I both know Lucifer would have known and would have never allowed it. He told me himself that love is a plague to be stamped out, that it was his true reason for being cast out of Heaven. So, that only leaves one true ending to this, and that is, that he did know. That he found out somehow, found out that my parents had fallen to that "Sin" and that's why they died, that's why he had them *killed.* I remember a conversation. I never paid it much mind until now, it never made much sense to me before, not until now. A child's mind is a very flexible thing, but one that is like a sponge, nothing lost, nothing forgotten. It is a conversation that is embedded on my very soul, the last conversation my parents ever had before ...'

He stops, his breath juddering as he takes a few deep breaths before speaking again.

'I was supposed to be asleep. We had had a busy day collecting things, blankets, herbs from the forest, things like that, nothing we hadn't done a thousand times before. We'd been out most of the day, so when we returned home, the three of us sat down to a meal. I remember it being very quiet that night. It made my father nervous, the halls were quiet, the Undercroft below us was strangely muted. Only way I can describe it is, like the pit was holding its breath waiting for something to give. It was unnerving because we always had a very lively meal, raucous conversation driven by the energy that fed from the world around us. My father would always tell the epic tales of old, of massive battles between one Warrior and another, his voice changing for each character. He would have me in stitches by his animated tone, and my mother would join in telling her own side of the stories, adding bits and tangents that I never truly understood. She was always very careful of what she told me.

'One thing that has always stuck in my mind though was that night, when I was tucked into bed. My father seemed tense, nervous, as if he was waiting for something bad to happen. I could see it in his eyes when he said his usual "goodnight my son". My fear mounted when it came time for my mother to say goodnight. She did something she never did, she held me extra tight. I was always given a tender hug and a kiss on the forehead by my mother, but that night, just like father she behaved differently. She then told me the words I always heard from her, *"You are my special boy Albion. You are different. You will do great things one day."* Then she hugged me tight again and walked out closing my door.

'I couldn't sleep, try as I might to fall off into slumber, it was the feeling in the air, the tension so thick I could have cut it with a knife, it was suffocating. So I fell back to what I would always do when I had trouble sleeping and turned to look out of my window. I was always so attracted to the stars in the sky, even though, from my home in the pit I was lucky to see it for even the smallest of moments; yet I would never admit that to anyone.

'The night was so quiet, it's probably what made sleep that night all but impossible, and I just lay there, listening to the wind and my parent's conversation. It wasn't what they were saying that has been etched into my brain, but the panic I heard in their voices. I had never heard it from them before, they were always so calm, so collected and yet tonight, that melted like snow in spring.

'I picked up on some snippets of what was said, little pieces like, *"it has to be now"*, and, *"there's no other choice, they are coming for us."* I couldn't help thinking "who" it was that was coming, what could ever make my mother and father so scared. Despite those memories being so fixed in my mind, it is the next words my mother spoke that have always stuck with me the most.

*"He is different, special, they will use it against him, they will use*

*him for Evil, and I will die before I let that happen!"*

'Those words, the sound of my mother crying, and my father soothing her, is all I remember. Despite it all, I must have fallen asleep. It wasn't until the next morning, after I'd made my way home, despite Garth and Glynnis begging me to stay, that the Dolophonos were at my door telling me that Lucifer himself wants to talk to me. I had no idea where my parents were. I had no idea who to tell in case my parents came home and I wasn't there. The only thing I did know at that point was, that you never said no to the Dolophonos, so I was dragged away to see the King of Hell.

'It was Lucifer who told me in his slick way that they were killed. He said it was in some sort of battle with Gabriel's Sleepers at the far ends of the forest, but, I think even then, I knew he was lying and it wasn't until years later that I found out my father's true fate, flayed alive by Malachai's father on Lucifer's orders. From that day, the smooth talking Fallen Angel of Hell told me my parents were dead. I became his protégé and learnt to never question my parent's death, even when I found out how my father really died. It's only now that I can remember more that I really question everything, everything I am and everything I really thought I knew.'

To say I am shocked at Albion's words would not be the truth. I have heard and witnessed the lengths that Lucifer will go to get what he wants, and truly believe he did indeed find out how different Albion was and that his parents knew and were planning on leaving before they met their timely demise. Then he had Albion, a child of both worlds, a very powerful little being he could brainwash and mould into the perfect soldier of Evil to stand by his side. He created a weapon of mass destruction. But, little did he know that he could never truly erase the Good that was embedded in his soul. He never really did have a firm grasp on that brilliant little boy.

'You're still as special as your mother told you Albion, even more so now that you've become a man. You being different is probably the only reason we have a special little person that we've created ourselves. She was right, you have done great things. You have learnt to love.'

# 13

## Revelations and Heartache

### ALBION

**'I knew this would be hard, but, this hurts worse than any-**thing I have ever felt, and I've been shot and stabbed by the worst of them and some of the better ones.'

I pull my Angel close as I feel her shoulders rise and fall, the sound of her soft sobbing tears my heart to shreds. Parting this way was something I had steeled myself for, but now, to be stood here only metres from the gates that are going to crash closed baring us from each other's side until our next union, is something I do not think I could ever really prepare for.

'Arianwen, I know this hurts, but we can't let anyone on my side or yours see the pain. I love you more than life itself, but, if this is what we need to do, to keep the status quo from tipping in the wrong direction then do it we must.'

She pulls me tighter, her fingers curling to the leather of my armour as I kiss the top of her head.

'No, I know that, but I don't want this moment to end. I only got you back and now they're tearing me away from you again. I just can't do it.'

I turn my head to the sun, my crimson tears searing my eyes as I fight the need to cry. I stifle a sob, my chest heaving slightly as I turn my gaze back to the weeping woman in my arms.

'My love we must do this, you know it, I know it. What we want right now, well, it just doesn't matter. We have to think beyond ourselves. I'll always be yours and you'll always be mine, but right now, we have a child that needs us both to be stronger than our own hearts.'

I lean down, my lips finding the top of her head as she turns slowly, as I graze them over her gossamer hair and satin skin until at last hers find my own. I taste her tears in her kiss, the frailty of the moment shattering me as I feel the hot passage of mine down my cheeks. I can't deny them anymore; I do not know why I did to begin with.

My thoughts careen through everything, colliding in a mass of pain and pleasure as my heart tries to tell me what my mind is still trying to hide, that I have to let her go. I break the soft and tender kiss, her pursed lips parted slightly as she slowly opens her eyes. The pale tinge of blue from her tears at war with the glistening violet that so swims with devotion and love as I see my own staring back at me from within.

'You're the light of my heart, and our child is the window into my soul. There's nothing I wouldn't do to keep you both safe. We'll make it through this, and if the mortal world is where we're destined to be, then, there is no one in this world or any other I would rather make the leap with.'

I cup her chin, her wide eyes melting my heart as I gently kiss her again.

'We'll survive this, we are stronger than this moment, and you know that. Together, Arianwen, we can conquer all. We have come too far, given up and found too much together, to let something as trivial as time and distance destroy what we have. I'm going to fight for us, for our child, for everything we are, and I know you will to.'

She leans against me, her hair catching in the thonging of my armour as I hold her tightly to me; the heat from her permeates my very core. I rest my chin against the top of her head as I sigh, thoughts of our life together dancing through my mind as I think back on all that has come and gone.

I would truly give my life for the woman I now hold in my arms. Nothing else in this world comes close to the level of love I hold for her, all of which is only equalled by the life she now has blooming inside of her.

'I love you Arianwen, with all my heart and soul, but, you need to go. I'll stay and watch over you from here until you are safely behind the Dragon gates. Just know this my love, no matter what happens, my heart, my soul, are forever yours.'

She pushes herself up onto the balls of her feet, her lips snatching mine before she turns and leaves. I am left standing there, watching as the woman I love disappears slowly from my sight. The gates crash closed with an echoing clang, the Dragons twisting, their eyes locking onto me as I stand staring at the brushed gold and brass that now stands between my soulmate and I.

I stand here, staring at the gates that stole the woman I love. I do not know how long I was stood, time ticking by, the rumble of the Dragons pulsing through my feet as I listen to the world around me. The trails of my tears, russet streaks on my skin as I turn, the pain welling in me again as I make the slow march through the forests and toward the cliff.

The ache in my heart is near to unbearable. We had only just found one another again and now, we are torn apart, fate slicing through the ties that bind us together like a hot knife through cold butter. The sting of losing her, even temporarily is all too real as I reach the foot of the fall. I turn, stone grating against my skin as I sink to the floor, my arms crossed over my knees as I lean my head against them. Pain, fear, anger, all of it tearing through me as I sink deeper inside myself.

I know this is only a temporary thing, and yet, it hurts more now than any wound I have ever received. No bullet, nor any blade has ever sunk as deep or bitten as fiercely as the self inflicted isolation and separation that now sits between me and the woman I love. I smile slightly at the thought of it. Love, who would have ever thought a Demon to be capable of it. But here I am, living proof that Demons truly can feel more than hate, anger or lust, and right now, it is something I truly wish I could not feel. How can something my parents so wished for me to feel, be such an unbearable curse. One filled with pain and anguish, so visceral it has left me little more than a quivering shell and yet all it proves is that, I am as Demonic I was taught to believe.

That is something I cannot answer, and something I am sure I will never truly know. All I can say right now, is that beyond those gates, carried beyond my reach and safe inside the walls of an army that has sworn to wipe my kind from existence, is the woman I would give all for, and the mother to my child. I cast my gaze to Eden one last time before I rise and begin the climb to the top of the fall, my eyes slipping to the trail that winds its way past me. I push it from my mind, the need to wash away the feelings that now assail me more deserving of the soul sapping climb I am now facing.

My arms ache, my shoulders burning as I haul myself over the cliff edge. I turn my backside sinking into the dust and grit as I stare back out over the forest to the shimmering glass and crystal spires of Eden.

I push myself backwards, tucking my legs beneath me and rising as I do, I cough slightly as dust whips up, cast into the air by the rising thermals from the forest below. I need to find a distraction, not only for my mind, but my heart as well; something into which I can pour every ounce of energy and passion that has flooded my every fibre into.

The scent of wood and leather drenches the air as I make it to Garth's door step, the timbre door standing stout in its frame as I knock. The dull echo rolling inside the squat building as I wait for an answer.

I turn, my legs weary as I sit, my body sinking to the floor with a thump as my muscles give out, the quivering lumps of sinuous flesh too taxed to bear even my own weight. I gasp slightly as my chest rebels against the impact as I lean my head in my hands. I sit there, mind wandering, listening to the dull chittering and garbled roar of the village when a voice cuts through it all, parting the fog in my brain like scissors through silk.

'Are you going to sit there all day boy, or are you going to come in? It's rather rude to knock on an old man's door and not accept the invite you know.'

I turn, my eyes meeting Garth's as I smile lightly, my mind too sapped by the day's events to form any quip or retort.

'Thanks old man.'

Garth brushes the sentiment aside, his body hunched and heat scarred as he shuffles back into his workshop.

'No thanks needed boy, your family did more for me and mine than any other Lord or Master that's come and gone over the years. Your father was a good man, a loyal man. He didn't deserve what they did to him.'

I stop short at the mention of my father, my mind dancing with questions as I struggle to think. My mind racing as I sink to the stool in front of Garth's work bench, the scent of tanned leather and oil soaked chainmail coating my throat as I rest my head in my hands. The stories and rumours slung at me as a child, of my father's demise and my mother's death in battle. Could Garth give me the closure I sorely need, to finally know the truth of what happened to my mother and father?

I lift my head from my hands, the sound of patting lips making me curious as I set eyes on Garth, the diminutive blacksmith now sat in one of the dining chairs, the coarse cut wood almost swallowing the pipe smoking bender of metal. I stare at the silent man for a few moments, the glowing briar of his pipe bowl illuminating one side of his face as he draws on the stem.

'I can see the gears turning Master Weisser, ask them if you've got them. Otherwise, I am to assume you're here to steal my work space again. So which is it to be?'

I cannot help but smile at the man, a sigh rolling up from me as I rest my elbows on my knees.

'Do you know the truth behind what happened to my parents?'

Garth's brow rises slightly at my question, the pipe bowl glowing a fierce orange as he draws on it deeply. His eyes thoughtful, gaze lost in deep contemplation as smoke curls towards the ceiling. I watch as he lifts the pipe from between his lips and wipes his mouth on the cuff of his shirt.

'Yes I do, but, for now it's not a tale you need to hear. I think young Weisser, what you need is time to clear your heart and mind, or am I wrong in seeing the sting of lost love in your eyes?'

My eyes widen as I stare at Garth. Is my face that easy to read, am I so wrapped up in my own misery that I have forgotten the one rule both I and my Angel set down? I must be, but then again, the wily silver haired fox that sits smiling at me is far wiser and more insightful than his modest profession would lead anyone to believe.

'I'll take that as a yes. If you're going to be making her a new Carapace, then I'd suggest you add a layer of padding to it. All sorts of changes can affect a woman's body, you never know what could come to pass, also flexible plating in the stomach area wouldn't hurt, but what do I know? I'm just a blacksmith.'

I cannot help but smirk, his flippant statement slicing through every doubt and hurt that clouds my thoughts. My knees and thighs groan in protest as I rise, my legs trembling as I feel Garth's gaze linger on me as I move towards the warmth of the hearth and the graphite stick and vellum that sits on the table.

A soft chuckle rolls free from him as I sit with my back to the fireplace. He grins and speaks as I cast a questioning glance at him.

'You climbed the fall didn't you, you daft bugger.'

I nod in reply, too wary of his sudden burst of perceptiveness to form any real reply.

'I knew it. I saw the same shakes and hangdog movements in your father more than once. You're just as troubled a romantic as he was. Too wrapped up in your own hearts to further much more than a grin after you have to bid your ladies farewell, for even the shortest time. Bloody idiots the pair of you.'

I stare at him, unsure of whether I should laugh, take offence, reply or stay mute. The wizened old soul before me has said more to shock and stump me in the last five minutes than he ever has before in my life time. Only one other moment can sit at the same level and that was when I sat at this very table, the life of my love in his hands and the damnable mask he had wrought into being.

'What else do you know of my father?'

Garth shakes his head, a chuckle worming clear as I watch him shuffle towards his work bench.

'I told you before boy, not now, you have work to do, and I have a job to complete. We will talk more of the past and all its secrets later. For now, you have armour to make, and I have a door to make hinges for.'

He moves through an arch way and into the forge he so closely guards.

'You'll find the calf skin leather and goose down padding in the baskets beneath the bench, the Demon steel and Angel glass is in the storage chests at either end, have fun.'

Fun, he says it with such flippancy and youthful vigour that I almost forget just how aged the old kook is. I stare at the paper in front of me, the graphite stick staining my fingers as I begin to sketch out the armour that I am so desperate to bring to life. It needs to be right, it needs to be perfect. Two lives, the only two that hold any meaning for me any more, rest on it being perfect.

The sound of the stick on paper fills the room as the crackle of burning timber filters through my mind. Pages flutter and fall as I etch out design after design. I need to get this right, for my child, for my Angel, I have to get this right. My eyes begin to ache as I cast aside the spent graphite stick, the dregs of it skittering into the glowing coals of the fire behind me as I reach for another, the floor around me littered with discarded ideas, notes and annotations.

Minutes drip into hours as Garth comes and goes, my mind so set on the task before me that I barely register the passage of his wife, the merest of guttural greetings tripping from me as I send another design floating to the floor before sinking once more into another.

I feel a hand at my shoulder, my head turning, my eyes sagging as I struggle to blink through the strain. It feels as if the insides of my lids have been smeared with sand as I set my gaze on Garth's wife. She smiles as I meet her stare, the motherly glint in her eyes makes my heart sink, even now, after all the years and the new growth that has sealed the scar my parents left. I cannot help longing for her to hold me, for my mother to simply scoop me into her arms and tell me it will all be right with time.

'Albion, love, you need some food and some rest. I can see how tired you are. There's a cot at the back of the workshop, go put your head down for a bit and I will make you something to eat later. Go on.'

My head throbs with the sheer over taxing tumult that crawls through my mind. I nod at her, questions bubbling like tar as I push woodenly from the table. My back aches as I rise a deep curling burn sinking through my bones as I turn, my mouth moving before I have any possible chance to logically think through what I am going to say.

'Why are you helping me? I'm a Demon, the personification of Evil. How can you possibly justify helping me?'

She smiles as she takes me by the arm and leads me towards the cot.

'Because child, you are neither a Demon nor Evil, not here, not anywhere will the soul you carry ever be that of a Hell spawn or be cast in the shadow of the pit.'

I sit with a sigh on the edge of the cot, her words twisting my thoughts as I cast my gaze to floor.

'But, I was born of a Demon, my home was the circles of the pit. I have killed the lost and Angels alike, sending all to the eternal sleep. How can you not claim me to be Evil, when all I have done is commit heinous and Demonic acts?'

She smiles as she sits next to me, her aura coating me in a balm of calm and peace.

'You, my dear, are born of far more than a Demon, but, as Garth said, this is a conversation for another time, and you need rest Albion. Get some sleep and we can talk later.'

I wake to the sounds of bubbling pots and the scent of frying pork, a rarity here in the village to be sure, but not one that surprises me. I stretch, working the knots and tension from my back and shoulders before rising to my feet and wiping sweat from my eyes.

I step towards the table, surprise working through me as I cast my gaze over the neatly stacked pile of designs and the carefully set allotment of materials that run its length. A soft chortle draws my attention as Garth makes his way in from the forge, his hands swathed in cloth as he wipes them clean of grease and soot.

'Yeah, Glynnis does that. She probably looked through that stack of yours, picked out the few she thought to be best, combined their best attributes into one and then selected what will most likely be the materials you'd end up choosing yourself.'

I cast a glance at Garth's amused face, his brow crinkling slightly as he grins at me.

'What? I thought you knew I couldn't draw to save my life. Glynnis designs it all, I just do the grunt work. Why do you think I married her?'

My brow furrows as I turn to face him, a question frothing at the edges of my mind.

'I was always led to believe that any one in the village wasn't permitted to marry, seeing as this is basically little more than a waiting room between Eden, the pit, and reincarnation.'

'Where there's a will, there's always a way.'

He winks at me as I hear Glynnis' voice filter in from the small bathroom to my right.

'That's not the only reason he married me, he can cook worth a damn either.'

I smile slightly, my mind still bubbling with unanswered questions, but somehow, at peace with the situation and all it has brought with it. Right now, as I stand watching the couple before me, their jovial jibes and playful banter, it gives me a sense of the life I and Arianwen could have, and it is one that I know we are destined for, one we are pre-ordained to live through. No matter what comes our way or how much it costs me to get there, I know that we will be together as a family, come whatever may.

I find myself smiling again as Glynnis hands me a plate and points to an empty spot at the table, with a short nod to her I sit, the metal plate clunking against the roughhewn table. Garth sits opposite me, the array of Demon steel and Angel glass dividing us like the walls of Jericho. I can feel his gaze on me as I dig into the food before me even as I struggle to find one particular question to ask when my mind is so riddled with those seeking my attention.

'Confused where to start aren't you boy, and I don't mean the food.'

I nod, my mind still boiling with everything I want to ask as Garth continues to talk around mouthfuls of meat and eggs.

'Okay, you asked me if I knew what happened to your parents. A broad question, but yes I do know, although it is not a question with a short answer. Well, I say no short answer. To be blunt he was betrayed, betrayed by those closest to him and for all the wrong reasons.'

I let the fork in my hand drop with a clatter to the plate beneath it, my hunger gone in a flash as Garth locks his gaze to my own.

'Before you ask anything Albion, how much do you know about your lineage, other than the fact that your father is a Demon Knight and your mother was a Fallen Angel?'

I stare at him, my mind a tumult of confusion and contradiction.

'My mother was no Fallen Angel!'

Garth lets out a barked laugh as Glynnis leaves the room, my ire mounting.

'You really think that, although I am not surprised they led you to think that, but by all that was sacred boy, open your damned eyes. Your mother was a Fallen Angel. How many Demons aside from the first to fall and all that he brought down with him, do you know to have black feathered wings?'

I sit mute as Garth pushes his plate aside.

'Well? Come on boy, think about it, after all those years you spent living there, how many Demons do you know sport black feathered wings? I mean, just look at yourself, have you ever wondered why your own wings aren't truly like those of your supposed kin?

'Your mother, may the saints keep her, was one of the few Angels to fall, and hers wasn't by choice, she was commanded to fall. Why, I was never told, but commanded she was, and I think that was the only reason she survived. Most of the Angels that end up falling from grace don't last more than a few weeks, maybe a month at most, but your mother, well, she was a force unto herself. She fought tooth and nail to stay alive, evading packs of Hunters, the Dolophonos, even a few of the higher echelons of Lucifer's personal guard didn't pin her down, well, that was until your father was sent out to claim her head, and I guess you know how that turned out, otherwise we wouldn't be having this conversation.

'But, that's not my point. I've known your family since before your Grandfather was born and Albion, none of your family were ever truly what the world, mortal or immortal, would ever call Evil. I've never seen a couple so truly belong together as your mother and father, from the moment he set eyes on her in this very room, I knew then, as I know now with you and Arianwen, that it was a fated and destined love; a fate so interwoven into your family's blood that it could never be undone.'

I watch as Garth lifts his steel mug to his lips, drinking slowly, his hand shaking slightly. I struggle to digest what he has lain before me. The fact of my mother's true nature, which if I am truly honest with my own heart, I always knew. The fact my father was once sent to claim her head, but instead had her claim his heart or the one irrevocable fact, that, through it all, I and Arianwen, just as with my mother and father, were always, by some twist of fate or irony of God, meant to be together.

'How do you know all this, no common lost soul could ever know all of this?'

Garth laughs once more, his head lolling back as he puts far more force into it than was truly needed.

'You still think I am just another condemned? Boy, I've been here since before Lucifer fell. I know more about this world, the people in it, and what the real meaning of everything is, than even some of the Arcs, plus, people talk to those they think don't matter, and I don't seem to matter all that much. But I digress, my story is not one worth telling, your Grandfather though, he was born of a union exactly like yours, a Demon and a Fallen Angel, although that tale's a lot less, adventurous, than that of your mother and father.'

I raise my hand, beckoning for silence as my mind turns. I pinch the bridge of my nose, struggling against the tide to root out the source of my question.

'None of this though, gives me the answers I need, what I truly need to know.'

Garth nods as he pulls his pipe from his belt.

'Well, your father, the Demon Knight, head of the Sixth Legion, he was as I said, betrayed. Betrayed by those he had sworn to serve and those he thought he could trust. With you here with me and he himself surrounded, what else could a loving father do, he surrendered, and let himself be taken for fear of them targeting you or your mother in reprisal for anything he did.'

It was at that moment that my mind seized, memories boiling through me as I remember everything and nothing all at once. The night Garth speaks of peeling away the layers of confusion and sanity all at once. Could I have really spent my parents last living moments in the comfort of a warm bed and the embrace of dreams? All the while they were cast into irons and dragged from my side like hogs to slaughter.

'Your mother, may the saints keep her, was a strong willed and powerful woman. She fought to the end, it wasn't her true end, but, you could see it from here. I watched, powerless to do anything else. I watched as Malachai's father beat her, carved her wings from her body, leaving only shreds of bone and flesh; just enough to prevent her from falling free of her bond to this world and into the realm of mortals. It's something I wish I could forget, the sound of her screams and the sight of her blood seeping into the dirt. She was a kind and loving woman and the way her light was stolen, is something she never deserved.'

Garth stops, his eyes brimming with unshed tears as I sit mute, unable to think beyond the words that are seeping through my every thought. He cuffs away the tears, a short snorted sniff bringing me out of my reverie.

'I know the truth of what they did Garth, what they did to my father. How they flayed him alive and fed him to Cerberus.'

Garth stares at me, his eyes red, pain streaking his face as he begins to speak again.

'You think that's what they did to him, no, what they did, was far worse.'

# Careful

## ARIANWEN

**The steps I take back to my own world are filled with more** confidence than they have been in weeks, but, they are also tainted with sadness. Sadness that I had to leave my love yet again to parade myself in the façade that has become my life within the walls of Eden. To finally be safely tucked within his arms and still having to walk away, is torturous on my heart. But, I know we will find a way and soon. But leaving will not be an easy task, physically or emotionally.

I will not let my mind wander to what it will mean to leave my family, that is a reality my soul is yet to accept. So for now I will return to the routine I have delved myself in for the past few weeks while secretly preparing everything I will need for my imminent departure.

I know the safest place to go is to the children's learning garden and try and blend in as if I had never left and just hope my absence has not been noticed. But, just as I hear the laughter of our worlds young, I receive a calling. It is loud and frantic, and I know I must not waste any time in reaching the poor soul in need, but, for the first time in my position as a Reclaimer, I hesitate.

I do feel as though my senses have gained more strength since I learnt about baby, but what if they are not powerful enough to conceal its existence. What if, when I step onto the Devils ground, he somehow senses baby? I have to believe in me, I have to believe in the reasons I am such a gifted Reclaimer. For as long as I can remember I have been able to almost knock on Lucifer's door and then return to my home without being detected. Yes, I have had his Hunters nipping at my heels on occasions, but not one has ever caught me.

The Dolophonos, they are a different story. I will extend my senses, and if I have the slightest indication they are near, I will do all I can to protect baby, even if that means leaving the poor soul in need, as much as it pains to think that. Baby is my greatest priority.

I turn and quicken my pace through Eden, desperate to release the soul from its final chains and return back to where we are safe the most. Just as I see the Gatekeepers come into view up ahead, I become very aware of a presence nearby. I slow my steps and just before I feel him reach my being I turn, to confront Gabriel.

'Why are you in such a hurry Arianwen?' I know I am supposed to seek a guard every time I need to perform a Reclaim, but I do not need the distraction they bring, especially with my fear about baby being discovered before we even have a chance to flee our worlds.

'I received a calling and I feel that it's most urgent. I wouldn't have had the time to seek out a guard. I must go now.' I turn, hoping he will just let me go alone, like I have been doing a lifetime, but I know he will not. I feel him close behind me when he speaks. 'I will accompany you Arianwen. I need to know you will be safe.' I have been safe, just fine on my own, but know I cannot speak those words to him. So I do the only thing I can. I try to completely tune him out, focus solely on the soul calling for me and the world in between that I am about to step into.

The stone Dragons are silent when we pass under, unlike recent times. I wonder what they think of me? Prancing around worlds with different males by my side. I have no time to think about that as my natural instincts kick in. I feel all creatures that are present in this eroding forest, from animals to bugs to creatures that are of the supernatural nature lurking on the edges. I sense Michael's spies in the thickest brush and a fellow

Reclaimer leaving the village on the far side, but so far no Hunters or any signs of the Dolophonos.

I slow as I near the first dwellings of the village and jump when Gabriel steps on a branch behind me. I almost forgot he was there. I feel the soul four buildings away and proceed to weave silently between buildings until I reach a wooden structure. It does not quite resemble a house or it could be best described as a house that was picked up by a tornado, spun around and dropped into the centre of Hell.

There is one window which is on an angle and oddly close to the ground, looking as if it is about to sink further into the earth. I move around to the next side looking for a door but cannot find one. Gabrielle brings his body up to my back and whispers close to my ear, 'I don't like this, I'm getting a strange feeling. We should leave Arianwen.'

I will not leave a soul if I am able to help them.

I ignore his concern and continue to search for a door. I run my fingers softly along the rough edges of thrown together panels of wood and then I find it. Down low, a small gap, a lip on the edge of one panel. I run my fingers along it and pull softly until it starts to give way. The panel that moves is only small, I have to fall to my knees to see inside. I can see the soul withering in pain on the floor, its body struggling with the war of seeking Good and expecting Evil.

Wanting to be extra careful, I close my eyes using everything I have to sense any foul darkness that may be lurking a little too close. Nothing alarms me so I start to crawl forwards, but a hand on my shoulder stops me in my tracks. 'Arianwen, this may not be safe,' Gabriel whispers in a panicked tone, so I turn my head and give him my most honest answer. 'It's never completely safe,' before continuing to crawl forward.

I sense him do the same as I stay low, wooden beams above me have all fallen at different angles. They look almost as if they are puzzle pieces and with one wrong move, it all falls down. I will not risk knocking them so I continue to crawl over a muddy floor with straw strewn sparingly across it.

I reach the soul who instantly starts to feel the peace I am going to offer it. He is a young man, seventeen in human years. I know he would have some of the brightest green eyes I have ever seen, if it was not for the effects this waiting room of Hell has had upon them. He has a solid jaw and kind face. He would have grown to be a very handsome man, yet one mistake, due to the lack of education and peer pressure, has seen him live on the doorstep of the Devil for way too long. One decision took away his chance at life.

But, his honest Good inside gives him the right to return to his true Lord and live eternity in peace. Good always wins over Evil in the end.

I take his hand in one of mine and place my other on his cheek. I cannot help but smile into his thankful face as I start to transfer some of my Heavenly aura into the shell he is about to leave behind. I feel his entire being. His hopes and dreams, his sadness and joy, his contentment and regrets. But most of all, I feel the light that is embedded within his soul. I start to lift the soul giving it the energy it needs to leave its human form behind and ascend towards the place it belongs. The body beneath my fingers starts to sink as the soul finds its strength and begins its journey home and into the arms of its creator. God.

I am standing, with my arms above my head still guiding the soul home, when I sense Gabriel's aura start to panic, then just as suddenly, I realise why. The Dolophonos are near. I use a massive surge of power to send the soul on its final journey which has me falling to the floor in a heap when I let go. I know I need to rise and move quickly, but I need a small moment to gather my senses back to myself.

Gabriel crawls over and places an arm around my shoulders. 'I know you feel it too Arianwen, we need to move now.' I place a hand over his to halt him. He looks confused before I explain. 'I'll be of no good to you or myself if I was to lead us out of here now. I just need a few more moments to gather the strength I moment-arily lost. It would be no good to face Evil when I'm still weak.'

I know he wants to argue, but I give him credit for accepting my words and having faith in me. It only takes a few more moments before I feel all of my abilities rise to their full potential. I would never risk baby's safety in leaving this shack with anything less than my best. I begin to crawl away from Gabriel and towards the hidden exit as he crawls close behind me. I stop, letting my senses guide me, before I push on the wood and move it to the side.

Once we are both outside, the Dolophonos' presence becomes almost overwhelming. They are heading this way, but I feel it is not because of us. They are seeking someone who is in the building beside us. They are gaining speed, we have to move fast without causing a noise or even a ripple in the stale air that surrounds us. I reach behind and grab Gabriel's cloak and pull him behind another building. I whisper to him, *'Don't breathe',* as I again pull him along quietly to the side of another building.

I freeze as I feel the Dolophonos come to a stop, standing still, not entering the building that was their destination. My heart skips a beat as I wait for them to make a move, praying to my Lord that they have not sensed us. I feel them each take a step in the opposite direction and again stop. Silence.

A haunting feeling starts to float through the air as panic starts its first bubbling in my soul. They again take a step away from each other and stop. Silence again as I feel Gabriel's aura begin to show signs of panic also. He too can feel that this is not right. I move my head slightly, trying to find a crack in the wood dwelling beside me to see where the Dolophonos are standing. When my eyes catches sight of one of their black cloaks, baby decides to turn fast in my stomach and one of the Dolophonos turns its head sharply in my direction.

I remain frozen, knowing that to run would mean certain death. I turn my head, my eyes widening as I sense Gabriel taking a few steps away from me. What is he doing? I turn back to the Dolophono and see that it has moved its head in Gabriel's direction too. This is just a disaster. I raise my hand slightly to stop Gabriel's movements. He stills, but when I turn back towards the Dolo-phono, it has gone from my view. I can sense that one is still frozen but one is indeed on the move. I will not let them anywhere near my baby.

I close my eyes and gather everything I have within, ready to fight if I need to. But then, I remember that both mine and Albion's abilities seem to have strengthened since the creation of baby. And all of a sudden, I know exactly what it is I need to do.

I bring both of my palms together, letting my natural energy flow from me, dancing between my fingers. The heated force that is brewing is invisible, but I can feel its enormous strength. I then raise my arms to shoulder height, I brace my feet apart and solid on the ground. I bring my hands back and then throw my hands forward with all the strength I possess and let go of the ball of energy I created.

It hits a dwelling about ten buildings away, and I can feel its explosive energy ripple through the air, the Dolophonos instantly moving towards the disturbance and it is then that I also feel Albion's presence within the village. I know he will be fine so I do not waste a second as I begin to run past Gabriel, whispering urgently *'move'* before I weave between buildings and out towards the forest. I run and run, not looking behind to see if Gabriel is following. All I am thinking of is to get baby as far away from those vicious monsters as fast as I can.

I sprint through this forgotten world, my whole body on high alert as I try and find any danger hiding nearby, trying to sense that Albion has stayed a safe distance from Gabriel and trying to hold down my panic at the thought of baby being in such close proximity to Lucifer's hounds. My whole body is buzzing with nervous electricity as the reality of the scene I just ran from, begins to hit me.

I created moving energy that was powerful enough to fool the Dolophonos, to fool Evil's most vicious creations. Instead of giving me the comfort that I thought it should, it makes me worry more. Worry over what would happen if either of our worlds found out about our hidden miracle and the power it may one day indeed possess.

I am so lost in my thoughts I do not even realise I have crossed the border into the safety of my world. All I am focusing on is getting myself and baby into the peaceful and safe cocoon of my family home. It is not until Gabriel firmly grips my arm that I stop. He turns me around, searching my eyes. I do not know what he sees, but he grabs me and hugs me closely to him in, an embrace that is all too uncomfortable.

I pull away slowly, not wanting to raise suspicions by pushing fast out of his embrace. He still holds on tightly to my arms, searching my face for what, I do not know. He swallows hard before he attempts to speak, only to stop and swallow again. The emotions falling across his face are foreign to what I have seen there before, his eyes saying more than any words he could spill over his lips.

'Arianwen ... I ... I feel as if I want to demand you never Reclaim again, that it is too dangerous, and I won't allow you to put yourself in direct harm like that again, but ... after witnessing the effect you had on that boy and the confidence and power that shone from you when faced with the danger of those Evil creatures ... I know I will never have the right to ask you to stop. You were born to be a Reclaimer, the best our world will probably ever see, and I know to ask you to stop because I fear losing you, would be asking you to not be yourself ever again. And I would never want you to lose the magical light that shines so brightly in your eyes. To lose that beauty would be a sin.'

I am too taken back by his heartfelt words to realise he is cupping my check with his soft hand and I am letting him. I aim my eyes down before I carefully lean back out of his reach. He frowns slightly but does not comment. The silence becomes awkward, but thank the Lord he breaks it. 'Have you ever encountered those ... things before?' He does not know their name? I thought our leader knew everything.

'The Dolophonos. Yes I have. That was mild compared to my last experience with them.' I regret sharing that information as soon as the words leave my lips. I think he is going to question me, but he looks to be in shock.

'*The Dolophonos?*' he questions with a look of disbelief covering his features. I nod yes. 'I knew of their existence, and I've heard many tales of what they're capable of, but, I've never been that close to them before. I could feel their presence from a mile away, their malice proceeded them, leaching out, clawing at the air before their beings were even close. It's been a long time since I've looked Evil in the eye, yet you do that sometimes on a daily basis.

I'm not sure how to feel about that.'

And I am not sure how to respond to that. It is not his responsibility to feel anything for me. I am not his woman, I am not his wife, nor will I ever be. I can feel he is genuine in his concern, but I want none of it. I just want to be in the arms of the man I love and never leave his side. I have just about had enough of all of these complications.

I need to move away from him, I need to clear my head. Without words, I gently pull out of his hold and start walking in the direction of the learning garden. He follows silently behind me. Both of us seeming to need this quiet after our close call. Just as we are about to reach the clearing where the children's laughter flows from, he grabs my hand to halt me.

He gently gives it a squeeze, before leaning in and placing a soft kiss upon my cheek. He then takes a step back, releasing my hand and gesturing that I go into the clearing before him. I am a little shocked at such a tender moment coming from Gabriel. Maybe he is not all I have thought him to be.

We both walk into the centre of playfulness, with the children playing a maths game that requires them to run around stealing numbered stickers from each other's backs. There is a light and fun feeling rippling through the air which makes it impossible not to smile at the children's antics.

I feel like I can breathe and relax when in the presence of these beautiful young ones, something I so dearly need my baby to feel. I play their games and read a few stories, while knowing there are eyes upon me. Not only from the smiling glances of Gabriel, who has stayed to take part in all the children's games, much to their delight, but I can also feel Michael's eyes boring into me as he wonders around the outskirts of this area.

I am also being watched by the two other girls vying for Gabriel's hand in marriage. They join in the fun and make pleasant conversation, but both their eyes are darting between Gabriel and I, as if they too can sense his eyes following me.

'He is very taken by you,' Mayloree, the tallest of the girls says quietly while stepping close to me. I just smile, wanting to take the focus off of me. 'I think he is quite charmed by us all,' I smile. She frowns slightly at my comment, but before it can get awkward, Sistelle, the other chosen girl, lightens the mood. 'He's *very* charming, he can have every female here blushing in three seconds flat.' She laughs at her own comment, and I decide to fake a girly giggle to join in. Mayloree grins slightly, but still does not seem all that comfortable. Even though she has always been a friendly, happy girl, her aura seems to now be slightly closed off which is very strange.

I decide the best way to shift focus from myself is to move it to the girls standing either side of me. 'He noticed you help that little one's grazed knee earlier Mayloree. He had a sweet smile on his face.' Finally she starts to smile, small, but it's there. 'And Sistelle, he seemed intrigued by the story you were telling the older ones about how the Dragons became stone. I'm sure he can tell how knowledgeable you are when it comes to our history.' This makes her already friendly smile bigger.

I leave the two to ponder my words and slowly make my way to leave. As I say my goodbyes to some of the children and their parents, I become well aware of Michael walking my way. I try to quicken my step, but as I make it to the edge of the garden, he grabs my arm, careful that no one can see his tight grip on me.

'A word Arianwen.' It is not a request, it is an order. We only take two steps before he stops, looking at Gabriel who is watching us carefully. He loosens his grip but does not let go. 'Where have you been lately Arianwen? I have not seen your busy self around for a least a few days.' I place the mask on my face I use when talking to Michael, not giving away any of my true feelings for this man.

'I've been helping just about everyone in this glorious garden of ours.' His grip tightens, not happy with my words. He once again looks up to see Gabriel walking our way. He grabs me tighter, digging his nails into my arm. 'My brother is too distracted. The sooner he beds you the better. *Make ... it ... happen!* That's an order Arianwen.'

He releases me just as Gabriel arrives, shooting daggers at his brothers retreating form. Not wanting to explain what just happened I plaster a small smile on my face when he is standing in front of me. 'Is everything okay Arianwen?' I make my smile bigger, just to cover my anger at Michael's crass words.

'Everything is fine. I'm feeling a little tired so I think I may return home for a rest.'

I turn but he grabs my shoulder and turns me back to him. He searches my eyes before speaking again.

'Are you sure you're okay my sweet Angel? You look ... there is something ... different about you.'

He frowns and inspects me further. *No.* He couldn't sense baby, could he? I breathe deeply, not letting the blooming panic rise to the surface.

'I think you are maybe a little more rattled by our encounter with Evil this morning than you are letting on. You know Arianwen, you don't always have to be the strong one. I'm here if you need someone to lean on. Please don't forget that.'

He once again places a soft kiss to my cheek then lets me go, obviously believing I am just a little worn out. I nod politely and slowly make my way down the path that leads to my home. I take a deep breath, now realising that my panic will be justified soon. Because soon, I will not be able to conceal that something, is indeed, different about me.

# 15

# Apathy, Anger, Hate and Longing

## ALBION

**The hiss of the hearth echoes the fall of my hammer, the** Demon steel in my hands bending slowly as I draw it across the padded and chainmail lined leather. The Angel glass rivets glinting softly in the flowing orange glow as I add yet another band to the plates of my Angel's armour.

The need to rend, to tear the life from another is burning through me as I slowly slip the rivets into place. My desire to send the hammer in my hand crashing down upon them with all the power I can muster, is almost too much for my slowly crumbling restraint. But, as I stare down at the burnished and tarnished armour that is slowly being wrought into being, my mind and heart both stay my hand.

I set the hammer down, slumping to the stool behind me. I have to do this for them, not for me. I have to do this for the woman who owns my heart and child who calms my soul, both of them deserve far more than I can ever truly give, but despite all my limitations, with this, I can surely come closer to being able to give them all I can.

I lift the hammer once more, my heart and mind in union as I softly piece together the last few plates of her armour. I stare at the budding creation before me, my eyes taking it all in, the play of light along the curve of the plates, the twisted reflection of my own shadowed form as I lift the armour from the bench and set it down atop a sheet of cloth on Garth's dining table.

I fold the cloth over it, the shimmering reflection falling away as I lift it from the table, the leather satchel across my back slaps against my skin as I pull it around, settling it against my stomach before dropping the armour into it.

'Not bad boy, not bad. Although, it's going to take a lot more tooling and finesse to finish it off, especially if it's for whom I think it is.'

I nod, my words staying glued to my tongue as Garth lays a hand on my shoulder. The blacksmith's wizened and leathery skin warm against my own as I reach up and close my hand over his.

'Thank you.'

He nods as he pats at my shoulder gently, before turning away and moving towards his forge.

✦✦✦

The door slides closed behind me, silence enveloping me completely as I move deeper into my hand carved home. The sound of trickling water echoes across the walls, filling my ears as I move towards my bench. The satchel slung over my shoulder hanging from me, slapping against my hip as I move closer and closer to the edge of my own private sanctum, the one place even in this cavernous home; a home hewn by the hands of my father, that I can truly say gives me the solace and peace when my Angel is so far from my arms.

I turn towards our bed, my satchel left, sitting solid and alone on the bench, surrounded by the regimented rows of my tools. Fatigue, anger and pain, steeped in loneliness and fear. All of it crashes over me as I stumble towards the plush, snow white covers of our haven, the source of our comfort. I collapse onto the mattress, my knees curling up to my chest as I feel the tears bite at my eyes, one image fills my mind's eye, one solitary moment in my life that soaks my heart in pain and anguish.

I bury my head into the soft cotton stuffed pillow, her scent wafting free, the image in my mind burning brighter as I feel the tears break free trailing over my cheeks as I pull the pillow away, crimson trails running across my skin as everything boils over. The anger, primal, searing anger at all I have let slip through my fingers, the shadow less depths of nothingness that sits as a testament to my inability to protect those I love. The pain overwhelming, dripping from my heart and soul, utterly ceaseless, merciless, unending agony bubbling from every facet, every memory of those I have failed, those that have fallen away from my reach, plunging into death and eternity, as their faces drift into the black.

Seconds tick into minutes, minutes into hours, all dripping from my soul and bones as I sink deeper and deeper into the miasmic despair that has so soaked my being. I feel my mind delving into darkness as I slowly drift off, edging ever deeper into a fitful sleep.

✦ ✦ ✦

I wake, bathed in sweat and fear as the scar carved into my chest burns, the ache seeping through me, shattering everything that was or could be. Lucifer's calling, and despite my hatred of him and all those that dwell in my former home, I need to answer, I need to play the game and keep his all seeing eyes from Arianwen and our unborn child.

My movements are sluggish, pushing my body at an awkward gait as I rise and move to the door, everything brushed to the side as I focus on the veneer that is slowly worming its way over all that I have fought so hard to reclaim.

I close my eyes, pushing back at the energy that course through the ether around me. As I open my eyes, my world a haze of darkness and silvered mists. I watch the walls of my home bend and twist. Lucifer's shadowed form swims into view, black shades moving past me as I am dragged closer by his sheer force of will.

'Albion, the world, our world, is under threat. The energies that so threatened our dominion are abroad once more, their strength is magnitudes greater than it ever has been. Come to my side Albion, there's more I need to share and at times like this, even the ether has unwanted eyes.'

The connection between my rune scar and Lucifer snaps closed, the world around me evaporating as reality once more takes hold. My stomach lurches as my mind and whatever fragment of my soul the connection tore away are sent careening back into my body, the force nearly lifting me from my feet as I struggle to stay upright. Staggering towards the door I cuff away the blood slowly dribbling from my nose, and then with the reluctance of a child about to be scolded by their mother, make my way out into the sunlight.

✦ ✦ ✦

'You summoned my King, I'm at your service, use me as you will.'

'Sit Albion, we have much to discuss.'

I move, my mind dark, filled with visions of Lucifer's battered and broken body and my taloned hand wrapped around his throat. Yet I find myself capitulating, moving towards the open chair with a near robotic gait.

'There was a time, once, when I was the left hand of God. I was the ultimate in vengeance and punishment, and Michael sat at his right. We were the ultimate power under our creator, we held sway over man and dominion, over all other life. But, now amidst the dust and chaos that has dogged my fall from the garden, there's another, something that eclipses me and Michael, it renders all, we are utterly impotent.'

I sit mute, my mind still casting out images of blood and rage as I stand over the decimated body of the Angel that calls itself the King of Hell. He stops watching me, studying, and for the first time in my existence, I can truly say, I do not fear the Devil. This personification of malevolence and viciousness, despite all he has and can do, no longer holds that yoke of fear around my neck. I am finally free of the crippling pall of terror that had so plagued my waking hours in his service. I am truly free.

I woke only an hour before, trembling at the thought of being before this shadow of hate, but now, as I sit here, I find only anger. Anger tempered by pity, pity at the image before, pity at the shell of the being he once was, twisted by the arrogance and pain that followed him from Eden and on into the waiting arms of Hell.

'I need you Albion, I need you to find this entity, this force, whatever shape it may take on and bring it here. Anything this powerful is something that we can't allow into the hands of those heathens in Eden.'

'My King, how do you propose I undertake this task? If it's as powerful as you say, how can I be expected to subdue it, if it does indeed eclipse your own strength and power?'

He stares at me, a cold pang of panic rises from my gut as my heart hammers in my chest. Did my façade slip, did I tip my hand to the fact that his hold over my mind is null and void? I let my eyes travel over line and feature, picking his face apart for any hint of deception or suspicion.

'You raise a valid point Albion, but I'm not asking you to subdue whatever this presence may be. I'm asking you to bring it into the fold, to make it one of us, before Michael and his gaggle of squabbling children find it or worse yet, Gabriel and his damnable Sleepers.'

The clatter of bone china and silver tea diffusers meets my ears as I curl my fingers into my thigh, willing myself to remain silent as my heart begins to hammer against my ribs. Water bubbles and steams as it flows over the diffusers in the slim handled cups. I watch as it turns a turgid green, my gullet clenching as my stomach turns. My hand rises as Lucifer offers the cup of steaming pond scum, his eyes watching me as I let the cup and saucer sit hot on my palm.

'It's a green tea before you ask, supposedly good for your digestion and in some belief systems, can aid in balancing your chi, although I'm not all that partial to the oriental doctrines, a few of the fellows in the Twenty First Legion tend to, shall we say, play on the orients Demonic and spiritual superstitions.'

I nod, keeping my face as close to passively neutral as I can, even as the tart and coarse liquid skates over my tongue making taste buds curl and quiver at the sudden burst of unfamiliar tastes.

'I can't impress on you enough, the gravity of the situation Albion. If Gabriel or Michael were to be the ones to gain the favour of this entity instead of us, well, it could be the end to all life here. There would literally be no possible way for us to counter it. You must get to it before anyone else, you simply must.'

I rise to my feet, my face a blank mask as I nod, setting the cup and saucer on the table as I do. One word and one word alone slips from my lips before I turn and move towards the door.

'Sire.'

My shoulders slump slightly as I hear the door click shut behind me, the ire and barely controlled anger that filters past the oak slab makes the air heavy. The syrup thick miasma coats my lungs as I turn and make my way towards the Undercroft. The small cache of weaponry that remains in the hovel that was my cell are my only remaining connection to this destitute pit of hate and depravity. I reach the end of the corridor before a voice washes over me, my heart seizing in my chest as it sinks through my soul.

'Well if it isn't my wandering hero, come back from the great plains to seek the solace of his woman. Oh please tell me that he has.'

I turn, my eyes alighting on the vacuous, Demonette that is slowly making her way towards me, the sway of her hips and the flick of her hair drawing memories from me, memories of my woman. Images of times spent locked in each other's embrace flow through my mind as this shadow of hate and malice continues to mimic her at every turn.

I pull my gaze away as my hand curls into a fist, the sheer force of my will staying it from the growling blade that claws at the edges of my mind.

'There is only one woman who could ever give me solace, Lilith, and I can say with surety, it'll never be you.'

Her eyes flicker as the glowing flames of manic rage burst from within them. I smile tightly as her claws push free of the soft leather gloves that sheathe her hands. That one display of uncontrolled anger is all I need to see, all I need to know that she, the Succubus Queen, is as far from the reaches of sanity as Gabriel is from the depths of Hell.

'You protest too much Master Hunter, you know as well as I,

that if Lucifer commands it, it'll be so and there is naught you, or your little feathered strumpet could do or say to change the tide of that inevitable fact.'

I let my hand settle at her throat as I slowly close my grip, her soft pliable flesh pressing between my fingers as I begin to squeeze. The soft pat of her gasping lips makes me smile as I tighten, slowly but surely around her supine neck.

'Threaten her again, mention her again in the same vein as any form of threat, veiled or literal, and it will be the last words to ever trip from your acid stained tongue, for if you do, Lilith, I will rend it from your head before peeling the skin from your bones and leaving you for the crows.'

I watch as her eyes begin to bulge, her fingers raking my neck as her face turns a tainted purple. I toss her aside, her gasping, choking body crumbling like a sack of rotten potatoes as she slumps against the wall.

'She will fear the nights to come Albion, of that you have my word. Her kin will feel the succubus' kiss before this week is done.'

Her words skate off me, my mind paying no more heed to them than I would the squalling of a child. I know my Angel is safe within Eden, nothing as foul as that mewling sack of guttural slime could ever hope to breach their walls. I know she is secure there, far from the reach of that carrion whore.

Thumping music, boiling alcohol and sweat laden flesh roll over me as I step through the door, bodies jostling and grinding in a glut of exorbitant ecstasy. The sheer avarice of it all makes me heave, my gut boiling with disgust as I push past the sweat slicked flesh and gyrating naked bodies. I take the steps up to the cells, two at a time, my legs heaving me upwards as I reach the third landing.

The sound of slapping flesh greets my ears as I pass its source, the thrusting loins of one male foot soldier driving into the twitching buttocks of one sodden Demonic slut, her naked body spread across the railings as her breast pendulum back and forth in sync with his pounding hips. I cannot avoid them as the foot turns and grins at me. I paste a smirk across my face and pat at his shoulder as I reach my cell, the cold hitting my face with all the impact of a sledgehammer as I let my door swing closed behind me.

I push the bunk aside, my fingers dipping into the mud pressed around the edge of one flag stone, the hollow beneath sits, lined with lead and layered with blades, firearms and armour. My eyes scan the small room, searching for any sign of intrusion as I drag a rough sewn leather bag from inside one of the draws next to me and begin to load in the myriad of weapons and armour I have kept hidden beneath my former homes floor.

The bag weighs heavy on my shoulder as I reach the main hall, the twisting walkway spiraling up from me as I stare at the thick pall of sulphurous smoke that rings the lip of the pit. My feet carry me onwards, the ramp beneath me pulling me higher and higher as I edge towards the final turn and the open air that waits beyond it.

# Suspicious

## ARIANWEN

**The taste on my tongue is something to savour. It is one of my** all time favourites. The recipe may be almost as old as time itself, but it tastes just as good as the first time my mother made it. And the flavour is even more divine when added to the laughter coming from our kitchen.

My sisters and I are helping our mother prepare a feast, just for our family of five. We have included all of our favourite side dishes, and my mother is working on a new sauce, while my father is stocking the fireplace with logs after earlier preparing the turkey for us to stuff and roast. Fingers are swiping at dishes, tasting before we are even finished, but when it comes to mothers special stuffing, which is a meal in itself, we are lucky to have any left to even place on the dinner table.

We joyfully make a mess, because that is half the fun, before all the dishes are finally ready to be placed upon the old wooden table that our father carved with the help of his father. When we all take our places I take a long moment to enjoy the ones I love. I look into their happy faces and feel blessed to be loved by these people. The only thing missing, here in our family home, is my man, who, if he was welcomed into this family, would be sitting beside me, holding my hand under the table.

At that thought, baby takes a moment to turn sharply, making me flinch in surprise. Baby also wishes that its daddy was close by. But, I will have to give all of this up, all of my family and the love they so selflessly provide me, for the start of my own little family. As unorthodox as it may be, I feel very blessed to have found two great loves in my lifetime. I just wish it did not come at the expense of my family surrounding me now and with such dire danger. But, I feel as if it is meant to be, and if God did indeed have a hand in the recent events of my life, then I have no way of stopping or changing what is about to be bestowed upon me. I push all of my worries out of my mind and enjoy this moment with my family tonight.

We have told tales, danced to old folk songs and done impressions of each other's favourite phrases while howling in laughter. I had not realised how distracted and busy I had become until my youngest sister Caronwen told me, as she said goodnight, 'I miss you' with tears in her eyes. To say I hugged her extra tight and extra long is an understatement. I feel saddened that I will not be around to guide her in life as a big sister should.

I head to bed with a very heavy heart and aching soul. I know I have to have faith in what fate has in stall for me, but at the moment it just seems to be filled with loss, heartache and danger. Yes, I have the love of an amazing man and a child on the way, but everything else surrounding it, is not filled with much happiness.

I will not let my soul fall under the spell of melancholy, so I close my eyes and imagine a happy place where Albion and I are free to love each other and a place that will always be safe for our child.

✦ ✦ ✦

I wake to the sunshine streaming through my window, feeding my soul, awakening my heart. I needed the family time I had last night, and I am determined to have as many as I can before I have to leave my home.

I am desperate to find a way back to Albion today, but know I still have to be cautious with Michael watching me carefully. So I decide to start my day in our fields of fruit, helping to harvest our latest batch, before making a short appearance at the children's garden. That way many people could vouch to have seen me if he decides to question where I have been.

As I am placing my cloak around my shoulders, tying it tightly at my waist, there is a knock at the door. My mother goes to answer it and then returns to me seconds later. 'It was a guard with a message for you Arianwen. You're required at a meeting in the great hall. I hope everything is okay. I'm sure it's nothing. I guess I better get used to you being summoned for meetings. If you're to become the wife of a leader you'll be required to attend almost all of them. How boring,' she laughs making me grin.

I give her a hug and move towards the door, but when my mum drops her arms from our hug, one brushes over my stomach as I walk past her. Her eyes widen as I turn back to her and all I can do is stare. The silence is deafening as I see the wheels churn in my mother's head. Thank the Lord I am saved by my little sister who comes bouncing through the door with a basket full of vegetables, chattering about her busy early morning.

I use this moment to make my exit, my head whirling with the thoughts of my mother somehow sensing my baby. My stomach is slightly swollen, but not so much that it is obvious. I know now how strong a mothers intuition is, so if she did not feel a slight raise of my stomach across her arm, she could have sensed baby inside.

I have to push those thoughts aside as I make my way to a meeting, a meeting where I have to be very careful at my reaction around others. A meeting where I have to conceal everything I am feeling.

I arrive at the great hall and make my way inside. I hear many hushed voices as a guard opens the door for me, but after one step inside ... I freeze. I see someone that has never attended a meeting I have been called to before. Claire. I mask my surprise and smile at her as she catches my eye and then proceeds to find a chair. I am not sure if I am reading too much into this, but I think she looks a little nervous.

Has she spilled my secret to Michael or been forced to reveal what it is I have been spending all of my hours in the library researching? I will not show my panic, I will not give into Michael's games if this is indeed his way to catch me out. I move quietly down one side of the table heading for a spare chair, when Gabriel catches my eye as he stands and motions to the chair next to him that he is now pulling out.

I cannot refuse, so I nod politely and make my way around to the other side. He smiles as I step closer to the table, giving him room to push the chair in behind my body. He smiles warmly, something he has been doing of late and settles down beside me, as a respectful silence descends upon the room when Michael sits down at the head of the table.

I look around, surprised to see all of my fellow Reclaimers also in attendance. I begin to feel the nerves take over, but I will not give power to them. I say a little prayer, hoping beyond hope that baby stays quiet during the meeting, as Michael begins talking.

'As most of you are aware, we have felt a large powerful disturbance in our land and beyond. We have had all of our resources out looking for what it could possibly be, yet, have not been able to find its source. It surfaced not so long ago, going quiet as quickly as it surfaced, only to then re-emerge all the more powerful. We cannot assume that this is the work of the Devil, nor can we focus all our attention on him and his Hunters, only to then be blindsided by another force. We must all be on high alert and take part in keeping watch outside our borders, as well as inside our own world.'

Gasps and sounds of disbelief echo around this room at his accusations that a threat could be coming from our own world. He is looking directly at me when he continues.

'We can never be too certain of what form Evil may take. Anything that looks suspicious or doesn't feel right, someone doing something that they have never normally done. It has to be reported to one of the other Generals or myself and Gabriel immediately. In the meantime we need to prepare for the possibility of war.'

I know he is waiting for a reaction from me. I will not give him one and I will not break his stare first. Protests break out around us. *Our kin is trusted, there is no way betrayal will be behind our walls, and the talk of war is premature.* On and on it goes.

I still do not understand why the Bookkeeper is in attendance and that makes me nervous. Michael breaks his stare to argue with someone about why war may be the only answer. The arguments seem to last all day, with everyone but Michael wanting to find another way to fight this mystery other than war. It has been centuries since the last war between both sides. Yes, there are battles between the two forces on a daily basis, but an actual major war? The last was well before my time.

By the time the meeting wraps up, I am exhausted. They have argued through lunch and dinner, and the only conclusion they have come up with is that everyone must work together to be more vigilant and no drastic actions will take place until we know exactly where the supposed threat is coming from.

I stand and head for the door while Gabriel is distracted by a conversation to his right. As Claire makes her way through the door just before me, she gives me a reassuring smile which puts my mind slightly at ease. I let two more kin go through the doorway before I attempt to walk through, only to be stopped by a hand on my shoulder.

I look up into the calm face of Michael. 'Would you mind waiting a moment Arianwen?' I know his polite request is anything but, it is a command I know I cannot refuse. I nod politely as we both stand to the side or the doorway, waiting for everyone to leave.

Gabriel is the last to approach, a frown masking his face as he stares down his brother. He places his hand out for mine, his frown disappearing for me.

'Arianwen, I shall escort you home.'

Before I even have a chance to decline Michael steps forward. 'I need a word with Arianwen. I'm quite capable of making sure she gets home safely brother.'

Gabriel stares daggers at his brother, who is not intimidated in the least. Gabriel snares at him.

'And *I'm* quite capable of waiting until you are finished to escort her home, *brother.*'

The tension is thick, suffocating the air that surrounds us as both men stare each other down.

'I need to question her alone. I don't want her *feelings* towards you to sway any of her answers, so if you would excuse us, I'd like to get this over and done with. You can wait outside if you insist on walking her home.'

Gabriel looks as if he is about to take a swing at his brother, but takes a deep breath to calm himself instead.

'As someone who will hopefully be married to this woman one day, I choose to stay and support her in your interrogation.'

He does not wait for Michael's okay. He grabs my hand and leads us to the two seats to the right of Michael's chair during the meeting.

Michael moves stiffly to his seat, barely able to contain his temper. When he sits he wastes no time.

'Did you go on a Reclaim all by yourself a few days ago?'

I mask my features, knowing that even though I snuck away quietly, it would not take much for him to walk around Eden and not see me in my usual places. But, before I can answer him, Gabriel speaks up.

'What are you talking about? She wasn't alone, I accompanied her.'

I know that it is not the time he is referring to. Michael stares at me with a sly grin and lowers his next words to a threatening sneer.

'The time before that is what I'm referring to brother.'

Gabriel turns slowly, his eyes staring into mine, asking me to explain. He then turns to his brother and asks.

'What are you talking about?'

'I'm talking about the day Arianwen was seen entering the forgotten forest, alone.'

My face still remains blank. I will not give him any fuel to burn me with. Gabriel swallows hard but remains quiet.

'Yes, I did perform a Reclaim alone.'

Michael smiles to Gabriel as if he has caught me out. But, I will not let any of these brothers try and incriminate me, so I continue.

'When I receive a calling, it's urgent as I know you understand. I was nowhere near the main buildings and didn't see any guards around. Time is a luxury I can't afford.'

Both men are staring at me when I look up. Michael in anger and Gabriel in … understanding.

'She's right Michael. I've witnessed it for myself. When a soul cries out in need, her body responds quickly, that's why she is so good at her calling.'

I am dumbfounded by his sincere words, so much so I cannot help the small smile that graces my lips. Michael is not pleased at all.

'How long were you gone on that calling?'

I know he is going to try and find a way to make me slip up. It will not happen.

'I don't keep track of the time for such things. My mind is occupied elsewhere and no two souls are ever the same, they all take a different amount of time to move on, some have taken more than a day.'

I say politely as he grunts in response. His anger barely contained. He leans towards me in a threatening manner.

'Did you see or feel anyone else wondering amongst the forest?'

Is this all he has? Nothing solid to ask me? I must be thankful for that, for at least I know I was able to sneak all the way to Albion's home without being detected. I can take some comfort in this conversation.

'I could sense a small group of your spies and two other Reclaimers, but no forces of Evil that day.'

I am being as polite as I can in my answers, but his content for me is rising. He goes to talk again, but Gabriel stops him by growling softly, 'back off brother,' before grabbing my hand and rising, making me follow suit.

'I will be taking Arianwen home *now*.'

He moves my chair out with his other hand and almost drags me to the door. I do not look back to see Michaels reaction, because I can already feel the darkness in his aura trying to seep towards me. He is getting desperate to find a way to bring me down or make me pay for my sins. Not knowing how far he will go is dangerous for not only myself and baby, but could also be dangerous to my family when I leave. Not knowing if they will be protected from his viciousness is hurting my heart.

Gabriel is still moving fast, out of the building and down a garden path before he feels me tug on his hand to stop his fast pace. He turns towards me, a vase of emotions playing across his face as he takes a few deep breaths before finally being able to speak.

'I'm sorry for my brother's behaviour. He can be a gentleman sometimes, but lately … he's lost that side of him. He has no right to verbally attack you every time he speaks to you. I'll will make sure it won't happen again Arianwen, I promise.'

I am not sure how to respond. I am thankful for his words, but I am also wary of then. I know how he sees me. Or more to the point, how he *wants* to see me, especially after his speech about me one day possibly being his wife, so I have to still tread carefully where he is concerned. I do not want to anger another leader, but I certainly do not want to encourage his emotions either.

'Thank you. I do understand though. His angry words are driven by his need to protect our kin. I'm sure you feel the same, but choose to express it differently.'

He smiles at my words, an almost shy look crossing his features. It makes me feel a little uncomfortable so I step away. 'I'm fine to make my own way home.'

He looks taken back by my need to retreat. I offer a small smile before I go to turn, only to be stopped by his gentle grip on my arm.

'Arianwen.'

He is not sure what to say. He looks down and swallows hard before meeting my eyes again. He steps in closer until our bodies are almost touching as he raises a hand to gently touch my cheek. I know how not to flinch at his touch, but that does not mean I want it. He stares into my eyes, and I can see what he wants, I can feel what he wants as his entire aura begins to change.

He leans forward, still looking into my eyes as he places a soft kiss to the corner of my mouth. My body is screaming at me to push away, to run from the man that is not my love, but I know I have to play nice to make it easier for me to leave this place for good, hopefully undetected. He pulls back, searching my eyes, before leaning in again. But, this time I know his target is not the corner of my mouth. He closes his eyes just before he intends to kiss me squarely on my lips, but at the last second, I turn and his kiss lands on my cheek.

He releases a soft growl.

'Please Arianwen, I'm desperate to feel your lips upon mine.'

This has to stop. I have to find a way to pull away nicely.

'We shouldn't. There's no one else around,' I whisper. A slight grin appears on his face.

'That's the point my sweet Angel,' he coos at me, leaning in again. This time I not only pull back, but I also take a step away from him and out of his hold. As nice as I need to be, I will not let him capture the lips he does not own. He frowns and coos my name again.

'*Arianwen.*'

I have to find the words I need fast, to politely tell him to back off. 'I'm a traditional girl Gabriel. Kissing a man in the dark while we're all alone, even if such man is one of our leaders, feels very improper to me.'

I am thankful to see a small grin grace his lips, instead of a frustrated growl. 'I can respect that Arianwen. You ... you are a surprise to me sometimes. But, I will respect your wishes and just hope that I can arrange our wedding day sooner than later. I'll not even consider one of the other girls, just so you know.'

He leans in to place a chaste kiss on my head before grabbing my hand and doing exactly what he told his brother he would do. He escorts me home safely to my door and leaves with a polite nod.

# 17

## Plan And Preparation

### ALBION

**The whispering cool of winter's frost, licks at my skin as I** finally push my way free of the heated oppression of my former home. My one and only goal sings in my mind as I march forth, the pit, my former kin and any vestige of my past falling away as Lucifer's orders and Lilith's words burn through my mind.

We are running out of time, if Lucifer is so readily searching for the source of the power, which I know is my Angel and I; our combined strengths, which are now pushed tenfold by the energies of our child, are what they so eagerly seek. We need to find a way free of these lands and soon, for if we do not, I fear my own skills and strengths will not be enough to stay the hand that strikes from the darkness.

War sings on the air, you can smell it. The heady stink of excitement and fear, it is rising from the soil, saturating everything with its eagerness for blood and death. I step towards the edge of the village. A vibrant sense of impending doom hangs over everything, the movements of the souls here are muted, their auras pinched and jagged as they move like rats. They know what is coming; they have all seen it before; seen it in their mortal lives and felt it in their immortal ones. The deep, throbbing sense of impending doom. No one will walk away from this war without scars, some of us carrying some that run far deeper than others.

My one driving thought as I wade through the ocean of fear and trepidation, is that of my Angel and our child and the need I have to see them both free of the looming malevolence that is closing in from both sides. With Michael and his coterie of minions and Gabriel, as blinded as he is by his besotted devotion for my woman, chipping away at the edges of our safety; all drawing slowly closer to the centre of our lives; and not only them but also Lucifer, my former King and Master. The fallen one, so intent on taking the throne of Heaven from his creator and father that he is blind to all else, although, he has already torn my world from under me once, but I will fall to the eternal sleep before I let him wrest it from me again.

I reach my home with nary a backwards glance, my senses strung tighter than any harp string as I brace for the merest of a hint that I am being followed. I pause for a moment as I sink to one knee. I slip my lone holdout dagger from inside of my boot and draw it across my palm. A whispered incantation slips from my lips as I begin to draw my palm across the stone façade that shields my home's entrance. I step back through the ruins of the small home, rotten wood and wind blasted brick and plaster surround-ing me as I head towards the crumbling doorway. The twisted lines and spattered dots marking the chipped and dust coated surface as I rise to my feet, the line of blood sinking into the walls as the incantation takes hold. The blood smeared runes fading to nothing as a soft glow flows through the brick and mortar hidden behind the layers of crumbling plaster.

I lift my blade, Enocian letters dancing from its tip as I carve into the remains of the wooden lintel above me. The dead language of the first Angels oddly fitting as I stare at the twisting script, *'Speak the name of the Queen of hearts and enter into the arms of her King.'* There is only one person, Demon or Angel, who will ever hold the answer to what I have indelibly carved into the wood above my head, and it is for her that I would willingly give my life.

Even if there was a chance of my Angel being stalked to our door, she would never need to speak a word, let alone utter her own name, to find the entrance to our haven. Her mere presence, the energy of her beating heart and guiding soul is enough of a mark of life to give her sanctuary when she needs it most.

I just pray that she never needs to enter with such caution. Our home is just that, our home, our sanctuary and a place of safety. To know that someday, possibly soon, could see it threatened by all that are pushing towards us, it is enough to drive anyone to madness.

I move through the entrance, the rune glowing softly as I utter her name and move into the cool darkness that sits waiting. I know time is growing short, the entire life Arianwen and I hold, resting on my shoulders. If one thing slips, if I miss one asset or forget even the most insignificant tool or object then our whole world could come crashing to the ground; shattering at our feet like an orb of carved crystal as we are drowned beneath the weight of both Eden and Hell. I stand here, staring at our home, what, if anything, can I truly start with? I run through the mental check list, food, water, weaponry and armour for myself and my Angel, as well munitions for my Iron Caster and Long Caster, all of this alongside a myriad of other objects large and small. No, I have to pare off the insignificant things, the frivolous ideals that we think we need in a moment, but, in the greater scheme are only dead weight.

As I step towards my small armoury, the glinting of the oiled barrels of my Casters catching my eye, thoughts of that Demon Harpy and her coterie of minion's bubbles to the surface. Could she pose as much of a threat to me and my love as I fear she does? I know in the depths of my being, I would be able to stop the machinations of her, or her despotic followers, but, if they all rise from the shadows at once, will I be able to stave off so many? To that, I truly do not know the answer and one slither of inadequacy, strikes me harder than any hammer or fist.

I pause for a moment, my mind running alive with angst and fear as I turn and face the ebony coloured armour, my father's armour. The images of him, swathed in the gloss black metal that hangs off the skeletal mannequin in front of me; my father standing proud before battalions of hunters as he held his Iron Caster in one hand and his blade in the other. A spike of pain and fear tempered by pride as I lift my Caster from its holster, the energy that courses through me bringing with it the memories of a thousand wars and a million souls that ceased to exist when greeted with the barrel of the weapon that sits heavy in my palm.

'Father, in my youngest years you were my shield and my sword, my guidance and my home. Next to you stood the temperate calm of my mother, the teacher and healer, both of you gave me guidance and faith in the love you showed and shared. Yet, here I stand alone and afraid, unable to offer the same comfort to the woman who now carries my unborn child. I beseech thee father, please, in my darkest of days, show me the path I must follow. You granted me the skills of a Warrior and mother gave me the wisdom of a healer and the heart to offer such love that allowed me Arianwen's in return. But now, I stand torn. I know not what I should do, what I can do. My mind was so scoured by Lucifer's putrescence that even now, I still find my thoughts clouded by indecision and pain. Father please, help me to find the way free from all of this, help me to find a way to protect those that have made me whole.'

Silence fills the air as I stand staring at the dust coated armour, my heart hanging in my chest. There is nothing that could stir me now, even as I turn away from the black reminder of my lost parentage and towards my work bench and the leather drum bag that sits beneath it.

I drag the oiled and water tight leather from where it sits, plans jumbling in my head as I pull rolls of oiled cloth up with it. No matter where we may be or what we do, I know I need to keep everything as battle worthy and ready to use as I can, even if that means tainting the breads slightly with mineral oil.

I pull my short sword and fist dagger from their slots in the armoury racks, moving over to my bench and the oil soaked rags that sit in a disjointed pile. One by one, I take the blades and run the oil brush along them before slipping them into the folds of cloth and setting them into a slot in my leather blade roll, the flat sheet of leather stained from years of use and abuse, the worn straps hanging loose as I tie them around the blade and handle. The task is laborious, but worth the time it takes if I am truly to ensure my woman and child are as ready and protected as I can make them.

Finally after what seems like an age, but with the slowly trickling sand in the hour glass on the wall, I know it has been no more than a few minutes, the blades are stowed and set into the bag on my bench, closely followed by blankets and bed rolls, rope and slings as I set in one by one each item from the mental list that is slowly ticking through my mind.

As hours slip by only a few items remain and those can only be done in the few hours that sit between us and our eventual escape from the clutches of all those that plague us both. Now, as I stand staring at the bag, my mind returns to the vacuous consumption that has so plagued me, the image of Lilith's sneering face swirling into view as I strip away the layers of doubt and fear, steeling my mind and heart for whatever may come. I know, as I always have, that she would strive to sink her talons into my heart and soul no matter the cost to those around us both. There is nothing I want less in this world, I would sooner cease my existence, casting myself into the waiting arms of oblivion before I ever let myself sink into that witches embrace. Now though, I have others outside of myself to consider, my child and my woman, both of them come well before my own needs, before my own wants and desires, before my own life.

A smile teases my lips as I think of her and my child, the violet eyed woman that owns every inch of my being and the unborn soul that sits within her, but it is a smile soon soured as my thoughts turn to what I could be leading them to.

What world will I be bringing my child into, the heir to my lineage? Will they be born an outcast, destined to live the life of a hunted animal, a plaything to be teased and taunted by Gabriel or whatever foul beast Lucifer sends snapping at their heels? Or will I be able to rest from this world or the mortal one, a life fit for them, a life where they can grow to be the man or woman I know my child should and could become? Now is not the time for these questions, of that I am sure. But still, here they are, souring my thoughts with their doubts and stinging pleading.

I need my woman, I need her by my side, where I know at least

I can be the one to keep her safe; in Eden and its spires of glass and crystal, she is for now safe, but even in there, snakes and scorpions roam. Michael and his guardsmen, the prancing lance wielding seraphim and their Arch Angel Master, zealots one and all. Alongside them and their scorpion stings slithers Gabriel, the foppish peacock so obsessed with furthering his own agenda and lineage that he is blind to all but the most self serving of goals. That being is more suited to Demons horns than an Angels halo and yet, there he is, trapped in a garden with my woman. Woe betides him or his masochistic brother if either of them lay a hand to my woman and child, and nothing, not even God will save them from my wrath; there is not a place in Eden, the pit, or any world that exists where they could hide, that I would not find them.

I step over to the fire and the smoke that slowly curls through the chimney above. I sit at the hearths side the scent of the slowly drying slabs of meat soak in spiced and fermented oils making my hunger begin to bubble up. Drawing a small knife from the carving block behind me I set to work, carving small slithers free and hanging them over the drying rack. Time drips by as oil hisses and snaps, the curing elixir dripping down onto the coals as I hoist the finished racks up through the chimney, away from the boiling heat.

A few days at most and they should be done, dry enough at least to see me and my family safely away from here and into the wild lands beyond the borders. I t hope we can find a safe way to another realm. Anything would be better than scavenging like dogs out there. I pray I am right.

The air shifts around me, dancing with purity and light as the door to my and Arianwen's cavern home opens, the Angel of my dreams stepping through like the summers sun parting the clouds.

'Albion?'

'Arianwen, my love, how ... how did you get here on your own?'

A soft smirk teases my woman's lips as she moves towards me, lifting her cloak from her shoulders as she moves. Her steps light, almost delicate, not even disturbing the thin film of dust that coats every flat surface. I watch with near fascination as each footstep matches my own. But nothing remains, nothing except the pattern of my own feet.

'Albion, I'm a Reclaimer, a pregnant one, but still a Reclaimer. I know how to move without being detected, just as well as any other Reclaimer and some Hunters.'

She glides her hands over my shoulders, pushing herself up onto the tips of her toes and presses her lips to mine. In that moment, my mind ceases to exist, every facet and flaw focused solely on the woman in my grasp. She moulds to my body, every line, every curve completely in sync with my own as I lift her from the floor, my fingers sinking into the pliant supple flesh of her backside as her legs ensnare my waist.

Her tongue dances with mine as our lips glide over each other. I can feel her soul as I breathe with her, every movement, every solitary caress a singing declaration of all that we are to each other. Arianwen breaks our tryst for a moment, her eyes searching mine as she leans in nipping the tip of my nose with her teeth. I try to hide the turmoil that is running through me, pasting over it the need for the woman in my arms, draping it in memories of us together and the thoughts of what life we could possibly have, but still, it bleeds through. The look in my woman's eyes skewers me as I feel her legs slip from round me, her feet landing with a soft pat against the stone floor.

'Albion?'

My name, her question, both drag my mind to the fore and set forth a cavalcade of emotion and fear as Arianwen steps away, holding me at arm's length.

'Albion, my love, talk to me.'

I can see the fear mounting in her as I struggle to give life to my thoughts and words.

'Lucifer, he's hunting the source, the power everyone is so in fear of. He's hunting us and ...'

I pause as she lets go of me taking a small step backwards, moving away from me as fear begins to slowly sink its claws deeper into her heart.

'He plans on using the Power as a weapon. If he ever got his hands on you and our child, I don't know what I would ever do. If I lost you and knew that I could have in some way prevented it ...'

She steps forwards and cups my chin, her gaze searching, probing, dissecting my mind and heart inch by inch as I feel her free hand slip across my cheek. Her skin is soft, soothing; like warm silk on a cold night. I turn my head, breathing deeply, her soft apple laced scent filling me as I kiss her palm softly.

'Albion, I know you, I know you would and will do everything you can to keep us and our child safe from everything that will ever assail us. Whatever happens my sweet Demon, I know it will never be from something that you failed to prevent. Fate has been kind and cruel in the same breath, setting us on a path that has brought us together, but even now is fighting to keep us apart. We may detest it, and rail against all it sets before us, but, you know as well as I, that we will never bow down and cry defeat.'

She rests a hand against her stomach, grasping my own and drawing it beneath it as she does. I stare down at my Angel, her skin glowing with the light of life and love as she looks up at me with tear pricked eyes.

'No matter what happens Albion, we've brought life to this world and that is a blessed thing to have given anyone, but, my love, I've something to tell you.'

I cannot help but feel a deep seed of panic crack and bloom within my heart as sweat pricks at the back of my neck, all of my past errors, every mistake that has ever befallen me or Arianwen.

'Michael called a meeting Albion, a meeting to discuss a possible war. Despite whatever alliance he has with Lucifer, he will do anything to protect our world. He wants to find the source of the Power as desperately as Lucifer and is not convinced that it is the Devil's doing. He is smart, for as much as he is arrogant; he's no fool, and the longer we wait in our worlds, the greater risk of him finding out about us and baby. We can trust the Bookkeeper my love, I feel it in my heart. She has more knowledge than anyone I know. When the time comes, I will go to her for help in escaping the safest way we can.'

'Well, you need to talk to her soon my love. We need to be sure she is someone we can trust. Someone, who, when their feet are put to the coals will not squeal out even the most shallow of secrets in the hopes of making the pain stop. We need to be sure of everything. Our escape, if we're ever going to make it, could hinge on the briefest of moments and we need to be sure that we have every exit open to us, no matter what happens.'

The look in Arianwen's eyes is part fear, part love, both of which are tempered by a resolute sense of urgency. I need to take her mind from the train of thought that is slowly drawing her deeper and deeper into the arms of an unassailable fear. The anger that gnaws at my gut flares for a moment before I softly push Arianwen from my grip and move back towards my work bench.

'I've something for you my love, something that I hope will keep you and our babe safe from harm.'

Her gaze narrows slightly as she steps closer to me, the soft swell of her stomach drawing my gaze as the her hips sway gently with each step.

'This ... this took a vast amount of thought, but, well, I want to ensure my Angel and my child are both safe and secure; no matter what happens to the world around them. So, I and Garth spent an age going over plan and etching until, after almost a day's age we settled upon one that well ... see for yourself my Angel.'

I set the canvas and oil wrapped bundle on the bench as my Angel reaches forth and begins to peel aside layer after layer. Her eyes crinkle slightly at the edges as she frowns. I feel my heart skip softly at the image as she begins to reveal the source of puzzlement. Finally, after what feels like an eternity the last shreds of canvas fall aside and her eyes alight on what was so deeply hidden.

'Albion, it's ... it's beautiful, absolutely beautiful, but, will it uh, accommodate everything?'

I cannot help but smile at her slightly worried yet excited tone, her voice rising a note or two as she runs her fingers over the slatted stomach area.

'Yes my love, it will more than accommodate anything that ... arises. It's one thing that I made sure it could do.'

I slip my fingers under the bottom edge of the armour and gently pull forwards, the sprung and riveted plates bowing around my fingers, each section moving against the rest as it flexes and extends. Even as it moves there is not a single gap or splayed edge.

I cannot help but feel a spark of pride in my work.

'Try it on darling. I want to see it on my woman. I tried to get it as close to form fitting as I could, well, except for a certain area obviously.'

I hold the metal and leather carapace open as Arianwen bends slightly and slips into it, the soft padded leather folds around her like a second skin as I carefully let the armour settle over her slim form. The bottom edge catches for the smallest of moments on her stomach as she turns in my grip, her eyes tracing over it, every detail sinking in her gaze.

'Albion, it's ... it's perfect.'

'No, this isn't perfect, you, my sweet Angel are perfect. You allowed my heart to grow and allowed me to show you the truth that lies inside. This may have been made by my hand, but it was your love that gave it form, that showed my hands the way to bring this to reality.'

The bands flex, stretching slightly as the Angel glass plates glow. Hand curled Demon steel springs bending, constricting as my woman breathes, the ring mail beneath glinting softly as she lifts her arms and slowly twists left and right. I watch, enraptured with her movements, the soft twisting of her hips as she bends and shifts. I stand transfixed liked a butterfly caught in a spider's web. I am helplessly in awe of her innate beauty.

'I love you.'

She stops and stares at me, her head cocked to one side as her golden hair flows effortlessly across her alabaster features.

'I love you too.'

'No, I truly love you, with every fibre of my being, every mote of my essence is yours; I ... am yours.'

Her arms fold around me as I draw her close, the cold metal between us oddly comforting as I lower my forehead to hers, her lips finding mine as I drink her in, the world blending into an all consuming miasma as her mouth opens slowly, teeth finding my lip as she gently bites down. The heat that rolls through me sends my mind into a vortex of lust and pleasure soaked pain. The feel of her teeth sinking into my skin is death to my senses; nothing filters in, not the feel of her fingers as she laces them through my hair; not the brush of the metal against my bare chest and stomach.

I am a torrid weal of pain and pleasure, the simmering heat of her teeth pressing into my skin, the taste of her breath on my tongue. All of it drowns me in a wave of pleasure even as pain seeps deeper into my mind.

I tear my head way from her, my skin splitting, my blood rolling down her chin as she stares at me. A look of fear pricked puzzlement soaking her eyes as she locks onto my own.

'We need to test our abilities, we need to know, and as much as I want you right now, we need to know what we can do, our lives and that of our child rest on us knowing what we can do. Also, I want to see just how well that armour compliments my woman's figure when she is walking away from me.'

A dirty smirk crosses her lips as she stares at me, a glimmer of excitement in her eyes as she nips at my chin, my blood still staining her skin as I feel my bottom lip begin to swell slowly.

'Okay then Hunter, let's see what we can find. I trust you Albion with my heart, with my soul and the life I hold inside me, I know you'll keep us safe no matter what we face.'

'Good, let's go see what we can find.'

# 18

## The Power Within

## ARIANWEN

**This forgotten place, between worlds, holds mixed feelings for** me. It has never been a safe haven. I never know what is lurking in the shadows or behind the rotting wood statues of the dying oaks, creatures from all worlds crawl and slither through the dying greenery on the same ground that ancient wars were once fought.

But, it holds a very special place in my heart, because within the decomposing green walls of this forest, is where my lips first met the man who would change the path my life was on and become the only one to truly open up my heart to its full capacity.

This place holds bittersweet memories, but even here, Evil and Good could never find a truce, in the past, present or future. But for now, it is the closest thing to an equal footing for Albion and I to test the strength of our combined powers.

We have been quietly testing our limits for the last hour, creating, testing, experimenting with this enormous force between us, that baby has made even stronger. Our little one has been gently tumbling inside my stomach each time mine and Albion's hands have touched, as if to say I am here to help.

We can individually harness an unseen force between our own hands, but when we join hands, fingers entwined with each other and try to harness the enormous force that rages between us, it is almost too powerful to control.

'Albion, don't let go! This is too powerful, this is stronger than the last one. If we send this flying out of our hands it could attract the attention of both our worlds, and I'm not ready for the war to begin today.'

'Trust me my love, we can control it. Use your mind as well as your soul to keep it contained to where we want it to stay. Feel it Arianwen, let it flow through your entire being. This is a part of us and a part of baby, it's not some sorcerers potion created for terror. This is Good I can feel it. Embrace it my love, don't fear it. We don't want it to shoot out of our hands like a bullet, we both know it would if we let it, instead, imagine it's a large soft blanket falling from the sky, smothering only what we want it to cover. Let's send it over this clearing. On the count of three. One ... two ... three!'

On Albion's last word we gently let go of our hands and wave them over the clearing, the energy between us slowly floating above our heads only visible as a slight transparent ripple of air, as it starts to descend on our minds demand. We visualise it slowly coming down, covering, smoothing everything that lies on this decrepit ground. As it makes contact, everything freezes. The shrubs and bushes are still despite the slight breeze that flows through here, the bugs that were flying through the air are now suspended in flight. The rats and strange immortal rodents that were running over the moss covered rocks are also as still as statues.

'Now try and squeeze our imaginary blanket tighter Arianwen, dispersing even the smallest of air pockets surrounding everything within our force as if we are draining the life out of all that so happens to be stuck within our grasp.'

I imagine strangling everything beneath this energy we are controlling and things start to shrivel before our eyes. I can feel the strength we have at our fingers tips, but I can also feel we have much more inside of us to give. If we wanted to destroy an entire world, I now feel confident we could indeed try.

There is a heat surrounding us, almost like the entire air is at fever pitch. Steam vapours start to rise from the earth as a slight rumble can now be felt beneath our feet. 'Albion stop! If this continues, it may be felt beyond this small clearing.'

We slowly let our hands drop to beside our waists, our created force now ceases to exists, as the clearing once again comes back to its dreary former life. A large drip of sweat is running down my forehead, over my cheek, down my neck, continuing its path over my collarbone, before making its final descent between my breasts. My body is humming with pent up electricity.

I look over towards my love and see that his eyes are alive with arousal. What started out as a test of our combined strength, has ended up as a prelude to foreplay. The enormity of what we could be capable of is not lost on me, but right at this moment, my love and fierce lust for this man is taking over all of my thoughts, especially when I see the corner of his mouth start to tilt up in a wicked grin.

'Arianwen, I ...'

Albion looks down and shakes his head in an apparent attempt to clear his thoughts, but when he raises it back up and stares directly into my eyes, I can tell there is no stopping the raging emotions I can see heating in his eyes.

He takes a slow step forward and stops, growling at his lack of restraint, before storming towards me and scooping me up into his arms and charging with speed towards our home.

'Albion.'

I try and talk but he stops me by slamming his lips against mine. I lose myself so deep in this kiss that I do not even notice we have made our way behind the stone walls and into our home, until he throws me on the fur covered bed.

I cannot stop the giggle that escapes my mouth, but Albion's smouldering stare soon silences it. I freeze, prey to this Hunter, as he places a knee onto the bed and slowly begins crawling over my body, his muscled form shadowing my feminine one as my breath starts to come in pants.

He stills, staring at me with so much heat I begin to whimper with need, my arousal starting to pool in my centre, my desperation for my love building to extraordinary heights. He reaches for my right hand, clutching it in his as he raises them above our heads. Our other hands follow suit as he uses his weight to restrain me.

His entire body is still hovering above me and as I am just about to beg for his heated weight, he slowly lowers only his head so his lips meet mine in the softest touch. I close my eyes, wanting more but he lifts his lips from mine, my eyes opening, ready to question his hesitation as I see the toll of restraint clearly in his stare.

'Albion, I need you, please. There is nothing to fear, you won't hurt our child I promise you. Please my love, please take me. Let go Albion.'

I do not have time to take a breath as his mouth smashes down upon mine, claiming me, giving me what I was so desperately begging for. His body slowly follows suit until I am pressed firmly into the mattress below, his solid manhood pressing hard against my centre. There is too many layers between us. I try to wiggle my hands free so I can begin to remove his clothing, but his grip tightens as he removes his lips from mine.

'You are mine Arianwen; mine to take, mine to control, do you understand what I'm saying?'

We have always shared our love making, neither of us have been the one in control, it has always been heated and primal, both of us moving with the other. This is different, the way he is looking at me is different, it is fierce. A shiver of sensual fear starts to wind its way up my spine, creating rivers that race over the surface of my skin.

Without breaking eye contact, he gathers my wrists in one hand, moving the other to above my head and beyond the edge of our bed. After a grumbled curse, his serious frown relaxes and a devious smile starts to spread over his features as he slowly drags his free hand back and rests it beside my head.

'Do you trust me my love?'

Albion's breathing has increased as he waits for my answer. There is only one way to respond.

'With my life.'

He growls as he once again claims my lips, biting the soft pink flesh just beyond pain, before plunging his tongue inside to dance with mine. I think I feel something cold against my wrist, but at that moment Albion presses his groin hard against my centre and I lose all train of thought.

My entire body is pulsating against his as I break out in a sweat of need. I try to break a hand free because I need to feel his skin under my fingertips, but I feel a cold tinge again. This time I pull harder and hear a click of metal and realise both my wrists are bound in chain. Albion sits back with a wicked grin as I once again try to free my hands. I turn my head and look towards my wrists.

Not only are my wrists bound together by links of silver chain, a length of the chain also runs to the top of the mattress and beyond. While watching, I tug again and realise with fascination that the chain is bound to beneath the bed. I am completely at my Demon's mercy.

I look back to my love to find him licking his lips. His hands slowly gliding over my ribs, down to the curve of my waist, a shiver of anticipation ripples through my body. He grips my hips, but before I can open my thighs with an invitation, his hold tightens and he suddenly flips me over, my face planting in the soft fur beneath, the chain around my wrists tightening. I feel him moving down the bed, his large fingers wrapping around my ankles, pulling my body down as far as my restraints will allow.

His fingers begin to slide up, tracing over my calf muscles firmly. He slows behind my knees, adding more pressure with his two middle fingers that elicits a moan from my mouth. He continues up, his thumbs sliding to the inside of my thighs, moving towards my centre. A rush of moisture floods my cotton panties before I feel his hot breath at the back of my thighs.

'These are in my way.'

His deep lustful voice, full of promises and sin, rushes over me like an inferno as his thumbs slide up the back of my panties, his fingers grabbing hold, slowly, painfully, he pulls them down my thighs and off my ankles. Each of his hands grab the flesh of my behind, kneading, pushing, making my want for him almost unbearable.

His thumbs slide down and push through my folds, I moan his name, begging for more. His fingers now join, parting my centre, and suddenly I am being attacked by his delicious tongue. I scream with pleasure, trying to push against him, but his grip is firmly holding me down upon the mattress as he sinks his wet flesh into my core continually.

Biting, sucking, licking, all of it is driving me crazy as my arousal begins to rise, taking me close to the edge of ecstasy, the sound of my wet centre almost pushing me over as Albion growls his satisfaction. He nibbles on my skin as if dinning on the most exquisite delights. His tongue begins to slide out, but before I can protest its loss, he slides it up towards my rim, the forbidden feeling has me gasping for breath.

When his tongue makes contact with that sinful entrance, I scream as the tidal wave of my explosion begins to rush through my body. I clench at the intrusion of his tongue as I continue to convulse around his sinful flesh. The pleasure he is creating is like nothing I have experienced before. The height I am reaching makes me fearful of the fall.

His strong fingers push inside me as his tongue still intrudes my back entrance. I feel my body start to rise again as it still continues to fall from my first explosion. I am panting, struggling to catch my breath as my heart pounds with force behind my ribs.

'Albion, I can't. I can't do it again.'

I plead with my love, the intensity of my feelings beginning to overwhelm me as he pushes harder, chasing another reward for his sensual talents. Just as I feel as if my body will give up, all contact ceases momentarily before I feel the heat of his thighs against my legs and his hard fevered erection brushing slowly through my centre. The sudden softness of his movements, a strong contrast to the pounding he was administering.

I turn my head back to stare him in the eyes and notice his hesitation. My Demon, relentless one minute and restrained the next.

'Albion my love, it's safe, take me how you want, please claim me, please own me. All of me.'

He takes a deep breath before pulling back slightly then thrusting in me with such force our bodies move up the bed. I scream with pleasure as my internal muscles contract and grasp his heated flesh, his growl echoes in my ear, I have lost all air from my lungs for just a moment in time.

'Are you okay Arianwen?'

I drag in a gulp of much needed air but I am still unable to respond.

'Did I hurt you my sweet Angel, did I push too far?'

The panic in his voice snaps me out of my trance. I take another deep breath before answering.

'I'm fine my love. No pain, just blinding pleasure. Keep going, please don't stop.'

He growls and pulls out slowly before ramming back in again, harder this time. My muscles begin to pulse as the build within reaches new heights. He grabs a handful of hair at the nape of my neck before pulling out and slamming back in, my body pushed further into the soft bedding beneath as ripples of arousal begin to roll through my flesh. With one hand still at my neck, the other comes down to grab the flesh at my hip, his fingers digging in giving him more leverage to thrust with his entire body.

My body is chasing ecstasy as my thighs begin to tighten. I am on the cusp of letting go, when I feel one of Albion's fingers seeking the forbidden path his tongue took moments ago. He circles the flesh at the entrance before adding pressure and pushing in slightly ... and that is all it takes for the explosion to begin. My flesh grips him tightly; the heavy drag of his manhood rubbing over my muscles as my centre tightens, has me screaming his name, my voice echoing off the stone walls surrounding us.

My loud excitement fuels him on, his finger between my buttocks pushes in further and his thrusts become harder as euphoria smothers my entire being. The new sensation has me floating with pleasure and thrashing about in painful delight as my Demon growls his own release, the sound shaking the solid rock above us as I feel his shaft become harder. The sensation of his release splashing my sensitive internal flesh causes shivers to race over my skin, as we begin to fall back down from the cloud of lust that was just holding us captive.

As the fog of release begins to clear from my head, the harshness of our reality starts to slip back in, reminding me that we are not privy to the joy of lazily lying in each other's arms half the day after making love. Our reality is that a war is looming, that instead of fighting it, has us preparing to run the other way, which is completely against both of our natures.

'Albion.'

His name painfully leaves my lips as fear of not having another moment like this starts to take hold. His hands reach up and release me from my restraints. He then turns me over and gently places his lips upon mine, while his hand softly rubs the slightly rounded flesh of my stomach. Wetness starts to fill my eyes and topple down my cheeks at this sweet man before me.

'Arianwen, I will keep you both safe I promise. We'll leave safely and find a place to raise our child without fear from either of our worlds.'

My love has the ability to read my inner turmoil and call me out on my fears, fears that are very real for the both of us.

'I'll go to the Bookkeeper Albion and confess all. She needs to know what she's getting into before offering to help us leave. I'll not let her unknowingly risk her own life for us.' He nods while still rubbing his hands over my tummy. He leans down and replaces his hand with his lips, giving baby a reassuring kiss, which has me swallow a sob that is threatening to escape.

I cannot fall apart now, I have to stay strong for so many reasons. Emotions welling over will not help us flee to safety. But, knowing I have to raise from this bed and leave the man I love, if for only a small amount of time, is torturous to my aching heart.

We both sense our intimate time has to end. Albion raises and reaches out a hand to help me up. He then grabs both my wrists and begins to rub life back into the slightly numb flesh with his thumbs, while wearing a wicked grin on his face. This makes me smile too as we both move around each other replacing the clothes that were thrown from our bodies. We then head to the exit of this cavern and use our combined senses to make sure it is safe to leave.

Once outside Albion embraces me fiercely, placing a kiss upon my hair, taking in a large breath of my scent as I do the same. Leaving each other, if only for a moment, is getting harder. We both sense the danger rising around us and the unknown threating to derail our plans of departure, but we have to have faith that fate has a plan for us and this will all end with us still being in each other's arms.

We let go in painful silence as I begin to walk away and back to the world I was born to. My sense of belonging has changed since Albion came into my life. I still adore my home, but it is now tainted with the fact that I know all is not what it seems and a feeling that Michael may not be the only one who has an alliance with the Devil.

Before I head to the Bookkeepers cottage, I need to mingle throughout my world so my presence can be validated if Michael feels the need to question my whereabouts these last few hours. I head to my favourite place, the children's garden as I linger around the edges, talking to proud mums, before making my way into the hive of activity and childish abandonment.

I feel eyes upon me before I even turn my head to see Mayloree, one of Gabriel's chosen staring directly at me with a straight face. I smile sweetly at her, but do not receive a smile in return. She blinks a few times before her eyes go wide, then she turns her head quickly to face the opposite direction. A feeling of unease washes over me as I remind myself, everyone in my world has their own unique gift or calling.

Maybe she can sense new life, maybe she sensed baby? I take in a large breath and let it out with control to stop the panic that wants to rise within. I continue to help the children, keeping myself busy, trying not to look in her direction again. Sistelle, the other chosen girl walks past my small group of singing children and says hello, offering a genuine smile which I return.

But beyond her, I catch Mayloree again staring at me with wide eyes. I instinctively pull a basket full of toys to in front of my stomach as if to protect my secret from being discovered. This time she does not avert her eyes, but instead continues to hold my glance while standing completely still as if frozen in place. My stomach rolls and I swallow hard, trying not to let the nauseous feeling take over.

I refuse to turn away, not wanting her to sense my unease at her eyes upon me. I am distracted by a child's question and have to break our stare, but when I raise my head again, she has gone. I turn, searching all around the clearing and beyond, but there is no sign of her. If she knows about baby, she may tell, especially if she wants me out of the way to increase her chances at the one to become Gabriel's bride.

I finish up the hymn that the children were singing and let them run away to play a chasing game. I move slowly, concealing my fear, as I move quietly into the background of this gathering before fastening my steps towards the Bookkeepers cottage. Albion and I may not have much time. Our departure may be more imminent than we had hoped or planned for. I may be leaving this beautiful garden very soon.

# 19

# Wrong Side Of Heaven
# Righteous Side Of Hell

## ALBION

**My mark burns, the searing, malevolent ache screams at me;** rattling my skull like the tumbling bones of the damned. I fight the need, the unquenchable urge to flee to the side of the man that set this mark in my flesh, the venerable butcher of souls, the Fallen Angel that set me on a path of destruction paved with the corpses of my own kin.

I know I must go, deep in my core the logic that drives me cries out in defense of my need to see this to the end, but, I would be walking into the very lair of Evil itself. No matter how much I want to stray from this path, to forge my own with the woman I love and the child we have brought to life, I cannot draw the ire of even one of the Hell spun Demonic spawn that had so called themselves my kin.

I step from my home and into the turgid afternoon air; I taste the air, her scent still lingering even now after her leaving my side not long before. I move, my movements mechanical, guided by the tugging strings of the Machiavellian puppeteer that even now, holds the gossamer threads of my life against the razor's edge. One false move, one foot in the wrong place, and my whole world comes to a guttering end, my strings cut and my bones crushed into the dirt through which I trudge.

I close my eyes, my sense honed to a needles point as I let them soak in the world around me, savoring the sounds and smells, keeping them locked and safe, a calming balm against what I know is to come.

✦ ✦ ✦

Smoke swirls around me, sulphur invading my every pore, choking the sweet taste of freedom before I am even past the first ring of this infernal ramp way. The sneering of the guards, the hulking behemoths whose every step could fell the walls of Jericho, turns my stomach. The foetid tinge of mould and rotting flesh staining their crooked teeth makes me cringe, my mind screaming at me as I catch site of a familiar, tribal scar, adorning a piece of skin crushed between the guard's misshapen teeth.

I turn away, memories flooding me, the sound of my own screams and the rippling patter of my own blood as it hits the gelatinous pile that was at my feet. The sight of my own torture torn skin wedged between the teeth of that mountain of hatred is one more lash across my scarred and pitted mind, as I make my way through fire and smoke and onwards, towards the Devil's lair.

Corridors twist and turn, my path beset by wickedness and contention as I pass minion, Warrior and former kinsman; all of them, to a man, casting scorn and hatred at my feet, all except for the one person I still cannot reconcile my doubts for.

'Albion, brother, what are you doing back so soon? Surely you can't hold the key to whatever insane elemental is causing all this tension and confusion.'

'No Alp, I honestly can't set my eye to anything as yet, I was summoned here, the only reason I stand before you now is because Lucifer tugged at my leash.'

'Ah, sorry brother, come with me then, for both of us are set to the same destination and the air around here is becoming a bit too … toxic for my liking.'

With his final words, Lilith rounds the corner, her sneering lips curling in a vicious grin as she sets eyes upon me. I follow Alp, my footsteps hastening as I quickly make my path away from that contemptible harpy.

'That bitch is too crazy even for half the Demons around here. Did you hear what she did to one of her own hand maidens?'

'No brother I haven't. I haven't been back to the pit in sometime as you know, and well, any Hunters I have come across while I was on my sojourn have mostly been at odds with my reinstatement.'

'I can understand why, you didn't exactly leave a welcome trail in which to follow, most of the Sixth are considering a vote of no confidence in you. I get the feeling Bara, 'Goth is going to challenge you for leadership over them, and to say he has a strong following is an understatement.'

'Thank you brother, for everything, without you I'm not sure I would've even ventured back once I was granted my freedom.'

Corridors twist and turn, descending into the bowels of this taciturn dominion of destitution. Everywhere I cast my gaze there are hovels and scrapings. Dwellings, little more than bowls cut into the dirt, with ragged and emaciated creatures lying curled within.

One cadaverous hand reaches out towards me. I feel my heart lurch as its eyes meet my own. The pleading, the unrelenting need for help pouring from it like water, my overwhelming desire to reach out and take the beseeching hand nearly undoes me. But, as I near my moment of utter undoing Alp pushes the hand back, growling at the cowering slip of paper thin flesh as his face contorts, skin twisting into a feral parody of a lizard.

The sight so confusing to the poor wretch that its body shrinks, ashen skin peeling apart as it bleeds back into the rocks beneath it.

Alp taps my elbow, nodding to the door as I stop, hesitating for a moment.

'Go brother, I'll be here when you return.'

My brow furrows for a moment as his eyes shimmer. For the briefest of moments, I could have sworn they took the same hue as my Angels. I shake my head slightly the thought vanishing as quickly as it appears.

'Yes brother, thank you.'

✦ ✦ ✦

'Come in, we've much to discuss.'

The room is dark, swathed in a thick miasma of wood smoke and incense. I step lightly, my gait even, tempered by a mix of fear and hatred; fear of the dance I am slowly being drawn into and hatred at who my partner is soon to be.

'My King.'

'Albion.'

I stop, my feet planted beneath me as I close my fist around my father's push dagger, the small form fitting sheath nestled at my belt line just above my backside. I watch Lucifer's eyes, his gaze approving as I square my shoulders and ready my blade, my stance proclaiming to anyone who looks no closer than the tip of their nose, that I am little more than an adoring soldier stood before his commander.

'Albion, what am I to do with you? I spend an arduous amount of time bringing you back from the brink of stupidity and treachery. Then once all that is said and done, the skin has slipped back into place and the wounds have long faded from sight. I send you out, and what do you do? ... You skewer one of your brothers and then ... then ... you fail me, you fail to bring what I sent you out for. Where is it Albion, where is that one prize that I so set your sights towards?'

I stand mute, my palm sweating around the handle of my father's dagger.

'Well ... *Where is it?*'

I struggle to find my voice as I watch Lucifer's aura swell, the edges rippling black as I take a half step backwards, my right foot shifting as the would be King of the world advances towards me.

'We need whatever is causing this flux Albion, without it we're finished. As we stand, the Legions, the legates and all the soldiers in between are naught if we can't bring unto our fold this spectral being that is wandering between my kingdom and the lands of my former kin. Do you not see what a tentative hold we have here? At a moment's notice, these realms could descend into the anarchic chaos I found them in when I was so readily cast from my father's side. Yet, there you stand empty handed and afraid of your damned shadow.'

I bristle at his words, his aura betraying his eyes as I watch it shimmer with repressed angst and ... it can't be ... is that fear I see hiding amongst the folds of self confidence and bigotry?

'Afraid ... I fear nothing, Angel nor Demon. I am the son of a Hell Knight, *they fear me!*'

'Albion I love the bravado, but, your stance and aura tell far more than your eyes and words. There's little that I fail to see anymore Albion, you're petrified just being here, your stance says flight more than any other I have ever seen and yet, well, you don't, do you? Some notion of foolish pride no doubt begs you stand fast when all you wish to do is flee from my presence and back to your cell or some other miniscule bolt hole you have no doubt fashioned for yourself. Very well, I will give you your out Albion. We are mobilising for war, that little skirmish you had with a coterie of Gabriel's Sleepers not too long ago was the lonesome spark we needed to get the fires burning. If my brothers want war then war they shall have, but hold no doubt, I do not hunger for this Albion. I want peace more than anything else in my entire existence. I want to be able to walk the paths unfettered by the threat of a bullet to my temple.

'If my siblings want that drawn from their own flesh then so be it, but know, that this war Albion, the one I want you to lead us into, was not of my creation but theirs, the so called Guardians of love and light, not the King of Hell.'

I cannot help but feel some measure of pride in the fact that the all knowing *King of Hell* has not seen through me, through my love for her and for the spell she wrought upon my heart that so drew from his malicious stain.

Very little he fails to see ... the notion is laughable. If there was so little that escaped his eye then he would have known long ago of the dissention that is so plaguing my former home and kin.

'Now go, go see to your men, that is, if they still wish you as their Commander. I do hear talk of one claiming the title from atop your skull. An ill fit I am sure, but never the less you know the laws of the Legions Albion, what was claimed in blood must be defended with it, that is unless you have lost your stomach for the fight.'

I feel my teeth lengthen as Lucifer smirks, my horns threatening to crest my skin as I stalk from his chambers, a throated chuckle following in my wake, slamming the door shut behind me.

'Brother?'

Alp's plaintive call falls foul of my mood as I wave him away and make my way towards the Undercroft and the halls of the Sixth Legion.

✦✦✦

I move through hall and passage, the cold bathes my skin as I spy the doors my Legions halls at the end of the corridor. My father set these doors here himself, the Legions Commanders that fell at his feet seeing fit to leave their backs open. Surely they saw the folly in their perceived safety. I smile tightly as a dark thought takes hold.

Does my own usurper see the error of his ways yet? Does he now sit cowering behind those very doors, the ones my father sealed with his own blood so that only those who bore the mark of the Sixth could ever walk through them? Does Bara 'Goth now sit cocksure atop my seat as I make ready to wrest it from beneath him?

It matters little now, my blade sits in my hand and for appearances sake I must sate it with the blood of a foolhardy child; a child who seeks a station he is no more ready for than a fledgling bird is for flight.

✦✦✦

'Behold people, the prodigal King has returned once again. Returned unto us; the loyal, the stalwart ... the betrayed. How can a Demon such as this lead us if he cannot even lead himself from the temptations of the enemy? We saw him cast from the arms of our King and dragged back to the fold, and now, here he stands. Here he stands expectant and doe eyed, wanting us to fall in line, to fall in step and be the wanton killers we were when he first clawed his way free of the pits and stepped up to become our Commander. Can any of you still say you hold any faith in this … this simpering, would be General?'

'So Bara 'Goth, do you mean to take the command from me, is that it? You mean to challenge me for the right to rule over the Sixth. You, whom I found cowering in a pool of his own filth begging me not to end his life when I first claimed this position, you, whom cowed at the feet of every General who walked before me and those who, no doubt you think, will come after I am gone.'

One thing always stuck in my mind, my father's first ever words of advice to me. I was just learning hand to hand combat with the other fledglings and was pitted against a Demon child that outweighed me in not only height, but also weight. After eight gruelling rounds I was left beaten and bleeding, the towering stack of meat looking down at me, rage and malice in his eyes as blood trickled from his split lower lip, my token gesture.

I remember my father's words clearly, more so now than at any other time in my life.

*'Make him angry Albion, make him angry and he'll come at you without thinking, he'll come at you fast and stupid so use it. You may be smaller at the moment but that won't last, what will last though is your speed, your power. He may be heavier and stronger, but he'll never be as quick as you so use it against him.'*

He was right and use it I did, I still do. I cannot help but smirk as Bara 'Goth's eyes begin to narrow as I watch his wings spill free and shoulders hunch low. I cannot help but mumble my father's words as I crouch slightly, bracing for my would be usurpers attack. Bara 'Goth roars, his arms flailing as he sprints at me, horns snapping free of his scalp as he bares his fangs and draws his blade from his hip.

'Make them mad.'

I twist to the left, his blade nicking the seat of my trousers as I deftly move from his path planting my foot between his wings and sending him sprawling. Bara 'Goth hits the floor with a shuddering thump as his blade skitters free across the stones.

He begins to rise as I calmly walk towards his weapon and kick it back towards him, the sound of metal grating over stone fills the silent hall as the Legion around us watches in raptured curiosity.

'Use their size against them.'

Bara 'Goth, despite his former cowardice, towers a full head taller than me as well as a half length wider across the shoulders. In any other situation, I would simply draw and put a bullet between his eyes, this dancing to and fro more of a hindrance than anything else I am forced into. Yet, dance I must, for the sake of my woman and my unborn child, I must bite hard on the proverbial bullet and tread through the motions of this antiquated and blood thirsty rite, lest I stir the ire of the entire Legion, well, more so than I already have. A lesser person would be driven to insanity contemplating the myriad outcomes that so sit before me.

The lumbering mount of flesh has finally clambered back to his feet, his eyes seething as his fangs lengthen. I really have drawn deep on his well spring of rage and bloodlust.

I crouch once more as Bara 'Goth charges, weapon held low as he spreads his wings. I close my eyes for a second, willing myself into another mind, another place; one where I don't see the opening before me; and one, where the palm of my hand doesn't itch incessantly for the chequered grip of my iron caster.

A dark almost whimsical sigh slips from me as I roll forwards, coming beneath the open swing of his blade, my own flashing left and right, lines of ichor opening along his arms as Bara 'Goth's blade clatters to the stone once more.

He bellows in pain and anger as his arms hang uselessly at his sides, tendons and muscles severed at the root.

'Yield boy, there is no need for you to fall to the eternal sleep today; yield and that will be the end of it. No honour lost and no more blood spilt.'

I stare at him as his fang and horns shrink slightly, his anger dulling to a guttering glow as he ponders my beseeching call.

'Yield to you? You expect me to yield to a blood traitor; to a Hell spun spit of gristle that lies with the enemy and then calls himself a Demon. Never more will I cow down before the likes you, the name of Weisser ceased to be one of respect and adoration the moment your mother spit you from her rotten cunt.'

I grit my teeth, the barbed slings of this child biting deeper than I wanted to allow. I find my hand tightening on my blades hilt as my own horns begin to breach the sanctity of my scalp. Before I even register my own thoughts, I have closed the gap between me and my squirming accuser, my clawed fingers sinking into his jaw as I lift him from the floor, his tongue slapping against my fingers as I set my blade against the centre of his chest and push.

My mind is screaming for me to stop as he thrashes against my weapon, my arm running alive with spittle and blood as I keep him held aloft. His body trembles, wings falling limp as he begins to pass over, the acrid stink of blood and bile fills my nostrils as I saw down through stomach and skin. His innards boiling free, spilling around my feet like wet wool as I feel my blade hit bone. I glance down, the blood smeared glint of Bara 'Goth's pelvis greeting my eye as I lean inwards, my teeth sinking into his heart.

With a twist of my head I tear it free, the sound of ice covered silk filling the air as it rips free of the dead Demon's chest, his screams and thrashing stilled beyond recant.

The silence is deafening as I let his body drop, the heat from his ashen dissolution eerily soothing as I spit his heart away from me, the bloodied organ curling through the air as it too begins to dissolve to ash. I turn to the men and women around me, their eyes locked upon me, letting my wings unfurl, my lips curling into a feral sneer as Bara 'Goth's blood stains my mouth and teeth.

'See what arrogance wrought! See what dishonour brings! Death! Death is all that awaits any who so seek to challenge me. That Demon sought my station and now here he lays naught but blood, ash and stone. I offered him his life and that offer was spurned with a curse to my mother's name. Let no man, Angel or Demon call into question the honour of my parentage. I may have strayed, I may have succumbed to the wiles of a tempting foe, but I paid my dues to our King and our courts.

'If that is not enough ....'

I snatch Bara 'Goth's blade from the floor sinking into the stone at my feet.

'Then let any who seeks restitution come and claim this sword and draw it from my flesh, for it is the only penance here, our blood and our flesh. I am the head of the Sixth; I am the Lord of this Legion, what say you?'

Their roar of acceptance is deafening, with smiling lips but a heavy tear soaked heart I leave, the taste of another failures blood still on my tongue.

My feet carry me, to where I cannot rightly say. My mind sits in a whirl pool of conflicting emotions. Why did that boy have to force my hand, why draw my family into a petty claim for power? Yet, as scornful and heart staining that barbed remark was, why did I end his life in such a malevolent and brutal manner? Why did I not simply lance his heart with my blade or snap the vertebrae of his neck? To tear his heart from his chest, with my teeth no less, what does this place do to me to illicit such hateful and diabolical actions?

What I did is not the action of a man who is soon to be a father; it is the action of a beast, a vile malediction that should be scoured from the face of existence, not left as the head of a Legion of killers and murderers.

I feel fingers curl around my shoulder, my pace drawn to a halt as Lilith slips from the darkness and curls against my side.

'I saw you lover, I saw you in the pits. What you did to Bara 'Goth, what you set down before them all, I saw it, it was delicious.'

Her grin is sickening, full of malice and wanton destruction, plastered across her face by insanity and a lust for death. This harpy before me, this carrion whore, she is all I despise, all that they draw from me with every second I spend in this damnable place. She is the epitome of all I was forced to become.

A merciless, lust soaked heathen that delights in killing.

'Get gone from my sight you malevolent whore, I want nothing that your diseased carcass can offer me. Our King may have set us together, but that is only in his eyes, to me, you're little more than the offal at the foot of a butchers block, something to be discarded and fed to the dogs.'

I push her away from me, snarling as I watch her sprawl across the floor, a guttural hiss leaving her as she stares at me before creeping back into her own shadow. No, I am not what I was forced into being, I am the man that my Angel loves, and I am more than the Demon I was lead to become. I know this at my core and yet, I still feel stained, my soul tarnished by all I have done.

I know my mother saw it within me, saw the Good that I have locked within my heart and mind. My father wrought it as only a Demon can. He turned his back on all he was raised to be and gave the light inside us both a place to call home through it all. Then when I once more fell prey to the darkness and all my failures, when I was swept away on a tide of malevolence and torture born hatred, Arianwen gave it life. She pulled me from the darkness and showed me I am more than the half breed of a Fallen Angel and a Demon Knight. I just hope, once more, that this place does not bury it or me too deeply, lest I never again am able to call my true self, the version of me that Arianwen fell in love with, the part she pulled from the darkness, home.

✦ ✦ ✦

I cannot help but feel the weight of my actions, the relentless pressure that is sitting atop my shoulders as I stagger and stumble towards the home Arianwen and I have taken together. Can we really call this a home, this hand carved cavern, hewn from the split of nature's skin by the hands of a man, a Warrior, a father, a Demon, that once held me aloft, safe and secure in his hands as I struggled and laughed with the abandonment of a child yet to see the horrors that the outside world so cruelly thrusts upon us all?

Can I ever claim to be that boy, that child that went running into the arms of his father and mother? The young whelp that would sit watching the world below with baited breath for a sight of his parents return or the roar of his father's triumphs over a foe, that has so changed my world and one of whom I now call my wife in all but paper and mother to my child. Could I have ever been that innocent? No ... I do not think I ever truly was. I saw my parents as the guardians they were and still are, but, the world around us, it had already changed me in ways I am still only just beginning to fathom. Its acrid putrescence sinking through my skin and into my heart and soul, more than any blade or bullet ever has, and the overriding fear, the one inescapable fact I can no more deny than the rising of the sun is, that now, that taint, the ichor that has so stained me, now clings to the soul of the child that is slowly growing within the core of my Angel. How can I be my child's protector when I have already so tainted their soul?

# 20

## Help Needed

## ARIANWEN

**After my strange encounter with Mayloree, I move carefully,** ever watchful as I pass through this beautiful garden, making sure no one else's eyes are following my footsteps, as I head towards the only kin of mine I can possibly ask for help. The warmth and safety I feel as the Bookkeepers cottage comes into sight is akin to the feelings I had towards my old mentor and teacher, Anatiamoros. What would he make of the mess my life has become?

He always understood why I felt different growing up and instinctively knew it was more than my once stunted wing. He knew it was something from deep within me, but Anatiamoros never once made me feel as if I *was* different, as if I could not achieve my calling as those before me had. He always believed that I would one day find myself, but I am sure he would be shocked at the path I now walk, one so entwined with both worlds that it led me to the one man I never thought could complete me. I just hope that his eternal soul still smiles upon the love I hold for Albion.

Even from my earliest memories, I could feel distant eyes upon me. Eyes from beyond my own world, and even though at times I would become scared, scared at the thought of something dark watching me, there would be others where I would find peace in the feeling I always had this invisible protector watching over me.

Spending what would be many human lifetimes feeling incomplete is taxing to one's soul, even though my home is the most beautiful place in existence. I have had a fulfilling and rewarding life serving my Lord and the humans we have been created to protect, but I always felt like there was a part of me missing. I never understood the feeling until I first laid eyes upon Albion, a Demon I should have been running from instead of staring into his eyes, staring into what felt like the missing piece of my soul.

I do not know if I will ever completely comprehend why this Angel Hunter is my missing puzzle piece, or why fate has drawn a path for us both to walk upon side by side, but I know how magical our love is and what we share is something I will never question. When reading my worlds history books about the great love stories in time, I never truly imagined it could be as intense as what Albion and I share.

Yes, many died for love, some even killed for it, but to have the feeling consume every cell in your entire body, that is a truly powerful emotion. It is no wonder that all wars are fought, won or lost because of it. It is an amazing piece of spectacular magic but can also create such devastating grief.

I reach the door to the Bookkeepers cottage and close my eyes, making sure I cannot sense another kin in the garden surrounding me or inside the cottage with Claire. When I feel it is safe, I place a timid knock on the door and only have to wait mere seconds before it opens and Claire is standing there with a welcoming smile on her face.

'I was expecting you my dear. Tea's ready.'

The enormity of what I am about to reveal to this wise and sweet Angel before me suddenly hits me and has my insides turning, upsetting babies restful sleep. I reach for my stomach to pacify my little miracle, Claire's smile growing wider as she stares at my hand rubbing soft circles over my clothes.

'You're still small, but that will change soon. Are you prepared for the ramifications of that?'

I know I will not be able to conceal my secret much longer which makes our imminent departure loom closer by the minute. I take a tentative sip of my tea, bracing myself for the words that are about to slip from my lips.

'I have lots to tell you, and I'm not sure as to how you will receive my words.'

I need to prepare her for the barrage of truths and the knowledge I am about to bestow upon her. I take another sip of my tea, ready to reveal that I have, in every literal sense of the term, been sleeping with the enemy. Her smile is so bright that I hate the thought of what it will be replaced with when I have finished talking.

'My child wasn't conceived with another Angel.'

She does not look shocked at all; her smile is still there as she lifts her head slightly as if asking for me to continue. I need her to know it all, right from the start; I need her to know that this did not happen because I fell prey to the darkened side.

'My entire life I felt as if something or someone was watching over me, more so when I was near the edges of Eden as it blended into the forgotten forest. I thought it was just a child's imagination running wild when I was young, but as I got older I knew it wasn't something from within my thoughts, but it was indeed real. I could sense it when it came near, and I could feel when it started to back away.

'At first I thought it was some type of entity, maybe a guardian spirit. As the years went on it felt more like a physical body, something solid. But, each time I tried to catch a glimpse of what was watching over me, it would vanish for the rest of the day. Never did I feel threatened by it, whether I felt it at the edges of Eden or following me as I went about my duties as a Reclaimer through the village of the damned. I always instinctively knew that if I needed help, or the Devils Hunters nipped too close to my heels, that whatever was following would make sure no harm would come my way.

'The day I finally stood face to face and looked directly into the eyes of a Demon for the first time, was the day I discovered what had indeed been watching over me for a lifetime. Shock was the first feelings that rushed through my body, then recognition, even though I'd never seen my guardian before. I felt as if the larger than life Demon before me, had somehow always been a part of my life. And the instant Good I saw within his eyes, and the light I could feel within his soul made me realise that he may have been living in the wrong world for all of his life. Then confusion took over as to why, why one of the Devil's minions who had been bred and trained to hunt myself and my kin, could possibly turn out to be the missing part of my soul I was always yearning for, and who had so silently been watching from afar for as long as I could remember.

'Our next encounter was just as intense as we both struggled as to why we had been so drawn to each other, why fate made our paths cross from such a young age and kept us parallel for so long until we finally met. One thing lead to another and love blossomed between enemies who found their true selves in the other. We both knew the danger our love could create, but neither of us could walk away. It feels as if this was always meant to be. Like this was how each of us were meant to live their life.

'But, now with the power we've discovered we have when together, which has only intensified since the creation of our baby, we know that we're all in danger and the longer we stay in our own worlds, the higher the danger and the riskier our escape will become. Neither will be accepted in the others world and even if we were, it would only be so the higher powers could use us, our power and once someone discovers that a baby has been conceived, they will no longer need Albion and I, our child will be their number one prize.

'We cannot stay, so I am here before you today, to ask for your guidance and help, in fleeing to a world that will be safe for us all. A world where we can watch our child grow and thrive without fear. I need your help, but only if you're comfortable in giving it. I understand if it's something you have to say no to because I understand the danger it may also place you in.'

After letting it all out in what feels like one big breath, I brace myself for Claire's reaction. With her smile still in place she grabs my hand softly, silently and starts to walk us towards the basement stairs and down towards the library. We walk quietly past shelf after shelf until she beckons for me to sit at a small table with two chairs around it. She walks down one aisle going directly to a book without even having to search for it.

When she returns and takes a seat opposite me, she places down what looks like a small book wrapped in ancient linen. I am suddenly nervous as to what it could contain, but her friendly demeanour puts me at ease. She reaches for my hand resting on the table and holds it in her gentle grip.

'I knew this day would come. I've known for quite some time it would be you telling me a story as to how you came to love a Demon and that you would create a special miracle together which would result in you needing a safe haven to escape to. Fate has had a plan for the two of you since the day you were created. The same day you were *both* created. I see the questions swirling in your eyes, but it's not my story to tell. But, you were right in seeing the Good in your love. His soul is pure and that is why you were gifted with a child. And you were right to seek me out for help, part of my fate is to assist this tiny secret of yours and make sure it remains safe.

'You see, you're not the only Angel and Demon to have fallen in love, there's been many in our histories to be exact, but you're only one of two couples to have achieved the impossible miracle of conceiving a child together. And that is not because of blind luck. It's because you were chosen by God as part of a master plan to ensure Good will always prevail. It's not my duty to reveal such a plan, but it's my duty to help you in whatever you request of me.

'You have always been special Arianwen, not different and so has your other half; that's why you've never been far from the other. Yes, you may reside in opposite worlds, but fate has ensured you have always been within arm's reach if needed. But don't think your love has been forced. Yes you have been designed to be part of each other's life when the time was needed, but your love for each other is all your own hearts' creation. True love is beyond anyone's power. It blossoms, it's not created.'

To hear our love is real and not part of some magic spell, brings me to tears. To know what I feel for Albion is real and comes directly from my heart and soul is magic within itself. Claire's hand tightens on mine before she releases it to drag the wrapped parcel on the table towards me. I pull at the twine that is holding the linen around the book, once loose, I part the ancient pieces of fabric to reveal a leather bound book. I cannot see a title so I gently pick it up and turn to see the spine. There is also no title there.

I lift my eyes to question Claire who indicates with her hands I should open it. I have never come across a book in here without a title so I am a little nervous as to what I may find when I lift back the cover. With gentle fingers and awareness of the age on this beautiful bound paper before me, I pull back the cover to reveal a blank first page. I crinkle my brow not sure what to make of this, but my curiosity has me continuing to the next page.

What I find is small eloquent writing in very ancient script, in what looks to be a woman's handwriting style. I have to bend quite low to actually make out the tiny words. But, once I do and begin to read, I know the words on these fragile pages will possibly change my life and the lives of the ones I hold close to my heart.

Once I come to the end of the book, with tears streaming down my cheeks, I look up to find that the old Bookkeeper is no longer with me. I can understand her need to give me some time to myself after reading what seems to be a hidden part of our histories. Part of what will become my future.

The book contained writings about the last and only know Angel and Demon to have conceived a child and all of the ramifications that came after it. The fact that the child was born safely in Eden in the Angels family home and with her Demon love beside her. It went on to tell that the family was able to remain safely in Eden until the child was six months old. Then there are reports that Lucifer somehow found out about this child and tried to bribe the Demon father to return to the pits of Hell with his new family, with promises that the greatest power will be bestowed upon him.

God, knowing that Lucifer could have only found out about the child's existence with the help of one of our own kin, decided that it was no longer safe for the child to remain within the walls of Eden, but to where they were sent to is still a mystery. Some myths say that they were sent to another immortal world, while other whispers indicate that Lucifer did indeed get his way and somehow the child is now a Dark Angel within Hell.

But, it appears that the strongest theory would be the correct one. That God clipped all of their wings and sent them to live safely amongst the mortals on Earth, and no word has been said of them since. I have read every book on our histories and yes there are stories of Angels who walk the earth, but I have never once come across a story of an Angel, her Demon love and the child they created living amongst the humans. I gives me hope that Albion and I can flee somewhere safe before Evil catches up with us. It also has me thinking about Albion's parents, whose story would have never been documented within our scrolls as it seems his mother had already left the sanctity of Eden before Albion was even conceived. I wonder where their history would be written.

I wipe my eyes before bundling this precious book back up in its covers and placing it back within the gap it left on the shelf from where Claire had taken it. I make my way slowly up the winding staircase wondering if this is the last time I will ever get to see all of the books containing my entire kin's history. At the top of the stairs I take a deep breath before opening the door to be bathed in the sunlight streaming through the cottages windows.

'I know it's a lot to take in and please do remember that not all of what you read is solid fact, but I think the first step you need to take is to request an audience with God himself and plead your case for your Demon love to be granted asylum here and to be protected as one of own.'

I know she means well, but after reading those ancient words, whether they are fact or myths, I know that if we did stay here in Eden, it would not last, just like the last couple, especially with Gabriel wanting my hand in marriage and Michael already knowing I have been sleeping with the enemy. My situation is too complicated to take the risk of staying.

'I know you mean well Claire, but if I was to stand before God and plead for his help in concealing a Demon within our walls and he refuses, Albion and I could both be immediately exiled from Heaven itself. It's a risk I cannot take with my child's life and the man I love. I know now more than ever that we have to leave and it has to be now.'

She nods with her smile still in place as if she knew that would be my answer to her suggestion. The love that shines from her soul is endless and blinding to the struggles I am currently facing.

'Then I shall help in whatever way you need my sweet Angel. Supplies are important to have ready to leave at a moment's notice, but the time is of the greatest importance. You need to make sure the moon is in the correct position to give you the most power and coverage the night you have to leave, then we have to make sure it's at a time where Lucifer's powers and those surrounding him are at their weakest. A moon that works for us, works against the tides of Evil. I'll consult my charts and let you know of the most suitable times. For now, be careful everywhere you go, even within your own walls.'

I should tremble with fear at her suggestions of Evil lurking within our world, but I have seen it with my own eyes so it comes as no surprise. I hug her tightly, trying to convey my thanks at the risks she will be taking with her own life in helping me, as there is not words strong enough to tell her what her help means to me and the ones I hold dear. I let my grip on her slip and offer a small smile before I leave the safety of her cottage and out into the reality that I may not have long at all in a place I have always called home.

I make my way past the children's garden, so I can again be sighted as being here within our world and will not have to answer Michaels incessant questioning as to my whereabouts. I smile at the young ones antics, desperately trying not to think about my own child unable to experience these simple joys of playing with their other kin, as I make sure to make eye contact with and say hello to the parents who are watching their children play.

After spending a large amount of time there, I leave for home. I round a garden bed on the path towards my home and I can sense Gabriel and Michael talking only metres away. Not wanting to bump in to either of them, I move into one of the small garden beds and crouch down behind a small shrub as their voices grow louder.

'You need to back off Michael, I'm trying to get her comfortable with the fact I want to make her my wife, but all your foul attitude and constant questioning is just making her pull further and further away from me. Enough is enough you hear me?!'

'Oh please brother, she wouldn't even be within your reach if it wasn't for *me* tainting her tea enough that she wasn't able to say no to the presentation ceremony. You should be thanking me instead of trying to chastise me for my behaviour, which by the way, is for the good of our kin and the peaceful world we all live in.'

'If I'd known that you were medicating her, you know I wouldn't have allowed it!'

'It wouldn't have been your choice! I did what I had to do for reasons you don't need to know about. Just concentrate on getting her legally bound to your side so you have the right trophy making you look good at all of our official ceremonies, while I take care of all the important stuff.'

'I admit that at the start I wanted her for her unchallenged beauty and what her powers as a Reclaimer could bring to my own gifts, but it's more than that now. I can see a beautiful future with her as my wife. My feelings for her are no longer shallow, but have grown quite deep, so you need to respect that and start treating her for who she will be, your sister in law. I don't want you doing anything that may destroy the love I'm feeling for her, and the love I hope she will one day return.'

'Oh my foolish young brother. Love? You've got to be more idiotic than I ever thought you could be. I've been telling you for half our lifetime that it will be a woman who will bring you to your knees one day and a dangerous one at that, but you never listened. Now you are here telling me that the one woman I suspect as being a spy for the enemy is the woman you love and want to make pretty babies with and live happily ever after with? Wake up and smell the roses Gabriel! She is not all that she seems to be, and the only reason I haven't removed her from our world and your sights is because it's best we keep our enemies close, so if she does indeed become your wife we can both keep a closer eye on her and her behaviour. But believe me, she will show you her true colours one day and don't get your nose out of joint when I say 'I told you so.'

I can no longer stand to hear the words dribbling from their mouths. I turn and crawl quietly through garden beds after garden beds, until I am safe enough to stand and escape without being detected. Gabriel knows of the poison tea, yet still has faith that his brother is making the right decisions for our world? They are both as foolish as each other, especially if they think I am still going to become Gabriel's wife, to become a further pawn in their dangerous games. Who knows what deal with the Devil Michael may make, when I legally become a part of his immediate family.

All thoughts of making the most of my dwindling time with my family goes out the window as my need to be in the comfort of Albion's arms grow. I need to feel his love and reassurance that we will be able to leave these worlds safely together. I quietly head towards the Gatekeepers, taking care in not being seen or detected by any of my kin. I want Michael to know I was last sighted at the children's garden if he feels the need to seek out my whereabouts.

As soon as I step into the forgotten forest I feel him, and I feel his concern at my urgent need for him. I only have to take a few steps before I sight the very worried face of the man I love. He knew, he knew I needed to be in his arms and he came for me, he came dangerously close to my world because he knew I needed him to comfort me.

When I step into his embrace his large arms engulf me with a need that rivals my own. He holds me close as I bury my face against his neck, feeling his heartbeat throb in the large vein just under his skin. He picks me up, and I instinctively wrap me legs around his waist and hold on tighter as he walks us towards our hidden home. I take a deep breath in smelling his scent that reminds me of everything we are.

I feel a desperate need to get closer to him so I begin to unravel my wings, slowly uncurling each feather, stretching them and setting them free as my love continues to walk at a fastened pace. I slowly stretch out the entirety of my wings down low towards the ground as not to obscure Albion's vision, before bringing them up and curling them around us both, cocooning us in a safe haven of love.

'My beautiful Angel, is everything okay?' Emotion suddenly

clogs my throat, unable to speak. I hold him tighter, closer, trying to convey my feelings through my body. I feel his worry as he starts to sprint towards the rock face that conceals our home. I kiss his neck trying to calm the panic I have caused. He growls at my lips contact and squeezes me tighter as we slide through the secret entrance.

As soon as the sunlight behind us disappears he leans me up against a wall, pulling back from me slightly to look into my eyes, seeking answers to my desperate need for him. 'Tell me my love, tell me what troubles you,' he says in a soft voice that melts me every time. Such a larger than life Demon, who was raised in the pits of Hell, has such a sweet and sensitive side that comes from the deepest parts of his true soul.

'I need you,' are the only words I can release as I gently place my lips upon his, seeking the love he so willingly gives. His movements are controlled and slow as he lets me explore the plump flesh at the entrance to his mouth, my tongue tracing the outline of his lips before brushing along the joined seem. He parts them and I slowly seek refuge inside. His grip tightens on my flesh as his hands slowly move down lower, grabbing my buttocks and bringing our heated flesh closer together.

Both of our control begins to slip as our need for each other rises. Our breathing quickens, and our hearts race in unison as our arousal begins to take over our entire bodies, enlightening every cell that feels the deep love we have for each other. One of Albion's large hands move further under me as his fingers seek my wetness. He pushes my underwear to the side and slips his fingers directly into my centre, both of us moaning at the delight his intrusion has caused.

I slide a hand between us, desperately undoing the laces of his trousers before slipping a hand down and against his throbbing shaft, his heat searing my skin as I grip my fingers around his flesh, pulling and teasing as he is doing to me. Before I know what is happening, Albion is shoving my hand away, lifting my dress aside and ramming his solid manhood into my soaked centre. I scream at the painful delight as he hits my resistance with force.

This is no longer slow, it is fast, frantic and hotter than Hell itself. We are grabbing, scratching, trying to become one in a fevered lust filled haze. I am panting and screaming, begging my love for more. My cries of ecstasy fuelling my Demons actions, making him lose control as I begin to tighten around his intruding flesh.

The wave of love is as powerful as it has ever been as we both reach the precipice of our peak before screaming out and taking the free fall of our explosion together, as one, as our love grows even stronger, coming down from the cloud of our euphoric high. As we struggle for a breath, while our hearts try to return to normal, I hear the most beautiful words that were ever invented.

'I love you Arianwen.'

# 21

## Love. Lust.

## Hate. Empathy.

### ALBION

**'You're the saviour of us all little one, but, you'll never know it.** You're destined for a life free of this world, free of the trials your mother and I've lived and fought through. You will grow up free, free to be whomever you wish to be, you will do great things and bring joy to the world of that I am sure. I pray that the world I was thrust into does not pass onto you my sweet child that would tear my soul in two, to know that I had left you with the stained past I so long to leave behind. You and your mother are my strength and my will, my very reason to push on and keep fighting. I love you little one, my tiny guiding star.'

I place my lips against the side of Arianwen's swollen stomach, her skin warm against my mouth as I feel her fingers curl softly into my hair, a small sigh leaving her as I raise my gaze to meet hers.

'I'm sorry my love, I didn't mean to wake you.'

Her smile lights my heart as I stare at it, her eyes glittering with love and tears, ones that I hope beyond hope are filled with joy.

'To wake to the sound of your voice and the touch of your skin as you talk to the soul we've created between us, Albion, I would die a thousand deaths if it meant having that moment for eternity. Never be sorry for allowing me to wake to such a sweet moment my handsome Demon.'

Her words filter down through every facet of my mind. Each tingling stroke against my love soaked thoughts sends chills across my heart and soul. The woman before me holds everything I am and ever will be in the soft clutch of her heart and hands; hands that now slowly skate across my side and chest as I shift up the bed, my lips finding her shoulder and neck as I nip and suck at her soft alabaster skin. Gentle sighs of contentment filters across my mind as I trace the pulsing line of her veins with my tongue, the lingering taste of skin drawing me in as I nip and bite along her taught flesh.

I draw my hand across the base of her stomach, the energy that pulses through me fills my heart with a song I thought had long since died. Her legs ensnare my waist as I bite gently at her collar bone watching the crescent indents of my teeth linger for a moment before they slowly fade to naught but a soft weal.

Her fingers roam across my ribs, my skin crawling with plea-sure as I feel her trace each one in turn. Nails rake my shoulders before slowly, with an almost tantric gait she curls them through my hair sealing my lips upon her own.

The soft velvet caress of her tongue upon mine sends my mind reeling as I tease my palms over the smooth swell of her abdomen, cupping one nubile, soft, breast, teasing her nipple between thumb and finger. The warmth of her flesh against my own is heady, her scent intoxicating as she pulls me tighter to her. Her wanton heat, the moist call of her sex against my barely concealed length calls to me as I begin to rise. I feel her silk against my head as I ease into her, Arianwen's own guttural moan driving me to madness while it slips down through me, her tongue still at war with my own as I draw away for the briefest of moments, catching her bottom lip between my teeth a wry smile teasing my features, watching lust and love vie for ownership of the violet orbs that hold steady with my own.

I nip the tip of her tongue as she grazes it over my bottom lip, the sweet taste of her soaking me as she arches against my sweat laced body. My mind races, images dancing past my eyes as I close them fighting the need to scream. My heart aches with the thought of the all consuming pressure that envelopes my very soul.

'Arianwen stop, I can't. I'm sorry my love. I want you more than anything but I can't ...'

I stop, breaking the hold and drawing free from her warmth, swinging myself over the edge of the bed before pushing to my feet and pad naked across the room. My hands ache as I feel my heart burn in my chest. I want her, I need her; I need to feel her engulf my soul in everything she has to offer. I want it all so badly that my skin burns, but, how can I? How can I allow myself to slip into that pit of desire when we have the calamitous spectres of death and hatred hunting for us both? How can I after all I did, just to save face with people I no longer care for or could ever truly be a part of? To force the tainted soul I hold inside to bond with hers once again, how, how can I bring that upon them both?

I have a child and a woman, both of whom are looking to me to keep them safe, when all I know is how to take a life not save one. I am a Hunter a damned half breed, forced into rank and file service to a despot King, a King of a world so full of hate and violence that it is etched into my very bones.

I cannot think, I cannot feel. There is nothing in this world that I need other than her and the child that now grows within. She is my beginning, my very reason for living and in her eyes I can see my end. I just pray I can stay this world from making me the one to ultimately become the reason for hers. I would gladly lie upon the swords of a thousand enemies if it meant that she continued on for even a few moments more. I watch as the skin of my fingers peels apart my claws sinking into the work bench as I drag them through the aged and tired timber, my mind so shattered by the thoughts that claim me that I cannot even keep my skin suit in one piece; the shell about me smouldering, a shell that I am so used to wearing, that even my own face in the mirror without it to hide behind, makes me start with anger.

The sudden touch of her hands on my shoulders stills my heart in an instant, everything crumbling, turning to dust in my mind as I feel her begin to envelope me. The silk kiss of her voice burns through every negative thought, every doubt that I hold inside washed away; cast into the blank hole that sits at the core of my own mind, scarred and burned into existence by everything that has sunk its claws into my flesh. I feel my body burn, the sallow skin suit that covers my true form dripping from me, my burnished red flesh greeting the light as she brushes the ash aside, the burnt and scarred truth I fight so hard to hide falling into view.

'Albion what's caused this, what's taken you from me so suddenly my love?'

I turn to face her, my eyes glowing with unshed tears as I stare down at the slim woman that rests against me, her naked body pressed against my own as she softly sighs laying her head against my chest. I bring my hands up, her silk hair rolling through my clawed fingers as she wraps her arms around my waist and draws herself tighter to me. I rest my hand between us as I feel our child's energy course through me.

'I can't lose you again, and yet, no matter what I do, how I try to protect you and our little one I do nothing but. The distance between us seems to grow with every step I take towards you. Everything I do everything I have done; its left me tainted and marked. My sins etched into my bones.

My hand softly plays across the skin of her stomach as I rest my forehead against her shoulder.

'And then, there's our little one. How can I be a father and protector to them when I can't even protect them from myself? I am tainted. Tainted by the world that I was forced into, tarnished by everything I do to keep them from us. All of it, all of it washing over my soul, a soul that gave a part of itself to our child. How can I be all that you both need me to be when I've already failed?'

She looks at me, her eyes slicing into all I am.

'Albion, you have failed no one. You've protected me and our child through everything, even now as you stand before me, scars and wounds laid bare, and the suit, the shield you hide behind gone; the "man" and Demon, that I love, standing clear before me.'

She clutches me tighter to her, warmth floods me as I feel our child stir, its power and strength dousing my mind as I tremble. My knees buckle as I tumble to the floor crimson tears trickling across my cheeks, sliding through her hair, staining the golden tresses as she cradles me to her shoulder and chest.

'I just cannot see it; my mind is nothing but a tumbling hole of confusion. The scars left behind by all that crawled inside; they made me forget, made me deny all we had. If I am so easily plied, led down paths that I've never before walked in my life, how am I to be trusted with the paths we're now forced onto? How can I know which is the one we're supposed to tread? When, for what felt like an eternity. I didn't even know the true owner of my heart and soul.'

I stare at her, begging the love of my life for an answer, praying that she can in some way show me the way free from the vacuous tunnel that is suddenly consuming all I have held dear.

'My love, you never forgot me or our child, there's nothing in any life or world that could ever scour that from you, for even if your mind loses the path. Your heart, your soul, never forget those that they are born to love. I never lost hope my sweet Knight, never.'

In that instant she knew, the one thing I needed, the one thing that would rid me of this cloud of soul shattering hatred and pain that clings to me like ice to winter's grass. It was her, simply and irrevocably her, no matter what I could do, I could no more deny it than I could the soft potted swelling of our growing child.

Her warmth folds over me, soaking my drowning pain and sorrow with equal measure as I begin to feel the soft glow of desire once more flicker into bloom within my heart. It grows as she softly traces my jaw with her lips, the embers glowing, rekindling all that had been drowned and lost as its delicious smoke fills my soul. She bites my neck as I moan, the sound deep, guttural, as I nuzzle at the side of her head, my lips grazing the tip of her ear.

My horns curl upwards as my arousal rises, the feel of her teeth on my Demonic hide sends a decadent and oddly thrilling chill up my spine.

I can feel the smile as she drags her nails across my stomach, fingers snaking through my waist band. A soft lilting giggle teases my ears as she feels me flinch, the sensation of her nails tickling my agates making me shiver. Each pluck and scratch making my throbbing length jump, softly slapping against the ball of her hand as she continues to bite and nip along my jaw and neck.

There comes a point, a point when the smoke bursts and the fire roars, where sense and desire bleeds away, when all you are left with is ... hunger; this intense need to feel the flesh and soul of another move against your own. I gaze at my Angel, her eyes glittering as she curls her fingers over the exposed ridges of my wings talons as they break through the skin of my shoulders, and pulls me in, her lips finding my own.

Her tongue forces its way in, capturing mine with a force and salacious hunger I never before knew my Angel could possess. She breathes in my soul and exhales life into every dead and decaying fibre that makes up the battered form she now cradles against her. I can feel the very marrow of my bones vibrate with energy as blood courses through my veins, heat rippling off me as I watch with a lust filled fascination as the very tips of my Angel's lustrous locks curl and twist. The molten want she draws from me spilling over us both as she rolls me onto my back and reaches between us, searching for my growing length.

I feel her heat swallow me whole, her soft rippling core soaking my thickness as she slowly begins to rock her hips. With each soft push forwards I sink deeper into her warmth, nails clawing my chest as she bends down, her lips ensnaring my nipple as I fail to stifle the deep rolling groan that is pouring from within. My hands move, tracing paths along her sides as I feel the swell of her breasts fill my palms, the granite stiff bolts of her nipples make her shiver as I pinch and twist. A mewl curls free of her lips as she sinks her fingers into my skin.

The copper scent of my own blood fills my nostrils as my fangs begin to lengthen, her rocking, rising, the slick slap of skin on skin echoing around us both as she drives me ever deeper.

I all but growl as she moves, twisting herself around my shaft, the feel of her moving around me almost pushes me over the edge. I stare at her slim and lithe body as she straddles me, her supple back filling my vision as she leans forward, her soft pink wetness blooming open as I watch her backside rise and fall. The sight of my hardened shaft splaying her pouting lips makes my heart hammer as I begin to push my hips upwards meeting her every downward stroke. I trail my fingers along her shivering thighs as I watch myself slip between her soaked lips. Her scent, her heat, the soft mewling that rises to my ears all swells within me as I feel her silk on my fingers, her slick wetness soaking them as I trail my nails along the sensitive patch of skin between her cleft and silk before slowly running them over her darkened haven.

She squirms and writhes as I run my clawed nails over her puckered star, the tender folds of her ring quivering against my touch. I press my finger harder against her hole as she sinks deeper onto my thickening length. I lean her back, her lips latching onto my neck as she moans. Her breath is warm and wet against my skin. I cannot contain myself, her scent, her heat; it is driving me beyond my limit as my fangs extend and I slowly drag them across her collar bone as I push between our bodies and sink my finger beyond the second knuckle, her guttural groan rippling through us both as she clenches on my invading finger and throbbing length.

I feel her shudder as I thrust deeper, my finger sinking ever further until my hand is pressed deep between her buttocks. The sensation of feeling my own invading girth as I move into my quivering Angel, sends me reeling lightly as I begin to slowly draw my finger from her heated ring before slowly sinking a second in beside it. She leans up slightly, her hair sticking to my chest as I move up with her catching her mouth with my own as she whimpers; our tongues dancing as I once more fill her to bursting point.

I feel my agates tighten, my limit drawing close. Her slick warmth sending me to heights or rapture I have only ever felt with the woman I now sink within. My pace quickens as she forces me deeper, pushing back against me, matching every thrust of my hips. I feel the throbbing rise, boiling up from the pit of my stomach and searing through me like a wave of boiling water.

She tenses in my arms, her back arching against me as she clamps down on my very soul, her body singing with pleasure as I finally tip over the edge, drawing her with me into orgasmic bliss.

Time seems to slip to nothing as we lie there; a tangle of sweat soaked skin and sated lust. I place a soft kiss on the side of her head as she curls her fingers through my clawed hand, staring at the juxtaposition of her soft alabaster skin and my heat scorned flesh. The livid red of my hand and bleached white of the bone tips of my fingers standing stark against her own glowing softness. Everything about her exudes love and safety, and yet as I stare of my own hands, all I see is anger and pain. I am struck once more at the implausibility of it all, that this Angel, this soft supine giver of love and light has given me everything another being can. She has given me a reason to be, a reason to carry on existing and reach beyond what I was born and raised to be. Even now as I lie here, devoid of my skin suit and cradling her in my own scarred and battle worn Demon arms, I feel as if I am living a dream.

I chuckle softly drawing a curious glance from my woman as she curls against me, the swell of her stomach sitting gently against my own. If this is a dream, I pray to anyone who listens, God or Demon, that I am never able to wake, and if that the one measure of happiness in my life is a mere figment of my own minds creation, then why would I ever want to live in reality again?

✦ ✦ ✦

I stir well before sunrise, the air floating around me sitting as a crisp reminder that I am alive. I scoop my slumbering Angel up and carry her to our bed, the sounds of her soft breathing making my heart thunder. How could a man, nay a Demon like me have become so blessed as to have the love of the woman I now hold in my arms? Surely fate is a twisted mistress to have my life so bound to another's, and yet have that other fated soul be so far from my arms, even now I know that as I let her slowly slip from my grip and into the soft cotton sheets and bear fur, that she will eventually be torn from me and forced back beyond the gates of Eden and into a place I know I cannot tread for fear of bringing the wrath of Heaven upon us both.

She knows as well as I, I would gladly lay my life and soul on the butchers block if it meant my woman and child were spared from any harm, be it at the hands of a Demon or an Angel, it would matter naught to me. As long as I knew my sacrifice kept her safe.

My armour clings to me like a second skin as I move towards the door, the chainmail lining hanging heavy across my shoulders and scalp as it pushes the thick calf skin sheathed padding against my hair. A soft rustling behind me draws my attention as she stirs. I turn to face her, my breath catching in my throat as she sits up, the covers slipping off her shoulders, the soft swell of her breasts and stomach greeting my eye as she stares at me through sleep soaked eyes.

I cross the room, my feet gliding with barely a whisper, reaching the edge of the bed in seconds and slip across the sleep warmed fur and scoop my Angel into my embrace planting a soft, longing kiss on her lips. My fingers tease her nipple drawing a moan from my soulmate before sliding down and slipping into her rapidly soaking silk.

She squirms and bites at my lip as I curl my fingers searching for the one spot, the one spot that I know drives her beyond pleasure and into sheer rapturous ecstasy. She sinks her teeth deeper into my lip, the coppery taste of my own life's blood coating us both as she gasps, her head rolling back as I feel her close around my fingers, her body quivering in my embrace as her cream drenches my fingers and palm.

I kiss her deeply as I slowly lower her back to the bed, the wanton lust glowing in her eyes as I nip playfully at her chin before slowly, teasingly, kissing my way along her jaw and neck. My tongue slips across her skin, tasting the soft and subtle scent that is wholly her own. Her hands tear at my armour covered head, pushing the leather back across my scalp while I drag the bavier down my chin, her fingers curling into my hair as I lash at her nipples with my tongue. My fingers dance across her ridged button as she pushes me lower, my lips tracing along her skin as I plant kiss after kiss across her softly swelling stomach.

Her nails rake my scalp, lines of heat radiating through me, curling through my throbbing length as I graze her tender button with my tongue. Her thrashes and whimpers as I sink my tongue through her fragrant silk, the subtle musk of her arousal filling my sense as she soaks my tongue and chin.

'Albion, for the love of all creation, stop, please ... oh ... stop.'

I cannot help but grin as I feel her gush again, her taste filling me as I drink her in, her thick cream making my head spin as I softly nip at her flushed and plump lips before flicking my tongue one last time across her shuddering bud.

She slowly strokes her hands through my hair as I push up the bed slightly, resting my head on her hip, tracing the outline of her belly button. I let my vision turn, the shimmering outline of our child shining brightly, watching the beat of their heart and the flex of their fingers as they join their mother in the soft embrace of slumber. I cannot help but smile as I feel them yawn in sync with my Angel, her fingers falling free of my hair as she drifts off into sleep once more.

'I love you my sweet Angel.'

A soft smile teases my loves lips, mumbling a sleep drunk reply as I push myself up planting a soft kiss on her stomach, whispering to my child within.

'Be good little one, look after your mother for me. I love you.'

I move over to the wash stand, rinsing my face in the ice cold water before collecting my weapons from my bench. With care I pluck parchment and graphite from the tray on my bench and scrawl a note for my Angel.

I cast my eyes over it quickly making sure it is as clear as I can make it. With a few swipes, I emphasise the one point I know I need her to follow, to bring back anything she thinks she will need, no matter how innocuous she may think it is, there is nothing we can leave to chance in our need to be free of this world and all that exist in it.

Setting it on my side of the bed I cast one last lingering look at my Angel as she lies curled in the thick layers of our bed, before, with a deep seated reluctance, I turn to the door and move out into the watery dawn.

✦ ✦ ✦

The village is thick with tension, I can almost taste it on the air. Moving in near silence, I scale the wall of one mud slathered building, the sun baked surface powdery beneath my feet as I crest the lip and roll forwards, my sense primed and vision shifting, slowly scanning the world around me. The shifting shapes of these dead apes huddled together in their homes and hovels drags up the memories of many a night spent surviving in the wilds that surround the pit, eating whatever I could dig up. One unpleasant memory makes my stomach lurch as the vision of the multi coloured grubs I once subsisted on surfaces.

I force it down for fear of losing what meagre contents remains in my stomach as I move on safe in the knowledge that I am all but alone at the hour of the morning. I am undoubtedly being tracked by some of Gabriel's minions, but their threat to me is negligible. If I allowed ever tickle or sensation rouse my suspicions, I would soon drive myself to insanity. I learnt long ago to set aside the notion of being able to move truly unobserved, for somewhere, somehow, no matter how good you may think you are, something is going to know where you are or have been despite how hard you try.

I drift from shadow to shadow, my senses strung tight as I shift past an open doorway, the stench of unwashed bodies and flatulence hanging like a blanket. Corners slip past in a blur, one turn after another taking me deeper and deeper into the warren of homes and shacks. I stop dead in my tracks as something tugs hard at the core of me, the soft wailing making my eyes sting with unshed tears as I turn, my vision shifting, searching out the source, knowing all too well what I will find.

The sight of a tired mother lifting the squirming bundle free of its bed makes me smile, the unbidden action sending one bloodied tear down my cheek as I watch her slowly rock the babe in her arms.

I cannot hide the thoughts that swim through my mind, images of what could be and all that I truly want, vying with the stark reality we face, a life of isolation and fear as we hide our love and lives from all that seeks to undo all Arianwen and I are building together. I stop for a moment, the crisp taste of a new day coating my tongue as I flirt with the scent of wet grass and wild garlic. The smell of it all twisting my mind into a fallacy of calm and collected thoughts as I stare at the shifting mists that twist through the streets.

Each step is framed in a twisting swirl of white, the world blanketed in a living carpet of air. Garth's door swims into view, an amber glow filtering around the edges as I near the golden warmth. The pitted and chipped plank door swings open, heat washing over me. I spy at Glynnis standing there, a tattered towel in her hands.

'So Master Weisser, what took you so long? Garth was starting to get worried you may never return. It's been a tense and trying time since you left with the gilded armour you crafted for Arianwen.'

I try to smile, her warmth is damned near infectious and as I draw closer the desire to turn the ridged line of pain and regret that stretches across my lips into a bow of contentment rises, but, there is nothing. Even the memories of last night and this morning do little more than stir my heart and loins. Despite the fluttering in my chest and the warmth of my soul, I cannot bring myself to smile. There is nothing in me that can turn my form to that simplest of gestures.

'Things have not been ... easy, they've been watching my every move and for a time ... I ... I wasn't myself. There is a lot that has transpired that kept me from you and from Arianwen.'

I move past her, the heat soaking through my armour long before I actually set foot in the home. Garth is watching me, his eyes searching, suspicious. I cannot shake the feeling that something has shifted, his stance is combative, not the open and welcoming warmth I once knew. What have I done to cause such a sudden rift between the diminutive blacksmith and I?

'We know all that boy, what we do not know is why you have been so drowned in self pity that you cast out a beacon to any dullard with a ken for aural reading. Are you daft or do you not care for the safety of your child and woman?'

I stand fixed to the spot, my feet rooted as if nailed in place. I would say this was an unusual feeling, but in recent days, I have felt more and more trapped by my own mind than anything else.

'You doubt my love for her, after all I have been through, all that you know I have done to see her safe? You doubt me?'

'No, I never said I doubted your love for here, ken my words boy, and know them well. This morose, self pity that you have allowed yourself to wallow in has been a candle in the dark for every sapient despot in this cess pool. Even your father's sigils and signs have not stopped it from leaking out of the home you so eagerly run to. If you do not drag your head from between your own cheeks and take true stock of the situation you have put yourself and your woman in, then … you will lose her and all that you love. Do you hear me now boy?'

I am struck mute, my mind a fog strewn whirlwind. Am I really putting them both in that much danger?  My heart sinks when I think over all that has transpired, all the pain, the suffering, the anguish I caused my Angel when I was taken and trapped inside the prison of my own mind. It took the will of the woman I love to break its hold on me, not my own, hers.

'What can I do?'

Garth swats at the air as he turns and walks towards the forge, his shoulders are tense and body cast a long spear of anger through everything around him, I can almost taste it.

'You can start with not caring one iota for those depraved zealots that fawn over that fallen sack of cow dung. Did he show any tender care to you when your parents were slaughtered, was it not he that ordered you bound and flayed as an example to the rest of those jackals? No, he didn't and he still doesn't, you're a righteous man Albion trapped in a world run by those that delight and dote on the wickedness of others.'

I find myself stuttering as I step away from him, the look in his eyes a dark and direct challenge to not only me, but everything in this world. I stay mute, saying anything now would only exacerbate a very tense situation further. What stays my hand is not fear or anything of its like, but something else and as much as I hate to admit it, its respect for not only Garth, but my father and the link this man represents to my past and the life that was taken from me.

'You need to decide Albion, decide where you truly belong. Is it at her side or with them?'

I glare at Garth, my anger rising as I feel my fists clench.

'I know exactly where I belong, I know exactly where my true home lies, and it's not with those howling winged monkeys that scrabble in the dust for a demented dictators cast offs. Everything I have done, everything I will do, it is all in the name of bringing a screen to Arianwen and I making our way free of this vile existence.'

Garth's body shifts, his demeanour changing in an instant leaving me wrong footed and confused.

'Good, now we can get to the reason you're here. Follow me.'

How can one being be such a conflicting melee of emotions and actions, only moments before he was stoking the flames of my anger and scolding me like a dog that soiled a rug and now, he is beckoning me to follow him to only who knows where? I swear on all that is true I will one day understand this man, although I fear it will be long after I am dead.

'Garth, darling … don't you think?'

Without breaking his stride, Garth casts a clipped and tired reply over his shoulder as I scramble to follow on his wake.

✦ ✦ ✦

The smell of dust is the first thing that greets me as I step through the small arch way, following the diminutive blacksmith down a shallow flight of steps. I find myself ducking, beams and chiselled stone passing only inches above my head. I struggle to see where Garth could be leading me, when, as quickly as we had descended, he stops. The harsh scratch of flint and steel greets my ears as sparks flare in the darkness before the wick of an oil lantern catches and fills the small strong room with an orb of flickering orange.

'What I'm about to show you, hasn't seen the light of day in more than a score and well, you should see why I'm showing it to you now.'

He reaches around his neck and lifts a small iron key from beneath his stained and heat scorched clothing. The smile on his lips makes me a little nervous as he brushes aside the thick layer of dust and detritus, the plain face of the lock falling into view, as his hand brushes across the oak front of the timeworn cabinet. I watch with the tender, raptured attention of a child as his hand turns, the key twisting in the lock, the sound of tumblers moving fills my ears, the room beyond deathly silent.

A dull clunk echoes for a moment before the door in front of him swings open, dust coated shelves filled with a mind twist array of oddities spills into view. With a delicacy and care I have only ever seen him show his most detailed works, Garth lifts one cloth wrapped bundle from the cabinet before motioning to the door, his head dipping to the side as he urges me to close and lock the cabinet as he moves past me.

I cannot help but wonder what the old smith has and why he feels the need for such pageantry and secrecy. I can only follow and wait, hoping that his next action will cast the nagging curiosity from my mind. Garth is stood waiting for me at the top of the small stair case, his eyes mirthful and mouth smiling, yet, his body language is pensive, almost scared at what is to come. I find the whole image almost too much as I hurriedly step past him and make my way to the table where Glynnis and the cloth wrapped bundle await.

'Albion dear, take a seat. Garth and I, we want to show you something.'

I frown slightly, the jumble of rags drawing my eye as I move taking a seat opposite them both, feeling a knot form in the pit of my stomach. Garth leans forwards and pushes the pile or cloth towards me, both of them smiling in a manner I have never before seen from either of them.

Garth's voice shatters my momentary reverie as I turn my gaze to him, slightly startled by the sudden burst of noise.

'Albion, this was left here by your mother. She left it in our charge and knew that it would be of use to you one day. I don't think she thought it would ever be in a situation such as this, but ... well ... she was always a far sighted woman and knew a lot more than anyone could ever truly ken. But, it's yours now and well ... I think you'll understand once you see it.'

I reach out, pulling at the cloth, pieces falling away the more I tease at it, as more and more of the age worn rags peel off and fall away the object within slowly comes into view. The hand wrought leather and cotton strapping puzzling me for a moment before I finally take stock of what is sat in front of me, memories flooding my mind.

'I remember this, I know a tale of my father making it for mother before I was born. She used to carry me in it. There was a small sheath in the bottom where she would stow her holdout weapon. I never truly thought on why when I was a boy, but, now ... well ...'

'Aye lad, she carried you everywhere she went, when she dropped this off she had the wife and make a few alterations to it.'

I nod, lost in memory as I run my fingers over the treasure of my childhood. A thought spears my mind as I look up at Garth.

'Why the alterations and ... why now?'

Garth smiles as he rises, a soft chuckle leaving him as he folds the cloth back across the carrier before taking it past me and to his work bench.

'The second, you already know the answer to and is all too obvious, Arianwen. The first, well, that's a story for another time, although, I dare to say you'll come to know in time. After all, it's a long way from here to there especially with a family at your side my boy.'

# 22

## Preparation

## ARIANWEN

**I slam the sixth draw closed a little harder than is needed** after not discovering what I am so desperately seeking. I have been in my family home alone for just over an hour, a rarity I have been making the most of. I have packed four bundles of necessities for babies impending arrival and some much needed items for Albion and I. Albion's note left little room for manoeuvre, and all I am packing falls well within what my love has said we will need, but there is one luxury I will not leave without. It is small, so it will not impact on trying to travel light, but it is a memory I do not want my mind to let slip by as time proceeds.

I place my hand in the seventh draw, reaching for the back, pushing past items long forgotten, my fingers searching for the bevelled edges of the ancient glassed frame, when finally, the tip of one finger makes contact with a cold smooth surface. I gently reach, sliding three fingers over the edge, pulling it carefully towards the front of the draw and into sight, the memory of that moment instantly brings tears to my eyes.

It is not as if I have not seen this exact moment in a much larger image that adorns the wall of our lounging area every day I pass it. It is the fact that this small photo of my entire family, taken when I was in early teen years, will be the only physical item I will have to remind me of the family I must leave, the family I will have to sit down soon and explain my departure to, a family I may place in danger even with my disappearance, a family I will have to beg to let me leave and to keep it a secret.

I turn and place the small picture frame onto the square of paper placed across the dining table and wrap it carefully, returning to my bedroom to place it securely into one of my travel pouches. Just as I am closing up the bag, I hear the front door open and scurry to place all of my bags under my bed, turning around just in time to see my parents walk into the kitchen with bundles of food under each arm as I head out to join them.

'I feel like I haven't seen you in days my dear girl.'

My father's warm embrace makes me miss him already. I know they will both be strong for me, but now that I am becoming a mother myself, I can understand their impending heartbreak of me having to leave our world behind, most likely to never be seen again. That last conversation will surely claim a piece of my heart.

My mother hugs me next and as much as I want to squeeze her tight, I keep it light, not wanting her to be able to feel my small baby bump that is becoming more prominent by the day. She pulls back, hands on my shoulders and stares into my eyes. She gives me a soft smile which says so much more than words. It says I am here for you, I understand and it is all going to be okay. It is a look I am sure to give my own child one day. If she suspects anything, she does not let it show, which is fine as I am sure when I do have to say goodbye, there will be plenty she will voice then.

My sisters soon walk in, and the joyous noise of my family makes all the stress and fear just float away, even if just for a small moment in time. After all helping to prepare items for tonight's dinner, while it is cooking, I make my way out into the garden and wander down one of the meandering paths until I reach the herb gardens. Travelling through the unknown and to a world that is not my own, I want to be prepared for any strange ailment that may come upon us.

I walk a few more steps until I am at the medicinal herbs, then carefully select and pick the leaves I may possibly need, ready to dry when I reach Albion's home. The right combinations can be used to cure anything that my powers may not be able to. I grab a large amount of each important herb and place them carefully into the pockets of my cloak, when I suddenly feel a prickling feeling at the top of my scalp, much the same as when one of the Devil's minions is nearby.

I swirl around quickly, ready to defend myself against what must be a powerful intruder, who has such extraordinary magic. They have breached the walls of Eden and Heaven itself. I turn and turn in circles, searching for any sign of the enemy, but my eyes land upon nothing. But, the prickly feeling only intensifies while I can only scent my own kin nearby.

I hear a group of girls giggling just beyond the herb gardens and as their laughter becomes louder so does the feeling of dread within me. I can sense that they are only my kin, but this horrible feeling will not leave. I make sure all of my senses are on high alert, ready to not only defend myself, but my fellow kin as well.

I search with my sight, my smell, all of my senses, but I cannot detect the Evil that is hiding. The girls finally come into view and smile as they see me, my panic concealed under my sweet offering of a smile, but when I notice one of them is Mayloree, my heart stops for just a moment.

She stares at me with a practiced smile, but it is what I see behind her eyes that has me ready to defend our world. Her eyes are swirling with an unknown colour, something that is not seen here in Eden, but something I have seen before in the village of the damned. I hold my breath, waiting for her to surprise me with an action or words, anything she could possibly hurl at me, but nothing comes. She continues that false smile and proceeds to follow the other two girls through the garden and then away from sight.

Did I imagine what I just saw? Is the stress and panic of my soon departure playing tricks on my own senses? I need to stay clear of that girl. If I did indeed see the strange colour in her eyes, it is alarming. Has Evil not only penetrated the Garden's walls, but also affected one of our own kin? If I go after her now it could spell trouble and as much as I am worried that some type of fiendish entity has possibly contaminated Mayloree's being and that fellow kin may be a risk, I need to protect my little secret first.

I need to go, I need to clear my head and make sure I am ready for anything, even to be surprised by one of my own kin. Even though the unsettling feeling has now passed, I am left with a horrible sense of unease. Albion and I need to be prepared immediately because something does not feel right.

As I am making my way back home, I receive a calling. I have no time to drop off my pockets full of herbs so I head directly towards the Gatekeepers and the forest beyond. The call is becoming urgent so I quicken my pace, still mindful of all that surrounds me, making sure Evil is not lurking too close.

I carefully enter the village edge, sliding along the walls of old broken down buildings, moving between the fallen timber of what used to be houses, stepping carefully on the pieces of debris strewed across the muddy ground. As I sense the position of the soul that is calling for my help, I become all too aware of another being nearby.

I can feel something strange, as if some sort of force is trying to mask what that true being is. I cannot tell if it is another soul, maybe someone clinging to their partner, not wanting to let them fly free. It is nearby in the physical sense, I just cannot determine what it is. A piercing scream shatters the silence as the soul retches out its pain. I know something is not right, but I still need to reach the soul with the hope of sending them safely to their maker.

Just before I reach the building where the soul is calling from, I scent a slight smell in the air, it tugs at my mind. I know I have scent it before, images fill my head as a memory tells me where. I can all but feel the heat of Lucifer's fires as that odour continues to taint the air. I slowly step through a low lying window at the building next to where the soul is and crawl across the old wooden floor towards a door that will face the building I need to reach. As I look through the crack near the doors hinges, I see the soul, lying in the doorway of the other building, one arm supporting himself, head bowed down low. Then I see the other being standing in the street and know that foulness is indeed at play.

It is a woman, quite tall, with luscious curves, all in tight black clothing, long raven hair flowing wildly over her shoulders. She must be a powerful Demonette if she is can still conceal her true vicious self from me. Even though I am looking directly at her and can see she is one of the Devil's own, my senses can still only pick up a natural being with a slight burnt acidic smell. If she is so good at concealing her Evil within, she is an extremely dangerous woman.

Baby turns so hard that I cannot help the slight gasp that leaves my lips. The Demonette turns her head, thankfully in the opposite direction, but I know she can now feel that I am near. The fiendish smile that grows upon her face is disturbing.

'I can feel you nearby my dear Angel. I'm mildly pleased with you. To know that Evil is so close, lurking in the shadows as your kind likes to think, yet your call to duty is too strong to ignore; so noble. Hmm, apple blossom, I hoped it would be you that heard this call ... *Arianwen,* no use hiding dear, I know just how close you are.'

I place a hand over my mouth to ensure no other noises escape as the shock of my name leaving her lips has my mind in a spin. How does she know who I am? She has obviously baited me here knowing I would show, but what are her intentions now I am here? I begin to shut down my body in hopes of hiding my whereabouts from this Evil temptress who somehow knows exactly what Reclaimer would be here at this moment. My temperature has dropped and my heart rate has slowed, as I take one long breath and hold onto only the oxygen that baby and I will need for the immediate moments.

'Arianwen that is you isn't it, or is there another blue blooded whore with your scent wandering around? Oh yes I remember you, I remember you well, your scent, your name ... I heard your pet Hunter calling it from his nightmares, night, after night; after night, after night. Quite a pathetic sound actually, wailing for a weakling that had no hope of saving him. See, you never came, you never rescued him from his prison cell and own personal Hell. It broke him. Left him quite malleable in the end, a fitting lump of clay for my master and I to tease and mould. But, you see, I can sense your power, that raw well spring you keep so closely hidden inside. I always wondered what it took to trick one such as the great Albion.

'A once powerful and commanding Demon, one of Hell's best, into falling in love with you. You know your power won't save you and ... ah, what do we have here? I can hear another heartbeat. Well, well, well, the bewitching Angel and her Demon lover have conceived a child, oh how deliciously perverted. I always thought it impossible for our kinds to conceive, and yet there it is, tucked neatly away inside your quivering quim, so very interesting, very interesting indeed. You must be more powerful than I first gave you credit, most certainly so, if you were able to make the impossible, possible. No wonder Lucifer is so desperate to have you out of the picture.'

I can feel her strength seeping all around her, looking, searching for my whereabouts. Desperation seeping from her every pore. I have never encountered a Demon as powerful as this before. She even surpasses the powerful presence of the Dolophonos, who legends says are almost on par with the Devil himself. I will not let my fear take over. I must remain completely focused if I am to survive this and leave her presence undetected.

'I suggest for your safety and the safety of your spawn, you walk away, turn around now and I'll let you leave. After all, we wouldn't want Albion to worry over you and the little bundle of impossi-bility that you're carrying now would we? Go and hide while you can little Angel, you won't have long to hide once Lucifer discovers your tiny secret. I promise it will end badly, and once I have permission, and I know I will get it, I will ensure that the only seed Albion ever sires will be mine, I promise you. Then again, maybe I won't wait for permission. Maybe I'll just kill you now ... because I could, *if*, I wanted to.'

I will not be baited. I am smarter than that. Her whole demeanour starts to change. She starts to pace in frustration and anger, from controlled to viciously frothing at the mouth within seconds. She spins and turns, perilously trying to find me as her sharp nails grow in size, ready to slice and attack at any moment.

'You're lucky really, lucky that your gifts can hide you or you'd be *dead* by now, so why not come out? If you come out now, I promise to make it quick. I won't even tell Albion all of what happened, you wouldn't want me to upset him after all, would you? *Where are you? Where are you, you stupid, fucking, whore?'*

Her aura flares, her malicious anger at not being able to detect me making it glow all the brighter. I watch, helpless as she starts to exert her rage upon the poor soul in need still slumped in the door way. She grabs at the young man, pulling chunks of flesh from his bones as he screams in pain, trying to wither away from her assault. She pulls on his hair and drags him out into the street where she was pacing.

'You truly are a lucky little Angel, lucky that I can't get my hands on you or you'd be lost to all eternity just like this poor *soul.'*

She then proceeds to grip his neck with both hands, and even though I know exactly what she is about to do, I am helpless to save the soul I can see before me, for I would risk not only myself, but the most precious thing I hold dear to my heart. My baby. And it is with thoughts of baby and Albion that I look away the moment this repulsive piece of Evil rips the head off the innocent soul that was destined to walk into God's arms.

'Where, are your great powers now *Arianwen?* You useless, pathetic, snivelling piece of Angelic filth! You couldn't even save the soul you came here for, and you expect to keep that squirming half breed inside of you safe. You're nothing, nothing do you hear me? Nothing. Know that no matter what Albion promises you, he will come to me. He wants me! We will be together, and I'll feast on the soul of your child as he fills me with his seed. Lucifer has ordained us both and will ensure I get what I want. Albion, he'll be the sire of my spawn and he'll take me as his queen. Do you hear me? He is mine you mewling little cunt, mine!'

Her screams rattle the ground beneath my feet as she turns and takes out her anger on the rest of the soul's body before her, viciously tearing at his flesh and bones. While she does this, she has let down her guard, too consumed by rage to even realise I am still nearby. I use her focus on the innocent soul to slowly slide away, slithering through the back window and then to the building behind that, then to the tent behind that, until I am at the edges of the village.

I do not waste time as I run through the dead forest, desperate to reach the safety of Albion's stone hideaway. I wish I could quicken my steps by opening my wings and taking flight, but that would just make me an obvious beacon for all of darkness to see, so I have to rely on my fast yet careful steps.

I have no idea who that horrific woman was, but her powers were of the extreme. To first be able to mask her Evil self, where all I could sense was a slight smell, is not something I have seen before. Then to be able to hear baby's heartbeat while I was using all of my powers to conceal us both, is astounding and terrifying at the same time. She is not someone I can ever encounter again, because I fear that next time, she will find a way to discover my whereabouts and despite the increased powers and abilities I have gained since baby was conceived, I would still be no match for that woman I just saw.

And to know that Albion was calling for me, even in the state he was in, is just heart breaking. My love was so lost, yet he still knew who I was and that he needed me. Evil may be no match for the love we share, but we still need to leave these worlds very soon, before we are unable to.

# 23

## Panic and Desperation

### ALBION

**Never before, have I felt such sorrow, such primal indecision.** I stand staring out over the clouded world, mist clinging to the trees like sand on wet skin. I cannot help but think that with this new day, Arianwen and I will be closer to the edge and running for our lives with the enemies of both our worlds snatching at our backs with clawed and talon sheathed fingers.

I cast my gaze to the cliff that rises sharply to the east, the shattered buildings at its feet hiding our home from even the most prying of eyes. Will my darling Angel be safe within those hand cut walls, or like every other time we have come to a point where we could see light at the end of this never ending tunnel? Will another hand come from the sky and tear us asunder, be it the *'flaming sword'* of Michael or Lucifer's shadowed killers? I can only keep hope alive in my heart that this time, this chance we are now taking, is the one we see through to the end and can claim our freedom from this oppressive realm and find solace in each other, for whatever shall remain of our lives.

The chill of dawn eats at my backside and legs as I sink into the wet earth beneath me. The smell of sap and the floral bouquet of my Angels world flirts with my senses. If it was not for the ever present pall of death and the threat both my world and Arianwen's poses to my Angel and child, I would actually find the scene tranquil. My mind heaves with the tumult hurtling through it, the irrepressible cacophony of doubt and anger that is piling on, one thought after another, dousing me with every shattered memory that has long sat imprinted on my nightmares.

The mists below dance and swirl as my mind's eye turns inwards, one thought tearing at my mind, screaming to rise free, but it will not. The roots sink too deep, lodged too solidly in the quagmire of all that I have become, all that I was, and the possibilities of what I could be. I screw my eyes shut willing the thought to the surface, my head throbbing, scalp burning as I feel pressure rise. Lancing lines of light course across my eyes, dragging pain and discourse with them. Images flash through me, dazzling, taunting, the faces of my mother and father, the sickly scents of sweat and blood mingling with the subtle odour of potpourri above the hearth.

The lilting singsong voice of my mother washes over me as the memories sink their claws into my mind. I feel tears well as I sink deeper into the warmth and love that I used to know.

*'Abara my love, we need to go, we need to leave. Lucifer knows, I don't know how, but he does.'*

I watched my mother turn, her hair shimmering in the heated air around us all. Sweat bathed her features, her glittering eyes drawing my own as she turned to face me, sinking into a soft crouch.

*'We'll go tonight, we have to move quickly. The window will not remain open for very long and we need to depart from here before the end of the moons highest cycle. We have to ensure that everything is as it should be. We can't come back to this plane once we are on the other side. Albion, you know I love you, you know your mother loves you, this world we are seeking, it's far from any prying eye or vengeful hand, it's a place where you can be safe, once we have found a way there, we'll all go together.'*

My father turned to my mother, a sad smile on his lips as he took her hand and pressed it to his cheek ever so softly.

*'There's nothing in this world or any other that I wouldn't do to keep you and our child safe Amunet, you know that.'*

He turned slightly and kissed the ball of my mother's hand

before looking down at me, worry beginning to eat at me as I saw the desperate sorrow and fear he was trying to hide. Mother turned her eyes away from both of us for a moment, my father's tenderness making them well with tears as she smoothed my sweat damped hair from my forehead.

*'Oh Albion, my sweet boy, I need you to know that your father and I, we're doing this for you. I hope one day you can find a way to forgive us.'*

I remember puzzlement furrowing my little brow as I tried to speak, to beg her to tell me what she meant, what anything I saw meant and yet ... even now ... with the passage of years and the will of a battle tested man, in the face of my mother, with the all knowing eyes only a mother could ever possess; ones that seemed to be able to peel apart my soul and turn me inside out with nary an effort, it all still is unclear.

*'Amunet, my love, it's time. Garth will take care of Albion until we return. Do you have your cloak?'*

I watched my mother nod as she lifted it from the bed. Casting over her shoulders before she pulled it tight to her, the discoloured fabric and crystal lining making my eyes itch, I knew my father made it for her, but even now I still do not fully understand why I always had that reaction to seeing it.

*'Albion, come boy, your mother and I are going to be away for a little while. We're taking you to stay with Garth and Glynnis until we return.'*

I remember clearly the look of love and panic in my father's eyes at that very moment; it is was look that will always sit clear in my mind for as long as I am alive. The chill breeze snaps me from my stupor as I feel my eyes burn with unshed tears.

I barely remember the time before my parent's death, and yet, here I sit with the memory fresh in my mind and the wraiths of my mother and father guiding me to the end that I so desperately seek. I know I need to dive deeper into my own mind, to try and drag free the hidden snippets and captured moments that my parents never thought I would see, the fragile fragments of time locked within my mind, locked deeper than even the roots of my own soul. I need to know what my parents were seeking, what had taken them to that edge of desperation where they were willing to sacrifice their own lives to ensure I had a way to exist free of the prison that became my home as well as my gaol.

The only other burning question that sits at the fore front of my mind is … the one that casts up more questions than I fear I will ever find answers for. All I now know, all I need to know … is that there is a way free of this cursed place, I just need to find it. My heart is hammering in my ears, panic and anger flooding me in equal measure. My parents knew something was coming, whatever it was or is I know not, but one thing is clear … I need to get home to my Angel, to the woman I love and then … from there … leave this cursed land and never look back, no matter what comes our way.

✦ ✦ ✦

The sound of my own heart beat resounds in my head as I sit and wait, the edge of the mattress beneath me digging into the backs of my knees, waiting with a growing maelstrom of panic and worry searing my stomach. The tension that courses through me is sending lancing lines of pain along my spine. Even now as I rest my head in my hands, I feel them scurrying along my back like vermin, unseen teeth gnawing away at my flesh.

Where is she? Never before has my Angel been this late for any of our pre wrought rendezvous. I am starting to rise and stride across the room towards my waiting armour and weaponry, when that familiar scent washes away everything that was slowly turning my mind to ash.

'Arianwen!'

I sprint forwards, snatching her off the floor and clutching her tight to my chest, my nose and chin buried deeply in her hair. The heady scent of my woman drawing tears to my eyes as I breathe in her calming balm.

'I was so worried my love, what kept you?'

She clutches at my shoulders, pulling me tight to her as I feel her shake in my grasp. The boiling cauldron in my gut rises once more, searing through any anger I had, replacing it with a cold unyielding worry and need, a need to see my love safe and our child to a home as far from God's eye and Lucifer's reach as I can make it. I softly pry myself from Arianwen's grip, casting my eyes down upon hers as she stares up at me, the lustrous violet stained with her tears. She opens her mouth to speak, and as she does, it hits me. The acrid stink, the throbbing vile taint that comes from only one source, Lilith. It drips from her like water soaking the air, squatting on my tongue like a toad. I heave slightly, her face turning puzzled as she feels the movement roll through me.

'Who's touched you? You reek of the scent of death and decay.'

Arianwen's eyes smoulder slightly at the tone in my voice, her mouth turning into a defiant line of anger as she tries to shrug from my grip.

'No one has touched me, no one since we were last together. I ... I can't believe you could ever think so little of me as to feel the need to ask that of me.'

I tighten my grasp, my tone hardening as she glares at me.

'Arianwen, I need you to think. Who has been near you today? There had to be someone ... something that didn't seem right, that sat so ill in your heart and mind that you couldn't help but see it.'

I watch at the soft twinkle in her eyes fades as she delves into her minds depths, brow furrowing deeper than I have ever seen it as she reaches forwards and clutches at my armour covered chest. I cannot help but feel my heart beat hasten, the scent of her filling me, twisting my mind away from the turmoil and urgency and sending me head long into lust and need as she leans against me.

'There was ... there was something. I didn't think it was anything to be concerned with, but, now that I think back on what I saw ... my flippancy with it all, it wasn't normal Albion.'

I run my fingers through her hair, the tactile sensation running through me like fire as I bury my face into the satin locks slipping through my fingers. I draw her as tight to me as I can, my mind tumbling as I fight the need to take her here and now.

I cannot fathom where this sudden overwhelming flood of lust and need has risen from. I force myself to turn my hips slightly, fighting to keep my loins from ruling my mind as I strain against the thonging of my trousers. My voice is strained as I coax ever more from my sweet Angel.

'What Arianwen, what was it? It doesn't matter how small you may think it is, *nothing* is insignificant now. We can't afford to overlook even the smallest of inconsistencies. Lucifer and my former kin are beyond devious.'

I feel her breath on my neck as she looks up at me, her lips grazing my skin as she softly replies, the silence in the room barely ruffled as I fight to hear her.

'Mayloree, her eyes Albion, they ... they were not her own. They held the glass of malice and madness. I felt the seal of fear and anger oozing from her every pore and yet ... those eyes, her eyes, they were everything she's not.'

The lust and wanton hunger vanishes in an instant, my heart freezing in my chest as I turn my eyes to my woman's.

'What do you mean? What did you see when you looked at her?'

She pulls away from me slightly, her hands pressing against my chest. I let my grip relax slightly, taking my queue when it pushes at me, even if it was overly obvious. Arianwen softens, her aura levelling out, the colours blending again into the vibrant swirl I am so used to seeing on the woman I love, instead of the fractured, spike laden coffin that was dogging her moments before.

'They were filled with a twisted whirlpool of malice and insanity. I could feel it chipping at my mind even in the fleeting moments we held each other's gaze, her mind was shattered Albion. The sweet innocent Angel I had grown with is gone, what is in her now has seen to that, it consumed her completely. She walks and talks like the Mayloree I once knew, but the thing that wears her form now, it is Evil Albion, and it taunted me with it.'

'No Ari, no. I don't think she is gone. No Demon can mimic an Angel completely, there are always cues and leads to the dead soul within. Even my former brother Alp cannot completely mimic one of your kin, and he is a shape shifter. I think my love, what you saw was the penitent's gaze, there are only a hand full of my former kin that can do it, myself, Lucifer, Alp and ...'

I stop watching her, waiting for her to take the lead I am holding out and fill in the gap that I dearly wish wasn't there.

'No, no I will *not* say her name. Never will I give that whores name the privilege of passing across my lips, *no.* Poor Mayloree, she was such a sweet girl, a little lost and smitten gazed, but sweet no matter what happened to cross her path.'

Her shoulders shake, soul drenching tears filling her body at the thought of what has become of the innocent giver of love and light she once knew, and for once in my life I find myself feeling the same sorrow. Innocence so wantonly corrupted by that guttural whore to hasten her own sycophantic agenda; a malevolent psychopath that was even now stalking my shadows edge. Anger begins to boil within my heart tempering my sorrow, I may now walk a line between Heaven and Hell, a twisted wind battered tightrope that at any moment could be wrested from beneath me, vanishing in an instant to send me tumbling into a void so filled with emptiness that I could find myself falling for eternity. But, despite that constant threat, the chaos and danger that vicious Evil soul represented to everything I hold dear, has only steeled my resolve.

I cast my eyes down to the woman in my arms and the blossoming seed of life she has growing inside her. No, nothing will keep me from reaching the other side of that rope, not Lucifer, not Lilith, not even God and his Legions of war dogs will stop me. I would slaughter them all for her, no matter the cost to myself.

'Albion ...'

Her voice shatters my thoughts in an instant, every thought of death and destruction vanishing like dust on the wind as I turn my entire focus upon the tear stained face of my Angel.

'That's ... that's not all that kept me from you.'

My grip tightens on her arms making her flinch. I let go in an instant, guilt lancing me as I pull her closer to me guiding us both to the bed. The soft furs whisper as I pull my woman onto my lap and hold her as close as I dare to.

'What else is there, you need to tell me Arianwen? I need to know.'

'It ... there was a Demonette, a tall willow thin woman, her aura soaked the world around her, but, it was clouded, distorted and hard to read. She was. I had a calling, I went to find the soul before I came to you, and, there she was, this thing. She was stood over the soul like a hyena around a wounded calf, and she was taunting me with it. Even as I lay hidden with my cloak smothering ever last ounce of my light she still sensed me near to her. She knew my name, she knew your name ... she knows about our baby. Albion, she knows about our baby. How ... how could she know? She said that Lucifer has promised you to her, said that you will be the father of her spawn and take her as your Queen. Albion I ... I was terrified of her. She held such darkness inside that it made me sick just to be as close as I was. Who was she?'

The name sticks in my throat, my need to warn her of Lilith all too consuming and yet, try as I might I can barely think upon that name let alone speak of it with the woman I love. To know she came that close to that vile harlot turns my soul inside out. Anger scalded by fear fills my chest as I bite down on my own childish woes and take one last lingering breath before forcing that name past lips.

'It was Lilith, she's the only thing that fits what you described. When I was lost to you, Lucifer promised me to Lilith. He wants to groom me to be his successor and wants me to replace him as the leader of Hell one day with that whore as my Queen. If you sense her again, if you even think she is near you ... run ... get away as fast as you can, as strong as you are, you are no match for her, she is the *only* female Knight of Hell, and there isn't a single soul in the pit that doesn't fear her. I have stood toe to toe with her in sparing combat and she's beyond formidable. If it wasn't for my father's blood in my veins, had I been a lesser man, I doubt I would have bested her. So please my love, if you feel her presence in any way, I want you to run, you did it then and I want you to do it again.'

She locks eyes with me once more, anger roaring through her as she glares at me, forcing herself from my embrace. Even in her current state, dirt smeared and weary, I can see the power and anger that rolls through my Angel and ... I cannot help but smile. Her violet orbs flare with anger as she watches my lips curl.

'*You find it funny Albion?* I'll not run from anyone or anything, I'm not *helpless.*'

I shake my head as I stare at her, her chest heaving as she shimmers with anger and fear.

'No, I don't find it funny my love, and I know you're not helpless. I know that you're hiding your true strength from everyone and that against the rank and file Hunters and Demons you are more than a match, but against someone as powerful as Lilith you may as well show up naked and hand her the knife to plunge through your heart. As painful as this is for me to say to you, you are no more a threat to her than you would be Lucifer. She is a Knight of Hell and the handmaiden's mother. She's the one who gave birth to the first of them and has led them through every conflict and war since God and Michael first cast Lucifer from Eden. I love you Arianwen, and would never doubt your abilities or strength, but against Lilith ...'

I let my words trail off, her face telling me all I need to know. I push myself upright and move towards her, my arms finding their way around her waist as she moulds herself against me.

'I'm scared for our child Albion. If she knows, then Lucifer will surely know. It'll find its way back to Michael and Gabriel, to my parents ... Michael will surely punish them in my stead Albion, how can I let that happen?'

'You can't and I won't. I promise you Arianwen, nothing will ever harm your mother or father, nor your sisters, I won't allow it. I would die before I allowed that to come to pass, but, you know what we have to do.'

She nods her head as I lean down, resting my chin gently on the top of her head.

'I know. We need to leave, and soon, I just wish we weren't leaving them behind.'

'It'll be hard enough with the two of us avoiding detection and finding our way free from here, the more we have with us ...'

I feel more than hear her sigh as she turns her back to me, my arms still locked gently around her waist as I feel her soft weight sink into me.

'I know. Can I at least leave them something, something to warn them of what could come to pass?'

I feel my jaw tighten, the next words that leave my lips are some of the hardest I have ever had to say to the woman in my arms, but say them I must.

'No, we can't let anything tie our disappearance to them, no note, not a soft whispered goodbye, nothing. To them, to Michael and Gabriel, to Lucifer and everyone in between, we must simply vanish. Nothing can be left behind that would give them any clue as to where we have gone.'

Her eyes brim with tears as she nods, turning from me and twisting free of my grasp. The silence that falls is deafening as I watch her move towards the rock pool at the far side of our home.

'One last thing Albion, before I take a bath ...'

I cannot help but feel my length harden as I watch her slowly disrobe, the satin material slipping from her like water over stone. I choke out a reply over the lump that is threatening to choke me. She smiles slightly at my reply as she casts a smoke filled gaze at me from over her shoulder.

'How long do we have left before we must leave?'

'Three days at the most.'

Nothing else could have sealed the hurt in her heart more than what I had just said, all playfulness leaving her as she slips beneath the water and drops from my sight. There comes a point when I look back at who I was before Arianwen brought me back from the darkness. I wonder if, through it all, it would have not been kinder on her for me to have simply pretended to never have returned at all, to leave her with the memories of who I was, rather than what I am now. Surely it would have been a kinder fate than what I am leading her to now. Fate has handed us war, but, our union, our love, is costing her, her entire world. Mine was stolen from me when I was naught but a boy, but Arianwen, my loving Angel; I am asking her to leave the only life and world she has ever known with family still left to love her.

It would have been kinder, better than what we are both now facing, would it not?

# 24

## The Greatest Pain

## ARIANWEN

**The time has come, that time is now. We need to leave within a** day, maybe two, and my heart is breaking, breaking as I walk back into my own world, ready to say goodbye to all I have known, to my family and a world I may never return to. This has been my safe haven for eternity and now it will only exist in my memories and in the stories I will one day tell my child.

I need to get to the Bookkeeper immediately. If we are to leave so soon, we are going to need all the help we can get. I know it is best to wait for the right position of the moon, for when the dark ones are at their weakest, but we may not have that luxury. I try not to run, despite my body feeling as though it wants to sprint. I do not want to let any of my kin witness me behaving erratically. When I do not return immediately, I need people to think I am just away at a difficult Reclaim so a search party is not sent out too soon after my departure. We need to gain as much precious ground as we can before either of our worlds come nipping at our heels.

I steady my pace along the winding paths, taking a moment to appreciate the abundant beauty of the Garden of Eden. The smell of the flourishing greenery intoxicating my senses as I commit everything I see, smell and feel to memory, hoping to give it all justice in the tales I will one day recite from another world.

My mind is ripped from this beauty as I suddenly feel a set of eyes watching me. I dare not turn my head, so I continue my even footing as I tune all of my gifts into sensing exactly who it is that is following me. It is not Michael or Gabriel coming to find me, I can feel their beings in the great hall. I struggle to sense exactly who it is, yet, I somehow feel it is one of my own kin. I continue following the path while using all of my gifts to try and uncover who it is, an uneasy feeling starts washing over me when I cannot pin point this being.

I decide to curve around and walk towards a place in the garden that is always busy, not wanting to face my unknown stalker alone. I walk towards the small fire pits, where some of our grand feasts are prepared, knowing that, even when a large celebration is not taking place, there will still be an abundance of families gathering to cook their own meals.

As I get closer, the presence following me becomes stronger, closer, gaining speed as its invisible oppression bears down upon me. I will not turn or even try to face it, I cannot risk causing a scene. I have put too many young ones in harm's way. I silently pray that this malevolence thinks as I do as I continue on my way, pretending to be unaware, heading towards the flow of noise and laughter that is echoing loudly all around me. There are families at every table, faces filled with joy and laughter, their grills and cookers piled high with slowly roasted meats. As I move closer I hear their voices, the deep tones of the men as they stand talking, the musical ring of ladies laughing, all of it topped by the high throated squeals of their children as they run around chasing each other. It surrounds me, the warmth of it all comforting in its normality. But, it is all quickly shattered for me as I step towards one of the ladies to say a hello and still feel the sense of someone close behind me.

I turn to talk to another of my kin and carefully look out the corner of my eye, trying to sight the person causing such unease in my being, but there is no one there, no one close to me. Knowing I need to be seen before I leave, I make my way around different groups, talking to as many as I can, all the while waiting for this uneasy feeling to leave me, or for its cause to make itself known.

A family invites me to sit at their table and share the meal they have so lovingly prepared. I know that every second of my time is precious, but with the feeling of eyes still watching my every move, walking away from here on my own would not be a wise choice. I cannot stomach much so I nibble and spend the time talking. But, too much time is wasting, I need to leave soon, I need to get to the Bookkeeper as soon as I possibly can.

I rise and say my thanks, giving hugs to the children and a chaste cheek kiss to my host and hostess before I finish saying my goodbyes to the others at the table. I go to leave, but have a strong feeling that the eyes watching me are fast approaching. Knowing that I am in sight of many people here, I decide to turn around to face the person causing such unrest to my soul.

I am surprised to find four young women I know walking my way with friendly faces, two of which are Gabriel's chosen girls, yet the horrible feeling in the pit of my stomach does not ease. Could one of my own kin be causing such a feeling? Could what I saw previously in Mayloree's eyes be causing this feeling? They all say hello and begin a conversation. Nothing seems out of the ordinary as they talk about their day of baking. Even Mayloree, who the last time I saw was acting so strange, which I believed was possibly because she could sense baby, is paying my stomach no such attention. She is as comfortable as the other charming girls, talking away with glee and not once looking towards my small, barely there bump.

I still do not want to be so near to her, especially with this odd feeling still causing a knot in my chest. I go to say goodbye, with the excuse that my family is waiting for me, when Mayloree pushes a wicker basket towards me.

'Arianwen, would you please try one of the muffins I baked today? I tried a new recipe and with you being such a great baker, I would love to know what you think of the taste.'

She smiles brightly at me, as do all the other girls. I feel as if I cannot refuse or come up with a reasonable excuse not to try one, and looking into her eyes shows no sign of the sinister swirling that was there at our last encounter, so I reach in and grab one that is sitting on the white linen lining. But, I will not eat it, not trusting Mayloree completely.

'It smells delicious and I can smell the fresh peaches you've used. I'll take it with me and share some with my sisters when I get home.'

'Would you mind trying a bite now? I'm not sure if I added too many peaches, and I'd love to get the recipe just right, so I can make some large batches of them for my family when the sun rises.'

Her smile is so genuine, her eyes so bright and hopeful, and with all the girls staring at me like every word I say really matters to them, I feel as if it would be out of character for me to refuse, and when I leave, I do not need any of these girls questioned and saying I was not acting myself. I quickly use all of my senses to ensure this muffin is not laced with anything that could be harmful. It seems perfectly fine, and when I bring it closer to my mouth, the only strong smell I can pick up is the lovely fresh peaches that are baked inside. I do not feel any urgent warnings swelling up inside of me, telling me to not taste it, and my gifts and abilities have not let me down so far.

Deciding I need to get this over with quickly so I can leave, I smile and take a bite. The peach taste is quite overwhelming and surprisingly completely overshadows the raspberries and walnuts that I can sense, but for some reason, not taste, which is strange. I swallow and with a smile, I give her my verdict.

'Your baking is as lovely as always Mayloree, but maybe use slightly less peaches so the raspberries and walnuts can also shine through. But, you have created a wonderful combination.'

She smiles shyly and nods thank you. As I say a goodbye and turn to leave, I realise her muffin has left an odd aftertaste in my mouth. I grab a glass of water from a table and take a few quick sips before placing the glass down and making my way from this gathering area and head towards home. I barely take three steps before a strange feeling washes through my skull. I stop, take a deep breath and the feeling passes.

Even though I realise, the feeling of being watched has now passed, I will not take any chances and decide to leave visiting the Bookkeeper until after dark, not wanting to draw her into any more of my complications. I take a few more steps, and the strange feeling in my head returns, this time causing my eye lids to suddenly feel heavy. I know I have had a busy day, but this feeling is more than simple tiredness.

Not liking this sudden sensation, I hasten my steps and head towards home, believing that I may need to lie down very soon. Suddenly the paths before me start to blur, making it difficult to find the one that leads to my house. I take deep breaths and blink my eyes, hoping to find the right path, feeling worried for baby, needing the safety of my home immediately.

I make my way down a path, but soon discover it is the wrong one, but when I turn to choose another path, none look familiar and panic suddenly starts to wind itself through my thoughts. Something not quite right is happening, but I feel a little too confused to figure out exactly what it is. Visions of Mayloree's smiling eyes play through my mind, yet her eyes do not quite look like hers. Could a sorcerer's spell been placed on her? I stumble slightly and reach a hand to my stomach, desperately wanting to protect baby in case I fall. I hear a noise in the distance. I think it is my name, feeling relived that someone may be able to help me make it to the safety of my home.

I walk, not knowing where I am going, only concentrating and the voice I hear. After a few more steps the voice is clearer. It is Albion's voice I hear and he is calling my *name*. He must know something is wrong, he must sense Evil is at play, if he has made his way through the gates of Eden to reach me. I walk faster, needing him desperately, only to hear a splash and realise that I have taken a step into the bathing lake.

I spin around, looking for my love, but can only see the forest trees surrounding this body of water. No one is here but me. Where is Albion? Where was his voice coming from? I struggle to catch my breath as my body begins to feel heavier, and I begin to sway. I am in disbelief that darkness has somehow made its way into my world, under the noses of my kin, and caught me completely off my guard and somehow found a way to weaken my defences. How could that be?

My eyes land on a blurry figure in the centre of the lake and my mind instantly believes that it is Albion, even though my soul is screaming that it is not.

*'Albion, I need your help.'*

I reach my arms out, but the figure remains still. I start to move through the water, wanting to reach what could be him, even though part of me is willing my being to turn away. As I get closer, my mind hoping the figure will come into sharper focus, but it remains blurry. If it is Albion, he could also be in trouble. I move my heavy body as quickly as I can, deeper into the dark water. Just as the water level laps at my shoulders, the vision of the figure suddenly sharpens and all of my senses scream to flee.

I recognise the figure, the vile Demonette who scorned me and butchered the poor soul in front of me. The one Albion scented on me, I know its name, as much as I wish I did not.

Lilith.

It is the powerful female Knight Lilith. I feel my head spinning, the world around me blurring. I can see her standing there, her mouth calling my name, and yet the sound coming from her lips is Albion's voice. The vicious tilt of her smile, the wicked shine in her eyes and her guttural, poisonous laugh. All of it drips with glee, as she revels in the fact that she has me right where she wants me, at her mercy. I can feel her immense power floating through the air, crackling like electricity around me. She is the spider and I walked straight into her web.

I turn away from her, not believing how she could have possibly gotten past the walls of Eden, when suddenly memories hit me. Albion explaining this Lilith's powers are almost equal to Satan himself, the strange swirling through Mayloree's eyes that I now realise must have been a possession of a spell by Lilith if not the Demonette herself, the strange aftertaste left in my mount after barely a bit of Mayloree's muffin. Oh my Lord, this vile dark bitch must have somehow made contact with Mayloree at the edges of Eden, played on such a sweet soul, twisted her to her will under a sorcerer's spell and gained entry to this world under the cover of an innocent girls soul.

*No, no, no. She is in our world. Evil is in our world.* I can feel the desperate trouble I am in, I am facing certain death. *Oh God no, baby, baby, baby.* The need to flee from her presence immediately is a sickening torture or urgency, but my body remains heavy, and the water is only making the heavy feeling worse.

Suddenly, I feel the water around me ripple and something press sharply into my back. I turn and see Lilith with her hands out, her eyes glazed with malice and rapturous pleasure as black vines slither through the water towards me. I look beneath the surface and see the vine winding around the outside of my body just before I feel it touch my flesh. I scream, but the sound is caught in my throat as the vine suddenly tightens, taking my breath away.

'Oh Arianwen, what have you gotten yourself into, soaked through to the bone and all wrapped up? I'm rather disappointed to be honest, I expected more from my lover's concubine. It wasn't any more of a challenge to get you here, than it was to rip that hairless apes head from its shoulders. Truth be told I was rather looking forward to the fight that I thought you'd offer me. Oh well, que sera sera, I will have to make do with what is. I mean, I can't very well get you to trot back and have that stupid little airhead come visit you with her poisoned peace offering again can I?

'If I can be candid though, it was all too easy to worm my way past your borders, all it took was a few whispered words about being a leader's wife, and helping to wrest Gabriel's affections away from you and that stupid little baker willingly let me possess her. I doubt she even realised I'm a Demon. Who knew God made such intellectually stunted Angels, quite sad really? She still does not know what hit her. If I had known it would be this easy to get to you, I would have destroyed that mongrel spawn you have growing inside of you long before now. I really must talk to my lover about where he sows his seed. He needs to pick his cattle more carefully in future.'

Pain lances through my stomach, my mind bursting white as I reach my hands down desperate to protect baby. I can feel the vines tighten, wrapping around both my wrists dragging me down, the water felling like solid ice encompassing every inch of my body, entombing me in its layered glacier mass. When my head dips below the surface, all my breathing is stolen, but I cannot panic. I know I have to concentrate all of my abilities on saving baby, hoping that I will be able to break free from whatever spell this vile Demonette has cast and the deathly promise it brings.

As I watch tiny bubbles of my air escape to the surface, I concentrate on shutting my body down, sending every ounce of energy I possess, even though it is weakened, towards my unborn child, trying to build a shield around its fragile form. Everything I have ever learned, every gift I was born with, works its way down to my stomach, and just as I feel a wall of protection starting to grow, the vines suddenly tighten, pain sheering through me as I feel my bones begin to break. The tightness is suffocating all the life within its atrocious clutch.

I become frantic under this watered tomb, losing my concentration, opening my mouth to scream for help, to scream for Albion, water rushing into my lungs as I try and rip the vines from my body. I am thrashing under the water with every piece of strength I have, but I can feel that all of my senses and power are unnaturally dulled, numbed by Evil's potion, a darkness that should have never been able to gain entry into my celestial world.

My body suddenly breaks the surface of the water, and I go to scream again, only to have the vicious black vine wrap around my mouth, silencing my cry for help. It pulls me beneath the water's surface, and with no way to hold my mouth closed, water once again rushes in. I need to save baby, I need to find a way to escape this horrendous nightmare. I need to find a way to *fight*. A severe pain slices through my stomach, making me curl in pain, but also fuelling me to fight harder for the life of my child.

I kick, I thrash, I even bite the damn vine, anything to find a release from these underwater shackles. I kick my legs to propel me to the surface, hoping eventually one of my kin will stumble upon the lake and raise the alarm that a Demonette has penetrated our world. Another slicing pain attacks my body, and this time I feel baby move sharply to one side, then still completely.

*No, no, no.* I must get out of this water. I must fight harder. *I will not let Evil take mine and Albion's child away from us.* I scream with such force that I actually push some of the water out of my lungs and watch as it causes a large splash at the surface. I do it again, knowing that such a large splash could also cause a large sound, and my kin may be alerted to something wrong at the lake.

With barely any energy left and the pain increasing in my stomach, I scream one last time, hoping that this will be the time that alerts my fellow kin. Suddenly, the vine disappears from around my entire body and I kick myself to the surface. Gulping for air, I spin around quickly, thinking this may be a ploy to make me rise, with Lilith waiting above to exercise more of her sorcery terror upon me, but she is nowhere to be seen. And there is none of my kin at the water's edge or through the surrounding forest.

I have no energy to scream for help. I try and wade through the water, to get to the edge, but pain cripples my body again, my entire being shuddering in pain, taking me under the body of water again. I push through it, kicking my legs to break free of the water. Once my head is above, I suck in as much air as I can, in case I once again slip below. I paddle slowly towards the edge, trying not to cause my body anymore pain.

My leg touches the muddy bottom, and I use its solid form to propel myself forward until my hands can touch the bottom also. My body is weak, all of my strength used to fight Lilith's witchery, so I can only crawl from the water to the grassy edge. I collapse down, gasping for more oxygen as my hands reach down to feel for baby. There is no movement, only cramping pain as I use one hand to crawl further from the water's edge.

Crippling pain once again strikes my stomach as tears stream down my face, with the realisation that baby is in grave danger, and I do not the strength to barely move. But, I will not lie here and let Evil have its win. I will crawl as far as I have to, to reach help, to find someone who can save my unborn miracle from the curse of darkness.

I feel something warm and thick between my thighs. I look down and see blue. My eyes rise back to where I came and I see a large trail of blood from the water's edge to where I am lying now, and at that moment, my heart stops beating. I throw my head back and open my mouth in a silent scream, as my soul shatters into a billion pieces. All of my gifts, all of my abilities, all of the recent gained strength of Albion and I, was nothing, was not strong enough to fight Evil's intensions.

*This cannot be happening.* We had a plan, we were going to leave our worlds, we were going to a safer place, a safer world, where we could live our life in peace, together. Albion and I and baby. *Oh God. Baby. Baby, baby, baby. No. No. No.* This is not how it was meant to end. No this is not the end, I will not let it be, I will crawl for help, my world is Good and light and forgiving and powerful and healing and, and, and ... *No.* We will watch our child grow, watch our child run beneath the sun, red rosy cheeks, a cherubs smile on its lips, joy and happiness running through its veins. Nothing to fear, nothing to worry about. Happiness, only happiness and love is what our child will feel. *Not this. Not this pain.*

This cannot be real, this has to be a mistake. *All this blood is not real. Why would fate bring us together to create a child, only to threaten to rip it from us? No. I will not let this happen. I will not let this end this way. I turn forward, dragging myself across the ground, fighting through the pain, fighting through the grief and fear, fighting for my child's life.*

I still feel numb, I still feel weak and soon realise, even in the state I am in, Lilith planned this out extremely well. She made *sure* my defences were already down when I entered that lake, which only made it easier for her sorcery to overpower all of my gifts and strengths. Albion and I have been so focused on keeping our secret miracle hidden from the leaders of our worlds, we were not aware that Evil could slip through the backdoor.

I crawl, my nails bleeding as I dig my hands into the soil beneath me, gaining some type of leverage to move myself forward, dragging myself forward like a slug dragging slowly across the ground, still holding hope that I can find help in time. I have no idea how far I have come when my head starts to sway before it hits the ground with a hard thud. My eyes gaze down towards my stomach, and I see a pool of blood surrounding my torso.

I squeeze my eyes shut as tears fall silently down my cheeks when I realise I can no longer sense baby's presence. My world turns dark. I do not bother taking another breath of air, with my heart no longer beating. What is the point in trying to stay alive? My hopes and dreams are fast slipping away. All of our careful loves, all of our careful planning was for what? We did not even make it past our own borders before darkness discovered our little miracle, our tiny creation.

Our baby.

I lie here, shattered, broken, destroyed. My will to live left the moment my beautiful unborn child's essence of life left my body. Why did God allow such a miracle and tremendous love to grow inside of me then allow it to be stripped away so viciously? Where was his protection of his creation? Where was he when I needed him the most?

I hear a whimper and turn my head, slightly opening one eye to look directly into the eyes of one of the Dragon Gatekeepers. I feel the earth shaking beneath my body as both Dragon's whimpers turn into growls that make the earth tremor more violently. I lie here, wishing for nothing but certain death to come and collect my remains, for now that it has collected my precious baby, I have no use left for my body and soul. I wish it to cease to exist.

As I close my eyes again, wishing for nothing but darkness to come and sweep me away for eternity and beyond, I have one, whispered word, left on my lips.

'Albion.'

Then all of my thoughts cease.

My heart refuses to beat again.

My body shuts down.

And my soul starts to slowly, float, away.

# 25

## From Three To None

### ALBION

**My mind races, desperation vying against sense as I once** more trail over all that I have before me. Weaponry and shelter, food and water and everything in between, I cannot risk leaving anything to chance. I made tentative preparations weeks ago, but now, now the day looms ever closer I fear that even my early steps will have me falling short as I look upon all I have collected together.

I know my Angel will collect together all she can, but, with her tender condition I know she would not be able to bear half the load I will be carrying. I need to ensure that everything I have with me will cover *every* eventuality, for if our child does bless us with their arrival before we reach safety, I need to know I can care for them as well as Arianwen and myself, for if the worst does come to pass, nothing will save those who dare to lay a finger upon either of my beloved.

My hands tremble as I begin to once more turn my mind inside out in fear laced desperation. I can feel the doubt gnawing at me, the overwhelming sense of inadequacy is threatening to breach my walls and drown me, unless ... no, I know for a fact I have already cached stores of water and pemmican in numerous locations, the oiled leather wrapped bundles buried five feet down should be safe enough should we need them, but, what if ... no

Albion, focus *damn it.*

Pemmican, a Hunter's friend. The thought of having to subsist on the ground meat and berries mixed with rendered animal fat is not the most appealing thing that has ever crossed my mind, but, I know that if I and Arianwen and our child are to survive, then we will certainly need whatever aid we can muster, no matter how bland or stomach turning the thought of it may be. I smack my knuckles against my temple, annoyed with my own indecisiveness and self induced panic. This is not the man my woman and child need. They need the Hunter, the survivor. The cached stores are proof positive that I know what I am doing, so why am I faltering now?

Suddenly I feel my heart seize in my chest, my knees buckling as pain runs through me, sending me tumbling to the floor in a sweat soaked mass of spasmodic flesh. I cannot help but scream at the pain that possesses me right at this moment, the brutal, callous tearing that rends me to the core is teasing the limits of my endurance as I fight to breathe through my clenching jaw and rictus throat. As I lie here, panting in a pool of my own sweat I feel it more than hear, the deep creeping rumble and grating roar that belongs to only one pair of beings in this entire accursed world.

I rip through my own pain, my heart and mind racing as one as I sprint for the door, my fear and doubt forgotten as their call resounds in my mind. Never before have I ever felt such a desperate plea. Only one thing has ever come close to the Dragons screaming my name, and that was the siren call of my Angel as she coaxed my soul back from the darkness that Lucifer had so gleefully wrapt me in.

My wings rip free, and I am in the air even before my door has fully closed, the roof of the dilapidated building that hides the entrance to our home does little to stop me as I shatter it completely, my mind focused on one thing only. My Angel, the woman who owns the very fibres of my being. Her Gatekeepers are calling me, screaming her name from inside my mind, nothing good awaits me of that I am sure. My own safety be damned, I let my guard fall, my cotton shirt and leather trousers falling to ash as my meat suit sloughs away, my true Demon self born to daylight as I race towards Eden. I just pray to … no … I pray to no one, my Angel is in dire need, prayers are as much use as a paper shield before a Dragon's fire.

I fold my wings back, plummeting past the edge of the fall, the forest below screaming in anguish as I race towards it, but, it is not at my arrival, it is not at any dark or Demonic presence, the very air around me sings in pain at the Dragons calls. My heart lurches as the full reality lays heavy upon me. I feel my fear return as I meet the ground, my clawed feet tearing through the loam and needle strewn dirt as I race the final yards to the gates of Eden. Grinding stone greets my ears as the granite beings turn their ire upon me, their eyes softening as much as any sentient stone beings can when they see that it is me. I look from them to the slowly emerging bundle between them, their wings parting as they move aside, my hide burning as my meat suit begins to twist and worm its way back over my body.

'Arianwen!'

My voice for all my panic and fear, is little more than a whisper as I fall to my knees beside her, the glittering blue pool that shimmers around her fills me with dread. What happened to her? Am I … Am I too late?

'Arianwen, my love … speak to me.'

I pull her limp form into my lap, the Dragons are mewling and moaning as they encircle us both.

'Why have none of her kin come to help, where's everyone?'

'Nan come, f'r nan can sense her sorrow 'r pain. She is between worlds, lock'd inside her own heart and mind, the dark that hath dealt this blow took that which was purest and ripp'd free of her mortal shell. If she is not heal'd of this lief, she will fall to the eternal sleep and from that, thither is nay return, not yea f'r one such as thou child.'

I cannot begin to comprehend what my heart and soul knew the moment I saw my love, our child, my child … gone … *no.* I feel the tears breach, scarlet trails sear my skin as I bury my head against Arianwen's neck.

'Sirrah, thou wilt hie, she dost not hast the time f'r thou to grieve the loss of a life unborn. If thou want to save the lief of thy woman thou love, thou wilt act and act anon.'

If her own kin are blind to my Angel's pain and sorrow then I know of only one other person with whom I can entrust my soulmate's life. I lift her as gently as I can before I force my meat suit from around me and set myself to flight, the Dragons angered roaring fills the air as they let their rage be known to all that could listen. There is only one being I know capable of what has befallen the shattered woman in my arms, and then not even the Legions will stop me from sating my vengeance in her blood.

Garth's home slips into view as I drop from the sky like a stone, not caring about the blinding agony that slices through my left leg as I feel the bones in my knee splinter and crack. Without preamble of even a moment's thought, I cast the door aside, turn and drive myself backwards through it. Glynnis' startled yells follow soon after as I careen into her home, words and curses flowing around me, all of it vanishing in an instant as both she and Garth catch sight of the blood soaked woman in my arms.

'Please ... save her ... I can't lose them both.'

Garth's eyes tell all as he snatches Arianwen from my arms and vanishes from sight, closely followed by Glynnis. I sit amidst a pile of shattered wood and crockery, knee already repairing itself, my hide burning, the scent of my cooking flesh filling my senses, but, I barely pay it heed, my mind too consumed by all I have born witness to in the last few minutes. I cannot help but chuckle, a few minutes, that is all it took for my world to once more cease to turn, life and time, much like fate, are fickle. None of them care for the other, or those that exist within their unyielding world.

I listen to the soft tones of Garth and Glynnis, my ears plucking their clipped and harried words from the miasma of noise around me. My eyes slip closed as I fight back another wave of crippling anguish. I cannot lose her, just the thought of it forced into my mind by the oil soaked snake that is Lucifer, was enough to send me across the edge and into an abyss so dark and deep, I no longer recognised my face in the mirror. If I truly lost her to the machinations of an obsessed psychopath, this world would cease to exist in an instant. Arianwen is truly the only good part of my life and world. She gave me hope in a time when all I could see before me was a path beset by wickedness and contention, a path that led me to a place few, if any, ever return from.

And now, now she lies on a table soaked in her own blood and clinging to the gossamer threads of her own life, while our child ... baby ... Oh Lord have mercy, would they have been a boy or a girl ... *will* they be a boy or a girl? Could they save them both? Is there still a chance? Tears flow free as I bury my head in my arms and shut the world away. All I can ask is for Garth to know the right choice, and if that means I spend my days raising our child alone in a world far from here then I will make sure that our little one knows who their mother was and what she did to give them the life they are living, but not before I raise this entire forsaken cesspool to the ground and leave it smouldering in its own ashen bones.

✦ ✦ ✦

A hand at my shoulder drags me screaming back into the world, the sun has dropped below the horizon so I know that it is well after the sixth hour, and yet I feel as drawn and tired as I did the moment I arrived. I stare blearily up at a sombre Garth, his face haggard and streaked with the track of tears and sweat. I know already that he was not able to save them both, the look in his eyes tells me that is a foregone certainty. I can do no more than steel myself for the blow that is about to fall as he squeezes my shoulder and softly tells me to follow him through the arch way.

'I did all I could, Glynnis as well, but ... she lost too much blood and the babes heart just couldn't take the strain, we managed to keep our girl with us, but, the little one ... Albion I'm so far beyond sorry my boy that words will never be able to find what I want to tell you. The little tyke fought hard and long to keep their feet in this life, they had their father's heart. I've never seen a stronger fight for life, even if their essence was all but gone. I'm sorry my boy, despite it all, the little one ...'

I can barely breathe, the walls pulse and shiver as my head begins to spin. Bile scorches my throat, my lungs burn as I swallow and try to breathe all at once, the acrid taste of my last meal sitting hard on the back of my tongue. I can hear Garth's voice, but, it is disjointed, wobbling in my ears as if he is talking through water. I take a step backwards, stumbling over my own protesting feet as my mind struggles to keep track of all my body is trying to do. I feel the warm stone walls grind against my back as I sink against them with a juddering thump, tears breaching everything as I slide to the floor. Garth rattles on, words tripping over one another before my Angel's name pierces the veil around my being and drags my attention back to the world around me. My legs shudder, my muscles as soft as snow as I force myself once more to my feet, Garth beckoning, guiding me through his home as I struggle to keep my mind in one piece. I cast my eyes down at the sallow and drawn face of my Angel, her breathing short and shallow. I cannot help but lean in and place my lips against her forehead, even now fighting back the tears that want to breach and flow free.

'Arianwen's a fighter boy, she'll pull through. If she can survive the mask she can survive this. Now, let's get both of you home, she needs rest and by the looks of you Albion, some sleep wouldn't do you any harm either.'

I wrap Arianwen's cloak tightly around her and lift the hood up, letting it rest gently over her face, shrouding her from view, my hands trembling before Garth lifts the handles of the cart and moves her out of my reach. I watch for a moment, my mind filled with fog before instinct takes hold and I slip my blade from its sheath, moving into the shadowed archway ahead of us, slipping past the hunched form of the blacksmith as he slowly follows on in my wake my heart and soul unconscious before him.

Cold air washes over me as I step through the door and into mine and my Angel's home, the sweat soaked cotton of my undershirt clings to me like a second skin as Garth stumbles in after me, the cart long since forgotten. I glance down at my Angel, her face pale and drawn as she pulls in a slow shuddering breath, her body all but weightless in my arms as I carry her towards our bed and lie her down gently, pulling a fur pelt over her form.

'Garth ... I ... I don't know if I will ever be able to repay you for what you have done for Arianwen and I.'

He nods at me slowly as he turns towards the armoury, my father's armour drawing his steady gaze.

'Boy, there are more things in Heaven or Hell owed to more souls than can be counted in kindness or favour. What I did, it will be rewarded in its own way and its own time, but for now, I have one more gift for you and this one comes from a path of love and protection so deep rooted that not even God himself could find its end.'

I watch with intrigue as Garth reaches down and pulls the mannequin stand away from the wall before reaching up to his neck and pulling a small chain from inside his soot and cinder smear shirt.

'Garth, what ...'

His hand comes up patting the air as he bids me to silence, a slender iron key dangling from his hand as he tugs the chain, snapping the links like a strand of hair. None of what I am seeing makes sense. I have scoured this cavern more times than there are grains of sand on the shore. I know this place like I know my own body and yet, here I stand, watching this diminutive blacksmith reveal a part of it that up until now, I had no more known existed, than I know the face of God. I cannot fathom what other secrets my father has hidden in this place.

'Just how many of my father's secrets are you hiding from me old man, what haven't I been told?'

Garth taps at the floor beneath the pedestal, a small glimmer of light flowing from each point he presses into the stone. I cannot help but stare as a square begins to form, Garth's key slipping through the line in front of him, a subtle almost imperceptible click issuing forth, the square sinking away, the inescapable sound of water rising past Garth as he reaches into the opening. Arianwen's soft whimpers pull my eyes from the spectacle before me as I turn and move to her side, Garth and his subterranean box of mysteries forgotten in an instant. Her skin is slick with beaded sweat as I smooth her hair from her forehead and whisper softly to her, lulling my Angel back into the arms of slumber. I cannot help the tears that threaten, they skate down my cheeks freely as I let go of her hand as gently as I can before sinking to the floor, Garth's shadow falling over me as I rest my head against my knees.

'This ... this was your mother's, I made it for her, well, it seems a lifetime ago now, certainly your lifetime at least. I tell you now I hold in my hands one of the greatest feats of craftsmanship and subtlety I've ever managed. Far more so than that *'flaming sword'* Michael carries around with him like a second phallus, or those dammed masks and coffins Lucifer had me craft. This my boy, will forever be my greatest achievement. Take a look.'

I run my hands over the slim plate in Garth's hand, as my fingers pass over the centre, flat almost transparent bands spool free before drawing with them paper thin sheets of Angel glass, the opalescent sheen unmistakable even drawn as thin as it is. I cannot tear my eyes free as it twists and bends seemingly of its own volition all the while a sheer carapace like armour growing from almost nothing.

'Garth, that ... it's ...'

'I know, it took me a very long time to craft, the wraith steel was especially hard to master, oddest metal I've ever worked with. Never in all my years, have I had to be polite to a hunk of tin.'

The armour quivers against my fingers as Garth smirks, a musical tinkling filtering through the air, its soft chimes somehow comforting, its living force bewildering.

'Oh grow up, it's not as if you don't have some tin in you. You have to be the most unaccountably temperamental piece of metal I've ever worked with, besides, you're a new owner now. The boy's girl needs better protection than he can craft and Amunet bless her heart ain't here to claim you, so, your Arianwen's now. Got it?'

The chimes ring again as the grumbling blacksmith casts his gaze upon me. Garth can see my mind racing and pats my shoulder before rising once more to his feet, a wry knowing look in his eye.

'Just tap the middle gently and it'll fold itself away until needed, now ... curl up with your love, she needs the comfort, I'll see myself out. Nice use of Arianwen's name as a password by the way, the riddle rhyme is a bit soppy for my tastes, but clever all the same. Call on me if you need me boy, you know where I'll be.'

I set the living armour plate on the stand next to my own before turning back and crawling softly into bed, my arms slipping around my Angel as she shivers, her legs and arms twitching softly as she slowly fights her way back to me. I turn my head biting my lip to keep from screaming. Despite it all, Garth's work and the small token he has offered us both, I know this was my own fault, my arrogance bringing this folly down upon us both. I just hope against hope, that when she wakes, my Angel, my love … can forgive me. But, I may never forgive myself for our loss.

# 26

## Cease To Exist

## ARIANWEN

**The believing, the praying, the faith in my Lord, what was it all** for?

Nothing.

*It was all for nothing.*

If a dark grief mourns over my soul such as this then all of my faith was for nothing. It has not saved me from Evil's clutches. It has not saved me from making the right choices. It has not helped me to save *all* of the souls that were bound for God that the Devil has taken for himself. It has not kept my home and my kin safe from Hell's minions. And it did nothing to help save the beautiful miracle that was growing inside of me. No, my faith has not served me well.

I strongly believed that Good would always prevail over Evil. I have been proven wrong. Good would never take a child away from its parents, it would never take a life before it even had a chance to experience the miracle that *is* life, it would never persuade fate to cross the paths of two people from different worlds, only to destroy them with a tragedy that can never heal. My faith was supposed to protect me and all I hold dear to my heart. It failed. I have lost faith in all I have ever believed in.

Now I am numb.

I have no faith, no beliefs, no religion, no feelings, no heart, no soul. It all desiccated the moment baby ceased to exist.

Oh my baby, my sweet, sweet baby.

I am so sorry I could not protect you like I should have, like a mother should have. Maybe that is why you were taken away from me? Maybe God knew my gifts and abilities were not strong enough to protect you from the Evil that would have tried to find you for many lifetimes. But, what I do not understand is, why, why was your beautiful soul gifted to me if I was not capable of keeping you safe?

Why? Why? *Why?*

So many *whys*. I have never known such cruelty as I am feeling now. I do not want to think, I do not want to breathe, *I do not want to live.* If I can never hold my precious child in my hands, I do not want these fingers ever touching another thing. I want to break these fingers, I want to scream until my lungs collapse, I want to run far away, I want to hit something, I want to scratch my nails down every piece of living flesh I can find. I want to drown in the dark that is all my eyes can see. I want to cease to exist. Maybe then I will find baby again.

I am vaguely aware of my body being moved about, but have no care to open my eyes to find out why. I never want to open them again. I do not ever want to see the bright colours of my world, or the dull greys of the forgotten forest, or the bright reds of Hell's pits. If I can never look into my baby's eyes, I do not want to look at anything else. If I could find a way to die, I would not hesitate. What I always saw as a gift, immortal life, now seems to be nothing but a curse, a curse that I will have with me for all eternity. All of eternity thinking about my baby.

I can sense flashes of lights behind my lids, I can hear faint noises, I can feel soft touches on my flesh, but nothing will persuade me to leave the deep recesses of my mind. The darkness and nothingness here, is all I want. If I cannot leave this body for good then I will endeavour to keep it shut down for as long as I can, even if that is for millennium and beyond.

Arianwen, the Reclaimer, will be no more.

Dark. Numb. Nothing.

Flashes of a memory invade my mind. As much as I try to omit them, they will not leave.

*I am a young child, near the water's edge, my mother is washing her hands in the lake beside me. I am distracted by a tiny Swallow, swooping past my head. I turn and watch as it flies up high, swooping around in circles, having fun and being free, only to then be caught in a large gust of wind. It falls down with force into the tree tops, bustling through the leaves and branches, before falling lifeless to the ground.*

*My little legs run, trying desperately to reach the small bird. I find it on the ground, its body still, and I feel a foreign pain inside my chest. I bend down and gather it up gently in my small hands. I turn for help, but can no longer see my mother. My eyes then search around for larger Swallows, thinking a bird this young would also not be far from its mother, but I cannot sight any others.*

*I stare at it, willing it to take another breath, feeling sad that it is fun and frivolous flight may have caused its death. I close my little eyes, feeling a sadness that my young self had never felt before this moment. My small thumbs rub over its little feathers softly, silently telling the bird that I care, that I want to see it soar up high into the sky again.*

*I feel a slight twitch under my fingertips and open my eyes to see the Swallow's eyes flutter open. I loosen my hold on the bird, and it shakes out its feathers, looks me in the eye and then hops down to the ground. It looks back to me, as if willing me to follow, so when it takes flight, low to the ground, I do. It flies a small distance and then stops, looking for my small self before taking a short flight again.*

*It comes to stop at my homes border of broken boulders and blackberry bushes and begins to peck at something on the ground. I walk over and lower to my knees, curious as to what the bird has found. I notice small red and blue, crystal like stones, sparkling in the sunshine's rays. I had never seen stones like that before, but even so young, I somehow knew not to touch the unknown.*

*I watch the bird pick up the stones with its little beak, flicking them up in the air, watching them scatter back down upon the ground. I find the bird to be so adorable that I cannot help but run a finger over its head and down its neck, giggling at the feeling of its soft downy feathers under my fingertips as I listen to its song of whistles and clicks.*

*I am so mesmerised by the tiny bird, I have not noticed that I am no longer alone, until another small hand reaches out from the bushes beside the Swallow and I, and their finger begins to pat the its tail. I feel my smile widen at seeing another child's chubby like hand enjoy the simple company of a baby Swallow.*

*We must tickle the Swallow as it jumps and shakes its feathers vigorously before resuming its play with the stones. Two young sets of giggles combine at the bird's antics, as we both resume patting the small animal. It is not until our fingers touch, does my young brain register that I should be wary so close to the border of my home, that the tales of Evil on the other side begin to replay in my fresh mind, yet, I feel no fear at the unknown hand that has just touched my own. All I feel is ... happiness, great happiness.*

*I finally raise my head, yet see nothing but blackberries scattered amongst braches and leaves. I look back down and the finger and the hand it belongs to has gone. My smile falls. Then I hear my mother calling for me to come and the memory fades away.*

I can remember very early memories, but this one is new to me. I did not realise I was so young when I first saved an animal from death, or when I first saw those red and blue crystals on the ground of Eden. I can feel deep within my being, that the other small hand and finger from this memory, belonged to a childhood version of Albion and what could have been our earliest connection.

And the significance that it was a Swallow who introduced us, is not lost on me, even in the dark state that I am so immersed in. Egyptian poetry describes the Swallow as bringing the first sign of a new love, while in ancient Greece, the Swallow was associated with Aphrodite, the goddess of Love, and was believed to be the bearer of good luck and happiness, and some cultures see the Swallow as a symbol of sacrifice and rebirth, as well as new beginnings.

The Swallow can also be found in the words of the ancient Romans, who believed that it was a totem bird for mothers in sorrow, and that it embodied the souls of children who had been lost before they had a chance at life. Most of history has seen the Swallow as a symbol of hope, but what hope do I have? My unborn child was taken from me. I am in love with the enemy and both our worlds are at the brink of war because of our love. That is what hope looks like for me.

As the memory completely fades, darkness once again consumes me, which is better than the heartbreaking memories of life before, before the greatest loss I have ever experienced. I feel something at my stomach. A flicker of hope starts to spark within my blackened soul, until I realise the feeling is coming from the outside of my flesh, not internally. I plummet even further into the despair of my now still heart.

I hear my name, I recognise the voice, but even my great love for Albion cannot pull me back to the land of the living. I have no will to ever return there, so I ignore it and concentrate on the numb feeling that consumes me and hope that he will one day give up calling my name, because as much as I try to ignore the sound, hearing his deep voice causes only more pain to my shattered self.

I feel my body shuffled around a few more times again, before I sense the beating of Albion's heart against my ear and feel the warmth of his arms surrounding me. I try desperately to ignore the feelings that are returning to my flesh, willing it all to remain resistant to his touch, but the life still pulsing through his large form, overpowers my frail self. I do not want to feel, I do not want to remember, *I want to remain numb.*

I open my mouth and scream as loud as I possibly can, trying to push out all of the pain and grief that is consuming me, trying to rid myself of this horror that has destroyed my life and the life of my child. I scream like I have lost my mind, because that is exactly what has happened to me. *I have lost my life.*

I feel Albion hold me tighter. I hear him trying to soothe me with his deep words, but I do not want it, *I do not want any of it.* I have no control over myself at this moment as I turn into something akin to a rabid dog, thrashing about, biting, scratching at anything I make contact with, wailing like a vicious animal, all the while Albion does not waver, his strength stands strong, his grasp on me just as firm, his words as steady as he rides the delirium I am expressing.

I slump in his arms and once again seek the darkness that has been my company for how long, I would not know. But this time, in the company of darkness, I also hear the very quiet words of Albion singing a soothing hymn, and with this, I think, I actually fall to sleep.

✦ ✦ ✦

Time has no meaning. Nothing at all has any meaning right now, but slowly, feelings are starting to return. My physical body aches, varying degrees of pain are all over my flesh. My heart aches, but I will not allow it to beat again, despite its yearning to. My soul is dark, and I fear it will never be anything more. But one thing I am feeling clearly, is anger.

Anger towards my God.

How could he stand by and let this happen to Albion and I. If fate brought us together to be a part of some master plan, why did God gift us with the soul of our child knowing things would become so volatile and deathly? He should have protected one of his Angels against feeling such loss, at feeling such grief, at feeling as if I will be in mourning for the rest of my *existence*.

Where was he when I needed him the most?

My faith has been nothing but strong and steadfast since the day I was first created, so why did God choose to leave me when I needed him the *most*. If I had not seen him with my own eyes, I would now believe he was nothing but a myth. But I have seen him. Yes, the sightings may have been rare over the times in my life, in fact only twice, but I can vividly remember seeing him, so I know he is very real.

Yet, when I was silently screaming for help, lying by the lake, in the blood of my unborn child, did he answer my call for help? No. My call was ignored. For what reason, I may never know. And right now, I do not even care. Caring has disappeared from my being, along with the need to breathe, drink and eat.

I can feel Albion trying to lift my head, water falling to the sides of my lips, his desperate plea just getting through to my vague mind. I feel drips of water reach inside my parched mouth, touching my sandpaper tongue and as much as I want my lips to remain closed, at the taste of much needed water, my mouth opens to accept more. It pours it and I begin to choke, straining to stop drinking, yet my body takes over, fighting with my internal stubbornness, and accepts his offer of water.

I sputter, spitting water out while it runs down my chin. I can feel it making a path down my neck, not wanting any feelings, becoming more agitated that my body has decided to awaken against my will. I try and shut it all out, shut everything down, but Albion's pleas to drink more, his roughened voice cracking as he begs me to come back to him, tugs at something deeper than mere feelings of water on my skin.

'Arianwen I beg you, please open your eyes, I need you, I can't face this without you my love. I can't go on unless you're by my side. Arianwen, my Angel, I love you, I need you; I truly cannot do this without you. I need my heart, without you this grief will consume. Arianwen please I can't do this alone.'

Grief.

Grief at the loss of our child. Mine and Albion's child. Albion. *Oh my poor love.* In all of my self pity and mourning, I have forgotten that he *also* has suffered a great loss, and he has been suffering alone, while thinking he may have lost me also.

The dam finally breaks.

I sob his name out loudly, using my numb fingers to try and grip him, any part of him, needing to feel him, needing to hold him, needing to offer some sort of comfort. I take large gulps of air, my body struggling to return to life, my heart beating painfully in my chest as it too struggles to grip the force of living once again. My eyes flood with tears that have been unshed for too long, a river running over my ashen skin, soaking into his soft linen shirt beneath my cheek. As much as this hurts, the thought of my love having to live with the loss of us both, shatters me beyond the realm of existence.

His lips kiss me with a tender force, on my hair, over my face, softly on my mouth. Broken words are heard by my ears, his voice as fragile as I feel, his own grief lying thick in the air as his grip around me tightens. Hearing his shattered sounds have me silently promising to never recede inside the dark mourning of my mind again. He also feels pain and for a brief moment, I was consumed with my own pain, my own grief, my own loss. But, there is two of us who created life, there is two of us who had hopes for the future and now there is two of us who are suffering a loss no parent should ever have to. We are not alone, we have each other to draw strength from and I will never forget that again.

'Albion, Albion, Albion.'

My whispered words are a plea to hold me tighter, to take away this pain, to never let me go.

'Oh my sweet Angel, I can't put into words just how mortally scared I was. Never again will I let you from my sight, never. I nearly lost you and this isn't the first time my foolish arrogance has come close to costing us everything. But, what it did take in penance for my pride, our child, I ... it tears my heart asunder to think of it, to know that if I'd only been more careful, our child, our little baby would be sitting here with us. I'll never be able to ask for your forgiveness, all I can say is, our love, my love, for you, for our little baby, will give us the strength to carry through. Together.'

I sob harder at the mention of baby, still in disbelief at what has happened, still in shock that we will never get to hold the precious miracle that was growing inside of me, now realising we have no need to leave this world. Because I am still angry, I am scorned, all my thoughts zone in on wanting revenge. Revenge on the world that should have protected baby and I, revenge on the world who destroyed our miracle, revenge on the vile creature who found a way into my own home and ended the life of our child. I am angry, and I want someone to pay for this sickening feeling that has taken over my being.

I scream a vicious blood curdling scream, a loud promise that I will avenge my child's death, even if I have to turn towards the darkness to do *it*.

# 27

## Life Over Death

### ALBION

***Lilith, Lilith, Lilith. That accursed Harpy.*** **How could I be so** blind, so unaccountably stupid in the face of such a devious harridan? That vacuous whore has slithered and cajoled her way through the walls of my life and Arianwen's world and, in the process, has wrest asunder my very existence. If it is the last thing I do, I will rend her head from her shoulders and flay her hide until all that remains of that contemptible whore are the bones that reside with the putrescent sow she crawled out of. Even now, her lingering scent causes bile to rise up my throat, searing my tongue and driving me to the edge of madness at all that her oil slicked aroma has brought to my door.

How could I have allowed myself to be so complacent, so damned irresponsible? It has cost me everything that I have come to love, everything that has ever held a shred of hope for me has been ripped apart on her razor edged talons. The love of my life now lies, curled and shattered in a bed that was once the centre of our passion, the very crucible from whence our family was seeded. Now all it is, is a bitter reminder of all that could have been, of what should have been.

Who can I lay blame with if not myself? I pressed home my own arrogance in a hope that it would be enough to shield my woman and child from the slings and arrows of a jealous xenophobe, a *woman* so enraptured with the beasts of her own making that she saw delight and delectation in the pain and suffering of anything that was born in a skin of its own making. Yet here I stand, helpless and as close to dead as I dare allow myself to be. I cannot help but cast my gaze to the woman I love, curled foetal in the centre of our universe. I watch her hands as they play over her stomach, shoulders shaking as she once more descends in rolling waves of crippling apathy and pain.

It skewers me deeper than any blade or bullet. She pulled herself free of the soaking pool of pain and anguish for the sake of my heart, of my pain and yet, I know, that the truth if it all is, I am the source of it. The sheer unadulterated agony that rolls through me, slashing away at the ropes that are holding my meagre sanity together, each twisting snap dragging me closer and closer to the precipice of madness. All of it, all that has fallen around us sits as a constant reminder of my failure as a father and as a protector. I cannot bring myself to even think upon asking my love for forgiveness, although there is not a shadow of doubt within me that she would not grant it in an instant. I simply cannot bring myself to ask it of her. How can I when I cannot begin to contemplate asking myself that same question?

I cast my eyes over to the bench in my barren and depleted armoury, the glinting disc sitting proudly as its contented music filters through the air, a sad almost empathic note to it as I listen. I cannot help but think, that if she had had that small token of protection then, maybe, just maybe, my love and our child would be whole, that Arianwen would not now be lying shattered on our bed and our darling child would not be cast to the eternal sleep before they had even had a chance to dream.

We need to find a way free of this. I need to find a path we can both walk, one that will take us to a place free of Lucifer, free of Lilith and away from the prying eyes and jealous hearts of Arianwen's kin. All I can reconcile within myself, is the fact that through my own faults I brought this down upon us both, but, in doing so, I have opened a door for us to find our way free of this world and through to a new life.

My Angel told me, through tear drowned words of pain

tempered solace, that she holds me no more responsible for what took place than she does the ground for supporting our feet or the air for filling our lungs. Turning, I move through the water of the bathing pool and sink to its floor, my throat burning with unshed tears as I slip backwards beneath the waterfall and let its chilled weight hammer down upon me as the warmth of the spring bubbles up from beneath me.

I cast my eyes once more to the love of my life, her form still, rising and falling with the ebb and flow of her breathing. My heart lurches in my chest, the love I hold for her, nothing will ever be able to extinguish and yet, I cannot bring myself to move to her side, not after all that has transpired. I need to see through the retribution I know I should seek, but, I cannot bring myself to leave her. Even if physical comfort is not a possibility I still need to be here, I still need to show her that even though our family is shattered, I, *we,* still endure. I just hope I can make her see this before she drifts even further from my grasp. My shoulders heave as my strength finally breaks and I let the silent tears fall, slowly staining the water red.

✦ ✦ ✦

The water hammers down upon me, how long I was sat in the maelstrom of heat and ice, I cannot say, all I do know is ... my chest ... burns. The mark carved into my flesh steams, its edges glowing with a dark yellow light as I force my numb arms to lever me away from the wall and I drag my tired legs beneath me. I know, to answer the call now will open wounds and doors I cannot hope to hide, but, to not heed the calling, to belay the cry from the would be King of Hell ... all that would reward me with is pain, anguish and death, and right now, I have had my fill of that, enough to last me the rest of eternity.

✦ ✦ ✦

The heat sinks into every pore, every fibre of my being is drenched in a warmth so cloying I can hardly breathe. I cannot fathom, how, for the first three decades of my existence I lived in such a place, the heat, the stench, the lurid debauchery that sits at the edges of my vision, no matter where I cast my gaze. I pass the behemoths, fellow Hunters and Legionaries, every one of them, to a Demon sneering at me as if I am the butt of some gargantuan joke. My blood boils in my veins as I pass them one after another, all with that same smirk smeared across their lips.

The closer I come to Lucifer's door the colder the air seems to get. I can sense the tension, I can hear the chattering teeth of the guards I pass, all of them standing, eyes fixed, lips turning a pale blue as they struggle to stay awake. My sight shifts, and I cannot help but grin as I watch them one after another, slowly freeze, their auras slowly turning black as I reach out and grasp the handle of Lucifer's chamber door.

My hand shakes slightly as I tighten my grip on the crenelated handle, the metal oddly warm as I take a slow, deep breath and push down before moving through and into the room. What hits me first is the vapid scent of ... apple blossoms, the room is replete with the over bearing scent, I take a heady almost turbulent breath, my head swimming as I lean on the door slightly, waiting for the wave of over powering vertigo to pass.

I cast my eyes around the room, searching for anything to give me a sign of what is to come, my sight alights on Lucifer, his body draped in a house coat as he sips at a cup held carefully between his fingers, his stance almost foppish as he watches the world beyond his balcony windows. I bite down hard on the inside of my cheek, the pain slicing through the red fog that was slowly enveloping my mind. Tentative steps draw me through into the room, the door swinging shut with a hollow thunk as I pass clear of the threshold.

'Albion, good of you to come, I do so hate having to tug on your leash, but, you do seem to have a penchant for straying out into the field for excessive amounts of time. It's getting to be a bit of a bother to be honest with you. I'm starting to ponder on whether or not I should have your orders reprinted on that rather vicious mind of yours.'

I ignore the wholly barbed remark as I stop six feet from the door, Fallen Angel or not, I should be able to make a fast retreat through the entrance behind me should need arise. I begin to run through all the possibilities of escape, although as I turn each option over in my head, not all of them leave me completely intact.

'You called my King?'

Lucifer smiles around his cup, the glow of his remaining ethereal grace casting shadows along his unnaturally smooth complexion.

'Yes, about that, it seems as if things are not ... shall we say, moving on as quickly as one would like, with regard to your finding the source of this "force" as it has been so quaintly dubbed. You seem wholly distracted, perchance by that fluttering little gathering of violet eyed feathers that so took your eye, or am I misinformed?'

I fold my hands behind my back, my father's push dagger once more held in my grasp, its edge biting into my palm as I choke down a barbed and vicious retort, my judgment twisting as I dig the blade deeper into my hand letting pain clear my mind.

'Yes my King, I am afraid so, wholly misinformed as to the situation and what has transpired in my absence from your side.'

Lucifer's brow rises, surprise registering tenfold on his aquiline features as I hold his gaze.

'Really now? Well, I must say that is a surprise. I had it on good authority that you, Master Hunter, were seen in the enemies embrace more than once, which would be quite the slight on the part of your betrothed.'

Bile lances up my throat as the scent of my own blood flirts with my senses.

'Betrothed Sire?'

I watch his eyes sparkle with mirth as he watches me, no doubt in my mind as to whom he speaks of, and yet, I cannot help the questioning tone that laces my words.

'Why *Albion*, have you forgotten me so quickly?'

My heart and soul freeze in unison as I watch the source of my worlds pain slink and slither from her seat in front of the fire. I flick my gaze between the vacuous whore that is Lilith and Lucifer, his upturned lips on the precipice of an all knowing smile as he studies my reaction.

'No, I *haven't* forgotten you, very little would make me ever forget the impact you have had.'

I hold my stance and ground as Lilith saunters over to Lucifer's side and drapes a sinuous arm over his shoulder as she moulds herself to him, crotch pressed hard against his hip as she lays her head against his arm. Through it all, I have not taken my eyes from either of them, my nerves tighter than a harp string as I viciously twist the dagger into my own hand, my heart screaming for vengeance as my mind vies for caution. Every fibre of my being is willing me to launch myself at the smirking whore, to sink my teeth into her throat and tear her head from her shoulders, but, for the sake of my Angel, I somehow pull myself back from the edge.

'Good, I do so want to feel your seed fill me, the pitter patter of little feet is something that makes my silk quiver with need. Do you want that too Albion, a little version of you running around and making mischief? I know I do.'

My eyes widen as I suppress my anger and pain, my mouth filling with the taste of my own blood, my gums twist and a fang snaps clean in two as I clench my jaw to keep from betraying all that boils within me. Pain lances up my arms as I sink the blade through my hand, bone grinding against steel as I continue to push and twist the dagger, needing the pain that it brings to keep my mind and heart from the war that is tearing my soul apart.

'Children ... an entertaining notion, but my mind as yet is divided on the issue. Possibly, when I'm settled, and war is little more than a memory, then maybe they may become more than a thought.'

Lucifer sets his cup aside, shrugging off Lilith's fawning and overtly lust filled grasp before breaking the tension and conversation with a coldly dismissive wave of his hand.

'Yes, yes, as nice as the notion is, for now, it is not something that is required of either of you. Albion, you need to step up the search for this "thing" be it person or object I couldn't care less. I need it off the playing field before my feathered brothers lay their pampered hands upon it. I'll not go into detail as what awaits you should you fail me again, am I clear?'

I nod, my body stifling any worded reply as I fight back tears of anguish and pain. Lucifer smiles, nodding in return as I wait on his word.

'Good, set to it then, dismissed.'

Seizing my chance, I break for the door not waiting on any further word from Lucifer or Lilith as I head to freedom and the solace of mine and my Angel's home.

Anger clouds my heart and mind as I break free of the sweltering heat that blankets everything around me. I need to let this flow, to let it free before it shatters my heart completely and spills into the purity and love my Angel has filled me with, tainting it beyond any hope of recourse.

My wings snap free, the sensation of my own tearing flesh falling flat, pale in comparison to the maelstrom that has so filled my mind and body. With quick heavy beats I send myself up into the star littered sky, searching for something, anything, to soak away the rage that fills my heart and soul.

I descend upon the wilds of the forest with a shattering roar, my meat suit long since banished to dust as I shed every semblance of restraint. Nothing hides with me as I sink claw and fist through trunk and branch. My heart sings with undiluted rage and pain. I watch as my fingers peel apart a tree, the screams of terrified Drewen fill my ears as I send the eviscerated tree twisting over the canopy. Time vanishes in a blanket of splintered lumber and primal screams, everything that has piled on top of my soul, pouring free in one tumultuous torrent.

I could not care any less for my own safety even if I was dancing through the jaws of Cerberus, soaked in the blood of swine and oxen. I let every barrier and wall collapse, my pain, my anger, my raw unadulterated power soaking the air as I rip a squealing terrified Drewen free of the sod and send it sailing through the open air, watching it shatter against the cliff behind.

Yet as soon as it starts, everything grinds to a stop, her face hanging clear in my mind. What am I doing? I am risking my own life and safety for what, to vent my anger like a spoilt child that was denied its favourite cake? This is not what I am, this is not what she needs. Arianwen needs the protector that watched over her from the first day she set foot in the village. She needs the man I was, the one who silenced his own kind, sending them to the eternal sleep to ensure that she, my Angel, was safe. Arianwen needs me to be that man now, to be all I was and all I could be.

I will be that man. I will protect the woman who owns me, now and until I am reclaimed by whatever power calls me home. I will restrain myself until the time for vengeance is right.

# 28

## Forward Doesn't Exist

### ARIANWEN

**The hand moves.**

Tick tock. Tick tock.

The gears behind the face, churning, forever turning, moving the hands always forward.

Around, and around, and around.

Time is as old as the Gods themselves, but I have no care for it now. I may have been lying here in this bed for hours, days or maybe even weeks, yet it means nothing to what is left of my blackened soul. My heart may beat again, but how do I take a breath? How do I throw the covers back that Albion so lovingly tucked around me, letting my feet touch the ground knowing it means I have to take a step forward? How do I walk outside of this rock shrouded haven and raise my head up to the sun again, knowing the rays falling upon my pale face will never touch the delicate skin of the baby that will not ever be?

Grief is not an emotion I have ever felt with such strength before. I do not feel myself at all, it is like I am a stranger in my own body. Due to the devastating loss I have experienced, I am no longer the Angel I was raised to be. Maybe I have changed, maybe I have evolved, maybe my soul now lingers between worlds, trying to find a home, a home that does not feel the pain that is currently rippling through my every cell.

All of my life seemed to lead to the moment I finally laid eyes upon Albion. As surprising as that first moment was, to realise my silent life long protector was a Demon, every twist in fate after that seemed to be leading to the fact that we were to become parents, parents to a special little soul who would eventually lead us both from the worlds we lived in. It was as if we were destined to protect our child by moving to a new world, a world where we all could be free of the restraints of our upbringings and the expected roles we were to play. But now ... what does fate have installed for us? What are we meant to do now? What world do we belong to now?

Even though the urgency to leave, to protect our growing family has ceased, what world could Albion and I possibly live happily together in? I feel as if the faith in my own world may never return. The once safe cocoon of Eden and Heaven no longer seem as peaceful as they once were. My own safety can no longer be guaranteed there, so how could I expect Albion to live safely there with me.

And with Lucifer's hold still glowing brightly on Albion's chest, I doubt our safety can be taken for granted even here, hidden under rock walls on the edge of the forgotten forest. This world, between both of our own, is fair ground for all immortals to roam. Either side could plan a surprise attack at any moment, like they have done once before.

So does that leave our only option, to take residence within the walls of Hell itself? To think that vile Demonette would be a part of that world day in and day out, is the only joy I hold for this option. If I was to become a Dark Angel and walk the corridors of the pits of Hell, I could easily get close enough to that vixen to be able to wrap my hands around her pretty little neck and drain the life from her before yanking her skull clear from her shoulders.

A primal growl boils free from my lips, just the thought of willingly ending another's life. Despite how much she deserves it, is going against every cell in my body, causing immense pain to ripple through my entire being. I want to cause her pain, I want to make her suffer. *I want to end her life.* But to do that, I cannot be in my current form. As much as my mind wills me to find a way to seek her out, to seek revenge and cause her as much pain as she has caused me, if it came down to it, my body would not allow me to take action on such thoughts, unless it was clearly in self defence of my own life or another innocents life.

No. If I wanted to end her life, I would have to give up all the Good that runs through me, and pray to the Lucifer to accept me as a Fallen Angel, to become Dark at his will. Then, and only then, would I have the power and complete will to slaughter the vicious bitch that has destroyed one of the happiest things in my life.

These dark thoughts that are invading my mind are causing me to curl up in pain on mine and Albion's bed. Feeling something so harsh and Evil is causing slithers of agony to race through my veins, as a way of keeping my light intact, a way of bringing me back to God's will, a way of keeping darkness away from my system.

But what if I do not want to keep it away? What if I want to welcome Evil into my soul? If it meant I had the power and mind set to seek out this Lilith and destroy her the way she destroyed mine and Albion's child, I would welcome the Devil to my doorstep. To watch her eyes slowing fade as I drain the life from her foul soul, to see her silent pleading fade to nothing as I ignore it, to see my own hands tighten around her throat until the last of her life runs from her body, would be something I may just sell my soul for.

A dark scream rolls through me as pain strikes again, blurring my vision as my thoughts fight with the fundamentals of the Angelic soul I currently have inside of me. A soul that I cherished, until the moment I no longer felt the joyous innocence of the child growing inside of my stomach. My faith in my world and kin died; it died the moment baby's tiny heart stopped beating. Now, now I do not know where I am meant to be or how to find myself once again.

'Arianwen, my love, speak to me. Please my darling Angel, talk to me!'

That voice.

The only voice to break me out of my black morbid thoughts, the voice of the only one who can save me from my current self, soothes some of the agony that has taken up residence within me. Just the sound of his deep sombre tones, calms some of the shattered and spinning pieces of my mind and reminds me that I still have to fight, that I still have to find a way out of the darkness to be able to help him through his own grief. He needs me. I just need to find a path back to him.

I feel the mattress dip behind me as his large form scoots up close behind my own, his entire body enveloping mine, creating a cocoon of safety and love. And it is with this love that my thoughts finally slow down and begin to find some sort of reason and calmness. Revenge is not in an Angel's nature, yet as I once again fall into a soothing rest in my loves arms, revenge is a word that quietly floats in my subconscious as I am claimed by sleep.

✦ ✦ ✦

I wake with a start, visions of Lilith's laughing face flashing behind my eyes, before I open them to find the concerned, sad eyes of the man I love. I have seen much trouble behind my Demon's eyes before, but what I see now, is a man that is barely holding on and one that has grief etched into his soul, embedded into it as deeply as my own. I grip him tighter, drawing him to me, trying to offer him the comfort he has so selflessly been giving me for ... I have no idea how long I have been here, in the caved seclusion of our home.

My family must be worried by now, and I am sure Michael and Gabriel have their spies searching for me. The only solace I have is that they will not come near this part of the forest; the part that lays in between worlds, and, that as a Reclaimer, it is not unusual for me to be gone for days at a time. But, if all the worlds felt the force of Albion and I coming together and then the power that grew when baby was created, then I am sure baby's loss was felt far beyond just Albion and I.

As if Albion can read my mind at the mention of baby, he lets out a soft pain filled growl as his entire body shudders. We hold on to each other tighter, our grips desperate as we try to get closer, almost crawling into the others skin as we both grieve the loss of our brave beautiful baby.

We lie here for some time, both of our bodies finally calming when I sit up straight, my heart beating wildly in my chest, all of my senses on full alert while I strain to hear what has startled me so. My body automatically preparing to rush to a Reclaim, when it suddenly hits me, I cannot remember the last time a soul in need called out to me for help. I have crawled to the edge of the bed, Albion's voice echoing in the room, asking what is wrong, what am I sensing, when I realise, I can no longer sense anything.

I try and scent any souls, in need or not, but come up with nothing. I then try and feel if any of my own kin is nearby in the forest, but cannot sense anyone. I close my eyes, almost shutting down my entire body, using everything I have to feel something, to smell something, to sense anything at all, but I am hit with silence. What is wrong with me? Why have all of my gifts suddenly deserted me?

My head starts to spin and when I feel my body begin to fall sideways, Albion is there, catching me, cradling me, desperately asking what is happening to me. I stare at him blankly, struggling to understand myself, let alone find the words to explain it to him. Have my thoughts already caused me to fall? Am I already on the path to Lucifer's doorstep? Am I turning into a Dark Angel of my own accord?

'Oh Albion.'

My mind starts to unravel again, pieces shift and blur, reality becomes unclear despite my larger than life Demon desperately trying to hold onto me, calling to me, pleading to not fall into myself again, begging for me to stay with him, to help him. He needs me, and I am failing him, as I failed baby.

*Oh my sweet little baby*. How can I go on without the joy you brought to our lives?

Fear, grief, desperation and despair are flooding my senses as I once again feel my grip on reality slipping. Why? Why is God allowing such dark feelings to overcome me? Where is he when I need him the most? Make it stop. *Make it all stop.*

I feel Albion grip my shoulders and shake me sternly.

'Arianwen, don't you dare leave me again! I need you. I can't get through this without you. Please don't go inside yourself again. I can't ... I can't bear seeing you so lost. Please my beautiful Angel, please hold on to me, hold on to us. I beg you my love, don't let go. I can't do this, I can't exist alone. Please ... don't leave me.'

His rushed words, the terrified look in his eyes, the warmth seeping through his fingers that grip me tightly, the love he is so desperately trying to shroud me in. All of it, all of it tethers me to him, to this moment. In this moment I need to hold on, in this moment I need to choose to be stronger. In this moment I need to choose to live.

'That's it my darling, that's it. Look at me, hold on to me, concentrate, focus solely on my voice. I ... need ... *you*. Do you hear me Arianwen? I need you to fight, this life, my life, everything I had before you gave me your love, was barely a whisper in existence. Before you looked upon me, holding my gaze, staring into my eyes without an ounce of fear or trepidation, all of it meant nothing. My world was dead, a swirling desert of death and emptiness, that was, until I had you, until I let the love I held for you free and allowed myself to feel. I stopped being a Demon the moment you first loved me. Everything I was vanished, Demon, Hunter, Murderer. All of it vanished in a tidal wave, a wave that was born the moment you looked into my eyes. You made me a man Arianwen, a man that will do anything to hold on to you. You are the single greatest thing to have ever happened to my measly existence. I love you Arianwen, and I need you to fight, fight for me, fight for us.'

My breathing is calming as I watch his lips, trying to concentrate on every word that slips from them, trying to hold on to them, to never let go. He needs me. He needs me more than his own life, and I feel exactly the same way. His love for me allowed me to be the Angel I was always destined to be. We each became more powerful when we joined as one and that has to be for a reason. All of this, love, loss, grief, it all has to be leading to a greater purpose.

I may have lost my faith in my own world, but I understand enough that fate is still at play. It has been from the very moment I first sensed another being hiding in the forest when I was the youngest of a child. The 'why' to everything that has happened in our lives, will eventually be explained to us, be it now, or many more lifetimes from this moment. I just have to have faith in the love Albion and I share and know, that a time will come, when all will be revealed as to why, one day, a Demon and an Angel fell in love.

# 29

## Vigilance And Fear

## ALBION

**My eyes burn, sleep, that torturous beast, the one that has so** eluded me, now stalks my shadow like a wolf after sheep. As much as my body cries out for its sweet kiss, I know I cannot give in to it. My Angel needs me more now than she ever has before, and I will not forsake her again.

I have not left her side in days, how many, I cannot say nor do I really care. When she sleeps I keep vigil, when she wakes, I keep vigil, never taking my eyes from her for a moment, never leaving her side from the instant her eyes open, to the time they close at night, I always keep my vigil.

Days have passed since ... since our world was torn apart, and barely a word has passed between us. My soft consoling and love tempered gentleness, little more than a blanket covering the gaping wound that sits between us both. Despite it all, despite my self imposed isolation and unwavering need to see my love safe, I cannot help but sense the overbearing spectre of death and calamity that is slowly looming large on the horizon. War is coming to our worlds, and Arianwen and I are caught between it all. We need to leave, we need to put paid to this world and seek refuge as far from here as we possibly can. I just hope my Angel is of a sound enough mind to see, that it is our only surviving option.

I know, despite how much I need to stay, need to know she is safe, that I must leave. I have to make sure our path is set, our way free of this world is secure and that this war, the one I have felt to the depths of my soul, is finally bubbling to fruition. The storm that is coming will envelope this world in a wave so violent, so wholly and all consuming that nothing, no soul, no Angel, no Demon will be able to escape its embrace. Eden, the Village, the pit, all of it will cease to exist.

'Arianwen, my love, I have to leave for a little while. I'm going to seal the door behind me, the crawl will always be open, but, as long as you are in here you will be safe, I promise. I love you little wing.'

I lean in and brush her hair back from her face, catching the gossamer thin strands behind her ear before pressing my lips lightly to her cheek. Her only response is a soft shrug of her shoulder as she pulls the hide cover tighter to her, turning her face away from me as she does so. The look in her eyes, those violet orbs that were once so full of life, shining bright with laughter and love, are dull and lifeless, the pain that skewers me as I watch her lay there, is insurmountable. But, I steel my heart and move onwards, turning away from her and heading towards the door, the heavy leather and mail of my armour pressing down upon me as I move the door aside and step out into the cold, mist laden morning that awaits me.

✦ ✦ ✦

Thoughts, feelings, words, images. My mind resounds with it all, a maelstrom of riotous noise and confusion that is tearing me apart, casting my mind to the winds. I need to find a way to spirit my Angel and I away from here, away from the pain and hardship that is set upon us. Layer upon layer of anger and malice, like slabs of granite, pressing down upon me, crushing the life from my heart and the air from my lungs. Try as I might to work my way free, it is there, forever, crushing the fight from my spirit.

I drag the cuff of my sleeve across my eyes wiping away the unbidden tears as I move into the maze like warren of streets and tenements. Guttural groans fill my ears as I slip past shadowed doorways, the darkened lanes hiding the pliers and pimps of life's oldest trade.

I need to gather the dregs of my life, the last slithers of my old self and old world, and spirit it away from that cess pit that spawned me. My parents set me on a path, a path that led to Arianwen, and yet, I am still struggling with the shackles of my past. Lucifer's leash locked around my neck, the slavers chain on my ankle; a chain that leads back to that whore and harlot, Lilith. Anger soars through me at the thought of her, her sneering face and ink black heart. That witch is the lynch pin of my pain, the instigator of Arianwen's agony, she stole from me, the true source of happiness that only comes from being a father. She reached into my heart and tore out its very core, and for that, for that my pound of flesh will be sought. I will tear from her hide and soul every inch of pain and penance that I am owed.

Above all, beyond the vengeance and pain, I still need to forge a path for Arianwen and I, a way for us to truly be free of it all. I just pray my parents plans bear the fruit they so desperately sought, otherwise, I fear, Arianwen and I may share their fate.

I head towards the Undercroft, the pulsing heart of Hell. Lucifer in his vanity assumes the mantle falls to him, the self proclaimed strutting peacock of the Demon realm, but, in actuality, the Undercroft has always been its life's source. In there, it matters not if you are soldier of General, Knight or Servant, in its pulsing lascivious embrace, all are truly equal, and its ruler, well, in a place such as that, there is only one person who can truly claim to lay ownership, to be the true King of all they survey, and they are forever locked behind alcohol soaked bars serving up whatever the clamouring court below desires.

Every time I step through these doors, I am immediately swamped, my senses pulverised in a deluge of pulsing music and sweat soaked skin. The heat that radiates off the writhing, naked flesh of the crofts denizens is so thick, I can taste it on the air. The sickly sweet, cloying sludge of lust and avarice, I cannot help but turn myself away from it all, the need to clear my throat drawing me closer and closer to needing to vomit. The sheer unadulterated assault on my senses all but unbearable as I make a desperate break for the winding stair case leading to the cell I once called home.

As I reach my door an all too familiar sensation washes over me, my rage flaring so brightly that I feel my skin begin to smoulder. Not now and not here, my grip tightens around the handle of my door, the metal buckling and twisting as I try in vain to maintain my composure and not give in to the burning desire for blood and vengeance that is roaring through my veins. I bite hard on my lip, I push forcefully against my cell door, sending the slab of banded and nailed oak, swinging back on its hinges hard enough to drive the handle into the carved stone of my cells wall. I step inside, the cold stone lending a soft chilled bite to the lurid heat that worms its way up the stair way.

Stepping through the doorway casts a hole so deep through my mind that I find myself momentarily lost in a reverie so utterly complete and all encompassing, that even my thirst for vengeance against Lilith and all that she surveys is dampened. I cast my eyes about the room, memories vying for supremacy as I move to the straw mattress and cot that masqueraded as a bed. Dragging it aside, I send it clattering into the corner. Scratch marks and chipped stone meeting my gaze as I kneel and sink my talons into the cracked edge around one flag stone. With a muffled grunt I pry it free, the dull thunk of stone on stone lost to the pulsing din that is oozing through the open cell door.

Lilith's familiar aura continues to tease my senses as I lift the bag free of the hole and lay it open, drawing my eyes over the contents looking for any signs of tampering and decay in the metal and leather that resides within. Snapping the bag closed, I send my senses out, tracing along the ether that fills the air, tentatively seeking out the saprophytic tendrils of Lilith's abhorrent aura. The taint that rolls back over me makes my stomach lurch, the acid burn of bile teasing my throat as I follow the path back to the source of its stench and decay.

'Hide at the peacock's side all you want, it'll do little to stay my hand or vengeance. You took my child from my love and I, not even the call of the seventh trumpet will save you from me.'

My words echo off the walls around me as I feel her aura shiver, the mental bridge between us screaming with panic as Lilith's aura shatters in a burst of pure unadulterated fear. I push up, rising from where I kneel and lift the bag with me, a plan burning through my mind as I sift and discard each thought and inclination. Slowly with each step I take, it begins to form, one that will see the end of not only Lilith, but my and Arianwen's life in this woe begotten vapid world.

The heat once more swallows me whole as I step off the bottom step and move through the gyrating mass of Demonic flesh, hands brush and grope my leather clad body, fingers teasing the strands of my cod piece, one lone hand cupping my buttocks as I move onwards. I keep my gaze level, my senses following everything around me as I move inexorably towards the exit and my Angel beyond it.

I catch sight of Alp as I finally breach the seething wall of sex and lust, his eyes studying the mass over gyrating bodies, his gaze predatory, like a cat stalking a mouse. I cannot help but feel a slight chill as I take in the look locked behind his eyes, as I study his face, a thought bubbles free. Do I truly know what my kinsman and brother is fully capable of? I have fought beside him all my life and yet, not once have I ever seen the true extent of the power he holds inside.

The sudden and unwarranted realisation sends a ripple along my spine, the hairs on the back of my neck rising as I let my hand stray to my caster on my thigh. One thing atop of all my skills and abilities has kept alive these past decades; my ability to perceive the world around me; to recognise a threat when I see it, even if it is only but a momentary glimpse. And now, what I see before me, my brother, my friend and kinsman, Alp, he has vanished, replaced with something else entirely. They say, the old guard, the Knights of the first order, those like my father, that you will never see the bullet that claims your life or the knife that strikes the deepest. Now as I stand looking upon Alp, the master deceiver, I may have caught sight of just that.

My father's voice echoes through my mind, an old adage wrapped in his deep baritone.

*'Albion hear me, and hear me well. Always keep your friends*

*close, but, above all, keep your enemies closer.'*

I step towards Alp, his eyes shifting to mine, the flint sharp orbs shifting, swirling, for the briefest of moments I could have sworn they glittered violet as I draw to within feet of him.

'Well met brother, it's been a while.'

I cannot help but find a smile easing its way across my lips as Alp claps my shoulder tightly in his grasp.

'Likewise Alp, likewise. Brother, I need your help, there is ... an obstacle that needs removing from my path, and it's not something I can achieve on my own.'

Alp's gaze hardens slightly, his eyes narrowing as I watch him step back from me, his stance wary.

'Well, what kind of obstacle are we discussing here? Demonic, Angelic ... Animal, mineral, vegetable? There are a lot of ... variables to be counted here Albion, I need more than "an obstacle" to work with.'

I nod, my mind skimming over everything that I am holding back. I take a short steadying breath before speaking further.

'One word Alp and one word only will explain all that you need to know.'

Alp's brow furrows further, I can sense him getting more irate by the second. I watch as he opens his mouth to speak and cut him off before a single word ventures forth.

'Lilith.'

His eyes widen, shoulders softening and stance turning, a grin claims him, rolling up through his eyes and aura as he replies.

'Okay, what do you need me to do?'

The scent of wild flowers flirts with my senses the closer I draw to my home, the dust that clings to my legs and feet mingling with the air, lending it a chalk like taste as the wind whips between the buildings and the cliff face. I relish in it, after spending the core of springs first hours locked within the sweltering heat of the pit, the flat taste of chalk and dirt on my tongue is a miniscule price to pay for such a sense of unattainable freedom.

Freedom ... that one word stops my joy cold, my mind flooded with the memories of the cell, of Arianwen's tear and fear soaked face as she sank into my arms. What has freedom truly brought me? It has brought me nothing but pain, after being the one thing I so sought after for the entirety of my adult life, freedom, in all its forms, has been my biggest curse. I push the door open, the crisp cool air of my home washing over me, the gentle kiss riding the fine line of pleasant cool and comfortable warmth. I drop the remnants of my former life by my work bench, the dull clunk of leather muffled wood and steel riding free on the wind as I settle my gaze upon my Angel.

'Arianwen, my love, I'm home. Are you awake my Angel?'

A soft stir of her shoulders and a muffled sniff tell me that she is, at the very least, awake. I move slowly, wary, my thoughts crashing over one another as I edge closer and closer to our bed. I shift my vision, casting my eyes over my Angel. Her aura is a wash of disjointed colours and spikes, movements slow and sluggish as she turns her face towards me.

'Albion ... I ... I feel ... empty, like my soul has been torn out of me.'

I crawl on to our bed, pulling my Angel towards me. I feel my chest tighten, tears fighting through every barrier I throw in its way. I kiss her shoulder, curling my fingers through her hair as I struggle to find anything I have not already said.

'I know my darling, my soul is too filled with holes and pain that I cannot begin to describe the depth of the emptiness. But you, my love, my life, my sweet Angel, you give me the strength to fight, but I am scared Arianwen. I am petrified that I can't protect you. We already lost our child, I *cannot* lose you too. I ... I need you to be safe, safer than I can make you here. These walls, our home, all of it was built for us, for our life together, but, this war, the layers of Hell that are peeling open, baying for our blood. Our home isn't the fortress it needs to be, and I know, in the very depths of my heart and soul I can't make it one.

'I need you to go back my darling, back behind the gates of Eden, behind the Gatekeepers and walls, back to where Legions of Gods war dogs wait. At least there, I know you will be truly safe.

Lilith will never lay finger to you again, that is my promise, but I can't stop her and protect you. I am only one man. I need you to go my love, go back to Eden.'

Tears burn my eyes as Arianwen turns in my arms, her fingers tracing my cheek as she presses her lips to mine, before resting her forehead against my chin, her reply soft, yet filled with a wilful strength I thought we had both lost.

'If it gives you the strength and comfort you need, to finally rid our worlds of the Evil taint she brings, I will. But know this Albion Weisser, never more, will any other man own me as you do, you own my heart and soul. Find me again when this is done. I love you my darling Demon.'

'I love you too little wing, I love you too.'

# 30

## Acceptance

## ARIANWEN

**The pain in my chest tightens.**

Sweat starts to bead on my forehead as a shudder runs down my spine.

My vision blurs as the ancient Gatekeepers come into sight, peering through the foliage of this deathly forest. Their larger than life granite forms dance in my vision, shifting between leaves and branches. Memories invade my mind, vivid recollections of the last time I was in their presence. I have come to accept that for some reason my fate is not to be a mother at this time. But, the only way I can move forward is to hold dear to my heart, the dream that Albion and I will be blessed again if fate allows it. Maybe that will be many lifetimes away from now, but one day I truly wish to be gifted with the feeling of an innocent little soul growing inside my belly again.

Now I have to focus on the Good to be able to move past this grief that is so debilitating. I need to cherish the moments we did have. The sensations of tiny butterflies taking flight from deep within, the moment Albion understood he was to become a father, and the way his eyes shone brighter than I have ever seen them shine before. Waking up to him lightly tracing the small bump of my belly, his eyes full of wonder and love as he quietly spoke to our child, as I watched silently, a smile curling my lips gently, as we lazed in bed. The amazement we both felt as we realised baby's life force strengthened our own, and the hope that we would one day find a world we could live together in peace.

Our baby will never be forgotten, neither will the pain of their loss ever completely leave our souls. There will be hidden scars for as long as we both exist and as much as we will try to be strong, try to move forward in what life has planned for us, there will be moments that the tears will not stop and the heartache will be almost unbearable. But in those moments, there will still be love, love for our child and for each other and that is what will keep us moving forward. Together.

I have to push down the trepidation that is churning up my throat as the border to my home comes ever closer. I cannot leave my home permanently yet. Our immediate departure now has to wait until Albion, and I know what the leaders of our worlds are planning, what they are thinking. For as much as we needed to leave for the protection of our child, I now cannot concisely leave without knowing that my family will not be immediately thrown into a war. I need to know they will be safe before I say my final goodbye.

As I begin to pass under the Dragons, their mighty souls encased in stone, I feel their grief for me fall upon my shoulders. But I also feel something else. Hope. They are trying to give me hope at one day finding my place in these worlds.

'Has't strength child as the sun will riseth f'r thou again on a new day. Thou will findeth thy way. Thy path may has't many twists and turns, but love will always be thy companion.'

I have no response but for a slight smile as I take a step onto the soil that is Eden. It is different now, not the safe haven I always knew it to be. Lilith found a way to breach the borders and control one of my own kin, a feat the Devil himself has yet to undertake. Maybe he can, but chooses to fight another way. Memories of Mayloree's eyes, the way they shifted, not looking as though they were her own, invade my mind, as does the fact I so willingly accepted a muffin she had baked, despite the unease I felt in her presence.

I push the onslaught of visions back, not wanting to relive the dark moments of grief I have been lost in. I need to face my family, and for that, I need to be calm and serene. They will be worried of the days I have been gone and to walk into their questions with emotions welling in my eyes will do me no good.

As soon as I reach for the old iron handle on the door to my home, a peace washes over me, one that I so desperately needed. Despite my world no longer feeling as secure as it should, this house, my home, surrounded by my family, it will always be my safe haven. But, as soon as I open the door and take my first step through, I sense that my mother knows something is not as it should be.

My father and sisters greet me eagerly with warm hugs and curious questions, but my mother stands back with a sad look in her eyes. I am rattled by her expression and knowing eyes, but I hold myself together as I answer my sister's questions.

'You are not normally gone so long Arianwen, you had us all worried. Gabriel has been here numerous times in the past two days very concerned. It has been so sweet to see.'

Caronwen's innocent young ideals of romance brings a smile to my face. I hope she never has to see our world for what it can be. Michael making deals with the Devil, a Demonette possessing a young Angel, things I hope she will never have to endure. The harsh reality of it all was almost too much to take in, even for my own prepared mind.

'I had many souls in need at the same time little one. It was Reclaim, after Reclaim, after Reclaim. It took time, but I was needed and performed my duties that God instilled upon me. I am sorry to have worried you all.'

My mother still eyes me with concern as a take a seat at our dining table, my middle sister handing me one of her delicious pastries. I bite into it with a ferocious hunger, only now realising that I had refused all of Albion's offers of food during my entire exile into grief. Brianne sits beside me, grabbing my hand to hold.

'It was very endearing to see Gabriel's concern for you sister, even after mother explained that it was not unusual for you to be gone days at a time.'

My eyes find my mother's once again as we seem to share a

silent understanding. Feeling as if she may know all of my secrets, is not as frightening as I thought it may be. A mother's intuition knows more than her children will ever catch onto. I now know that myself.

'But, when that pompous Michael came knocking on the door asking your whereabouts and demanding that he and his men come inside to search our home, as if you were hiding under the bed or something silly like that, if was quiet humorous to see the veins rise under his skin on his forehead when father refused his entrance. Father told him politely, but oh so firmly, that his angry aura was not one to be welcomed into our home, but, that he was more than welcome to return once he was in a more peaceful state.'

Brianne's slight giggle snaps me back to our conversation. Michael wanted to search my family's home but was refused and walked away. I am sure he will not always walk away so easily. But, I hold some peace knowing my father can be forceful towards our leader if need be. He may need that very attribute when I have gone, to protect mother and my sisters from the interrogation our leader will likely put them through.

I finish my sister's delight then head towards my room, not needing to turn my head to know that my mother will be right behind me. I shrug out of my cloak and place it on the end of my bed as I hear her light footsteps enter the room and the soft click of the door closing echo around the silence.

'I feared you may not return to us.'

'Oh mother. You know some souls need more help than others. And at this time, there were many in need.'

She smiles lovingly at me despite her face telling me she does not believe a word that I have uttered.

'My child, you are wise beyond your many years and have been that way since you first opened your eyes, cradled in my arms, instantly absorbing the entire world around you. I knew then you were destined for greatness, but I also knew it may come at a price. You know the immortal worlds are not all that they seem. Even our own world conceals many secrets, secrets kept to protect our kin. But despite that, Good and Evil still need to lie on separate sides, to blur that, could end in disaster, not only for yourself, but for your own kind.

'Evil has a way of tempting even the strongest of minds, making its victim feel as if they are still in control of their thoughts, until it's too late, until they are in so deep it becomes impossible to find their way back to the light they were born to. Tread carefully Arianwen, for love also blinds some to the truth in front of them. Fate doesn't always choose our paths, sometimes we try and choose our own, only to fail when reality slaps us in the face.'

Watching my mother wipe a lone tear at the corner of her eye, has me seeing her in a new light. My always strong, yet loving and happy mother has pain hidden within her soul. I see it clearly now. In her words, in the soft contralto tone of her voice, in the language her body is speaking, she was in love with another before my father.

'Who was he?'

I am unsure if she heard my soft question until the sound of her swallowing loudly fills the silence. She does not seem surprised by my question as she moves to sit beside me on my bed, a slight smile gracing her lips as she reaches for my hand, holding it dearly in her own.

'He was touted to be a leader of our kin, many, many moons ago. He was confident and so very sure of his every action and the words that he spoke. He was also a little mischievous, always finding trouble, or creating it for his own amusement, all harmless things. But his greatest trait was that he loved fiercely. Everyone he held dear to his heart knew of his ferocious feelings, even myself at one time. Yes, I was in love before I met your father. I was intrigued by the contrast of this man's arrogance to the love that also shone from him so brightly. I had lived a quiet life until the moment his lips lay upon my own. I was instantly captivated by his interest in my quiet self. Yet one day, the love that started to grow for him, began to blind me to his true intentions.

'He wanted to be the leader of our kin and didn't want to take no for an answer, despite already being one of God's right hand men. He wasn't satisfied with what he had, which went against the core of who we are as Angels. He wanted more, he wanted to love more and to be loved by all in return, and soon his ambitious ways began to tire the likes of our current leaders, whom, he knew, were slowly pushing him out of the power that he'd already gained. Eventually God saw his true colours and his ambition for what it was. His fierce love for what he wanted was his ultimate downfall, and he was banished from Eden and Heaven for eternity.'

'Oh mother. I'm so sorry.'

'Nothing to be sorry about Arianwen. Ultimately it was for the best. I could see the warning signs of his true being long before my heart fell, yet I still let it fall. I could see the darkness lingering behind his eyes, but I still willingly loved him. I thought that my love could one day be enough for him, yet he always sought out more. Of course, it was never with another close companion, but from everyone. Darkness comes in all shapes and forms, even in the hearts of some Angels. They try and fly into the light, but in the end, their fate eventually lies in another world. Dark Angels or as others know them "The Fallen" are not just a myth, but I have a feeling you already know this to be true.'

I do, I do know. I feel as if Albion is more Angel than Demon, but because of his upbringing, who his parents were, and the world they all lived in, he would always be seen as a Dark Angel by my kin, instead of what his heart truly is, which is all light. The reality of Albion never being welcomed into Eden hits me hard and solidifies the fact that, to be together, Albion and I must one day find a world that is neither the ones we were born into.

'You don't need to look so sad my child. I found your father and loved him more dearly than I've ever loved another, and we were gifted with three of the most beautiful girls any parents could ask for. This is my fate, here, between the walls of our home. I'm where I'm supposed to be and very happy with the life I cherish. You need to remember Arianwen, to trust your head as much as your heart, it will be harder for the blindness of love to take over.'

She kisses my head and walks from the room, leaving me with more questions than answers. Who was it that she loved and where is he now? Did he fall to earth or did he become a Dark Angel, to sit beside the Devil? And yes, I have seen the effects of a blinding love, sometimes in the eyes of the souls that I have freed from the village of the damned. Love has made many humans act out of character, leaving them with lifelong consequences, to the point that they end up with one foot in Hell.

But, my heart is not the only thing invested in Albion, the Demon Knight. No, my heart is not alone in loving him. My head, soul and entire being, every fibre and cell that make me who I am, is invested in the man I would follow to the ends of our worlds to be with. I am far from blinded. I am more awake than I have ever been in my entire existence.

I am lost in my own thoughts when I hear my sisters call out that they are heading to the bathing lake. My first thought is of fear and to warn them not to go, but I know the darkness that lurked there not so long ago, was there specifically for me. That vile being achieved what she set out to achieve. There is no need for her to venture back into Eden now. I do not want to risk falling back into my dark thoughts, so I busy myself tidying my room and then walk out to help tidy up the rest of the house. I leave my parents quietly reading as I slip out of my home with the intention of being seen in my world on my way to the Bookkeeper, to inform her that mine and Albion's departure has lost its urgency for now.

After waving a greeting to some of my kin, I round the corner of the herb garden, heading towards Claire's cottage, when I feel as if a tree trunk has sprouted from the ground and collided with me.

'Where in God's name have you been for the past eleven days Arianwen? And don't you dare spin some fucking speech about Reclaims!'

Michael's furious expression fills my entire being as his heated breath rains down upon my face. His grip on my upper arms so tight, it has pain rushing down both my arms. He walks me backwards, quickly, until my body slams into a tree, while still continuing to scream in my face.

'Where have you been?'

I can vaguely hear Gabriel's voice in the background as my ears ring with the force of Michael's words. Gabriel is trying to pry his brother's hands from around my arms, but this only makes Michael tighten his grip.

'The truth is Reclaiming. If you don't want to hear that, please don't ask again.'

I am surprised by the strength my voice holds in the face of such anger. But, I will no longer bow to his forceful ways. Even his threat of torturing the truth from my lips holds no fear. As I have recently lived through my own personal torture, no amount of pain will ever compare to that.

'Brother, let her go, now!'

'Back away from me Gabriel or I will turn my ire upon you dear brother. We need answers and she has them! You will speak Arianwen. In your absence, this mysterious power changed, it became stronger, darker and then ... silence. And silence is just as dangerous. Things seem to happen every time you leave the safety of Eden, so telling me you know nothing, you were focused solely on the ones you were called to help, will not work this time you stupid bitch so start talking!'

He is gripping me so hard I feel my body protest under the strain, but I push my feet further into the soil below and stand my ground. I will not bow to his will.

'Have you lost your mind Michael? I beg you, stay your hand unless you are looking to break her bones? The look in your eyes Michael, I haven't seen it so dark since Lucifer fell. You're bordering on the manic, near crazy. Let her go and we can all go and discuss this somewhere more appropriate. Brother, I'm telling you now ... let, her, go ... or I'll be forced to make you!'

With a sickening grin on his face, Michael turns to face his brother while still continuing his hold on me.

'You are completely clueless brother, clueless to what this Angelic slut is capable of, blind to everything she is. Ever since you first laid eyes upon her blossoming form you have not seen beyond the rose tinted glass she has lain over your eyes, and your judge-ment where she is concerned, the less said the better all will be. Tell me "little brother" how you cannot see that she *is* working with the enemy, it is plain for all to *see*. Are you so besotted with her you continue to side with this traitor, at the risk of the safety of your own kin no *less*. You are a leader Gabriel, start acting like one.'

Michael pulls his arm back as if to strike me, causing Gabriel to rush at him, pulling him from my form. Michael's grip on my arm does not ease, and I go tumbling forward with them both, falling to the ground as Gabriel tries to pin his brother down, screaming at him to get a grip of himself. Michael's hold now gone, I crawl backwards, not wanting any part of this, knowing that Michael will never let me live peacefully in Eden again.

Fists fly as they wrestle to each to gain force over the other, a fight for supremacy taking place right before my eyes. If our leaders cannot see sense and work together, how are they going to work at keeping our world safe? If Albion and I leave, will the threat of war still hang in the air? Could I solve all this by running to Albion now and insisting we leave immediately?

I look up to see both men now on their feet, standing apart, chests heaving, with deathly stares flying between them.

'You walk a doomed path Gabriel, and hear me now, when it all falls down around your ears, I'll not be there to save you from the fall.'

Michael storms away as I rise to my feet. Gabriel turning to me instantly, concern filling his eyes as he sees the large angry welts rising on my arms, he steps forward with his arms open, as if his about to embrace me. With no thoughts of controlling my reactions to this man, I take a step back, eyes wide open, a horrified expression on my face in regards to the affection and comfort he was about to offer.

'Arianwen?'

The hurt that furrows his forehead will not hit my emotions. This man, the Angel before me, is not the man I need comfort from. I do not say a word. Instead, I slowly take silent steps back, until I turn, not caring that I wounded the emotions of one man and ready to run into the arms of another. Into the arms of the one I love.

# 31

## Hounds of War

### ALBION

**The scent of my own burning flesh drags me screaming into** reality, my mind so lost in the twisting miasma I had been wallowing in since my Angels departure that I barely register the pain at first. The stench of my own melted skin doing more than the searing heat that is slowly eating through my chest. I roll from my bed and stagger into the bathing pool, water bubbling and steaming as I sink into it, ripples lap at my chin as I finally quench the heat that was threatening to boil my heart in my chest.

I know I cannot ignore this call. I need to find a way through the veil of death and deception, to gain ground enough so that I can finally sink my blade through Lilith's chest and once and for all settle on whether or not something as wholly Evil as her can actually possess a heart.

Dragging myself free of the water, I pad silently across the floor, a glittering trail of water logged footprints mark my path as I move towards my armoury.

As much as loathe the very sight of my former King and home, I know I have to keep the veil in place. Lucifer still yanks on my chain. I cannot remember a time when he could not, the memories of my parents and my life before lost. When Arianwen and I make it free of this place and the seal on my chest no longer holds sway over me, I will gladly carve it from my flesh, no matter the pain I have to endure as a result.

Moving through the village, I cannot help but feel the curling fingers of fear along my spine. The silence that follows my every step is wholly unnerving. It bathes this world in a blanket so thick, so utterly impenetrable that I can hear the flow of my own blood through my own veins. It is as if the very ground beneath my feet waits with baited breath, a breath I fear when released, will bring with it an outpouring of violence so pure, that nothing, Angel nor Demon, will escape its reaching grasp.

My feet send up a skittering cloud of dark red dust, the acrid scent of sulphur and ash flirting with my senses as I draw close to the edge of the pit. I can feel the gallows stare of the outlying watchers, their skeletal forms wedged deep into crevice and crack, long casters trained on my wandering form. Should my need for a rapid retreat arise, I cannot help but wonder just how far I will manage to fly before one of their shells finds my heart or spine. The cadaverous wretches are more than a match for any Angelic marksman.

Stepping free of the cool air I sink into the swirling mire of heat and anger. Even in this sweltering hole of fear and death, I can hear little more than the soft hiss of the sulphur and steam as it swirls upwards, the soft babble of rain as it falls, hissing against my skin, sending a cadent laugh through my mind as I move deeper into the bowels of Hell.

I cast my eyes about me, halls and cells empty, the pop and bubble of molten stone echoes off the walls, the hot bulbous belch of magma hissing as it slops across the floor. I cannot help but feel the pull of fear, something is wrong, the village, and now the pit itself. They have never, in all my years of existence, stood empty and now, I could march a Legion of Angels through the halls and encounter little more than air and empty rooms.

I watch as the air turns cold, the lick of ice lacing the walls around me the closer I draw to Lucifer's chambers. My mind boggles at the sudden change, for as long as I can recall, the sweltering heat of the Styx has bathed these halls, but now, now it is colder than anything I have ever felt. Have I truly found myself in another world or ... or has Lucifer simply dropped all pretence of entrapment and finally made his power and dominion over this world truly known?

I cannot bring myself to think upon it now, the frozen and rigid corpses of Lucifer's chamber guard flank the doors, the dullards simply too loyal or too stupid to know when to break rank and flee. Lucifer's charisma can bring even the most arrogant and head strong to heel, these idiots never truly stood a chance. I rest my hand against one, pushing with minimal force, watching as the lump of meat centred ice rocks, gaining momentum as its weight shifts, before, finally toppling all together and crashing to floor. Shards of frozen leather and skin burst in all directions skittering over the flag stones like diamonds, shaking my head I turn back to the doors before me and twist the handle.

'Was that really necessary Albion? Balo'c could have been returned to normalcy, you and I both know that a frozen death in these halls isn't a lasting one.'

I have to play the role, I have to keep the façade in play for as long as I can. I have come too close to slipping of late, and I need to make this fallen bird think that I am back to heel once more.

'Balo'c was a cur and a pathetic waste of flesh, even the mid level rank and file of my Legion held no respect for him. He had no place guarding your door let alone continuing to live. He's better off as a frozen carpet.'

Lucifer stares out at the river Styx from the balcony opening out before him as I approach and take point at his side. Charon's bloated and twisted form bobbing, lost to the current as it strains against its moorings.

'Fair enough, a purpose is a purpose I suppose. I assume you're wondering why I sent such a forceful recall. I must apologise if it caused you any undue distress, but, well, time is short and I needed my best at my side.'

Lucifer waves his hand at the table and the two small wooden dining chairs that reside next to it. Moving at his direction I take a seat, my back ridged and stance fixed as I wait for his cue.

'Patient as ever, it's one of the qualities I so adore in you Albion. Your father's knack for it was quite a feat and one I must say I did childishly test from time to time. Being monarch here can be a rather tiresome affair.'

I bite my tongue, my need to bite back swelling within me as I sit and listen, waiting for the moment that I know is coming, a moment where Arianwen and I are finally granted the window we both desperately seek, a window that means we can rid ourselves of our accursed worlds and find peace within each other, wherever we may end up. Anywhere has to be better than here.

'I need you Albion. I need you to head to the forest border and sow discord and murder, as much as you can. Anything that steps from those gates and into the wooded stain of no man's land is fair game. Reclaimer, Sleeper, Legionnaire, I care not who they are. I want you to send them to a sleep so deep and eternal that not even my accursed father can find their soul again. Take as many of your fellow Hunters as you wish and go. I want you to soak the soil of the forest with their blood, I want not a single inch of ground left untainted. Am I making myself clear Albion? I want you to slaughter them all.

'War is coming to us Albion and I'll be damned if I'm going to be struck by Eden's first stone, their sins weigh far greater than any of us have ever committed. The Legions have gathered and are awaiting the call, even now they wait with baited breath for the sound of the trumpet. These are the end times Albion, pray that we're the ones standing atop the high ground when the flood finally does descend.'

I would be the most crass of liars if I was to say, even to myself, that I wasn't surprised by this and yet, it still opens the path that Arianwen and I so sorely need. Using this as I know I can, I may just be able to weave a path dark enough that even the light of Michael's sword would be lost to its depths.

I pray that my sweet Angel does not turn against me for what I am about to do. The ethereal blue of her kinsman's life essence will surely be a deep stain upon my soul, but for her, for her it is one I will have to bare. Taking a pure life, I cannot bring myself to think upon it. For all the Good that resides in me, it seems now, as we draw close to my and Arianwen's final days here, I am calling more and more upon my darkness to see me through. I cannot dwell on this. It is not what will finally see Arianwen and I to a safer home, and the longer I take in responding to this featherless peacock the greater chance I have of my time worn mask slipping away.

'Yes my King, thy will be done.'

I stand and turn, not bothering to look back at the petulant former Angel. I will certainly grant him his wants and desires, but, through it all, his selfish need for power and lust for adoration will ultimately keep him blind. He may be the former right hand of God, an Angel so torn by his own needs that he was cast from Eden, but like us all, he is still a being that wants to be loved and accepted, even if he cannot see it for himself.

I push open Lucifer's chamber door and make my way through the halls and towards the Undercroft, the pulsing beat of its heart, one I have become so accustomed to hearing now, sits silent and dead, no music, no raucous laughter. Simply silence. I turn away from the bare and barren hall and down into the twisting corridors towards the darkened cells that house my former comrades, men and women I am soon and all too willingly sending into the jaws of death.

✦ ✦ ✦

The forest stands cold and silent. I scoop a handful of snow from around me holding it in my mouth. The chilled ice stopping my breath, I swallow slightly, melted water flowing down my throat. I glance around me, *my* men and women ready, waiting. Sharp hand movements sends each pair scurrying away, their passage into the forest below silent as a mouse. In another life, with another me, I could have been proud of them, but now I truly loathe the skills I gave them.

I can feel her, I can feel my Angel. My heart seizes in my chest as I see her appear in the distance. I lift my long caster from where it sits, my Hunters moving like wolves as the gates of Eden swing open, a coterie of Sleepers and Reclaimers marching free. They surely must be fearful of the coming clash if they are taking such desperate measures, sending out Gabriel's minions with my Angels kin. Still it will keep them off of my Angels scent. My gut clenches, my Angel, she is down there, I cannot let them lay a finger to her. Lilith, the contemptible whore already took too much from us both. I will be damned if one of these pups will take any more.

I move, with haste my wings snapping free as I jump from the fall and plunge through the canopy as one by one, Sleeper and Reclaimer, vanish into the layered flora, twisting and rolling past branch and bush. I spy her, away from the rest, her glittering eyes a beacon to my heart as she steps out into the woods beyond her gates. A flash of glittering dust glows around Arianwen as she ducks low. I reach for her, my path blocked by the snarling body of one of my former kinsman. I all but scream as I watch his blade rise, my Angel twisting away from its path, rolling back across her shoulder as the razor edged sword slices through empty air. My mind falls blank as hard won training takes over, as, with practiced ease I reach forth, cupping chin and crown, and viciously twist.

The hollow crunch of a shattered spine and throat rises to my ears as Arianwen runs towards the safety of the woodland that surrounds us. I try to call to her, the sounds of the dying drowning me out as she sprints deeper into the trees. Snatching up the silenced caster of the slowly vanishing Hunter, I turn and kneel, tracking my Angel, my sight shifting as I softly squeeze the trigger.

Shot after shot, Hunter, Sleeper, anything that dares draw too close to her, I slay them all. Dropping the now empty weapon I rise, dragging my blade and iron caster from their holsters, the sound of battle rings through the stillness, carving it to pieces. The world around me dances with colour. Arianwen's pale blue and gold aura twists like fire through the trees, guiding me, calling me. With a speed born only of my want for her safety, I move, my blade arcing as I shear through all in my path. One of my kin calls my name as I move between them, the voice of his compatriot dying on my blade as I lift my caster and send him to sleep.

I crash through the branches before me, Arianwen's flushed and determined face turning to greet my gaze as I duck low and lift her from her feet, my wings snapping open moments later and dragging us both skyward, the sound of my dying former kin fall fainter with each passing second.

✦ ✦ ✦

My feet bite deep into dirt and snow the rest of creation lying miles below as I draw my wings closed with still six feet left before I even meet the safety of the ground. My knees buckle beneath me, as I let my body go limp spinning myself onto my back at the last moment as my Angel lands atop me.

'Arianwen, my love, are you injured, do you hurt anywhere? I need you to tell me.'

I can feel her heart beat through my hands as I clutch at her back, holding her as tight as I dare. I feel her fingers against my neck as she turns her head resting against my chest, our bodies in near sync as we both struggle to bring ourselves down from the high of a battle's rush.

Her words are soft, almost a whisper as she replies.

'I'm fine Albion, nary a scratch, but please my love a warning would've been welcome. I was terrified some wayward commander had sought to start the war on my doorstep.'

I bury my face in her hair, inhaling her scent as she begins to tremble softly, the pulsing energy of nearby war and flight seeping free of her as I cradle her in my grasp.

'You handled yourself well, I'm proud of you. A lesser Angel would've fallen to the blow that was cast at you. You dodged that better than some of the Hunters I've commanded.'

I trail my fingers along her cheek as I speak, the soft touch of her skin against my own sending bolts of wanton desire through me as I feel her smile.

'Arianwen ... Lucifer is making his move, it was at his order that I commanded those Hunters close to the gates. I could no more turn my back than I could hide my love for you. I tried to find a way to get word to you, but these orders came to me only hours ago. It's pure luck that the party just before you came through as I sent my men to war. Had they not taken the opening salvo, I can't bear to think upon what could have befallen you.'

Her body tightens against my own as she listens to me speak, not a word leaving her as I stroke my hand up her back. My fingers slipping across her sides, the soft swell of her breast as she rests against me teases my fingers before I coil the stray golden strands of her gossamer hair through my fingers.

I lever us both upright, my stomach quivering as I lift our combined weight free of the clinging snow and ice around us.

'Arianwen, we need to leave, the sooner the better. I have enough prepared that we can leave now. Just go, leave this all behind. Lucifer is blind to everything that is us, but the thought of crushing his brothers and toppling his father from the Throne of Heaven. All I need is for you to say yes and we can go, go and never look back.'

She looks up at me, her eyes wide. Tears prick the edges of her crystal violet pools as I stare, waiting for her to speak.

'Albion ... I'd love nothing more than to leave, to put these worlds and all the misery they hold behind us, but, without baby, without our child to find a safe and peaceful home for ... is there any dire need for us to leave in such haste? I need to find a way to say goodbye to my mother, father and my sisters and be at peace that they will be safe once I'm gone. I need to do that at the very least Albion, and it's not something I can do on a whim and chance. I just can't Albion. I'm not as strong as you.'

'Not as strong as me? Are you in all honesty being truthful with me at this moment? You're the strongest of us both. Hell, you're the strongest person I've ever met. After all we have been through, everything that has been cast in our paths, from being locked away in that infernal mask, living in a world where I wandered lost in my own mind and losing our child to that black hearted whore. Any of that would have crushed another Angel or Demon, no matter how strong they claimed to be.'

I lean forward and press my lips to my Angels forehead as she pulls herself tight to me.

'The memory of baby, of everything that has happened, all of it. I can't bear the thought of living in the world that stole our child from us. God forsook us both, and I'm never going to be able to see his world in the way I once did.'

I close my eyes and hold my Angel close as memories flood me with images as dark and hate filled as any I have ever had. Biting down on my own pain and fear I force my voice to stay level and begin to speak.

'If time is what you need, then time is what you shall have. You know our window is small, but, I think we can wait another two or three days before we *have* to take our chance unless we lose it all together.'

'I love you Albion.'

The smile that coasts over my lips is the first genuine one I have felt in a very long time. I hug her close as I rest my chin against the top of her head. Arianwen snuggles deeper into my grip as I begin to push up to my feet and head down towards the outcrop and the crawl that leads down into our home.

'I love you too Arianwen, now let's go and get warm. I have to leave soon to ensure that Lucifer hears my version of what transpired before any stragglers or survivors make it back to the pit. Besides, I have *something* to take care of before we can truly be sure of our escape from these accursed worlds.'

# 32

## To Cross A Line

### ARIANWEN

A line drawn in sand
Two opposing sides
Safely in their own worlds
Until in comes the tide
The line is blurred
Confusion sinks in
A battle brews
And a war begins

**Leaving Albion's side again is painful, but I know it must be** done. Staying in our worlds is no longer viable for either of us, despite the urgency waning. Michael will forever be suspicious of me, and if I was to be brave enough to ask the high council to consider Albion's exile into Eden, I am sure Michael would do all in his power to make sure he was never granted entry into our community. And for me to receive safe protection inside the walls of Hell, would surely come at a price too high for my Angelic soul to be able to pay. I need to be prepared to leave now, at a moment's notice. Any chance for Albion and I to live in peace, I am taking it.

Just as I near the line of trees that stand to the left of the entrance into my world, I hear Albion calling for me. The sound is strange and not a way I would have thought he would chance calling to me if he needed my help, but it is definitely his distinctive deep tone. For him to call for me out in the open of this forgotten forest there must be an urgent reason for me to be by his side.

Panic starts to creep into my aura as I carefully but quickly rush through the forest and start to wind through the crumbling buildings of the village. I can sense him now I am closer and even though he is no longer calling my name, I can feel the urgency he has for me. I can scent that he is not alone, two dark beings, his own kin are nearby. He would not risk me being seen by any of his kin unless it was absolutely necessary or ... he was terribly injured.

I fasten my pace but still careful as to not make a sound, as I slow down and crawl the last few metres to where I can sense Albion standing. I prop myself up upon a wall and slide slowly towards a crack in between two boulders to get a closer look at my love in need. I can see that he is able to stand as the back of his black leather top comes into view first, my eyes slowly travel up, searching for any obvious injuries he may have sustained. I see his long midnight black hair hanging loosely over his shoulders, but what I do not expect to see is the feminine hand with long scarlet red nails weaved in his hair, gripping the strands tightly.

I only just manage to hold in my surprised gasp as I try and divert my eyes quickly to the left, trying to see whose hand those red nails belong to, pressing my eye closer to the stone in hope of getting a clearer picture. I then see the ruin of my world. That vicious piece of scum, Lilith. My body begins to heat with a ferocious anger as I witness her and Albion seeming to be sharing heated words, both scowling at each other with hate and anger. But, before I can even begin to wonder why her hand is threaded in my Demons hair, she throws herself against Albion, smashing her lips to his.

I push my eye closer into the boulder, the sharp pieces of granite sure to leave an imprint when this disgusting spectacle is over. My hands ball into fist as I wait for the mere second to pass before Albion throws that vile slut away from him. But suddenly, time seems to stand still as Albion's hands move to her hips, and instead of moving her away, he grips her flesh and pulls her tightly to him, her other hand wrapping around his neck, her mouth devouring his as he turns his head slightly to deepen their sickening kiss.

I push away from my stone peep hole, in utter shock at what my eyes just witnessed. It must be a *trick*. Lilith must have lured me here by imitating Albion's voice and has now somehow placed a spell on my vision to make me think the man she is kissing is Albion. I take a deep cleansing breath, willing my mind to be free, trying to shake the possibility of a sorcerers spell as I once again lean in to see the incorrect vision again.

My heart pounds loudly against my chest as I witness, what could not possibly be my Albion, slowly, seductively, move his hands up the sides of the Demonette and weave his own hands in her long tresses. I still hold out hope that this is all just a spell of smoke and deception, until I hear the very familiar aroused growl of the man I love. I have no doubt now that that man, holding sensually onto that pathetic Demonette, is my Demon, my love, my Albion.

Bile drives up my throat, but I swallow it away as I silently slink back into the shadows I came from, slowly slipping away from the most devastating scene I have ever witnessed, my heart and soul still in disbelief at what my eyes just saw. It cannot be true. Albion would never kiss the murderer of our child. He has spouted hate for the woman each time he has spoken her name, even giving her credit in helping Lucifer to keep Albion's mind chained in the deepest crevices of Hell, keeping him from returning to me. This cannot be real, it cannot be true.

My heart is refusing to believe that Albion could cause me the pain that is ripping through my body, but then my mother's words come to my mind. Listen to your head ... and my head is telling me that it was clearly Albion who made that noise of sensual delight.

Oh dear Lord. I fall to my knees on the wretched soil between two decrepit buildings and empty the contents of my stomach. My body shakes with the war that is rising inside. Thoughts are swarming, colliding, fighting for recognition in my mind. Albion would never, but that was his distinct sound, a sound I thought *I alone* brought out in him. Lilith has mimicked Albion's voice before, but it all sounded and looked so real without the haze of a spell surrounding the vision. Why would Albion even risk getting that close to such a powerful Demonette? Why would he even risk the chance of shoving another stake through my heart after recent events?

An aura is chasing me, a feminine scent, the smell of mating and arousal, tracking me, taunting me, trying to send me mad ... and it is working.

I flee.

I run.

I try to escape the madness that is starting to grip my sanity.

I am careless in my escape. I aim for speed and not safety, my only need to get as far away from here as quickly as possible. I run through the dense brush of the forgotten forest, pushing past branches and vines, entangling myself in the process, falling to the ground, my delicate hands speared with the prickles that lie over the soil.

I stand, disorientated, turning in circles, not caring to move with my normal silence, frustrated at the threads of my clothing catching on the thorns of the blackberry bushes I have somehow found myself in. I step forward, ripping the cotton of my cloak, yanking so hard it almost tears in half as I try to run again. I want out of here, away from the turmoil that is threatening to undo my already strained sanity.

I push past trees, not caring that their jagged branches are tearing at my arms. A piece of Drewen tree catches strands of my hair, pulling me to an abrupt stop, the scream of pain that releases from my throat, a sound I have not heard before. I pull at its braches ferociously, screaming, crying, wanting to be free, to leave this place and all that has happened behind. I break the branch, leaving it caught in my locks and continue to sprint through the forest.

I feel the stale air flying past my face, my vision blurring through tears I was not aware were falling, my heart shattering as my head struggles with what to believe. I fall again, slipping on the sludgy moss covering the ground, falling forward, landing on jagged rocks, the flesh of my right palm slicing open. The pain is nothing, nothing compared to what is happening inside my soul. I run, I fall and continue this on repeat, until I sense the border to my world and scent the giant lily pad lake that is just beyond.

I take off in an all out sprint, flying through the think growth of thistle bushes until my feet land on the soil of Eden, my passage is with ease as my Angelic lineage gives me the right to enter. I scramble with haste to the water's edge and fall down, immersing myself in the waters pure essence, desperate for a relief from the heart breaking feelings that are starting to consume me.

I am confused, I am hurt and I am trying not to believe all that my eyes witnessed. But it all looked so real. What if it was real? What if Albion's constant slandering of Lilith was just a deflection of his true feelings? I believe he loves me dearly, but what if he also has feelings for one of his own kind? They might not be as strong, but they could still be there. What if, in his struggle with grief, she caught him in a moment of weakness? A moment he thought I would not never discover.

*No.*

*This cannot be happening.*

The sickness I feel is poisoning me from the inside. I look out to the giant lily pads, once a place of my peace and mediation, somewhere I flew when I needed to think, to heal, but now I do not even have the strength to stand, let alone fly. I fall to my side on the muddy bank and curl up into a ball, hugging my knees, trying to hold myself together as my heart endures another scar, in a way I fear will leave it in ruins for eternity.

My heart and soul is screaming at me to not believe what I saw, yet my head is giving me a true possibility that what I witnessed was real. I do not have the strength or clarity of mind to figure this out, my entire being, so utterly drained from the traumatic loss of baby. Oh baby. How could Albion place his lips on that murderer? The vision of her lips on his, her fingers entwined in his hair, her body pressed up against his, are haunting my thoughts, making it impossible to fight for a clear path to think.

Sobs rack my body as I begin to lose control of my tightly wound sanity. As much as I wish not to believe what I saw, the visions of Lilith in Albion's arms. It is all I see and the pain of that sight, it is truly something I cannot handle. My body shakes as I feel grief start to sink into my aura again. I cry, I whimper, I gasp for breath and fist my hands as my still healing body falls once again.

I considered going to the dark side for Albion, what world do I reside in now?

I feel the mud beneath me start to cake on my cheeks and my body start to chill, as I continue to shed a river of tears at the confusion raging inside my mind. I hiccup as I breathe, my entire body shivering, as I desperately try to find some type of reality to cling to.

I scent someone nearby, one of my own kin, but have no care to raise my head and see who it is. I would prefer them to pass by, leaving me here in my state of self pity, but no Angel would leave another in such distress. My ears are pounding with the sound of my own heartbeat, the rhythm thumping erratically in my head, blaringly loud, drowning out everything, so much so that I do not hear his softly spoken words the first time. But, when he repeats them again a little louder, there is no mistaking the words that belong to Gabriel.

'Oh dear Lord, what's happened to you Arianwen?'

His question and the deep concern in his voice has me crying harder, trembling at the irony that Gabriel's the one to find me here in such a state. He truly is the last man I want to seek comfort from. Yet as that thought settles in my mind, I realise, I do feel a slight amount of comfort, that it is one of my own kin who has found my distraught form. I know, no more harm or pain will come to me in his presence.

He kneels down beside me, his voice echoing in my ears as my heart beats louder to a deafening roar, as a torrent of emotions flood through me.

'Arianwen, can you hear me? Are you injured? Can you move?'

I cannot answer, I cannot respond, my breaths coming in short pants as a panic starts to ripple up through my body, and I have no idea as to why. Gabriel steps behind me, scooping his arms under my muddy form, lifting me into his arms and pulling me tight to him, cradling me to his chest as he begins to move away from the lake and head towards two grand buildings.

'I've got you, you're safe now. Hush now my sweet Angel. I'll take care of you.'

His words make me cry harder as I bury my head into his chest, his arrogant and confident smell, not nauseating me as it once had. I fall further apart, gripping my hands on his linen shirt, desperately trying to hold onto something so I do not fall further down the rabbit hole. I feel his steps quicken, then feel them rise quickly up steps, before the crisp fresh air of our world stills and turns warmer. The sense of being enclosed takes over and the familiar scent of the grand halls invade my airways.

He turns a few times, taking more stairs, turning again, until I hear a click of a lock, heavy wood moving one way and then back and the soft click of a lock again. I feel Gabriel's steps slow. He raises a knee then shuffles our bodies slightly. I chance opening one watery eye just a crack, to see that we are propped upon a bedhead, silky white linen below Gabriel's legs and my dirty dishevelled form lying across his lap. I swallow a strangled howl knowing he must have brought me into his home and now, he sits cradling me in his arms upon his own bed. Just as Albion did.

The panic that was starting to grip me, now runs like a bull through my veins and makes it harder to breathe.

'Hey my sweet Angel, you're safe now I promise. I'll look after you. Breathe for me Arianwen, please. Take slow deep breaths.'

I cannot. I cannot breathe. I try but feel my throat closing fast. I know I should use my gifts to help, but my body does not want to respond. The last thing I remember is Gabriel pleading with me to take long slow breaths before everything, suddenly, turns black.

✦ ✦ ✦

I feel my body heave with the remains of a silent sob as my senses start to awaken. I know instantly where I am. I can scent

Gabriel surrounding me, my entire aura bathed in his. I want to pull away from the hold he still has on me, my body snared tightly in his arms, cradling me against his chest. But, I honestly have no strength left to fight. I feel as if that is all I have ever been in, an enduring, never ending fight, constantly battling emotions, trauma, raging conflictions within myself, love worlds apart yet constantly colliding, all too much for my supposedly sweet, innocent, Angelic soul.

Despite my conflict at who is holding me, a sense of calm flitters over me as I let out a sigh. At least here, I have no Evil chasing me down with distressing visions or a sorcerers spells. Here I can just ... breathe.

'How are you felling now?'

Gabriel's soft words make me flinch slightly before I settle further into his chest, not wanting him to see the war of emotions and betrayal flittering through my vision. He rubs one hand softly up and down my skin, reassuring me that it is okay, that I am indeed safe in his arms and in this very moment, I feel that yes, I am safe.

I chance a look into his eyes as I slowly raise my head, his concerned, furrowed brow cannot be masked by the smile he is attempting for me. I just stare, for the first time, deeply into the eyes of the leader I thought I knew, the leader who has been so aggressively pursuing me, into the eyes of the arrogant man who seemed he would not stop until he got his own way. But now, there is no trace of the man I thought he was. All I see now is genuine concern and affection for the woman he is holding so gently in his arms.

My confusion must register in my eyes which has his frown deepening, the emotions he is showing me are all too much for my fragile self to handle. I look away and instantly know it is a mistake. My eyes zero in on the open fireplace that is crackling softly in the corner of the room, and as my mind registers the orange flames, flickering softly through the air. My thoughts take me back to all the times Albion and I have lain in front of his fire, making love to the soft glow of the amber light.

I gasp and turn my head back sharply, colliding with Gabriel's chest, my hands flying up to my face, trying desperately to stop the tears that want to flow. I catch sight of the dried mud on my fingers and pull my hand back, staring at the mud and scratches that are plastered all over my skin. A sob escapes as I look down at the rest of me and notice how much of a messy shambles I am. I hold my emotions back, no amount of tears will make anything right at this moment.

'Shh my sweet Angel. It's fine. We can clean you up.'

Before I let a protest escape my lips, Gabriel is lifting me in his arms and carrying me towards what must be his personal bathing room, something only seen in these large grand buildings. Important leaders and members of council do not always have the time to venture all the way out to the bathing lake.

He sits me on the top of a large wooden bench, one arm still around my shoulders as he leans over beside a large hand carved bowl next to my hip, grabbing a stone cut crystal decanter and begins to pour water into the bowl. He grabs a handful of soapflakes from a small china bowl and drops them into the water, using his free hand to swirl them around, while the both of us watch in silence.

When satisfied with the milky tinge of the water, he bends down slightly while still holding onto me, bringing back a washcloth from the shelf below and drops it into the water. He turns back to me with a sweet smile as he slowly, careful not to hurt me, pushes my ripped and dirty cloak off my shoulders and sets my arms free. He then takes one of my hands and brings it over the bowl and uses the cloth to wash away the caked mud from my skin, careful not to brush too hard over my many scratches.

The sweet and gentle way he cares for me is surprising, yet, it is not. My opinion of Gabriel has been tarnished by his need for me to be his bride. Before he took notice of me, I respected him greatly for the way he lead our kin, with friendliness and grace, but when things changed and he started to look at me in a more personal way, I pulled back, worrying that one day he may request that I no longer Reclaim.

But seeing him now, concerned over my dirty skin and red

welts, washing me tenderly yet meticulously, I am seeing a whole other side of Gabriel I would never had thought existed. He swaps to my other hand and washes that too, dragging the cloth up my arm, making sure to wash away all the mud he can see. He then steadies my shoulders, making sure I am able to hold myself up right, before he falls down to his knees to inspect the dirt and scratches on my lower legs. Once I am all cleaned there, he rises again.

He stares into my eyes, holding me captive as deep emotions swirl through his vision. He gives his head a little shake, as to break away from whatever spell he was falling under then leans in to ever so gently remove all the branches and leaves that are still stuck in amongst my long locks of hair. He brushes the strands softly through his fingers, trying to dislodge the knots then uses the wash cloth to remove specs of mud that have also ended up in my hair.

He turns away and lifts the bowl of dirty water, walking it over to the waste hole and pours it down. He brings it back and fills it with fresh water and more soap flakes, swirling them around the water, lost in his own thoughts. He grabs a fresh cloth, dips it in the water a few times, wrings in out and then faces me, a soft grin playing at the corner of his mouth. He takes a step closer, raises the wash cloth and softly runs it over my face. Around each cheek, over my forehead, down my neck then gently over my eyes then smiles when I am all cleaned.

This tender moment making my stomach twist in knots. I do not want this, this affection from him, but I have no fight left or clear thinking to try and find a way to escape it. He places his hands under my armpits and lifts me down from the bench, my feet touching the ground, legs feeling weak as he raises his eyebrows, asking if I am capable of walking. I look down and take a step and instantly feel as if I am falling sideways.

He quickly scoops me up in his arms and carries me back to his bed, silently crawling to the middle of the bed head and settles down, once again, holding me across his lap. I shift, trying to move to sit beside him instead of on him, but his hold tightens.

'Please Arianwen, please let me care for you. I never thought I'd see such a strong Angel in this state. You have me worried. What happened to you? How was it that I found you curled up in a ball on a muddy bank? Who did this to you my sweet Angel?'

My breathing hastens as memories try to invade my mind at exactly how I ended up back inside the walls of my own world. I hold them back, refuse to give them the power to cause me pain anymore. If I let them free, I am not sure I would survive the onslaught of emotions that will inevitably tear me apart. I hiccup a large breath and try again to pull out of Gabriel's hold.

'Please Arianwen, I beg you, please don't tense in my arms, please don't pull away from me, please don't run. Let me take care of you like I so desperately want to. I don't know exactly what I did to make you so nervous around me all the time. Maybe I was too forward or too crass towards you at times, but whatever it was, I will be eternally sorry for it. I *am* sorry. I am sorry if I have treated you more like a possession at times, than a woman who deserves nothing but my unyielding love and respect. You deserve more and I'm sorry I haven't seen that until recently. But please, please let me care for you now, please let me look after you, even for just a small moment in your time of need.'

I take in a large breath, unsure on how to respond, unsure of how I *want* to respond to his outpouring of such honest words. Maybe he has not been so bad all along. My stubbornness of not wanting to stand by his side as a trophy, risking losing the biggest part of myself as a Reclaimer, may have clouded my mind to who this man really is. Yes he has been arrogant and forceful, but maybe it was more confident and headstrong, and I was blinded to see the truth by my fear of becoming just a pretty mute by a leader's side.

His quiet words break me out of my silent thoughts.

'I know I'm one of the leaders of our world, but I'm also an Angel, a man, who is completely spellbound and in love with the beautiful woman in my arms.'

I gasp and hold my breath, his words piercing through my heart. They are real and honest. I can feel the sincerity of his words soaking through his aura as his eyes plead with me to see his truth, to understand the words he has spoken. He is begging me to reciprocate without saying it out loud. We are both holding our breath while he waits for my reaction, the only sound in the room is the quiet hiss of the fire place and the wind blowing softly outside.

He reaches up and runs a finger cautiously down my cheek, a smile pulling at the side of his mouth as he lets his entire hand make contact with my skin, cupping my face as he leans in slowly, gauging my eyes for any hesitation to his touch. I am frozen, unable to move, his scent completely enveloping me as he moves in closer again. I see his intention, clear in his eyes, yet I do not move. Why cannot I move?

I move my eyes from his and down to his lips, two plump, pink cushions of flesh, wanting a taste of my own. His breathing increases as does mine when he closes the last little piece of space between us. I can feel his fast breath against my mouth as panic starts to rise inside my chest. Yes, he may be much more than I ever gave him credit for, but to go so far as to let him be intimate with me, is not something I should be encouraging. So why is it I cannot pull away from him? How is he captivating me so?

I close my eyes the moment his flesh touches my lips, the taste of him instantly flooding my mouth. This is wrong, I cannot do this, I cannot fall under the spell of someone I have been trying to run from. He presses his lips harder into mine, my stomach turning as I feel the feather light touch of his tongue dart out to make contact with the seam of my lips. These are not the lips I want to kiss. This is not the tongue I want to taste. This is not the man's arms I want to be in. Albion. Albion is the man I want.

Just thinking about him has visions of that Demonette wrapped around his body. Vile rises quickly up my throat and takes all of my effort to not come out as I pull back from Gabriel as far as I can in his tight grasp. There is a large knock at the door which has Gabriel groaning as he places his forehead on mine, unaware that I was trying to pull away from him.

'Do you think if we are quiet, they'll go away?'

He says this with a boyish smile on his face. I try and smile, pretending to join in his joke, while praying that whoever has interrupted us, does not go away at all.

The banging gets louder, more insistent. Gabriel moans, places a soft kiss to my head, moves me to the soft sheets beside him and moves from the bed to go and answer the door. I hear Michael's angry hushed tones and instantly grab at the blanket near my legs in an attempt to hide from his vicious words. Michael raises his voice louder, making it clearer to understand his words.

'Your foolishness could endanger us all!'

His comment has me moving from the bed. I stand and begin to sway, my body exhausted from my recent emotional and physical strains. But, I stand still for a moment, willing my body to cooperate, trying desperately to channel everything I have that has helped me push through all the other difficult moments in my life, and begin to take unsteady steps forward.

I enter the bathing room needing my cloak. I pick it up from the bench and shake it out, trying to dislodge as much dead greenery as I can, hoping to make it look decent enough to move through my world without questioning eyes upon me. I have to steady myself on the bench two more times, my head dizzy with emotions trying to release. I hold it all in and concentrate on threading my hands through the sleeves of my cloak and shrugging it over my shoul-ders. I pat down my wayward hair and walk into the bedroom.

Just as I am sitting on a chair, tying the straps of my sandals around my ankles, Gabriel comes back in. He is silent while I continue to tie my shoes. I raise my head slowly and instantly see the disappointment in his eyes.

'Why ... why are you leaving Arianwen?'

'I need to get back to my family. I have no idea of how much time has passed.'

'You were gone for eleven days and they knew you'd be fine. Stay, please.'

I shake my head slightly and stand, taking careful steps as not to sway on my feet while I leave this room. Gabriel steps forward, gripping my shoulders gently, pleading with me through his eyes so full of love. Yes, it is love that shines in his eyes, so clear for me to see.

'Stay, spend the day with me, here, alone, no prying eyes upon us. Please Arianwen, please don't leave.'

# 33

## The Price Of Vengeance

### ALBION

**Her fingers are curled tight into my hair as her lips grind into** mine. The scent that fills me is one that I never thought I would find filling my senses, and yet, it does now, every fibre, every facet of my mind sings with it.

'Alp said you wanted me here, I didn't think it would be like this Albion.'

She grinds herself against me as I curl my fingers deep through her hair, Lilith's tongue skating across my teeth as they begin to extend, forcing their way through my gums as my horns tear their way free of my scalp.

'Oh I wanted you here Lilith, I wanted you here so badly.'

I close my grip, a soft gasp leaving her as she feels the tension of my hold sing through her.

'But, not as you wish it was.'

I wrench down twisting my hand as she falls. I watch fear and pain sail through her eyes as she screams at me, guttural Enocian like words slithering across her lips as I bend her backwards over her own spine.

'My brother did exactly as I bid him to. Alp called you here at my request. You vacuous whore have dogged my shadow and life for too long. You took all I held dear and ripped it apart, you instigated every horror that has befallen me ...'

I lean in, my lips barely millimetres from her ear as she begins to turn a pale shade of purple, pain over shadowing her breathing.

'You murdered my child! You lay hand to the woman who owns my heart and soul ... all because a would be child King gave away something he never owned, to a whore it was never destined for!'

I feel Alp's hand at my shoulder, his voice smooth as syrup as I twist my grip tighter, her scalp peeling apart the further I push. I cannot help but smile, a sickening joy blooming in my heart as the rippling sound of collapsing cartilage fills my ears as her mouth opens in a wordless howl of pain, the pale skinned meat suit that sheaths her form, sloughing away to reveal the putrid Demonic sack of flesh beneath, her aura glowing as she tries in vain to conjure forth any sort of defence or sorcery against me.

'Brother, do you really think ending her life will right the wrongs she has caused you, all the pain and anger you feel now ... do you honestly think it will just disappear the moment she falls to the eternal sleep?'

'Alp, you have helped me come this far, why are you staying my hand now? She has wronged you, just as she has me. Can you truly say her death will not benefit you as much as it will sate my need for vengeance?'

He steps in front of me, his body fluid as I glance up at him, my mind quivering in confusion for a moment as I look into his eyes. I cannot say for sure what I see, but, I swear his eyes were those of my Angel. I cast my gaze back to Lilith, too caught up in what I am about to exact to bare my confusion any heed.

'I don't know brother, and as much as I want to say that she deserves everything that is boiling within your brain, I can't say the same. She's one of our kin, a General and Commander of a Legion. Surely she deserves clemency, especially with all that is coming.'

'No Alp, she doesn't! For some crimes, especially those that she has committed, the only punishment is death.'

I sink my other hand into the soft pliable flesh of her throat, curling my fingers inwards as I drag downwards. Lilith's hand rises, claws snapping free as she sinks them into the side of my face, I feel the tips of her harpies talons grate against my skull as I lean forwards, my weight bearing down upon her.

A primal flame burns in her eyes as her spine buckles, the hollow crack echoing off the walls around us as I close my fist through her throat. Steam coils of blood bubble free, the acrid green slopping over my fingers as I drag backwards, tearing her windpipe free.

She thrashes and claws, her nails rake my arms, glittering trails of my own blood running free along my arm as I curl my fingers open, dropping the blood soaked wad of flesh and cartilage into the dirt. My mind is a sheet of primal rage as I spear my hand downwards, my fingers sinking past her ribs and closing around the bitter lump of flesh she calls a heart.

I feel its sallow beating within my grip, pump after pump, all of it growing weaker as I twist my grip, her neck bulging against itself, spine cracking as I draw my arms backwards, her fear smeared gasping head twisting free of her shoulders as I drag her heart from her chest, the pulsing organ throbbing in the palm of my hand.

I hear a stifled, quivering gasp from my left. Turning, I catch sight of Alp's ashen features. Striding forwards I drop Lilith's severed head and take hold of Alp's hand. With a callous flick of my wrist I drop her blood drenched organ into Alp's shaking hand before reaching down and once more curling my hand into Lilith's twisted and matted hair.

As my skin suit moulds itself across me once more, Arianwen's familiar energy washes over me. I close my eyes suddenly when, as much as the rage has soaked my every fibre, I am filled with a cleansing calm.

I turn and take off at a dead sprint towards my Angel, her energy and aura drawing me like a fish on a line. I can hear Alp's pleading calls behind me, his plaintive cries falling on deaf ears as I move towards my one source of happiness as a cold fear wraps itself around my heart.

Did she see what just come to pass? Did she cast her eye upon the lingering deception that was the kiss between that gutted contemptible whore and I?

I pray not, in my haste to rid my life of Lilith's putrid self I foolishly negated to tell my Angel of what I had planned. I cast a prayer to anyone who will listen that she did not see it, if she did ... I cannot bring myself to think upon the implications it will have on my life hereafter.

I turn a corner, the sour tang of blood settles on my tongue with every breath I take as it slowly drips from the twisted remains of Lilith's neck, the overwhelming scent rising on the wind as it drips from the whore's head in my hand.

As I draw nearer, the sensation of calming happiness increases tenfold, my heart and soul basking in a bountiful ray of pleasure and comfort. I close my eyes, the air around me cool, twisting over my skin, caressing and easing the tension from my every aching muscle.

'Arianwen ... I.'

I am too late, her scent, her comforting aura, all of it, a mere shadow of the Angel I so love. She has gone. I cannot fathom the pain that must have rolled through her if, and I hope beyond hope that she did not, that she saw only the first few fleeting moments of what has just transpired.

I drag phlegm and spittle up from my throat, vainly trying to cleanse my mouth of the taste of that butchered whore. I shift my vision, my mind reeling briefly, my body still not in tune with my senses after what I had just put myself through, staying the course, forcing my body and mind through something that every cell of my being is screaming out against taxed me beyond compare. I stare at the slowly fading lines of my Angels glittering aura, her passage away from here, tearing me apart as I watch the wavering colours, a pattern all too familiar to me.

I can taste the pain and betrayal in the air. Tears sting my eyes as I race forwards, desperate to reach her before she moves beyond my grasp, the borders of her lands already teeming with Michael's zealots and Gabriel's Sleepers. Never would I have a hope in ... well ... a hope in Hell of breaching their lines to reach my love, to explain to her just what she saw.

As I reach the precipice of the fall, all I can do is sit and watch as she passes through Eden's gates, hair gnarled and twisted, thick lines of red weaving across her body as thorns snag and tear at her soft cotton dress, the need to drop from my perch and go to her, to sweep her up in my arms drives me mad with need. But, as I watch one sound echoes free, the clang of the Dragon's gates rolling through the air shattering my heart as they close behind her, sealing her away from my love and life.

I bury my head in my folded arms, as I lean in against my hunched legs. I am such a fool, all this pain, all of her heartache. Everything I just created, all of it could have been avoided if only I had set aside my need for haste and spent the merest of moments and explained to my love what it was I was about to do, and now … for the want of a few simple words, I may have lost her once and for all.

✦ ✦ ✦

Night begins to settle in around me as I feel Alp's presence tease the edges of my perception. He is good, his movements soft and subtle, his aura dampened, but to me, he is as loud as a full march-ing orchestra. I do not bother to turn and look in his direction as I speak, calling him forwards, my voice low, cautiously paced. The pain that soaks through my words all too plain no matter how careful I am. I feel Alp stop short of my side, his breathing soft and even, but his energy, his aura, both betray his fear.

'You left this with me.'

He drops Lilith's heart in the dirt beside me, the shrivelled black lump of flesh oozing clotted blood and viscous puss. Even for a Demon it is vile. How much hate this woman contained I cannot say, but, for all she was it was only matched by the level of her avaricious lust for what she could not have.

'What do you want to do with it? You know if you give her enough time, without "dealing" with it, she will convalesce, all of her kind are capable of that, Lilith more so. I dare say she can hear and feel all that is going on around her. We need to decide Albion. *You* need to decide, exactly what we are going to *do*. If or when she comes back, this kind of slight against her will redouble any hate and anger she held for you. I have seen her and Lucifer, hang, draw and quarter people for far less than what you did, what I am party to. I love you like a brother, but I'll not go to the butchers block for this. Not when we can silence the issue for good.'

I scoop it up, weighing it in my hand as it continues to drip blood and filth from between my fingers.

'I'll deal with it, as you say. I am the one who drew it from her so I should, by rights, be the one to seal her fate. Leave it to me Alp, go and forget all that happened here, make yourself seen in the croft. If you have to twist and bewitch one of the lines women to gain an alibi do so, they're too dull to see the difference anyway. As far as I'm concerned you were never here brother, and that is what I'll say should anyone ask or question me on what has transpired.'

Alp stands fixed to the spot as I stay still, staring out over the darkening expanse of the forest below.

'Albion ... I ...'

'Go Alp, I'll deal with it as I said I will, just know ... I'll never forget this, now go before someone stumbles upon you here.'

Alp's steps filter away as he vanishes into the village, heading I hope, towards the Undercroft and a lust and sweat soaked alibi between the legs of one of our kin. Setting my eyes upon the heart in my hand I close my fist. My rage, my pain, my fear, everything she dragged through me pours down into my tightly curled hand and what I have ensnared within.

The scent of charring flesh begins to slip from between my fingers as I close my eyes and whisper to myself. The Enocian words dance off my lips as I repeat them over and over, heat building, the pain beginning to seep into my mind as my hand and Lilith's vile heart begins to burn.

I open my eyes and watch as the flesh of my fingers begins to flake and fall away, rivulets of ash and smoke curling through the gaps as I squeeze my hand all the tighter. The last of my own flesh falls to dust when I stop, my mind screaming at me as the pain floods in. Everything I had just endured drowning me in one torrential downpour. It will take some time for my body to reconcile what I have sacrificed to that particular rite, but, the smouldering pool of ash that was Lilith's heart is all the comfort I need to help me endure as I watch it drain from my fingers. I drag my gloves from my pocket raising the left to my lips and catching the cuff between my teeth as I slip my hand inside before, carefully and tenderly sheathing the slowly healing remains of my right hand inside the other.

As I stand here, battered and soul weary, on the precipice of the fall, Arianwen's soft and warm embrace flows around me. Her energy pours through me, filling my heart and soul with a soft effervescent light I can feel cleansing the darkness from my every facet. The smile that flows across my lips is so complete I actually start to laugh, something I have not done, since ... I stand, stunned, I truly cannot bring to mind the last time or even the first time I have ever felt laughter flow from within me, and yet, here I stand, the soft exultation of joy tripping from me in droves as I cast my sights to Eden and the source of my happiness.

I stretch my senses to breaking point, my body weary but my spirit willing and open. I caress the edges of my Angels aura, the pain and loneliness that pours back over me shatters anything that had come before. Can she have truly seen what transpired and took it as truth? I cast my senses wider, my aura recoiling in fear and panic as Michael and Gabriel fill my mind's eye. Those rutting hogs cast a thickening shadow over my love as I feel all hopes of reconciliation boil away to nothing. I know in my current state I cannot hope to even get close to see my Angel, let alone hold her or even have the chance to explain to her what she had witnessed only hours ago.

Drawing back within myself I sink once more to the floor, my heart, crushed shards in my chest as I stare down at my Angel's home land, its towering spires and gilded fence a prison, not only to my heart's desire, but to my hopes, my dreams, to everything that had ever made me complete. Lilith's blank eyes and slack face stare up at me, anger curling through my chest as I stare back.

'You took all I had left in this world, I hope the sleep tears your soul to shreds, it's the least you deserve.'

I toss her head away from me, watching as it twists through the air and sails free to the twisted rocks and groaning trees below. A dark sigh wells within me as I stare down at Eden. All I can do now is wait, wait for the chance to see my Angel again, if she is still mine when those gates finally part.

# 34

## The Need To Flee

## ARIANWEN

**Confusion reigns supreme through my mind as I steady my** feet to a normal pace, stifling their efforts to run, fast, from Gabriel's residence. I declined his request to spend the day with him, alone. His disappointment was palpable, and for but a moment I thought he was not going to let me leave, but manners won out as he gave me a sad nod before stepping back so I could continue walking to the door. The sound of his quiet words, just before I pulled the wooden door back to leave, were quite melancholy.

'Arianwen ... you are welcome here anytime. If you need a quiet place to ... think, I'll make sure you have the clearance to always walk into my private residence. And if you need me, for anything, I'll always be available for you. Please don't forget that.'

The sadness mixed with a slither of hope, shining clearly in his eyes, caused an emotional response within me that I was surprised by. But, Gabriel's affections are one more thing I have to add to my ever constant woes, and the fact that I have not received a single calling from a soul in need since the parting of baby, is all starting to weigh upon me heavily.

My life before Albion was set in stone, or so I thought. I was an Angel of God, a hard worker for my community in every way, always spending time helping anyone who needed a hand. From my earliest memories I have had to keep busy, boredom always looming the moment I sat still. So the hectic life of a Reclaimer was a welcomed one when my gifts reached their full potential, and I was official granted that title by God himself.

My life was simple. I would save the souls that the Devil was trying to claim for himself, I would help my kin; be it teaching the children, tending the gardens, helping to prepare feasts for a celebration. And in my rare downtime, I would continue to read and research, something I have been doing a lifetime. Apart from the obvious risks of walking to the edges of the Devil's home, my life was a neat little package of routine.

Yet now, now I have no idea what direction to step. I feel beyond lost and terrified that for the first time in my existence, I do not know what is expected of me or where my place is in this world or any other is. Who am I supposed to be now?

If I were to stay here, in my own world, how long would Gabriel remain passive without his affections being returned? Would Michael forever be hounding me, berating me, trying to get me to confess to still sleeping with the enemy? Even if Albion and I were no more, how long would Michael still feel the need to interrogate me? Months, years, decades? I do not think I would ever again find peace in my own world.

And if I do return to Albion's arms, will there ever be that same trust, will I ever believe I will never find him in Lilith's arms again? That painful vision sends sharp lines of agony through my heart. Here I was, thinking my love was still grieving the loss of our child as am I, that that type of grief will always be a part of our souls then I walk into a haunting vision of a harlot wrapping her lips around his own. Nothing will ever purge that sight from my mind, regardless of it being truth or not.

I know better than most, Evil seduces the truth, in many ways, and I have witnessed and experienced what that Demonette is capable of. So why is it so hard for my head to believe it may have all just been a trick? That the man I love, who held me dearly for days on end while I was lost within the devastation of my own mind, was not willingly taking part in such a sensual scene with that slut?

Oh Albion. Even if it was all truth, my love for him has not diminished in the least. We have shared and created so much in such a small amount of time, I will be eternally grateful for all that he has made me feel. But to never feel that again from him ... would be tragic.

I wish I could knock on God's door right this instant and demand he tells me why. What did I do to deserve all this upheaval and heartbreak in my life? What are his plans for me? What do I do now? I feel as if I am standing at a crossroad without a path at all to walk down. I need answers. I need truths. I need guidance. Maybe I should plead with Claire for some insight into why my world has been torn apart.

My thoughts are ripped out from under me as a large hand grabs my arm and another fist a handful of my hair.

'After the intimate time you just spent with my brother, you still walk away from him, you're still reluctant to become his *bride*. I could sense your distaste for him the minute you left his room, I can see it in your eyes now. So tell me Arianwen, what game are you playing at?'

Michael's vicious words drip with anger and hate as his hand tightens painfully in my hair when I do not answer him immediately. We both startle when voices are heard coming our way. Without letting his hold on me go, he moves us further down the path before kicking open the door to one of our many garden sheds, walking us inside and slamming the door shut, bracing his back against it with me still in his hands.

He pulls me tighter to him, his body running up against the whole length of my own as he waits for the noisy interruptions of a family to walk on by. My heart beats faster as I realise I am locked in a small space with hostility pouring out of Michael's aura like lava, boiling and ready to burn.

'At least maybe my brother will have a clearer mind now that his hunger for you has been sated.'

He pushes me forward, my hands splaying out on a low lying bench to stop my fall.

'I don't know what you mean.'

My words, even whispered, seem to echo loudly around the

silence of this small space.

'Oh come on Arianwen, don't play coy with me. Every time an Angelic piece of female arse is seen sneaking out of my brother's room after the midnight hour or at dawn, he's a much happier man the next day. Every. Time.'

I know he is baiting me with his words. Little does he know that his brother was gentle and kind in the way he was taking care of my dirty, scratched up body. But, it does have me thinking that the side of Gabriel I recently experienced, could all be just an act, just to sway me towards accepting his obvious proposal.

'You're making my brother so distracted, he's not thinking clearly. How do you suppose a leader who's not thinking clearly can make sound decisions for our world? Putting all our lives, including your own families lives at risk.'

I turn around to see Michael take the two steps needed to stand right in front of me, his words hitting me exactly where they intended.

'Then let me go, and I promise to stay clear from him from now on.'

If I did not think that his face could be angrier I was wrong.

'Too late for that you stupid little cunt!'

Before I even have time for his vicious words to register, he grips my shoulders and spins me around, a forceful blow to my back has me flying down over the surface of the bench before me, his large hands grabbing my wrists and pinning me to the rough wood as he looms over my body, forcefully pinning me down.

'No Arianwen, you cannot walk away now. He wants you and only you. No amount of my coercive words have had an ounce of impact on him. You *will* be his bride and it better be *soon*. We have urgent business to attend, a war is brewing, and I need his full concentration at my side.'

His hot breath is pulsating right behind my ear as I feel the full length of his body pressed angrily into mine.

'No.'

My squeaked response has him pushing me further into the bench, his heavy weight threatening to squash me beneath him as he rams his body into mine out of frustration.

'Yes, yes you will! Or ...'

I feel him bend his knees into my legs slightly before he forcefully pushes my thighs apart, my feet easily sliding away from each other over the sandy surface of the floor. I am horrified to feel the length of his arousal pressing firmly into my cotton covered buttocks, sickened at the thought that he is aroused by his rough treatment of me.

'Maybe I should impregnate you now, right here, so you have no choice but to immediately sleep with my brother and insist on a wedding very soon. Mmm, maybe if I take you, get myself off using your body, maybe I too will be able to concentrate on more pressing matters.'

I gasp at his words, which has one of his hands grabbing over my mouth to silence my objection to his disgusting intention. I try and fight my way out of his hold, but he is too big, too strong and has an iron hold on me as he cages my body between his and the wood beneath me. This will not happen. I will fight to the death before I allow him to take me as he wishes. I bite one of his fingers, but it causes nothing more than a malicious laugh to roar from his chest.

'Don't fight me Arianwen. If you can give it up to an ugly, stinking Demon then giving it up to one of the leaders of your own world, should be a more pleasurable experience for you. If you fight, I will *not* be gentle.'

He holds my mouth tighter, leaning into me further, as he uses his other hand to roam down my body roughly. I feel him gripping at the hem of my dress, raising it up to slip his hand between my legs. I try and scream, thrash my way out of his hold, but he has me firmly in place. I feel his thick fingers slide over my cotton panties as tears leak out the side of my eyes.

'I can feel your heat you filthy Angel slut. You want me, you want this.'

He drags my underwear to the side and pushes a finger down my intimate folds. I bite him again, numerous times, hard enough to taste his blood on my lips, but he just laughs it off and pushes harder against my centre. Rage starts to boil inside of me as I silently call to every ability I have within to come together and give me the strength I need to stop this ordeal. I feel something begin to boil, a force that has laid dormant of late, a power I have been trying to hide from all the worlds around me that may just help me to escape the clutches of this sickening man.

But, if I am to show a man, a leader like Michael, all of the cards I hold, revealing all that I am capable of, I may end up in a state worse than I am now. I may even be traded to Lucifer himself. If Michael knows what I am capable of, there is no way in this world, he will let me anywhere near his brother or to roam the gardens of Eden at all. Do I fight him and reveal that I can indeed overpower him, or do I remain silent and as still as I can and wait until this torture is over to flee this world for good?

Before I decide, he lets out an enormous roar and the pressure of his body disappears from mine.

'I can't believe I almost fell for your sorcerer's ways you stupid little cunt! To think I almost gave in to my own weak desires, would have made me as stupid as my brother is. No, I will not teach you a lesson this way. But, you will not walk away from my brother again, do you hear me? You will willingly go to him tomorrow and announce that you have had a change of heart and are happy that he has chosen you as his bride to be. I will make sure a wedding is planned immediately.'

The defiant look in my eyes when I turn and watch him over my shoulder, must be very evident to him; his nostrils flare with rage as he takes a threatening step forward before stopping himself, a sickening smile starts to replace the anger on his face.

'Mmm, maybe I have another idea that would be more suitable and agreeable to us all. Maybe I can sweet talk your middle sister who recently came of age, to start taking an interest in one of her leaders. She does look a lot like you Arianwen, so I'm sure it wouldn't take too long for Gabriel to start to notice her in a more, shall we say, mature way. But then, if my brother's stupid brain is still clouded by thoughts of you, maybe I can then step in and offer my hand in marriage to the sweet and luscious Brianne. To have a leader forgo a presentation ceremony with other girls and just ask her directly for her hand, well, how flattering would that be?'

The sickening anger I feel is indescribable, but before my

words of hate can spill from my lips, he takes the last step to get to me and grabs the hair at the back of my head and rams my skull down hard against the bench. My vision starts to turn black as I hear his laugh slowly disappear into the distance.

As I fall to the floor, trying to remain conscious, I know that I will never have a place in this world, but that will not stop me from protecting my family from the perverse plans that Michael may put in place. I will not go to Gabriel tomorrow and confess my sudden desire to become his bride, instead, I think I need an honest talk with my parents, to inform them of the other side of Michael I have become all too familiar with. They need to have some warning in case this impending war brings Evil a little too close to their front door.

# 35

## Hastened Revelations

## ALBION

**The air of my home is stale, still and stagnant as I pace like a** caged animal. I need to see my Angel, I cannot bear this separation any longer. She has been gone too long from my side, any longer and I will surely descend into manic mania and ultimately madness. The Legions of Lucifer and God are both primed to descend on each other, all the while Arianwen and I are caught betwixt the two, like mice between a cats paws. There is little we can do except prepare and evade them all long enough to wind our way free of these lands to a home ... a home where we can truly be together, where we can once more forge our union and be what we have both always wanted to be with each other, a family.

The thought of it sends a spear through my heart, my darling child taken from us before you even gifted this world with your grace and love. I hope you find rest in the eternal sleep my little one, and know that your father sought restitution from the despotic harridan that took you all too soon.

My teeth grind together as I cast a harried glance towards the doorway, willing my Angel to appear. I long to see her there, violet eyes glowing with love and passion as she carries in the final pieces of her old life.

Old life ... I scurry through the cave, snatching whatever my mind seizes upon and piling it up on the treated canvas sheet cast across mine and Arianwen's bed. Clothing, wind sheets, bundles of dried meat and pemmican, anything I think can be of any rudimentary use ends up in the pile. There is zero order to my urgency, everything and anything is tossed atop the burgeoning hillock. Turning towards my armoury my mind stops, thoughts crashing into one another as everything grinds to a shuddering, migraine inducing stop.

Arianwen. Panic grips my chest as my sense burn, something has to have happened. She knew to be here by now, nothing would have kept her except ... I race towards my armoury, my armour already draped about me, buckles and straps half tightened or left hanging as I snatch my weaponry from where they hang and move through the door, my body slipping through the doorway before it is even fully open.

I breach out into the watery sunlight, the eleventh hour hanging high in the sky as I cast my senses out, everything I have searching for my elusive love, the lingering fragments of her scent tease me as I breathe deeply. Closing my eyes I follow each tentative trail to its end, Arianwen's glowing, lingering aura twisting through paths and alley. Over stream and woodland trail, yet none of them lead to her. I set my sights to Eden, not caring what or who picks up on my searching gaze as I dance through doorway and window. The copper scent of my own blood filters through as the strain of my far flung searching begins to take its toll. My blood drips from my chin as my knees buckle, still as I skate my mind across the crystal waters of the bathing pools and the open communal parks, I find no sign of my love.

Finally, as pain lances along my spine, shearing through my mind, I admit defeat and draw myself back, retreating within myself as I fall to my hands and knees, retching and gasping for air.

'Where are you Arianwen?'

I sink to my stomach before slowly, my joints aching and mind screaming at me, roll onto my back as I struggle to slow my breathing. I truly cannot fathom what has kept my Angel from me ... unless, could the thoughts of what she saw be driving her from me, can she not see the kiss, the most repugnant and stomach twisting act I have ever committed, as the ruse it truly was? I pray she can, I pray to whomever will hear me that my Angel, my love and soulmate, can truly see through the smoke and mirrors to the core of what was before her. I cannot fathom my life without her, nor do I ever want to.

Time seems to crawl as I lie here, chest heaving, trying to regain my composure enough to rise to my feet, yet I remain, still and drained, in the dust in front of my home.

The sun is passing, evenings rise by the time my body is willing to allow me to rise and move onwards. The need to find my Angel is all too apparent, yet, if she is to ever see me again, as the man she owns, as her one true soulmate, then I must abide by my own discretion and allow her to reconcile within herself what I know she saw. Yet, the pull to my Angel's side is one that is slowly choking the life from my soul. I know before long, I will be tearing down the gates of Eden in my need to once more hold her in my arms.

I just hope, a fools hope, that my resolve holds out longer than my Angel's doubt.

✦✦✦

Garth's home sits squat and tired before me, my feet guiding me to his door as I sit lost inside my own head. Before I truly realise where I am, I come face to face with Glynnis, her smiling face a picture of warmth and happiness as she pulls me tight to her and plants her lips upon my cheek.

In my fugue of worry and fear, I seem to have gravitated to the only place that, until Arianwen made my life and soul complete, I have ever truly felt loved. I cast my eyes around me, my gaze alighting on the racks and holsters adorning the far wall, the final few weapons that I have yet to sequester.

I cannot help but relax slightly in the warmth the hearth is slowly pouring into the room. I step inside, Glynnis' firm grasp pushing me down into one of the chairs at the pitted and rough-hewn table. I trace my fingers along the surface idly as she clatters and bangs through her meagre kitchen, throwing together a meal that is all at once, mind bogglingly fast and as complicated as any trial of God's creation.

I sit trying to take in the sudden swarm of kindness and affection when a bowel clatters down in front of me, a mix of meat, lentils and spices soon following as ladle full after ladle full is set down, the thick mixture coming so close to the lip of the bowel that I fear it may spill free if I even breathe sharply in its general direction. Finding my voice I call out to Glynnis as she moves away from me and back into the kitchen.

'Glynnis, it's not that I don't appreciate the vittles' and affection, but I have to ask ... why?'

A soft chuckle filters through on the sea of steam that is flowing across the ceiling.

'Albion, my boy, you should know asking Glynnis that question is akin to asking God why he didn't just revert Lucifer back to the particle mist he conjured him from. It's a secret that only she will *ever* know the answer to.'

I turn towards Garth, his wizened face split by a grin as he steps towards me and sets a hand on my shoulder. Glynnis' voice floats through the curtain shielding the archway leading through to the kitchen.

'Just you remember Garth, I cook *every* meal in this house, no telling which one I'll put something extra in and I don't mean alcohol.'

'You keep saying that woman, but you've yet to follow through.'

A hollow chuckle is Glynnis' only response as Garth sinks into the chair next to me, his gaze questioning, face set in a curious yet soft smile.

'So Albion, what brings you here?'

I sit silent, my mind spinning as Garth waits patiently for a reply. What did bring me to their door? Why of all places was I drawn so inexorably towards this of all places? Nothing I bring forth can give me anything in the way of a logical and cognitively sound response to the simplest of questions posed to me, by one of the only other people in either Heaven or Hell, who have shown me a shred of kindness.

'Honestly Garth, if I knew I'd tell you. At the moment I am

struggling to figure out whether I still have a reason to be, to even continue living in this twisted plane of existence, much less a reason for anything I've done in the last few hours.'

Garth's brow furrows as he turns to face me directly, his elbows coming to rest on his thighs as he clasps his hands in front of himself and stares directly at me.

'Albion, there's only been one other time in my life where I've seen that look in a man's eyes. Your father had the same gaze when he and your mother left you in my care the night they ...'

Garth trails off, his head falling forwards as he stifles a soft sob, his shoulders bobbing once before he looks back up at me and draws in a slow, softly shuddering breath. As I sit there looking back at him, I find myself drawn to the one question I have longed to ask; what possessed me to ask it now, I can only put it to the fact that I am now staring at the possibility of never more seeing Garth after this week sees its end.

'Garth ... I need to know what truly befell my parents, why did they leave me with you; what took them from me?'

Garth sighs as he nods, rising slowly and moving towards his work bench. I listen to the soft pop of a cork as he sends it bouncing across the desk top, the chipped cylinder of cork coming to rest in a pile of rivets and sewing needles. The rhythmic ripple of liquid hitting glass flirts with my hearing as Garth pours us both a much needed drink before returning to the table and setting the glass in front of me.

'I know what you've said before, I know what I've told you before ... and to an extent it was true, your mother was cut down after they took your father and flayed him alive, but ... it wasn't for the reason you believe. Time here, in these worlds of immortals and the dead, it doesn't behave the same as it should, it ebbs and flows, the longer you live here the more you see time repeat itself.

'I have thousands of lives come and go. I have seen Demons turn to the light; I have seen Angels turn to the Darkness, and yet, they *all* had one thing in common; to a man, they all did it for love. Love is the most singular emotion anyone can experience, it can make us fly or fall; it can make a man weep joy and a woman scream in rage, above it all though, it is the *one* thing Lucifer covets most, and it was because of love that he took your parents' lives.

I stare at Garth, unable to speak, unable to think. My entire life, my years of loyalty and blindly following orders in the name of a Fallen Angel I once called my King, all of it was a lie, as bold faced as any I have ever been told. The look in my eyes draws Garth's attention as he nods and continues talking.

'Your mother, Amunet, she was a gorgeous and wondrous person, a soul so pure and clean that not even rain dared to fall on her skin. She fell in many ways, but the most striking of them, was how fast and how suddenly she fell for your father. From the moment she saw him here, which is how they met, your mother was far more adept at hiding her aura and presence than *any* Angel I have ever met, and believe me, with how long I have lived in this world, I have met many a feathered flyer, but I digress. From the moment your mother saw Abara, she was destined to fall, the look on her face was the same one I have seen on yours each and every time Arianwen's name is mentioned.'

He points at me with a sly grin turning his features.

'Yes ... that *exact* look, she was so enamoured with the all powerful Hunter and Knight that stood before her, that when she finally dragged herself out of your father's amber yellow eyes she actually got her message backwards *and* in Enocian no less.'

'Garth ... I appreciate the story of my parents first meeting, *but*, it doesn't tell me all that I asked or indeed anything close to the fact.'

Garth raises his arm and pats at the air, his voice filled with mirth and sadness as he smiles.

'Patience Weisser, patience, all will be clear at the end, now ... shut up and listen. Your father, he was never one to toe the line or follow the pack, forever the free thinker and lone soldier in an army of collared wolves. Your father, instead of flying to the sword and striking down a stunned and helpless Angel, a doyenne of Reclaimers no less, he turned to her, bowed low and set his weaponry on the ground at her feet.'

I cannot help but feel the surprise that smothers my face, my brow rising so sharply I am set with the thought of my eyes bursting free of their sockets.

'Any other Demon, as you said, would have cut her down in an instant, but ... he disarmed himself? I can't hold that as truth Garth, you must be mistaken. My father, a Knight of the first order, would *never* lay down his weapons for any being regardless of who they be.'

'No lad, Garth's not mistaken. It was a beautiful sight to see, and one that I can say is as true as the nose on your face. I've never seen two people so better suited or destined for each other than your parents ... that was, until I saw you with Arianwen.'

Glynnis levels an even gaze upon me as I drop my eyes to the floor, staring at my feet as I run through everything that has transpired in my world.

'Over the weeks and months that followed I watched their attraction and ultimately, love, deepen. It wasn't long before our home became their "secret" meeting ground. But, none of this was secret for long. Lucifer is and always has been a very vain and jealous Angel, even before he fell. He had his eye on your mother even when he was in the welcome embrace of Eden, although she wasn't the only one he sought affection and devotion from. The castes of Angels are a complicated lot, but when Lucifer walked among them, let us say that it wasn't always the most, chaste of places.

'He used a few names in Eden not that I can name many of them, and was gifted the moniker of Satan after his fall, how that came to be I don't know, but when it came to his ear that Abara had taken his cherished Amunet off the playing field and made her his, well, jealousy is a cloak that's an ill fit for many, even a Fallen Angel such as Lucifer. Lucifer engineered many a mission, many a task. It put your father in harm's way, the task of a Demon Knight, well you know better than I just how perilous that life is, but, Lucifer went beyond the pale with Abara. The tasks he levied, the distances he pushed both your father's safety and the sanity of you mother; it was quite simply villainous; so much so that eventually it came to a point where Amunet made the decision that many an Angel has made for those they wish to protect. She fell ... she shattered her halo and renounced God as her master and keeper and left the light of Eden behind, but not before being given a soft push, from who I don't know, but despite her love and adoration for your father, the order was always there.'

I sit quietly, ruminating over all that Garth has been telling me. Lucifer, the vapid self proclaimed King of Hell and Fallen Angel, was in love with my mother, so much so that he engineered my mother's fall from grace? I know he is that devious, that maliciously foul he would go to any lengths to gain what he wanted.

Truly to find that, after all the years of doubt about my families true origins, to know that my mother was what, in my heart, I always suspected her to be and that in truth, her descent to darkness, her rebirth as a Demon of Hell was all because of one Fallen Angel and his jealousy at her loving another. And now here I sit, destined to make the same actions a reality, my love for Arianwen and everything we have been through has pushed us to lengths that would surely destroy a weaker willed pair.

I shake my thoughts from their track, focusing back on what Garth, the one true link to my past, in now telling me.

'So, yes, your mother walked from Eden, well ... I say walked, but, you understand my meaning, and marched into the mouth of Hell. Over the years that followed, I would often hear from your father his storied words of how Lucifer was in many ways trying to slowly drive a wedge between them both. How he knew that the birth of their child, you, would bring about the seeds of change for both worlds and that, in short, despite Lucifer's own manic jealousy and desire, could never be allowed to happen.

'It is one reason why your parents tried to flee, to leave to a world free of Lucifer's reach and God's watchful eye. When they left you in my care and went in search of a safe path, wherever it may have led, all they wanted was to see you safe. The last words your father ever said to you were, *"Be strong and behave, we will be back soon."* As I watched your parents leave, the world changed, the entire pit shook with rage and fear and at that point it was all too clear that he knew. I have no idea how Lucifer came to know of their plan, nor who it was in the end that divulged it to him. But, when he finally came to know of it all, there wasn't a place in this world that they could have hidden.

'In the end one irrefutable fact remained, that if Lucifer couldn't have her, then no one could. But, the folly of love is, that no matter how much you hate the person for their actions, you still can't in truth be the source of their pain. So, in the end, Lucifer simply removed the problem.'

Garth stares at me, his eyes drilling the truth into my skull.

'He killed my father.'

Garth slowly nods, his eyes tracking to the door and the streets that lay locked beyond it.

'Not three streets away, a band of his damned Dolophonos came at your father, all vapour and steel. There was little he could do against them, their bodies little more than mist when he served them the cold blade of his sword. They danced around him, blades rising and falling as he fended off blows and advances, but, in the end, it was simply too much, there was too many of them. Your mother ... I can still hear the scream of your father as he bellowed for her to run, to flee while he kept their attention fixed solely on him. You know already the name of the one who clipped her wings, and I can take some solace in the fact that, despite all that happened before, that vile being is finally at the beck of vengeance, all be it vengeance taken in the name of another. Your father's fatal blow, the one that finally silenced him, that came from Lucifer himself.'

I still remember seeing that blow land, as I stood powerless to help. You can think of me whatever you wish, but had I, the skill or power to help your father that day, I can surely say I would have gladly fallen in line with him. Lucifer's blow was a coward's one. As your father knelt, struggling to rise and parrying strikes and blows left and right, Lucifer raised his blade and sank it through your father's back.'

As I stare at Garth, unwilling to listen to the fate of my mother, I rise heading towards his front door. I can hear his calling plea, begging me to stay my path and find a way free ... and that is exactly what I am to do, although as I close my hand around the handle of his front door, I cannot find the words within me to say so. I will be free of this place, I will find a world where Arianwen and I can finally be together without fear and reprisal. I have to find a way back to my Angel, even if I have to storm the gates of Eden and wrest her from the hands of that fluttering messenger myself.

# 36

## Stay

## ARIANWEN

**I pull the hood of my cloak down slightly, not too low, but** wanting to cover the bruise on my forehead that my body has not completely healed yet, without it being too obvious that all is not right to the kin I pass on the paths through the garden.

My body is a riotous mix of anger and fear as I walk away from Michael's violence, savagery and threats. I feel my blood boil as I contemplate my next move. I need to talk to my parents, but not until I have calmed my aura and started thinking clearly. I now know that if I leave, either alone or with Albion, Michael would indeed find a way to follow through with what he threatens. I will not risk my sister having to endure what I am at the hands of our leaders.

No amount of words with my parents will ever encourage them to leave this Heavenly world, even if they were to take my warnings as truth, they would want to stay, to make peace, to find a way around Michael's or even Gabriel's demands. To think my sister could become a pawn in a game of power and deception, makes my stomach clench with a fierce anger. I would rather stay and find a way to live through many lifetimes fighting off Gabriel's affections and Michael's torment and torture, than for my sister to discover and live with, the reality that is our world behind closed doors.

Despite my lost faith in God and the devastation at losing baby, I could never turn to Evil. My soul is and always will be pure light. I could never turn my back on anyone in need, be it family, kin or a soul calling to me. Even a Demon that was lost inside himself. My need to help and nurture at all costs, will forever be at the core of my soul. I was born an Angel, a spiritual being who is a celestial attendant and messenger of God. Full of beauty, purity and kindliness, whose actions and thoughts are consistently virtuous and who, to the humans of Earth, is often a guardian spirit. I will forever be an Angel.

I need to find a place in my world where I can live in a semblance of peace. If I am to consider enduring Gabriel and Michael's behavior for eternity, then I need a place I can escape to when the burden becomes too much. After war is fought, win or lose, the forgotten forest will no longer be an option of a mutual ground to reside in, I am certain the Devil will make sure of it. So what will become of mine and Albion's home?

Albion.

My heart weeps at the very thought of him. Will we even be in each other's life when the war is over? Are we still in each other's lives now? The pain I feel at the visons of his lips blending with Lilith's, is indescribable. The confusion surrounding that heartbreaking scene is tearing me up inside. Everything in my entire being is telling me that all is not what it seemed, that it was Lilith's intended deception to make it look as intimate as my eyes laid witness to. And the love I feel for Albion is holding strong, telling me that Albion had a plan and what I saw was only a small glimpse at what that was about.

So do not I owe it to him, to us, to hear him out, to let him explain the horrendous act my mind believes to be truth? But, why do I feel a reluctance rise within me, at that thought? Is it because I am fearful that he will say yes, he did kiss her, he wanted her, that it was just a moment of weakness he promises never to repeat again? If the truth is not what my heart wants to hear, how far will those words actually go in snapping what is left of my thinly veiled strength? In such a time of turmoil and upheaval in both our worlds, our love could be all that holds us both together.

Love.

Our love.

Our love is strong. I need to focus on that. I need to focus on what I know, the facts, the certainties that are not at risk of being tainted by spells or the smoke and mirror trickery that Evil is so fond of. I know mine and Albion's love is so strong and pure that no amount of venomous influence could ever sway its bond. That is what I know, that is what I have to concentrate on.

That is what I have to believe in.

Oh Albion. How could I have ever doubted your love for me, for baby, for the life you have been fighting to create for us? You deserve a right to explain, to tell me exactly what occurred and why you needed to have it happen that way. Was it a way of keeping her quiet until we were safely on our way, or was it a means to an end that I was not privy to? No matter the reasons behind it, I need to see the man I still love with every facet of my being and hear his own voice explain away my fears.

I continue to walk along the paths of Eden, nodding politely to my fellow kin, praying to anyone that hears that I do not get stopped in conversation along the way. I need to get to Albion with as much haste as I can, without sprinting through my home like a storm.

I am almost at the end of the gardens when I scent him, fear and worry rolling from him in ferocious waves, desperately seeking my essence to calm his mind turbulent thoughts. I round a large oak tree, the Dragon Gatekeepers coming into sight and standing between them, vibrating with restless energy like a caged animal is Albion.

The moment our eyes meet, all of my doubt and confusion instantly evaporates. The desperate love I see in the deep crevices of his troubled eyes, tells me all that I need to know. Albion crosses the border and sprints towards me, ramming into my body like a freight train as his arms wrap around me like a vice, lifting me up into an envelope of pure, untainted, love.

*'Arianwen, Arianwen, Arianwen, Arianwen.'*

His broken words spoken on a sob breaks my heart. The distress in his voice has the tears in my eyes falling down my cheeks like a torrent, releasing all of the hurt and worry I had been holding onto so tightly. He walks backwards with me still firmly in his embrace, taking our bodies back over the border of Eden, to a ground he feels more secure on.

'I love you Albion.'

My whispered words, the only ones that seem important at this moment as my Demon crumbles in my arms. He falls to his knees, but does not let me go, my knees hovering off the ground as I feel his shoulders shake, his body racked with deep, unrelenting sobs, my own emotions tumbling forward and flowing out like a torrent.

How could I? How could I have ever doubted this man in my arms, the man that I love, the Demon who is shattering right in front me?

'Arianwen, I wanted to tell you, I needed to. But, not doing so was the only way to keep you safe. What you saw, what I did; it will haunt my mind for eternity, but, it was all for you, I had to give her what she wanted for but a moment. I needed her close, locked in a sense of self indulgence, it was the only way ... the only way I could get her close enough to end her once and for all. She is gone and nothing, not God, not Lucifer's black arts can bring her putrid soul back to this world. I couldn't risk her harming you, harming us again. I had to make her pay for all that she did, to you, to us, to ... to ... I failed. I failed you. I'm sorry my love, so very sorry to have caused you more pain. Will you ever forgive me? Please my love, please forgive me.'

My beautiful man before me has done nothing I need to forgive. I knew his actions would have been part of a plan, yet my exhausted and grieving mind could not come to that conclusion until now. The pain that is seeping from his every pore and floating over me, is agonising. My faith in God may have waived, but it should never had where this man is concerned.

I hold him to my chest a little longer, calming him with whispered words of love, but knowing we do not possess the luxury of time, especially in a place so close to my world, we need to move from here. I encourage him to loosen his hold, long enough for us to stand and begin to move towards our hidden granite home, ready to discuss our plans. I take two steps before

Albion gently scoops me off my feet and cradles me in is arms, my cheek lying against his chest, feeling his heart as it still beats at a rapid pace.

He walks quickly but cautiously towards home, his eyes darting around more than usual, an unsettling feeling creeping over me as I feel the unease tensing his shoulders. It is as if his waiting for something to strike, expecting it to at any moment. We need to be in a safe place now, before we discuss where our future lies and what we may have to do to keep the scale tipped in Goods favor.

Albion does not release me until we are safely behind the walls of our home and standing at the foot of our bed. As soon as my feet hit the ground, I see the unorganised pile of supplies we were hoarding to take on our escape spread all over the bed. The first thing that hits me is the pain, the pain at knowing that the reason we were leaving with such **urgency, is no longer growing within me. And the second is that we can no longer go, not** yet, not when my family could be in danger, of not only Michael's actions, but also the war that is bubbling just beneath the surface of both our worlds.

'Albion, we can't go!'

My panicked outburst surprises him as his brow creases in confusion at my words.

'Arianwen, my love, we have to and it needs to be now. Believe me when I say, our time has well and truly run out.'

The urgency in his words tells me that Lucifer has begun his plans of war against his former brothers and creator, more the reason we have to stay and protect my family, protect my kin, and fight on the side of Good.

'Michael made threats against my family, and I believe that in my absence, he will follow through with them and much more. He can't be trusted Albion. Even if he had some alliance with his former brother, I feel he is still preparing to go to war just to be a victor against his former sibling.'

As I speak these words, Albion reaches a hand up to my forehead and sees for the first time, the small evidence left of Michael's brutal handling of me. His body tenses, veins start to rise more prominently along his neck and forehead as he just stares at my head with a deathly glare. He goes to step past me but I grip his arm, nails digging in, to stop him from storming out of here and all the way to Michael's doorstep.

'No Albion. You *cannot*, within my own world would be suicide, and now is not the time. We need to fight with the light, not against it.'

'*Arianwen.*'

He desperately pleas for me to let him protect me and avenge any wrong doing upon me, let him do the job his love for me urges upon him, but the resignation in his eyes tell me he understands that seeking out Michael now, is not the best course of action just before a battle is to begin.

'There is going to be a war. Be it a small scuffle between former brothers, or an all mighty battle between Lords and their immortal worlds, it is going to happen. We both feel it, we both see it, and we both have lain witness to the provoking words of leaders. The disturbance our love has caused has rocked both side's foundations and threatened their power. If only they knew that it was *love* that is this all mighty force that has so upset the balance of their worlds, maybe war wouldn't be consuming their thoughts.

'I've no idea why fate or God or some other entity brought us together if war would be the result of it, but there must be a reason, an explanation as to why, why the two of us must stand together and fight side by side to ensure the preservation of Good is upheld. I need you Albion, I need you to see my family as your own, to protect them as you would your own. I need you to help protect my world because it's rightfully yours as well. I feel it Albion, I have since the first moment I raised my head and looked into your eyes. My mind was telling me to feel fear, to flee to save my own life, but my heart and soul were at peace standing before you. Because, I finally felt whole while standing in your presence. My entire life finally made sense while I was staring into the eyes of a Demon, who has a soul very much like my own. No matter what world we live in, you'll always be a part of who I am.'

He stares at me, eyes searching my own for the truth to my words. He is understanding the honesty of them, finally allowing himself to believe that yes, he is from light, he was also from my world, from Good, from Eden. The reason he ended up in the world of Evil is no longer important, when I see the acceptance start to flood his aura. Whether Michael, Gabriel, the high council or God himself may not see fit to grant Albion life in my world, he belongs there. Always has and always will. Hope springs in my chest that one day, just maybe, we will find a way to live in Eden, in Heaven, together.

'Arianwen, the darkness I was raised in, it is dead and gone. I pledge to you here, and now, I will fight for Eden, for your family, for your kin. I will fight for *you*. I will forever stand by your side no matter what the fight. I am yours, for all eternity.'

His large fingers gently whisper down my cheeks and ever so slowly make their way to the back of my neck, where he cradles me tenderly like I am made of glass. Slowly he leans in and brushes his lips over mine; the taste of him floods my mouth and awakens my body. I thought I lost him, I thought the worst of him; I thought I may never get the chance to be in his arms again. How foolish was I?

I eagerly grab his black jacket in my fists and pull myself closer to him, begging him for more, begging him to reconnect, begging him to give me all that my pent up body is craving, but his pace remains slow and tender as his mouth lazily takes my own. I am frantic, yet my love is the pillar of peace and calm.

His hands slowly move down my neck, soothingly over my shoulders and down my arms. He then wraps them around my back and just holds, holds me to him while he leisurely makes love to my mouth. The brush of his tongue over mine ignites my desire further, my body heating beyond the pleasure of arousal, my hands releasing from his leather cladded chest to wind up into his long midnight hair.

He starts to walk backwards, taking me with him, until I feel the heat of the open fire on the backs of my hands entwined in his hair, the only part of me that is not protected by my Demon's large body. He remains slow and gentle as he comes to a stop, still consuming my mouth with sweet, lush strokes of his tongue, taking me away to a moment that is not filled with fear or an impending war and the unknown of our future together.

I move my hands down to tug his shirt free of his pants, wanting to undo the ties, needing to feel his flesh with my hands. It takes a few tries, but I finally pull it free as my fingers raise to his chest and begin to untie the ribbons of soften leather that hold his shirt in place. I fumble in frustration, the ties become more tangled than free, Albion's fingers stilling mine and taking over, easily opening his shirt. I go to rake my nails down his chest but his large hands grab my wrists.

'Breath Arianwen. Slow down. Savoir.'

His whispered deep tone vibrates through my body, causing a shiver to rush over my skin as he bounds my hands in one of his, while slowly walking behind me. His other hand brushes my wavy hair over one shoulder, exposing the delicate flesh of my neck, the fast beat of my heart evident in the pulsing vein lying just under my pale skin. He licks over the beat that is trying to jump out of my skin, all of my nerve endings coming to life as I feel his hot breath brushing behind my ear.

His free hand glides over my shoulder and down between my breasts in a feather like touch, his fingers pulling on the end of the lace strap that is holding my torn white dress still in place. He languidly pulls the lace through each eyelet until the soft cotton falls open, my breasts exposed, my buds hardening at the low groan that emits from his throat.

He flattens his whole hand against the centre of my chest, feeling my heartbeat underneath, before slowly moving it over to gently grab a handful of my breast, kneading it with a slight amount of pressure. He moves his hand up, taking the fabric of my dress with him, pushing it over one shoulder then repeating it on the other side. My dress pools at my feet, Albion's appreciative hum further fueling my need for him as he releases my wrists and uses both hands to run down my sides, stopping at my hips, my panties under his hands begin to slide down and then fall to the ground.

His hands brush faintly over my stomach before moving towards each other and directly to the apex of my thighs. He pushes both hands over my centre, the pressure making my head fall back against his shoulder as I moan his name, the sound echoing off the rock walls surrounding us. He growls, I hear the restraint in is voice, yet his movements are still controlled, measured, memorizing every touch under his fingertips.

He pushes a hand down further, his fingers slipping between my folds, my hips automatically pulsing forwards, chasing more friction, craving more of his touch. The sound of my wet core is loud in this silent haven. Albion's fingers remain, but I feel his body move, dropping to his knees, his stubble jaw rubbing over the tops of my buttocks. All touch disappears for a moment before he grabs my hips, turning me around, his tongue instantly spearing my centre as he buries his face between my legs.

I moan to the ceiling, legs feeling as they will give way at any moment as Albion takes his time lapping up my arousal. He grabs my hips and pulls down gently, a silent plea to join him on the ground. He sits back on his hunches, and my knees fall either side of him as he grabs my mouth, the taste of my desire mingling with his own unique flavour. He reaches behind, grabbing my rear and pulling me up his body. My feet come forward, knees bending as he settles me upon his upper thighs.

His mouth once again, slow dancing with my own, our breathing heavy as we share the love we feel so desperately for each other. Albion's hand moves between us, the sound of his leather trousers shuffling about until the searing heat of his tip brushes over my hard bud of arousal. He now fastens his movements as he lines himself up with my core and surges up as he pulls my hips down.

'Albion!'

I scream his name as I feel him throb against my most intimate muscles, his steel shaft filling my entire core, his heat making me break out in a sweat. One hand grabs the back of my neck, his careful restraint broken as he loses control, his mouth smashing to mine, his other hand grabs my hip, urging me to move. I push up with my feet slowly, enjoying the drawn out growl that flows from his mouth and then let all my weight fall back down with force, landing back against his thighs.

His head flies back and the hiss he lets out tells me his control is completely gone. Both of his hands now grab the flesh at my hips and lifts me up, pulling me back down his hard shaft with so much force, spikes of pain shoot through my body, soon turning to pleasure as he repeats his movements over and over again.

My body rising fast to sit upon the edge of ecstasy, desperately waiting for my love to take me over. Albion's fingers dig deeper, his movements faster as he bites my lip in a frantic state. His mouth captures my scream and his tongue soothes the pain. I feel his length thicken inside of me, causing my muscles to clench him harder, wanting to claim him, never wanting to let him go.

I lose my breath as the wave finally pushed my body over the edge, my voice screaming out his name as my head flies back, my loves own roar of release drowning out my voice as we both ride down on the cloud of euphoria.

We cling to each other, desperately trying to get closer, wanting to crawl into the other's skin and hold on for eternity. But, deep inside we know that we need to leave the safety of our loving arms, the safe walls of the home surrounding us. The worlds beyond our home are much bigger than just Albion and I. War is coming, Albion and I, my family, my mother, my father, the sweet innocence that are my sisters, the youngest of my kin all caught in the middle. I cannot, *we* cannot abandon them. As I lie here in my Demons arms, I know as I can sense he does, that we *must* stay. I just pray that we are left standing after it all, so that when the dust does finally settle, we can have the life together we both desperately want, no matter what world we call home.

# 37

## Something Old; Something New.

### ALBION

**The stone above me drifts in and out of focus, the pain in my** chest fading as quickly as it descended. I cannot help but feel a semblance of peace having my Angel back in my arms and life, even if she does now sit beyond the gates of Eden if but for just a brief moment. I cannot help the feelings that creep through me, the fear, and the panic, everything riding on decisions I am truly terrified of facing, absolutely and unequivocally petrified of all that awaits not only me, but also the one true love of my life, my Angel, Arianwen.

I know my life lies with her, and only her. I have come too far, given too much to see it turned to ash because of the jealousy of an Angel. Could Gabriel truly have his gaze so firmly set on my soulmate? Have I been so blinded by Lucifer and his machinations against my family, that I have missed the threats at my doorstep?

I know for certain that I cannot serve a cretin such as he, the jealous petty child that is Lucifer, the man who ended my family with the thrust of a sword through my father's back. The one who condemned me to a life of utter hopelessness, that was, until I found my Angel. I need to get us both away from here, away from the pain, away from the heartache, safely to a world where, we can, I truly hope, have a chance at once more bringing a new life into our world and being a true family.

Now though, I know I need to stay, if only for a short while longer, but this home, my and Arianwens home, is no longer the bastion of safety I once thought it was. Michael and Lucifer have already breached its sanctity once, even though it was only the plateau at the mouth of the crawl, I still cannot set my hopes in a place. I cannot trust to keep the one I love the most free of harm, and now, with my departure from Lucifer's shackles waiting only moments from my grasp, I know it will never truly be what I need it to. I have to leave that destitute world of pain and madness, I cannot abide it, not knowing what I do about the man who molded me into the killer I am now. How can I?

I need to make my love see what I do, the looming specter that is Lucifer. His pale horse and spiteful, jealous heart intent on bending all to his will; to worship him as a God in rapturous love, but she is too blinded, blinded by the love for her sisters, her mother and father. Can I really begrudge her that? She spent a lifetime in the comforts of a place I never could, a true loving family. As much as I can see how she cannot want to leave them for fear of what Michael and Gabriel will bring down upon them ... can I truly say I fully comprehend it? No, I cannot and here I am once more alone, in a home threatened by the life I am leaving and the one my Angel is tied to.

If we stay, if we continue to exist in this world, war will surely find us. It is as inevitable as the changing seasons or tides of the endless seas. Arianwen and I simply cannot remain in a world that, through all its Goodness, will be our demise. This wretched existence has already claimed the life of the innocent, my child, Arianwen's child, our unborn babe; a life taken by the jealous hand of a Demonette twisted at the hand of Lucifer.

Once more, every inequity, every pain and arrow slung at my back comes back to him, the *King* of Hell, that spoilt heathen that sits atop a throne of corpses. Truly it is he that is the root cause of all the foulness and agony that has befallen my love and I, and now, all I am left with is one choice ... to flee this life and everything it contains, to find a world where Arianwen and I can, once and for all, be truly free.

✦✦✦

Sulphur, the acrid stench invades my every breath. How I spent so long in this place I will never be able to comprehend and yet ... once more I find myself sinking through this putrid pit. My destination for the first time in my meager existence, is not the sweat soaked embrace of the undercroft, nor the vapid chilled corridors of Lucifer's chambers, no, it is a place I have, in the last five and twenty years, never once considered returning to.

My father's refuge, the hand hewn cavern Arianwen and I call home; that place was my fathers respite, a place of solace, of peace where he could shed the guise of murderer and sadist; a place, where my father could truly be himself, and in time, when my mother captured his heart and drew him completely from his dark and dismal path, it became their home; their true home, where Angel and Demon ceased to matter, where Abara and Amunet, were, quite simply husband and wife, living out a life they so wished was eternally at peace. What I stand in front of now, the house in Hell which I was born, in which I was raised. For my mother and father, it was little more than a constant stage, a set piece for a play they performed for an all too willing audience of masochists and perverts.

I push open the charred remains of the door, the stale scent of burnt wood invading my senses as I move into my parent's old home. The hollow shell that was once filled with warmth and love casts a dark halo around my heart, furtive memories dance past my mind's eye as I move through the small hand carved house. The crumbling remains of chairs catch at my feet, the charred and buckled remnants of the table that once seemed so large and foreboding now lies in a pile of its own ashes as I drift silently past.

The singed and holed curtain that hides the bed my parents once shared hangs limp and soot stained, the heavy material defying all logic as it stands amongst the fire gutted remnants of the place of my birth.

I cast a glance to my right, the small hand cut window drawing my gaze down into the frantic halls of the Legions, and I cannot help but smile slightly as a dust covered memory bubbles up, my child self kneeling on the small settee that once sat in place of the pile of ash I now stand in.

I close my eyes, my mind swirling as I focus in on the long hidden and pain laced memories. As I turn back to the small room and it is now a dead and vacant hearth, I cannot help but feel a deep sense of melancholy as the world begins to bleed back into life, a feeling of lost warmth and completion boiling through me.

Slipping into these memories, it is a deep comfort, akin to tugging on a pair of time worn shoes, they may well be slightly too small or a little ragged, but, they have a fit and comfort all their own. The room shifts, the black walls and ash covered floors melting away as amber light flows around me and the scent of cooking meat fills the air, even now as I stand in the mirror of my memories, I still feel, alone.

*Looking now at the crackling fire, even though the smell of damp and soot still clings to my throat telling all too clearly what reality lies beyond these shades of fantasy, I feel ... content. My love for the sweet Angel who has given me her heart and soul is beyond comprehension even now as she carries mine with her. I watch as the memory conjured ghost of my father strides through the door, his broad, muscular frame stretching out his plated leather armour as if it were a second skin, each move a testament of control and finesse.*

*I know what is coming, the look in his eyes tells me it all too well. Why I chose this memory I simply cannot say, but, for what is coming, the life altering question that is perched upon my lips, it is the only one that will show me what I so desperately need.*

*'Amunet, gather Albion and your armour, we are leaving, now!'*

*I stand transfixed as my mother springs from behind the curtained archway, her body half covered in the form fitting mailed leather of a Huntress. She hastily ties down the straps as my father moves past her, the sound of metal on metal filtering back through the heavy cloth.*

*She turns in the direction of my four year old self, her eyes soft but, frightened. Kneeling she tugs at the cloak about my shoulders as my hands begin to shake. It is an odd sensation to feel the lips she places upon that shadows brow, upon my own. I cannot help but lift my fingers and trace the area where the once tender love had met my skin. My father returns as my mother rises to her feet, fear plain on both their faces, even as my father straps his caster to his hip, handing my mother hers.*

For a moment I break the scene, glancing down at my own hip and thigh, the glinting weapon of blackened wood, brass and steel sits heavy and comforting against my skin. The one true link I have to my father, more so than the blood that flows through my veins, I carry his life and that of my mother, locked within me. But my Caster, my father's Caster, the revolver that now sits at my hip its grip and barrel cold against my leather sheathed thigh, its value to me ... is something I can never truly put into words.

*Turning my sight back to the tableau that is slowly unfolding, I watch my father kneel, his hand heavy upon my shoulder as he looks me dead in the eye.*

*'Albion ... your mother and I are taking you to Garth, we need to do something very important, not only for us, but for you, it will mean you can be safe, but, if ...'*

*He turns from my gaze his throat heaving slightly as I see a lone claret trail snake down his cheek. Before now, I never let my mind take me this far, and as I reach out my small fingers brushing it away, I watch as my father pulls me tight into a hug that now, as I stand here watching this memory, has tears of my own slipping past all the stoic barriers I tried to keep within myself.*

*'If ... if we do not return, there is a box, hidden beneath the fifth stone from the corner in our bedroom, it is the one just below the right bottom corner of the window. Use it all with pride my son and there is one other thing in there, a gift from your mother, you will know who to give it too when your heart and soul tell you it is right. I love you Albion, you truly are the best of me.'*

*I stand rapt as my mother takes my hand and leads me from our home, my father staying behind for a moment. What happened here next I cannot say, but, from what I remember hearing, I can guess all too well.*

My need to know burns brighter than anything in that moment as I walk through the ash and soot, the world of my memories now nothing but a blackened shell as the curtain and light falls away. I kneel at the side of the table, half burnt runes scratched by a thick talon into the oak surface. I smile as I trace them with my finger, the magic within glowing, damp wood smoldering as I feel the power my father possessed from even these age worn relics of my past.

I kick my way through shards of timber and piles of sodden ash towards my parents' bedroom. I cannot help the smile I feel as I brush aside the curtain and move towards the window. Stopping short I set my gaze to the floor. With one eye closed, I lift my hand and slowly, carefully, count out from the corner. My brow furrows as I spy the stone, its edges clean, all too smooth for the rest of the floor. I know my father told me what it was ... but ... now that I am here, can I really break a seal on my life that has waited all this time?

My feet draw me onwards, the prize only inches away from me as I find myself kneeling and fingers tracing the edges of the stone before lifting it clear. I cannot deny the chuckle that floats through me.

'I guess my heart wanted to see what my mind didn't.'

Bundles of oiled canvas and a small rose wood box sit before me. I reach in, lifting the secreted treasures from within and laying them at my side. My senses, my training, all the experience I have carved from the flesh of my enemies these last five and twenty tell me exactly what is within each bundle, weaponry, munitions, everything a soul will need to fight for their life in a world gone mad. But the box, that small rosewood box is one secret I cannot recognise.

I pluck it from its resting place on the floor as I turn myself, my legs crossing beneath me as I sit, my eyes locked on the box as I slowly flip it open, a part of me all too scared at what could lie within. The glint of a silver ring and the thick aquamarine stone band that runs through it draws me in. I remember my mother wearing this, the tale of its origin a soft story of a families traditions and a mothers love.

I never knew my mother's parents, but, I know of them. The pride they held for my mother, the pain they held at her leaving their home and choosing the path that flowed from her heart, it is something I know all too well, and now, as I stare at the band of silver and blue … I can think of only one person with whom this belongs and I know, in the depths of my heart and soul, my mother, my father, would be proud to know she was the one who claimed my heart as her own.

I lift the ring from the box, its weight settling in my palm, for all the intricate workmanship that it contains it is near feather light. I turn it over and over in my palm basking in its simplicity.

I close my fist around the ring before slipping it into a small pouch on my waist and picking up the rest of the items and making my exit. I have no doubt someone will have seen my passage through the pit, but, with what little time I have left in this wretched place, it matters not.

✦ ✦ ✦

The chill of my home is a welcome reprieve from the spite and malice laced heat that I once called home. I need to tell my love, I need her to know; to know that I am not merely a Demon, that my mother was like her; a true Angel. An Angel that followed the same path Arianwen now walks, the one guided by love and by her heart. The same paths that led me free of the life I loathed and allowed me finally, to be free of the chains that so tied me to the nightmare into which I was born.

I need her to know that my parents, the Knight and the Angel, had found a way to be free of this twisted, murderous existence, set in a world where Angels fear the light and Demons lust for it; a world where Arch Angels make deals with the Fallen, and walk hand in hand through shadows so thick it is hard to tell where the Arch end and the Demon he walks with begins.

My parents gave their lives for a chance at freedom. If I turned my back on all that now … their heartache, their sacrifice and fear, all of it would be for nothing. Arianwen though, she is the light I call home, she is the one that gave me the life I hold so dear. My father knew and felt the same and now, his footsteps echo my own, all that they went through to forge this path to a new life. I will not forsake it, but now, now I have a new way, a new reason to fight and survive just for a while longer, in a world that wholly wants my heart on a plate.

I sink back on to our bed, the soft furs and the plush mattress cradling me as I let my body fall. As I sink deep into the smooth warmth I cannot help but conjure up the image of my Angel, her scent, her taste; the way she moves and the way she sounds, all of it rolling over me as I let my eyes slip closed and sleep claim me, even if it is only for a short while.

✦ ✦ ✦

The fall opens out before me, my eyes taking in the crisp green of the trees as the spires and towers of Eden rise from within them. Closing my eyes slowly, I capture the image of my Angel in my mind and send it floating free on the wings of my aura, the twisting scarlet lines flowing across my mind's eye as I watch it dance from one feathered bird to another.

I feel more than see her, as she senses my touch. A smile blooms across her features as she dips her shoulders, her head tilting into the curling lines of my auras caress as she turns and looks right into my eyes. I know in my mind that she cannot see me, but at that moment, as we stare through the distance into each other's eyes, I could not love her any more than I do right at this moment. She owns me so completely that I am struggling to see where her heart begins and my own ends.

She turns away from me, her mouth moving as she smiles, laughing slightly before turning back to me and moving beyond my sight.

A deep rush of energy rolls through me, my mind twisting as I stagger slightly, my heart racing in my chest as the Dragons growl softly in the distance. A smile tugs at my lips as I turn back towards our home, my Angel already making her way to the heart of our existence.

My patience bleeds through my heart as I wait for my love to arrive, ever nerve and thought poised on the single notion that my Angel is out there, alone and vulnerable. I know she is more than capable, but, my need to see her safe, to protect my soul's keeper is ever present. My mind starts to drag through the darker parts of my being, pulling every wayward, panic stricken thought to the fore. I cannot help but become overwhelmed by images of my Angel, thoughts of her ensnared in the grip of an enemy agent, his hands tearing her clothes from her body as he sets about having his way with her. I start to move, my armour beckoning me just as the door to our home opens, the sweet scent of apples and honey filtering through the air as I watch her slowly step in from the glaring light of day and into the flickering light of our torch lit home.

'Albion, my love? Is everything okay? You've never before sent such a soft and tender calling to me. It had my mouth smiling, but slightly confused. Are you all right?'

I cannot hide the grin that spreads across my features as I sweep my Angel into my arms and ravage her lips with my own.

'I, my love, despite all that is circling us, have never been happier and I have something I have to tell you, I just didn't want to alarm you with an urgent call. I know you would have run to my side had I made it as forceful as I wanted to and what, with Michael and Gabriel dogging your every step, possibly sensing your imminent departure, I couldn't risk you catching their eye as you made your way here.'

I pull her tight to me, burying my face in her neck and hair, inhaling deeply as she loops her arms around my neck and draws me in.

'I ... I need to tell you something ... it's important.'

Arianwen pulls away from me, her face quizzical as she stares up into my eyes. Her eyes sparkle, the pensive puzzlement behind them lending a cute furrow to her brow that only draws me deeper into her gaze. I cannot help but lose all semblance of what was to be said as her fingers tease my hair, her head tilting to the side as she patiently waits for me to speak. Closing my eyes, I breathe deeply before opening them once more, drawing my thoughts back from the far flung reaches of my mind, pushing visions of war aside, even for but a moment.

'My parents ... they ... they were searching, just as we are, they were seeking a way free of this place, free of everything; that is where they were going the night they left me with Garth ... the night they died.'

I slip from my Angel's grip and move towards the bed, my body suddenly weary as I begin to draw to mind all that had been said with Garth. I look up at my Angel as she trails in my wake, her body slim and lithe as she curls in beside me.

'What are you trying to tell me Albion, you know there is nothing that could shake me from you, not after all we have both suffered through and sacrificed together.'

'My mother ... she ... she was a doyenne of your caste, she was an Angel, she shattered her halo and followed my father into Hell, all because of love.'

I cast my eyes to my Angel, a soft smile on her lips as she moves towards the centre of our bed, pulling me gently towards her.

'Albion that is one thing I have known from the moment you set foot in Eden. There had to be Angelic blood in your veins, it is the only true explanation for what the Gatekeepers told you so long ago.'

'I know my love, but the fact that she did that, just to be with my father, she renounced the only life she had ever known, willingly giving up all that connected her to Eden, embracing the darkness and turning from the light ...'

I shake my head as I pull Arianwen into my embrace once more, my chin resting on the top of her head as she rests her legs across me, fingers idly tracing the top of the branding in my chest.

'To do all that for the man she loved, it, well, it gives me a hope for us; they forged a path we too follow; my father renounced the darkness, renounced Lucifer, all for my mother and to protect me ... but ...'

A deep sigh wells within me as I recount once more just what befell my mother and father.

'Lucifer killed them, he killed my father for loving my mother, and had my mother killed because she wouldn't devote herself to him. Lucifer wanted something from my mother she could not and would not give him ... her love, and ... he killed them both because of it. It's one reason they were leaving, because they knew that

Lucifer would stop at nothing to make my mother his. He's a petty, vain and jealous man Arianwen, he was cast out of Eden for demanding too much of too many and that ultimately cost my parents their lives.

They gave us a path to walk and a place to shelter from all that comes against us. My father carved our home from this mountain himself. They did that, for themselves and us. I know that together we will finally finish their journey, but, I will not leave this world until I know your family ... *my family* ... is safe. Eden may never be my home, but as long as I'm by your side, I don't care what world we live in, all I want is to be with you.'

I turn to face her, my nose inches from hers as I stare directly into her eyes.

'Arianwen, I want us to be free of this place, to be free of these wretched worlds that are tearing us apart every chance they get. I want us to build a life and a family together, if that means renouncing everything I was, casting aside the shadows and darkness then I will. I have already told you, I am yours, where you go I go. I will gladly give everything I am to see you safe my love, but ...'

I slip from the bed, taking two steps, my fingers falling to the pouch on my waist as I draw my mother's ring from within, snaring it between my fingers as I take a short walk back and lower to one knee.

'I want to do it as the husband I know I can be. I can't live this life without you, war will come, war will go, I'm by your side and you are in my heart and soul come whatever may. I am yours for eternity. Marry me Arianwen, without you as my wife and soulmate ... I truly have nothing.'

# 38

## Beauty Before Destruction

### ARIANWEN

**The fresh breeze that is brushing lightly past my face carries** the scent of apple blossoms, lavender bushes and roses, a collection of spring growth from the Garden of Eden, floating on the pure air of Heaven. Sunshine beats down upon my skin, giving a warmth and peace only my home can give. But, the most beautiful part of this Heavenly place, is the man standing beside me, holding my hand, smiling with an ease I have not seen before. His entire body giving off a soft celestial glow revealing his true self.

For anyone who would dispute Albion's place in my world, you would only have to look at him now, to know this is where his home should have always been. His heart and soul sing with true peace as we walk hand in hand along the far edges of Eden. We stick to the thick line of growth and trees to not be seen, but it still feels as if we can comfortably walk amongst a place that should truly be both our home.

We are heading to the furthest reaches of Eden, to the place not many of my kin venture. To a place that best represents the predicament our lives have been in. The Edge of Never. It is the edge of our world where only myths survive. Beyond it, over the edge is, oblivion. The water that falls over its edge, fed by the river that runs through Eden, never lands. Some water may escape, floating to mist, bouncing, suspended in air while the rest of the water falls forever. It never ends, yet is final. No coming back.

But, to stand on the edge of the waterfall, looking around at the most exquisite beauty and out into the endless azure blue sky, is one of the most beautiful sites you could ever see, something I so desperately wanted to share with my love and a place that seemed the most fitting for us to profess our undying love to each other.

We walk in silence, each of us with similar thoughts of the impending misery that may come our way, trying to hold strong for the other, yet knowing that one, if not both of us, may not survive the war that is about to begin between our worlds. No, not between our *worlds*. Between our *world* and the world that is Hell. Albion will fight alongside me for *his* world, the world of light, the one he rightfully belongs too. The world his mother was born to.

To think, Albion's father, also a Demon Knight, fell for an Angel too, is astonishing. But, the fate they were both dealt is a frightening truth that Albion and I will not speak words about, but I am sure is in both our hearts. They were about to make it out, so sure that they had found a safe passage, they left their precious son in trusted hands until they returned to also take him away. Yet, Albion never saw his parents again.

The heartache he had to live with and the feeling of always being trapped in a body and world that did not feel his own, is a testament to the strength he was born with, the strength he inherited from his parents. What they must have gone through to be together and then live together within the realms of Hell, is beyond what I thought Albion and I could endure. Their story, as sad as its ending was, also gives me a ray of hope, hope that Albion and I will one day find our place together in a world we will call home.

But, first we need to survive the upheaval that is about to explode upon our world. I plan on telling my parents all of what I safely can tomorrow, knowing that they will see the truth in my eyes, and that they deserve to be ready for a war that will land on their doorstep, if not inside their very own house. They will be the best people to protect my sisters so it is only right that I warn them of what is to come and of Michael's plans for Brianne if I was to refuse Gabriel's hand or not return to Eden at all.

I know they will ask questions and I am not yet certain of exactly how much I will tell them, about Albion and I, about the alliance Michael had with Lucifer that was witnessed by my own eyes, about how both men still seem set on war with each other and that alone has me worried as to where Michaels loyalties lie. My mother already knows something is terribly wrong, I could see it in her eyes when our glances met earlier. It was as if she could see it all, everything that is going on, everything that is inside my head, everything that words could not say.

Her eyes widened as if she already knew, that very soon, I would be asking for a word with her and father and warning them of what is to come. The same way I had a feeling she knew about the loss of baby. The way she looked at me when I first returned home, the love and understanding that shone from her eyes, and the grief that was reflected in my own, spoke scrolls of a hundred words all in a moment of silence. If she does indeed somehow know everything, it will make it easier not to voice all of the painful truths.

Tomorrow will be the day I turn my family's world upside down. Tomorrow will begin a chain reaction. Inform my parents of the truths, then we have to fight a war, protect the virtues of Good, ensure the safety of my family and kin, survive, win and then, then Albion and I can find our place in a world we can call our own, be it our birth one or another. As long as we are together, then it will be home.

Albion's soft laugh breaks my train of thought as I turn to see a brilliant smile gracing his lips as he watches a tiny Swallow swoop up high, then come down low to do a rather brazen fly by, right past his nose, daring him to try and catch it. My childhood memory of a Swallow that guided me to my earliest encounter with Albion floods my mind as my smile spreads across my face. Even back then, a Swallow knew that Eden was Albion's world too, as does this little one still taunting him playfully.

You can hear it before your eyes can see it, the mighty roar of a body of water riding over the edge of a precipice and falling into infinity. The sound gives you an image of the sheer force of such a moving mass and the power contained within. Even the most powerful of men could not swim away from the Edge of Never if they were to fall too close to the lip.

Albion stills as the Edge comes into sight. I hear his audible gasp bedside me as he takes in the overwhelming beauty of this part of Eden. He grips my hand tighter before turning to me, eyes rimmed with unshed tears as he slowly shakes his head. Confusion mars my features as I struggle to read the emotions playing through his eyes.

'I … I know this place. I know I've never been here before, but somehow, it's all so familiar. My … my mother, I think she spoke of it. She told me stories of her young life, living here, my earliest memories are of her, and I sat in front of the hearth as she painted pictures with her words, pictures of gardens, lily pads on water and floating mist that hid everything in its watery embrace, it all tugs at my deepest memories. But it's more than that, more than a tale. If I close my eyes I can actually see this exact area, her voice, her words, all of it is bursting through my mind.'

He turns left and right, looking for something until he stops, his eyes focusing on a Narachion Whispering Oak, one of a rare few that exist in the Gardens of Eden. He takes a single step towards it before stopping.

'The Narachion Whispering Oak stands tall, its beauty reaches high and wide, its roots deeper than a soul, forever standing strong, its branches move in an arch, up and over, reaching like fingers, dipping into the water that flows from Heaven's sanctuary. Its leaves floating away on the winds of fate.'

His whispered words are haunting as he recalls what I assume is his mother's words.

'Why do I know this Arianwen? Why, when I have never recalled these memories before, do they suddenly seem as fresh as the suns golden light?'

I smile brightly at the man I love. I know why, it is because this is his rightful home as it was once his mother's. His grin tells me that he has come to that same thought as he once again looks around and takes in all the beauty surrounding us. He looks at me, then back at the tree, before pulling on my hand to follow in his steps as we head close to the lip of the Edge where the tree is standing proudly.

The mist of the water soaks my hair and dampens the delicately beaded, white silk dress I brought from my family's home, knowing it was the only one I could possibly be dressed in when I stood before the man I love and declared myself his for all of eternity and beyond. My body shakes but I am not cold from the water, as the sun's rays filtering through the trees is warming my skin. I shake with excitement, with nervousness, with a desperate need. I truly cannot wait to become Albion's bride.

We walk past the blossoming gardenias, their fragrance floating through my senses as the rainbow coloured Gerberas and exqui-site Parrot Tulips fill my sight with blinding colour. The soft rich green moss beneath my bare feet feels like clouds of cushions as we walk the last steps up the rise the come to a stop beneath the ancient Oak.

I cannot help but admire my handsome Demon, who still wears his weathered, black leather trousers, but instead of one of his woven black leather shirts that always adorned his wide shoulders and chiselled chest, for the first time he is wearing a soft white linen one, making him look more at home here than I ever thought possible.

He takes both my hands in his and as I raise my head to meet his eyes, I fall further in love with him. His peace, his joy, his soul deep love is shining clear, as his mouth wears a slight smile. The growth of stubble over his chin, the scars, some small, some large, that mar his face, the deep set of his entrancing eyes, all giving him the appearance of a slightly broken, somewhat dark Adonis. How did I ever stand a chance of not falling in love with this Demon the first time our eyes met?

Be it fate, destiny, or God's plan, regardless of what brought us together, it was I who fell hopelessly in love with the enemy, with a Demon, with my Albion.

I squeeze his hands with excitement, trying not to bounce on the balls of my feet, but failing terribly, making my love chuckle at my childlike excitement. But I *am* excited, despite the turmoil surrounding us and the horror that may come as soon as we walk away from this peaceful spot, I cannot wait to vow that I will forever stand my Albion's side. Through good or bad, in sickness and health, no matter what comes our way, we will conquer it, we will face it together.

'My sweet Angel. My love, my little wing, my Arianwen. I don't have to stand here today and vow to you to be a better man, because you, you have already made me just that, with you in my life and heart I *am* truly the best man I can be. Because of your undying love, encouragement, guidance and strength, I finally found myself, the person my parents always knew I would be, but I was too blinded by pain, hate and Evil to see.

'You opened my eyes, to not only see myself, but to see my dark world and the ones beyond, in an entirely different light. I thought that I'd forever be shackled to the chains of Hell, destined to stand at the right hand of Lucifer, to be forever left questioning why I felt so out of place, never truly belonging to the world to which I was born. I was left set to a life of never truly finding the answers my soul so desperately sought.

'But, the moment I looked into your eyes, everything started to make sense. The ever shifting pieces inside my mind started to finally fall into place, allowing me to see with a true clarity, that until that moment, I had only dared dream of. You made that possible, you gave me the answers to the deepest questions of my soul; that newfound clarity allowed me to see you, the missing piece of my heart. An Angel, my kins enemy, a being I was raised to believe was the embodiment of faithless sin. The path I was set to walk, the one that Lucifer marked my life to, it was a cold, joyless existence. Every one of those around me rejoiced in the hunt, revelled in the kill, yet, for all of the years I spent locked in that mire of Evil and death, there was never a place for me in that world.

'But, when you were stood before me, eyes wide, defiant yet showing a shadow of fear, I knew where I wanted to be, even if at that moment, it sowed more confusion than understanding. You saw past the armour, past the death and anger that coated my skin and soul. You saw the real me, the one I was so desperately trying to find and yet hide all at once. In that moment, that one infinitesimal instance was the first time I ever felt hope. Hope for more, a desperate need for acceptance that could only ever come from you.

'The way you were looking at me, opened up everything that I was, peeling away layer after layer, the source of my very being exposed to your gaze as you lay bare all that had haunted me. I watched as you sank through all that made me a Hunter and Demon to the core of my being and the light and Goodness that waited within. When I saw the truth bloom in your eyes, when you knew in that grasping moment of realisation, that I'd been the one watching over you, guarding you from all that sought your life, even though in truth, neither of us will ever understand why, I knew my life was never to be the same.

'You showed me affection, you showed me love; you gave me all that I needed. You gave me the chance to truly be the man I always knew I could be, even though that knowledge, until then, had been lost to depths of my pain and misery. You gave me the light to find all that I was. You Arianwen, made me whole.

'Angels and Demons have always been enemies, yet I found my freedom in you, an Angel, *my* Angel. At first I thought I'd imagined it, it was all too much for my mind and heart to reconcile. Childishly I hid from the truth, refusing to believe what I knew my eyes had seen, but, at our next encounter I knew, I knew what I saw in your eyes was true, all that I held within echoed with you, your feelings for me, for a Demon, a Hunter, found their home and mirror within me. I didn't allow myself to believe, to accept how strong they were, but in my dreams, all logic and fear ceased, and I dared to imagine that what I saw, what you showed me, could in fact be what I wanted most, what I needed it to be. Love.

'I felt foolish, angry even, that a Demon, a Knight such as myself, a General and leader of a Hell spawn Legion, was secretly hoping that an Angel loved him. Confusion made me lash out, trying to rid myself of such joyous hope. But it was no use, your aura just kept pulling at me again and again, until I had no choice but to believe what was before my eyes, what my body was feeling, what my heart was falling for.

'Arianwen, the man I am stands before you because you showed me the light, you defied the natures of our kin and the laws of your God. I am the man I am because, you, love, me. I vow, here today, to spend all of eternity returning the love you so selflessly gave to a man who couldn't even love himself. '

Tears, they used to be such a foreign concept for an Angel, fall naturally and freely down my face as I take my hands out of his to place them on his cheeks, cupping his beautiful face in my grasp, the breathtakingly beautiful ring he placed on my finger when he asked me to be his wife, catches the sunlight and sparkles like a thousand fireflies, as I fight the emotions that have clogged my throat at his heartfelt words of love for me.

I use my thumbs to wipe the wetness that has pooled just under his eyes, my legs feeling weak with overwhelming love and devotion for this amazing man. For all we have been through, I cannot wait to spend many more lifetimes with him in any world, as long as he is by my side.

*'Albion ...'*

That word comes out like a cry, needing a moment to contain the emotions that are welling up inside, just about to break through the dam wall. I take a deep breath and stare into his eyes using his unstoppable strength to fuel my own.

'Albion, my love, my man, my life. You are the missing piece of my soul, the one that I needed to finally feel whole. I felt out of place and slightly unsure of myself, until you fell from the sky and landed in front of me. When I found you, I found myself. I devoted my entire existence to my God, to my kin, to our way of living. My life was so wonderful I was afraid to give in to the feelings that I wanted more, that I *needed* more in my life. I felt like it was greed to desire more than what God had provided.

'But, that longing instantly vanished the moment we were standing face to face. Even though fear was trying to force its way to the front of my mind, it never did take hold. When your eyes held mine, I felt like I had finally found me. The feelings themselves were frightening and exhilarating and oh so confusing. I always felt that my mysterious guardian was more than a spirit, that it held the body of human form and to know my instincts were right, was a relief, until I realised exactly what type of form you held. The form of a Demon.

'I instantly felt emotions for you, feelings that were so foreign to my life until that very moment. I had loved before, but it was the love I held for my family and fellow kin. But, what was bubbling up inside of me as we stood silently staring at each other, was a love so fierce it almost knocked me off my feet. I was horrified and felt like I was betraying who I was, betraying the world that I lived in, because an Angel shouldn't be feeling anymore for a Demon than fear and loathing. But, as betraying as those feelings were, they also felt so very right.

'As much as I knew I should resist the feelings you were creating within me, fighting them felt even more terrifying. Why would I want to resist them when those exact feelings were making me feel more alive than I had ever felt in my entire existence? I knew in those first moments that you were more than just a Demon. I could see it in your eyes, something hiding, something fighting not to be seen, but I saw it and that's what kept me coming back to you. That's my reasoning as to why I allowed myself to continue to feel for you what was so forbidden.

'Albion, even if I had tried to walk away from the love your presence was conjuring up inside of me, it wouldn't have worked, I would've come back. There was no way in Heaven or Hell our love was going to let go of each other. And I feel so blessed every day that I have you in my life that we have both held on with everything we have to the fierce love we share for each other.

'I stand before you today, to say thank you, thank you for enabling me to feel such soul deep, out of this world love. And I vow to you in this moment, that I will forever stay by your side and in your heart for all of eternities to come.'

He crushes me to his body in a ferocious hold, his love burning through our layers of clothing and flesh to seek out my heart and soul and to officially join with his. His body shudders, his shoulders vibrating with silent sobs as tears run joyously down my own face. This Demon, this man, is mine. No matter what fate brings our way, we will never be parted again.

He pulls back from me, holding onto my shoulders, looking into my eyes, a nerve ticking on one side of his jaw, telling me he is desperate to seal our vows with a kiss, yet knowing there is one more vow we have to make to each other that is older than time, beautiful Latin words that will forge us as one no matter what world will become our home.

'Arianwen ... Manus mea, vulnerasti cor meum in omni anima vestra nunc aeternitatis tenere.'

Then he lowers to his knees and kisses each of my hands that are captured in his. When he stands his smile is as blinding as the morning sun and has my body shaking with pure happiness.

'Albion ... Manus mea, vulnerasti cor meum in omni anima vestra nunc aeternitatis tenere.'

I softly sink to my knees and kiss both of his strong, large hands, before he gently helps me to rise again. Now, now there is nothing stopping us from sharing our first kiss as husband and wife.

His boyish, mischievous grin has a giggle rising up my throat, but before it escapes, his lips are upon mine with a beautiful gentleness, a vow without words that will stand the test of time in all of the immortal worlds and beyond.

So lost in the sweetest moment, it takes a few seconds for us both to register the sound of large rustling coming from behind us. Our lips part with questioning gazes as the noise becomes louder, howling, like a tornado is roaring through the garden.

I only have a split second to see the flash of movement flying through the trees towards us, my mind screaming in recognition at what it is, who it is, as Gabriel, wings stretched back to a point, hits Albion with such a force it sounds like an enormous thunder clap, as he screams a vicious curse in his face.

'She's mine!'

It happens so fast, my mind is having trouble catching up with my body's movements as Albion pushes a hand to my chest, the force sending me backwards just as Gabriel makes contact with him and sends them both flying through the air and over the lip of the Edge of Never.

My body scrambles to the edge, on hands and knees, just in time to see Albion's wings start to open underneath Gabriel's body, the leather flesh, with talons at their peaks, not quite opening to their full span, just before the mist of the water and

white trans-lucent clouds swallows them up from my view.
Gabriel took Albion over the Edge.
Over the Edge of Never.
Edge of Never.
Never.
Never.
Never to return.
'NO!'


# The End

**If you loved this book, please take the time to leave a review
on Amazon and Goodreads**

## WE LOVE TO CHAT TO OUR READERS

If you want to get in touch with or stalk (in a healthy way)
either author, please use the links below.
You can email them both on:
**cooperbooks100@gmail.com**

Take an intimate look inside Heaven's Scent at our **Pinterest**
board: www.pinterest.com/tmcoops/heavens-scent-series/

## FIND RICKY ON HIS:

**Facebook** www.facebook.com/R.C.books

**Twitter** https://twitter.com/RJwC20

**Instagram** www.instagram.com/ricky_cooper_1/

**Website** www.ricky-cooper.co.uk/

## FIND TANIA ON HER:

**Facebook** www.facebook.com/taniacooperbooks

**Twitter** https://twitter.com/TaniaTmcoops

**Instagram** www.instagram.com/taniacooper100/

**Website** www.taniacooperauthor.com.au/

# PLAYLIST

Music can set a scene or just be soothing background noise, but either way, we cannot write without it. Here are the songs that inspired Between Worlds:

Path 5: Grace Davidson & Max Richter
Lost: Zoe Keating
Reminiscence: Olafur Arnalds & Alice Sara Ott
Written in Stone:
Letters of a Traveller:
Silence: Delerium feat. Sarah McGla
Nothing Else Matters: Metallica
Hello: Adelle
Into Darkness: Thomas Bergersen
Radioactive: Imagine Dragons
Levitate: Hadouken
Crushed Like Fruit: InMe
Wherein Lies Continue: Slipknot
Just Tonight: The Pretty Reckless
Desire: Poets of the Fall
Cold Reader: Stone Sour
Gehenna: Slipknot
I am Bulletproof: Black Veil Brides
My Demons: Starset
Orchids: Stone Sour
Guts Over Fear (feat. Sia) Eminem
Firefly InMe
Sulfu: Slipknot
The Gilded Hand: Radical Face
Born to love you- Oddworld Remix: Elodie Adams
Running up that hill: Placebo
Wrong side of Heaven: Five Finger Death Punch
Follow you: Bring me the Horizon
Throne: Bring me the Horizon
Answer: Sarah McLachlan

# ACKNOWLEDGEMENTS

This is for all those chasing their dreams; go as far as it takes, and fight to become what you want to be, no one ever succeeded by standing on the starting line.

And a huge endless thank you to our readers. Thank you for loving our characters with a fierce passion and always wanting more. Your support is priceless.

**Ricky.**

Thank you to our cover artist Paul. Yes we are fussy with every little detail and probably drive you crazy, but you love us anyway.

Thank you to our editor Maria B for jumping in blind and not drowning and for understanding our craziness and our writing instantly.

Thank you to the talented Max Henry for making our words look so pretty.

Thank you Megan Davis for helping to spread the word about our steamy series.

Thank you to all the bloggers who love our writing with a passion. Your endless work at promoting authors is amazing!

To the support of beautiful friends, Nicole Layton, Anne Gardner and Casey Patton, thank you for always believing in me, when sometimes I don't believe in myself.

To our amazing beta readers Jennifer Cothran, Denise Taylor, Nicole Layton, Bec Butterfield and Alicia Butterfield. Thank you ladies for your honesty and keen eyes, it's great to know what's crap and what's not before we hit that publish button.

To my amazing co-writer and best friend Ricky. Oceans apart yet so much alike, no one else gets my crazy, ridiculous humour like you do. You actually make me feel normal LOL.

**Tania.**

# INDEX

## NAMES & PHRASES

**Arcs:** Angle of movement and shorthand for Arc Angel.

**Avarice:** extreme lust for ownership of objects or people and or gold and wealth.

**Balo'c:** Demon guard outside Lucifer's chamber.

**Bara Goth':** Demon soldier that challenges Albion for leadership of the Sixth Legion.

**Bavier:** Also called a Bevor; a Bavier is a piece of armour attached to the Gorget that protects the lower face from the nose down.

**Bruvou:** Favoured drink of the demons in the under croft.

**Carapace:** A hardened armour shell.

**Cerberus:** Mythical multi headed dog that guards the gates to the underworld, cited as the "Hound of Hades" and the mythological off spring of Echidna and Typhon in ancient Greek legend.

**Doyenne:** The most respected or prominent woman in a particular field.

**Eddy:** A movement in air or water that causes a whirlpool effect.

**Enocian:** Said to be the language of the Angels, found in the book of Enoc who was its creator/discoverer.

**Gaol/Gaolers:** Traditional English spelling for Jail/Jailer and is pronounced the same way.

**Gorget:** A high collared piece of armour that sits across the shoulders and collar bone and just below the chin, designed to guard the neck and shoulder area from sword cuts and other forms of injury.

**Harried:** A term meaning harassed or put upon, by the demands of others.

**Incantation:** A series of words said as a magic spell or charm.

**Latin wedding vow:** Manus mea, vulnerasti cor meum in omni anima vestra nunc aeternitatis tenere – Translation: My hand, my heart, my soul, is now yours for all of eternity to hold.

**Lilu:** Father of Albion's father's Commander Gilgamesh.

**Mayloree:** One of Gabriel's presented girls/possible bride.

**Miasma:** An oppressive or unpleasant atmosphere/odour which surrounds or emanates from something.

**Penitents gaze:** A stare that bewitches and controls those that are subjected to it.

**River Styx:** River that leads deep through hell, associated with Greek mythology as the gate way to hell.

**Sigel:** Symbol generally carved into an object or area that marks it as belong to a person or group.

**Sistelle:** One of Gabriel's presented girls/possible bride.

**Sword of Damocles:** A feature of mythology, art, literature and fiction. Used as an allusion to imminent danger and fear, first seen in the story King Dionysius in Ancient Greece.

**The walls of Jericho:** The walls of an ancient city that were, according to biblical sources, fell by the approaching army sounding trumpets.

**Vellum:** A fine parchment made from animal skin, typical calf skin.

# COMING SOON

Heaven's Scent series: Book 3

## Shattered Halos

"There's no need to fear the light; just the shadows it brings."